Calamity at Conclave

(Book III of The Osten Chronicles)

Author: Daniel Thorman

ISBN: 978-1-963913-32-3

Imprint: Native Publishers, The

The Osten Chronicles

Dedicated to:

Anthony Muñoz

(for his charitable heart)

CHAPTER ONE

The Headmaster

"Friendship is born at that moment when one person says to another: 'What! You too? I thought I was the only one."

~ C.S. Lewis ~

I sat waiting patiently. It had been at least ten minutes since Roy had been let in, but it had felt to me like hours had passed. I wondered how my cousin's interview was going and wished I could be a fly on the wall in the headmaster's office. Had our situations been reversed, I knew Royland could accomplish just such a feat. But lacking his facility with insects, I was left to wonder.

We'd arrived at Conclave near midday, nervous about what we might encounter. We had entered through the trade gate, our mules stepping in time to the jaunty tune that heralded our caravan's arrival. Conclave was a sprawling village far larger than my hometown of Meadowfork. Its streets were alive with the rich conversational babble of its teeming residents. Above this could be heard barkers peddling their wares, the distant bellowing of an ox, and the ringing strikes of hammers from smithies nearby. We settled in on a side street that had been

1

made ready for our arrival. The weather held clear, and the crowds grew thick as the merchants among us joined in the clamorous chorus of commerce.

It had taken several days to arrange this interview with the conclave's headmaster. With our trunks and other gear piled in the back of the jester's wagon, Taylor had guided our team to the postern gate at the appointed hour. Roy was seated beside Taylor on the driver's bench, and I sat atop my trunk in the wagon's bed. As we approached the low stone fence that separated the mage's quarter from the rest of Conclave Village, my chest swelled with a sense of eager anticipation.

"Whoa," said Taylor, drawing in the reins and causing the team to clatter to a stop.

I spied a youth arising from a stone bench just inside the gate. I supposed him to be around Royland's age. He was well-dressed in a gray doublet with a silvery sheen. Below immaculate black breeches he sported hose that were a deep burgundy in hue. These matched the red feather that hung down at a rakish angle from his floppy hat. He approached, looking up and inspecting our wagon.

"Would you be Royland Wagge and Lucas Harper?" he said with a slight frown that shed some doubt on the identification.

Before I could answer, Roy spoke up. I was unaccustomed to my cousin taking the lead in a conversation. A year ago, he had barely spoken at all. Recently, this had changed. He was speaking up more often and more aggressively in a manner most contrary to his former inclinations.

"I am Royland," he said. "And if you are the escort sent to guide us to our appointments, I would know your name also, Sir."

"I am Victor Brubaker," the young man returned. "Journeyman to Master Brownyng. I must say, I hadn't expected a mule-drawn cart. How ... pedestrian."

This elicited a short bark of laughter from my cousin, causing both Taylor and I to stare over at him sharply. For this too was out of character for Royland's typically aloof and dispassionate manner. We'd been meant to arrive in Baron

Westarbor's elegant carriage, but that had to be abandoned back at Barony Stein.

"I should think riding atop a wagon is quite the opposite of pedestrian," quipped Roy. "After all, you're the one on foot, journeyman. If you'd care to climb up, you can ride in comfort while showing us where we must go."

Looking a bit chagrined but still undaunted, Victor soon stepped up onto the buckboard and hoisted himself over the wagon's lip to alight beside me in its bed.

"I'm Lucas," I unnecessarily added.

And so under Victor's guidance, we proceeded through the gates and onto the pristine streets of the mage's quarter beyond. We wended our way past large estates and their carefully manicured grounds. We eventually found ourselves here at the conclave's heart, the academy. I thanked Taylor for looking after us these past several months and bade him a final fond farewell after our luggage had been unloaded. We were ushered into the grand stone edifice that was the academy and through its baffling maze of corridors.

"They've been at it a long time," said Victor, breaking my reverie. "Master Prowd usually keeps entry interviews rather perfunctory."

"Does he now?" I responded rhetorically. I wasn't sure just why, but I had taken an instant dislike to the young fellow sitting across from me in the headmaster's foyer. I hadn't neglected to mark his surname as belonging to Royland's true grandfather. Most likely, he was some distant cousin of Roy's. I had only recently discovered that Roy and I were technically unrelated. He was descended from the Brubaker line of mages, his father having been abducted by my grandmother some twenty-five years ago. But family is as family does. I would always think of Royland as my cousin of the heart.

"And remember to address the headmaster by his preferred title: Preeminence," Victor reminded me.

I considered the word. Though I knew it to mean 'superior before all others,' I couldn't help but to think of it as meaning 'not yet important.' I stifled a grin at the thought.

Just then, the outer door to the foyer swept inward. A red-faced young man stumbled in, pausing to catch his breath before sliding into a seat near the door.

"You're late," Victor chided him.

"Sorry," muttered the lad. "I was practicing and lost track of time."

He looked over at me and cocked his head.

"Is this one of the new chaps? The ones from Westarbor?"

"Indeed," Victor replied tersely. "This is Lucas Harper, newly arrived. The other is within, being interviewed by his preeminence. Lucas, this unpunctual fellow is Journeyman Aspirant Lloyd Bridges."

"I'm pleased to meet you, I'm sure, Aspirant Harper."

"Well, if your sure then," I said, "you can just call me Lucas."

Finally, the door handle to Master Prowd's inner office turned. As the door swung inward, the trailing end of laughter was heard.

"Royland, It's been a pleasure meeting you," announced a cheery masculine voice. "I'm certain you'll get on splendidly here at the conclave. Your lineage as an heir of Brubaker combined with the stellar reports on your progress by Master Chadwick bodes most favorably for your future here."

Victor stiffened at this latter remark. It was subtle, but I marked it in passing as my heartbeat quickened. The time had arrived for my own interview to begin. The door swung wider and Royland strode briskly out to join us, an amiable smile upon his face.

"Victor," commanded the headmaster from the doorway, "escort Aspirant Wagge here to your former house. Introduce him around and see that he's settled."

As the man turned to face me, my mind became ensnared in a jumble of memories not my own. Beneath his steely gray hair and sternly lined face, I glimpsed a younger man standing amid a field of flowers and shouting angrily. I shook my head to dispel the vision. I knew it to be a fragment of a dream I'd had since shattering the witch's heart. Abigale had known this man. And from the way my stomach twisted and the acrid taste of bile that arose at the back of my throat, their parting had been less than amicable.

"You must be Lucas," remarked the headmaster. "Come in, and we'll discuss what you have to offer us."

I meant to say 'Yes, your preeminence' as I'd been instructed. I was mortified that what emerged in its stead was 'I have a great deal to offer to him whose heart is true.'

Never had the dreams and emotions that plagued my sleep so intruded upon my waking mind. I lurched to my feet, trying to keep her animosity from my face, and moved to enter the office. Roy and the others cast me startled glances. The headmaster, with a similar expression, watched me step past him and quietly closed the door.

The headmaster turned from the now closed door, paced over to his writing desk and sat with his back to me.

"Find a seat, young man, I will be with you shortly," he said in a clipped tone.

I knew my remark had given the man affront, but I wasn't sure exactly why, or how I could repair the harm. He was perusing a thick letter, and I noticed the envelopes with Master Chadwick's broken seals stacked neatly nearby. The room was a study in orderliness. It had a barred window looking out upon the street below and afforded me several options to secure said seat. Without a word, I settled onto a bench beside a heavily laden bookshelf at the room's center.

After jotting down a few notes, Master Prowd turned his chair about to face me fully. His expression was rather cold until a frown emerged, as though he'd been reminded of a disagreeable duty or distasteful chore.

"Young man," he began, "I don't know what you meant by that outburst in my foyer, but I assure you I can recognize a tone of disrespect. Have a care. No master of the conclave will coddle an undisciplined journeyman. Such a mage is a danger to all around him and to the tenets we live by. So I'd suggest you curb your insolent tongue and think about your future here."

I wanted to object and plead my innocence, but the headmaster was right after a fashion. I hoped we could simply move past it.

"Your grandmother was much the same, and as a result, it ended badly for her."

Liar!

I struggled to keep the reaction from my face. It was clear he bore some grudge against my grandmother. From my visceral reaction to the man and his words, the reverse was certainly true. And from the derisive scorn behind these feelings, I was convinced I didn't want to know the tawdry details. So I bit back an angry retort and muttered: 'Yes, preeminence.'

"Now, on to business."

"I have assigned you to Aspirant Stein's house. There you will be brought up to speed on all you will need to know of our rules. As I told Aspirant Wagge, there will be a ceremony at the standing stones, an initiation of sorts. It will take place at the full of the moon a fortnight hence. This gathering is mandatory. There you will be officially welcomed into the conclave."

I had a hundred questions, but held them all at bay. I knew better than to interrupt. Megan had once counseled me to give people a chance to finish their thoughts before rudely interrogating them.

"This is also where journeyman selections are made," he continued. "If you should be so fortunate as to catch a master's eye, you might soon find yourself a journeyman. But I wouldn't get my hopes up were I you. Most of our masters have a full roster at the moment. And of course, preference is given to those with the most promise or the proper bloodlines and attitude."

Meaning not me, I thought. Reaching back, he retrieved my letter of introduction from his writing desk and reassessed it.

"On another matter," said Master Prowd, brightening. "Master Chadwick gives you high marks on reading. Like your fellow aspirant from Westarbor, he claims you are somewhat of a prodigy. You'll soon learn that all mages at the conclave must contribute to our community. Each is assigned a primary duty.

For yours, I shall recommend teaching the children and newer apprentices their letters. Some of our most recent recruits are woefully untutored if not completely illiterate, especially the young women. You can hash out the details with Mistress Julia. She is presently in charge of the program."

The headmaster stood. Recognizing my imminent dismissal, I stood as well and made ready to depart. He gestured toward the door, and I preceded him, turning the handle and opening it partway. Determined to part on a positive note, I waited until I was certain those without could hear me clearly.

"Thank you, preeminence. I shall heed your advice and try my utmost to learn my proper place here."

"Aspirant Bridges," said Headmaster Prowd. "you are to escort Lucas here to your house and see to his accommodation. Get him settled in and set an appointment for him with Mistress Julia."

"Yes, preeminence," the boy responded.

Within me, I felt a surge of resentment as the witch fumed. No longer content to haunt my dreams, it would seem that this familiar place and its people had emboldened her to encroach upon my waking thoughts. Well, I'd had enough. I would purge the venomous old hag from my soul, even if it took a grand working. In a magical academy, I should be able to discover the proper means.

***

I was dismayed to discover my new home was not the same one to which Roy had been sent. Thus was I to be shorn of the last vestiges of familiarity as I embarked upon my new life here. Lloyd had proven to be a talker. In this, he put me somewhat in mind of Kevin Monohan, a baker of my acquaintance back in Meadowfork. As Lloyd set an appointment for me to meet with this 'Mistress Julia' and summoned porters to carry my trunk, he had filled me in on all manner of details about the house to which I'd been assigned.

At the conclave, each master wizard maintained an estate similar in size to those of Osten's nobles. As we passed by some of these, Lloyd would remark on their owners, naming each and summing up his or her role. Unlike the nobles of the kingdom, master wizards could be either male or female. The unmarried women among them could even hold title to their own estates and have their own apprentices and journeymen. Such progressive allowances had proven a necessity because the gift of magic could be found in anyone heedless of gender.

This Mistress Julia was one such. Moreover, she occupied the unique position of being the only Elven master to live here at Conclave. There were other Elven masters, but almost all returned to their homeland of Lorédon upon attaining mastery. Why she had chosen to remain was anyone's guess.

The house where we were heading was a different matter. Masterless aspirants such as Lloyd and I were assigned common houses on the campus and expected to manage our own affairs until such time as we were offered journeyman positions. This process could take years in some cases. Lloyd himself had been trying to achieve that status for nearly two years. And Franklin Stein, our head of house, had been passed over four years running. No master as yet had elected to take in a necromancer. I was eager to meet Franklin. I had several private missives to pass on to him from his parents. The lad was noble-born. Surely that had to count for something.

Most of the estates we saw were built of a distinctive brown stone, and icicles hung from their roofs and lintels. These sparkled under the midday sun. Each had an extensive frontage and were set back from the roadway by well-sculpted hedges and gardens. The smoke that curled lazily up from brownstone chimneys suggested warm, friendly interiors to match the elegance apparent from without.

"That's Master Martin's estate," observed Lloyd, pointing out one of the more modest villas. "He's only just recently arisen to master. I thought you might be interested 'cause he's from your neck of the woods."

"Westarbor?" I asked, at once curious. "What's his given name?"

The baron had told me that before Roy and me, no mages had been discovered in our barony for well over a decade. I didn't know of any Martins in Meadowfork. His family must hail from one of the eastern fiefs.

"Martin *is* his first name," said the boy with a chuckle. "He insists on it. His full name is Martin Edward Bates. I first knew him as 'Journeyman Bates.' Since rising to master status, he uses his given name after his title to avoid any unfortunate associations."

It took me a moment, then I burst out laughing.

As Lloyd prattled on pointing out various landmarks and sharing tidbits of conclave gossip, I felt myself relax. The porters trudged along after us, bearing my trunk and other gear. So much was new. I caught my breath with excitement as we approached a most curious sight.

"Here we are, then, Aspie Rowe," Lloyd announced.

Where a well-trodden footpath branched off from the cobbles of the avenue, sat a large piece of statuary. At its top perched a trio of mermaid statues spouting water in bubbling arcs. These jetted down into a stone basin resembling the bottom half of an enormous clam shell resting at about shoulder height. Into this great shell, the waters swirled and churned eventually to dribble over its lip into a larger circular reservoir below. What made the water issue forth from above in defiance of the pull of the earth? Was there a water sprite trapped inside? Noting my bewilderment, Lloyd paused and remarked.

"Oh. That's the fountain. The water mages enchanted it to do that. It keeps the water fresh. I'd quite forgotten how strange it can seem to a newcomer. You get used to such things living in a community of mages. Why have a mere well when one can have an ever-flowing fountain?"

I could see life at the conclave would require some broadening of my thinking.

Staring beyond the fountain and down the path, I made out several structures. These weren't so grand as the estates we had passed earlier, being made of wood and seeming rather plain by comparison. Still, they were large as buildings went. And although appearing to be only a single story in height, they looked spacious enough and sat upon ample grounds. Unlike the crowded confines of Conclave Village beyond, it seemed the mages valued a sense of privacy and distance.

"Come on," Lloyd cajoled me. "This one's ours just down on the left. I'll introduce you to the others."

To the porters the boy said: 'You can just leave that stuff on the porch. We can take it from here.'

"Hail House Blue Jay!" shouted the boy, racing ahead. "Our new housemate has arrived! Come on out and give him a proper welcome."

Lloyd's excitement was encouraging, and I strode forward with a feeling of hopeful anticipation.

Stepping up onto the front stoop, Lloyd shoved the door inward and thrust his head within.

"C'mon guys, he's here."

The boy retreated several paces as the door swung wider to reveal another young man with a mop of dusty blond hair. He was nearly as tall as Royland, and though slender, was more well filled out withal. I noted a strong resemblance to Lord Leopold, so I took him to be Franklin.

A moment later, the man was joined by a dark-haired girl. She shouldered in beside him in the entryway to peer at me curiously. She had the smooth, dusky complexion I had come to associate with southerners.

"Well, what's wrong with this one?" she sniffed.

"That's just rude, Lory," Franklin berated her. "Is that what passes for manners among your folk, or is it merely a result of your own uncivil nature? You should at least wait until you're properly introduced before casting disparagements on a man's character."

"Lucas here has been assigned to us," Lloyd announced. "The other one went to the falcons. Lucas, this is Franklin Stein, our head of house. The girl with him is Doña Lorraine Cordova of Alamendra. We call her 'Lightshow.'"

"Only you call me that, klepto."

"I don't do that anymore! I have it under control." The boy protested hotly.

"Please, won't you come in, Lucas," interrupted Franklin. "Lloyd will show you where you'll be staying. I have some tea brewing in the kitchen. I'll go fetch it and we'll all meet back at the parlor. We can share unpleasantries there."

At that, the young man pivoted and stalked off.

"Where's Mudslide?" asked Lloyd, peering expectantly within before entering.

"Sholeena? Where else?" sighed Miss Donna, rolling her eyes as she made way.

My head was beginning to ache from the many unanswered questions that were piling up. I followed Lloyd into the house to commence my initiation with the Blue Jays. Though patience was never my strong suit, I was cautiously optimistic all would be explained eventually. Tea sounded nice.

***

It turned out that Franklin had brewed a most delectable pot of tea. After I'd gotten my possessions settled in the room I'd be sharing with Lloyd, we reconvened in the common area of House Blue Jay they called their parlor. In it were several comfortable and serviceable divans positioned before a cozy hearth.

I learned there were presently three hostelries for aspirants awaiting selection by a master: our own, House Falcon, and House Owl. The origins of these ornithological designations were a bit hazy, but it had been thus from time immemorial.

In theory, all the houses were deemed equal. However, according to Franklin, those aspirants who were considered the most promising in Master Prowd's estimation had a way of finding themselves in House Falcon. Those with whom he found fault would wind up here. I wanted to blame my outburst in the headmaster's foyer and subsequent poor interview for my placement. But there must be something else, for it seemed the decision had already been made days prior to my arrival. That's why Lloyd had been summoned to be my guide.

Royland had been sent to House Falcon. Perhaps there was a clue in that. The headmaster had remarked on Roy's fine lineage as a Brubaker with enthusiasm, whereas he'd touched

11

on the fact that *my* only known magical ancestor was Abigale. If such were his criteria, then perhaps my new housemates had more to offer than I had begun to suppose. Bloodlines didn't determine one's character or worth, after all.

The others drew me out. They were a friendly lot, but their curious stares as these disturbing facts were unveiled begged the question; what precisely was the matter with Lucas Harper? The intimate setting and the refreshing drink were conducive to frank discourse, so I shared my suspicions on the matter.

"Interesting," Franklin remarked once I'd related the tale of my grandmother and her betrayal of her oaths. "So you don't actually know who your grandfather was?"

It was a tender subject. I suspected the fellow in question had to have been someone living around here twenty-five years ago. I made no response.

"Tell me," he continued. "What is the nature of your magical gift? What do you envision as you work your magic?"

I explained that my magic center resembled a green field from which I could cause vines to sprout. These ropy vines, visible only to mage sight, would slither about to do my bidding. A look of shock crossed Lloyd's features, and the girl seated next to him crossed herself and made a quiet utterance.

"What?" I exclaimed. "What's wrong with vines?"

The girl Lloyd had dubbed 'Lightshow' was the first to respond.

"You know we are at war, Lucas. Down in Freemark where I am from, there are frequent encroachments by the dark druids and their horrid creatures. It is rare that one sights one of the enemy mages, rarer still that he is spotted by someone capable of mage sight. But on the several occasions when this has occurred, their magic is worked with just such vines as you have described."

Master Chadwick had once told me that each mage's gift is just as unique as a snowflake. I didn't know what he was going on about. Unlike mages (who were rare) there were millions of snowflakes fluttering about, and they all looked pretty much the same. However, the particular magic one possessed was also known to run in families. Why hadn't Master Chadwick cautioned me that my gift bore similarities to those of our enemies?

"That explains a great deal, Lucas," Franklin stated. "You'll be starting with that against you as well."

I felt we had dwelt on my shortcomings long enough and it was time for some others to come clean.

"I believe I know why Franklin is here," I said. "What about you, Miss Donna, why do you think they put you in the blue jays?"

She tilted her head and gave me a quizzical look.

"My name is Lorraine," she said.

"But Lloyd introduced you as..."

"Ah, I see," she said with a smirk. "Doña is an honorific we use in Freemark before a lady's proper name. It is like your 'miss' or 'madam.' As to how the headmaster may find me lacking, I suspect it is a simple matter of gender bias. Female wizards *always* have a harder time proving their worth."

"I'm not quite sure that's the entire picture," Franklin countered. "There are several female aspirants in House Owl, you know."

"Maybe it's because you can't do the normal stuff like levitation very well," put in Lloyd.

The girl frowned and glared at the boy.

"I'm getting better at the standard tasks, unlike *some* people I could mention."

It was Lloyd's turn to frown.

"Well, *my* power's unique, and I can do more than make pretty lights. They just haven't picked me yet because they don't know how to train it."

"I warned you we'd get around to airing unpleasantries," Franklin grumbled, refilling his tea cup. "Is there anyone *you* would like to castigate, Lucas?"

"I think," I replied, "I'll have to get to know you all better before joining in the innuendo and scathing rebukes. Just what is *your* magic center anyway, Lloyd?"

"Oh. It's nothing really," he said with a sly wink.

The other two groaned.

"I'm sure it's not nothing..." I trailed off encouragingly.

"Then you'd sure be wrong," he returned, his grin broadening a notch. "My magic center is literally nothing, a void. It took me forever to even find it. But now I can put things inside it and pull 'em back out later! Watch."

Lloyd scowled and glared down at his empty teacup, which promptly vanished. Even with mage sight, I could discern no trace of it.

A moment later, Lloyd relaxed and said: 'Now check in your pocket.'

Doing so, I was perplexed and a little uneasy to find his cup there, still slightly warm.

"Lloyd the Void, they'll call me once I've earned my mastery..."

"Lloyd, the peeler of potatoes, we'll call you this afternoon," interrupted Franklin. "Tonight's the welcoming feast for Lucas here, and it's your night to cook. Best you hop to it."

Pursing his lips in a bellicose frown, the boy stood and trudged reluctantly toward the kitchen. Once he was beyond earshot, Franklin turned to me and spoke in low tones.

"He's not a bad sort, Lucas. You may hear ill spoken of him around town, but try not to give it any credence. When his gift first became active, it wasn't under his conscious control. Things that he desired or admired had a way of just disappearing. In the morning, the missing items would be found at his bedside. His parents thought he had a terrible problem."

"Good lord, whatever did they do?" I asked.

Lorraine looked sad as Franklin resumed the tale.

"They made him return the items and apologize to his friends or the merchants he'd supposedly wronged. But word spread, and he was soon barred from most of the shops in his village. The matter grew even worse when a dead puppy was discovered in his bed one morning. It seems there's no air in that void of his."

Franklin drained his cup and set it aside before continuing.

"In desperation, his parents appealed to the Lord Mayor for help. After reviewing the case, his lordship decreed that as a petty thief, Lloyd should be placed in the stocks to be released only after he'd shown proper remorse for his misdeeds. He was there for the better part of a day because he wouldn't confess to having taken anything."

"Stars above!" I exclaimed. "And I thought I had it rough in the stocks. At least I knew why I was there."

Lory looked over at me sharply.

"You were in the stockade?" she said with sudden disdain. "What was your crime?"

"Nothing serious. A story for another day," I hastily averred. "Go on. What happened to Lloyd?"

"Sometime that afternoon, a curious thing occurred. Tired of jeering at the boy in the stocks, some passers by of a crueler bent took to lobbing spoiled vegetables and other refuse at Lloyd. Yet even through his tears, the boy continued to profess his innocence. And suddenly, as if in answer to his prayers, whatever was thrown at him began to vanish in mid-air. After a time, it would reappear on the ground before him. In due course, he was released and sent to the conclave where it was determined he possessed the gift."

"Well, at least he's here now," I remarked. "Where's the kid from, anyway?"

"That's the problem, Lucas," said Lory. "Lloyd grew up right here in Conclave Village. He still gets harassed every time he tries leaving the mage's quarter. We don't make him go into town for supplies any more."

I stared into the flickering flames of our fire. And for a time, the crackling as it consumed the orange-gray logs and an occasional clatter of pans and cutlery from the kitchen were the only sounds to disturb our somber thoughts.

"Hail Housh Blue Jay!" we heard from outside. "I'm back with fresh fish for our feasht!"

"Sholeena's returned," Franklin remarked unnecessarily. "Lucas, will you go fetch us a fresh pail of water from the fountain? She's a bit bashful, and this will give her a chance to clean up while we bring her up to speed on your arrival."

As curious as I was about my other new housemate, I could see the sense in this, so I nodded my affirmation.

"There are some buckets in the mudroom by the back door," reported Lorraine, pointing toward the rear of the cottage.

I arose and made my way to the indicated area.

Sure enough, just within rested a pair of wooden pails near the outer door beneath several sets of jackets and scarves hung from pegs on the wall. A pile of muddy boots lay strewn about the narrow room.

I was no stranger to hauling water, having done so at Fowler Ranch for the better part of three seasons. If I took my time, perhaps I could examine that fountain. Mayhap with mage sight I could suss out its strange enchantment.

The day was milder than it had been in weeks, and most of the snow had melted, leaving bare the slimy dirt of the path I trod. As I came around the house, there was no sign of the girl. Evidently, she'd already gone within. I did, however, spot a fellow entering the house across the way. It was like our own, but bore a placard with a painted hunting bird hanging from its eaves. And there stood Roy, stepping out onto its front stoop and clasping hands firmly with the chap, a crooked smile upon his face. I'd rarely ever seen my cousin so animated and wondered yet again what was up with him.

He glanced over. And though I knew he'd recognized me, Roy made no gesture of acknowledgment. He simply turned away and slipped back within.

***

Dinner was splendid. It featured perch fillets fresh caught from Lake Placid. Potatoes had been sliced into long, stout planks and pan fried in butter to a crispy outer texture.

I was introduced to Sholeena. I didn't know what I had expected, but the strange girl captured my interest at once. As I'd been warned, she was extremely reticent and withdrawn. Her people were called the Paludaria, which loosely means 'marsh-dweller.' She had peculiar brown eyes. They were generously sized and set farther apart than most people's. They shimmered strangely when she blinked, which she seldom did. Her nose wasn't very prominent, and it sat above a mouth that seemed a tad too wide. Though not unpleasing to the eye, the whole manifested an exotic effect, as if her face had been squashed just a bit.

I thought to put her at her ease.

"So, Sholeena, is it?" I said. "What's your surname, then?"

She stared at me with those soulful eyes, and her skin darkened a shade.

"It's Blorlafargalish, as near as we can pronounce," Lloyd quickly put forth.

I tried once again to pierce the uneasy silence that followed.

"These fish are delicious," I declared, stabbing into one. "However did you manage to catch perch in the wintertime? And in the middle of the day at that?"

The girl blinked, and her mouth formed into a broad grin. I could tell this topic had caught her fancy. It was good to know my time at Lakethroat Village hadn't been entirely wasted.

"You have to dive deep," she replied in a throaty whisper.

"You mean in the water?" I asked, seeking clarification.

"Of course," she returned. "Thatsh where all the fish are."

I was stunned. Certain the waters of Lake Placid were bitterly cold, I thought I must've overlooked something here.

"You like fish?" she inquired. "Which fish do you like besht?"

I considered her question.

"I enjoy most kinds of fish," I answered, "but I was recently introduced to eel. It's very succulent and has a flavor I find I fancy."

"I love eel too," said Sholeena with rising excitement. "We don't have any here, them needing ocean water to breed in. But I know a great place to catch catfish. Maybe you and me can be canoodling at the lake tomorrow. Do you want to?"

So much for her being the timid type. I quickly took an overlarge bite of steaming potatoes to forestall an immediate response. I didn't want to hurt the girl's feelings, but we'd only just *met* for star's sake.

Lorraine cast me a devilish smirk, then turned to Sholeena.

"Sholeena dear, your speech is getting much better, but I'm certain you meant to say 'go noodling.' 'Canoodling' is something different."

"Go noodling," Sholeena slowly repeated, then focused on me once more. "You want to?"

"Sure," I replied hastily.

I wasn't completely certain what I'd just agreed to, but I was eager to move past the awkward exchange. I grabbed up my tin tankard and drank deeply from it. Those potatoes had scorched the roof of my mouth.

"Excuse me a minute," mumbled Lloyd, biting at his lower lip. "I think I left something in the kitchen."

Not long after he'd exited, we heard a burst of whoops and guffaws from back that way. The boy later swore he'd swallowed something wrong, but I suspected they'd arisen from a different cause.

"We have to leave before the dawn," Sholeena added. "Catfish are feeding moshtly at night."

"As long as we can be back and cleaned up by midday, that should be alright," I returned. "I have an appointment with Mistress Julia in the afternoon."

"Well, in that case, we'd best call it an early night," announced Franklin. "Lorraine, you're on clean-up duty."

The girl pouted but made no argument. As she set to clearing the dishes and cutlery, I headed for my room. I was soon joined by Lloyd, who was still all grins and would occasionally erupt in suppressed snorts.

"What bait and tackle will be needed for this 'noodling,' Lloyd?" I asked as I turned down my sheets.

For some reason, this set him off again. When he'd settled and began changing into his nightgown, the boy finally answered.

"You'll have all you need," he giggled. "Sholeena will fill you in in the morning. She'll help you *tackle* the problem quite . . . *handily*, I'm sure."

"What's that?" he asked, glancing over sharply.

I had taken out my flask of the green elixir and was measuring out a teaspoon.

"It's just something to help me sleep. Without it, I tend to suffer night terrors."

"Oh... Lucas?"

"Yes?"

"If anything of yours *does* go missing, simply ask me about it and don't be cross, alright? I really have gotten much better, but if I have a lapse, know it's not something I do deliberately."

I let this sink in.

"Alright," I agreed.

The boy brightened.

"Vines. I'm gonna call you Vines," he announced as he slipped beneath his blanket.

"I've been called worse," I quipped.

If Lloyd had some need to assign nicknames, who was I to quibble? It was likely he did so to feel in control of a situation that had treated him rather badly. I would accept Franklin's judgment that Lloyd 'wasn't a bad sort' and roll with it.

"Why do you call Sholeena 'Mudslide?'" I asked instead.

"It's one of her tricks," he replied with a yawn. "She's kind of a water mage. She can do stuff with earth too, but only mud, silt and sediment."

"And Franklin?" I queried. "What do you call him?"

"I haven't decided as yet. He gets grumpy about most of them I've tried. But I've thought of a great one to spring on him tomorrow."

"Care to share it?" I asked as I swallowed my medicine and re-stoppered its bottle.

"Aabra-cadaver," he whispered.

As the potion began to take hold, I wished the boy good luck. Franklin seemed a little too straight-laced to appreciate the humor in that. I hadn't seen him crack so much as a smile the entire evening. Lloyd made no response. It seemed the sandman already had him in his grip.

The last thing I heard as I drifted off was the marching cadence of a goblin drum from across the way. Roy was probably regaling his new housemates with the tale of the siege of Westarbor. I could scarcely credit how outgoing my shy cousin had become of late. A year ago, he'd have cringed at the thought of performing before relative strangers. At least it shouldn't bother my sleep, I thought, as the numbing draught bore me down to a dreamless slumber.

***

I stood shivering on the banks of Lake Placid. The sky to the east was only beginning to brighten. I had always been an early riser, but any earlier and I would have called it late. Sholeena had awoken us in the wee hours by beating upon our door. Lloyd had merely rolled over, moaned, and covered his head with his pillow. So here I was watching the Paluda girl unlace her boots.

"You can't mean for us to go *into* the water," I argued. "It's freezing cold."

"Don't be a crybaby," she said as she slipped a foot free. "I'll show you a magic that will help."

Her foot was most irregular. Though not much larger than my own, her toes were far longer, being divided from one another halfway back to her ankle. As I watched, she wiggled those toes and moaned with relief. More curious still, her feet then splayed out to twice their former width. Between each digit stretched fleshy membranes akin to those of a waterfowl. The Paludaria were a more divergent folk than I had imagined.

Noting my gaze, Sholeena returned it, a frown of worry creasing her brow. I smiled and shrugged and began unlacing my own boots.

"What's this magic?" I asked.

"It'sh for keeping warm. My app-mashter taught it to me."

I was always game to learn a new spell. My own 'app-master' (which I took to mean the master under whom I'd apprenticed) had been quite stingy with them. Master Chadwick had always insisted that doing a few things well was preferable to doing many things poorly. Still, I had chafed under this maxim and yearned to learn more.

"Well, let's see it then," I prompted her.

She stood and said: "Watch carefully now."

I invoked my mage sight and observed as Sholeena folded her arms across her chest to rest her hands upon her opposite shoulders. As she bowed her head and incanted 'internum calorem,' I glimpsed her magic center. It was a pond amid a lush green meadow. Unlike my own inner garden, there was a sense of closeness, as though dripping vegetation surrounded it and gray clouds hung above. The waters poured forth from this pond to flow up her arms and enfold the girl like the warmth of a mother's embrace.

I knew it wouldn't be the same for me. But having observed it closely with mage sight, I felt certain I could create a similar effect after some practice. I deepened my breathing, duplicated her gestures and connected to my magic. At my call, the vines which sprouted from my inner garden lengthened and came twining up my arms to my fingertips. From there, they went on to enshroud my body in a fine lattice of tendrils which pulsed out a warm radiance as they snuggled close to my skin.

Had I done it? Rarely had I succeeded at a new magic on the first try. But as I lowered my arms, the pulse of warmth continued. I felt the sustained draw upon my magic. Unlike my darksight, another spell that needed to be maintained, this drain was significant. With my limited endurance, I doubted I could maintain it for even a full hour.

"Feel better?" Leena asked as she removed her cloak and spread it upon a rocky outcropping nearby.

I heard the slight note of condescension in her voice and was disheartened that she took for granted my prodigious accomplishment.

"Much," I replied, still basking in inner warmth.

To my dismay, the girl proceeded to undress. She first shrugged out of her overcoat, folding it and laying it atop her cloak. She then began stripping off her other outer garments. Underneath, she wore tight-fitting nether garments. The baggy apparel the girl seemed to favor had given me a neutral impression. However, once she'd shucked them off, I couldn't help but notice that the Paludaria were most definitely mammals. I blushed.

"Hurry up," she admonished me. "It'll be daylight shoon."

Unaccustomed to such public display, I nonetheless tugged off my own boots, stood, and did likewise. If I was going in that lake, I sure as sunshine wanted to return to dry clothing. I remained warm in the embrace of 'internum calorem,' but the drain on my magic center nearly doubled as the wind off the lake caressed my bare skin. I quickly revised my hopeful estimate of one hour downward sharply.

Sholeena was staring unabashed at my bare feet. Turnabout is fair play; I supposed.

"How do you people shwim with those shtubby little things?" she mused aloud.

"Poorly by your standards, I would imagine," said I. "They're great for running, though."

I demonstrated this by bouncing on the balls of my feet. The girl's mouth widened again in what I was coming to recognize as a Paluda grin.

"Before we go in," she said, serious once more, "I'll tell you about noodling. It's the sport of catching a large fish by hand using your fingers as bait."

I shuddered at the thought. As she spoke, the slurring sibilants of her speech seemed to all but vanish. I could still make them out when I thought about it, but my ear had adjusted and made them much less noticeable.

"You see, catfish like to feel protected," she explained. "So they hide in holes and crevasses along the cliff face. In this lake, they feed mostly on sludge worms and slugs that come wandering into their lairs. To get at them, we reach slowly into their burrows while wiggling our fingers to look like food."

I thought I saw where this was going, and I was aghast. Noodling, indeed. Still, I listened intently. This outing had obviously sparked the girl's interest and caused her to open up to me. As she warmed to the topic, her erstwhile shy manner deteriorated. There was a growing excitement in her voice.

"When the fish strikes and tries to swallow your fingers, you need to be quick," she said, demonstrating the disgusting maneuver by catching her wriggling fingers in her opposing hand. "Before it can pull back, you shove your hand down his throat and grab him by the gills! Then you can drag him from his den and toss him up on the shore."

"Won't the fish tear into my arm?" I protested nervously.

"Oh, he'll fight back alright. They can wrap their tails around stuff to anchor themselves, and some of them like to roll. A big one can twist your arm near out of its socket. Their teeth are sharp, but not very long. A good meal of catfish is worth a few scratches. Plus it's fun," she finished with a shrug.

I glanced down at the gently lapping waters of the lake. We stood atop a prominence about ten feet above its surface. The breeze brought me a musty, earthy odor akin to that of our mill pond back home. The dark waters had a brownish cast as revealed by the first pre-dawn light arising in the east. There was no beach below. Here, Lake Placid's rocky rim plunged straight downward to depths unknown.

"Alright," I agreed. "We'd best hurry, then. I doubt I can keep this warming spell up for very much longer. Where are these holes?

Sholeena stepped up beside me and spread her arms wide. 'Aquam claram,' she softly incanted. This was accompanied by a burst of brilliance from my mage sight as a cloud of mist emerged from the girl to drift out and settle lazily upon the lake's surface. It billowed out to enshroud an area as large as a plowed acre. And where it touched, the waters cleared. I could sense the suspended silt and sediment falling out to be deposited on the lake's bed far beneath.

"Is this safe?" I asked.

Her frank reply was fraught with enough qualifiers to render it far from reassuring.

"It's pretty safe here by the shore. All the dangerous predators stay mostly out in the deeper parts of the lake."

With this, she dove. One moment, she was standing beside me, and in the next she was flowing in a graceful, high arc to plunge head-first into the basin below. She made almost no sound as she knifed through the surface and shrank from my view.

Well, I told my suddenly shaky legs. We agreed to this. It's best we get on with it at once. Despite their reluctance to heed my encouragement, they nevertheless bent, and their muscles bunched to prepare for our upcoming leap of faith. I stumbled from atop the cliff's edge, my unsteady legs giving one final twitch of effort to gain some distance from the rocky escarpment. I flailed my arms about in an ineffectual effort to right my swift descent. I struck with a mighty splash, which must have surely alerted all nearby lake dwellers that new prey had arrived.

The wind was knocked right out of me, and the bracing shock of encountering the frigid waters momentarily wracked me as I sunk straight down.

Now, I could swim. But I wasn't well practiced at it. I enjoyed splashing about in the mill pond in the heat of the summer, but only rarely went out beyond where my feet could touch bottom. As the pressure built, causing an unpleasant popping in my ears, I scooped the water downward and kicked as I had learned as a child. In this manner, I made my ungainly way toward the surface. At least I *hoped* that slightly brighter, ripply patch of water was indeed up.

As I resurfaced, I drew a deep breath into my beleaguered lungs. It was accompanied by an unfortunate helping of bitingly cold lake water. Choking and flopping about, I stroked eagerly toward the cliff. Perhaps there I could find purchase on some stony protrusion. Achieving this at last, I looked earnestly about. Sholeena was nowhere to be seen.

Then an indistinct shape emerged from beneath me to my right.

"I see you found a likely catfish lair," she said.

I stood on a rough shelf protruding from the cliff face in water nearly up to my chest. Noting what I was gripping, I released it at once and snatched my hand back. Sholeena's eyes had that shimmer again, almost as though they produced a light of their own. I was later to learn that the Paludaria possessed a second, inner pair of transparent eyelids. These nictitating membranes would snap closed momentarily if the girl blinked and would remain closed when she was submerged in water.

"Ah, yes," I fibbed. "I thought this might be a good one."

"It's a bit too high on the cliff. You should try deeper down. But stay on the ledge. Catfish are strong, and a big one can drag you straight down under."

Marvelous, I thought.

And with this, she sped away. I watched her go, admiring her fluid grace and the economy of the languid strokes with which she cut through the water with ease. She more resembled a bird in flight than a swimmer. On the way here, I'd had a few unkind thoughts about Sholeena's bandy-legged stride, but now I understood why this was. Here, she was clearly in her element, and not just magically.

I'd read of mermaids, and of sirens and selkies, but the Paludaria were something else again. The way her hair fanned out behind her and undulated about when she turned was hypnotic, as were her shining eyes. In this environment, she was the most beautiful of women (save perhaps for one). I felt crude by comparison. Who was I but a graceless buffoon who couldn't even manage a decent dive? And yet she'd been so happy when I'd agreed to come. She must be terribly lonely.

As Sholeena poked and prodded about the cliff face, I considered my other problem. Since entering the lake's thermally challenging embrace, the draw upon my magic had increased yet again. My inner garden was becoming dangerously depleted. I suspected the Paluda girl had other defenses against the water's chill, that or a much greater magic reserve than had I. I did, however, possess another gift I thought might help.

Since shattering the witch's heart, I had developed a secondary affinity, this one for earth. It manifested as a small hump at the periphery of my inner garden. The hump had since grown into a respectable hillock. Using it, I could perform some basic earth shaping that had proven quite useful on several recent occasions. Royland had shown me how to establish a conduit from this to my primary magic to share power betwixt the two. I formed such a conduit now and immediately felt the replenishment of my garden's resources.

I returned to probing the cliff side, reaching within likely holes and wiggling my fingers enticingly as I edged along.

Sholeena had already found two and had joyously held them up for display before releasing them back into the lake. Each big, flat-headed fish must have weighed at least thirty or forty pounds. I think she was waiting for me to find one. Lucky me.

If it was a snake, it would've bitten me. As it was a fish, it tried to bite me anyway. My fingers were engulfed by a slimy scraping and then a sharp snap snared my wrist. When the creature began to disengage, I almost missed my moment to thrust my arm deeper within and scrabble for a better handhold. I found a firm purchase as I worked my fingers behind its gill cover and heaved.

My heart was racing like the staccato beats of one of Royland's drum solos.

The fish resisted my pull and clung to something within its tunnel. I planted both feet upon the cliff face and tugged harder. That did the trick. A sudden release sent me spinning out into the water while the catfish thrashed about.

Although I outweighed it by far, my writhing adversary was in his native environment and had been driven into a frenzy by fear. I was only barely able to get my head above water to snatch an occasional breath as our struggle wore on. Relief came when a nearby experienced swimmer noted my distress and helped tow me and my aquatic nemesis back over to firm ground. I made a mental note never to try this alone.

"Oh," Sholeena remarked brightly, "you caught a little one."

I glanced down at the oddly elongated piscine still struggling in my grip. With my other hand, I seized him about his slimy, squirming middle and lifted him up onto my shoulder as the girl had done.

At nearly the length of my arm, my catch probably weighed only twenty to twenty-five pounds, certainly no more than two peck bags of flour. He glared over at me and thrashed his tail as if already planning his escape. With Sholeena trailing watchfully behind, I made my way back up to the top of the cliff. On arriving, Leena lifted the lid of the over-sized bucket she'd filled earlier. I released my captive to coil within it.

"I think that's it for me, Sholeena," I declared.

The sun had by now fully arisen. It cast its first early rays to glitter upon the lake. A family of swans launched silently from a cove nearby to begin their daily foraging.

"We've got enough for our dinner," she amiably agreed.

Sholeena muttered a strange spell that caused the water to slough off of us. Even my squelching nether garments remained only slightly damp. Once bundled back in my dry winter clothing, I released my spell of warmth and was relieved to note I still retained some small store of magic. We gathered up our belongings and headed for home, toting the heavy bucket between us.

***

"So how did you like noodling," asked Sholeena as we strolled along.

"It was exhilarating," I replied with a grin.

The trail up from the lake wound about several estates set on hilltops and soon joined a cobbled walkway bordered on both sides by lush grounds. These, I was to learn, were the conclave's extensive gardens. On the left were uniformly planted orchards that provided a variety of fresh fruits through the warm season. Among these were the peaches which Taylor Allen had described. Sholeena assured me they were delicious, but I remained skeptical, having never encountered a hairy fruit before.

To our right stretched a semi-wild area that was home to more exotic flora the conclave cultivated for various uses. The Paluda girl explained it was Mistress Willoughby's private glade and was forbidden to all save for masters. Supposedly, some unnatural horrors prowled within, and once, a student who had entered unaccompanied had been lost. It struck me as a strange way to run a garden.

My arm was tiring from lugging the heavy pail between us, so I suggested we switch sides. Sholeena had been uncomplaining thus far, but I sensed her uneven strides starting to falter. With relief, we set down our heavy burden and stretched.

My wrist was still sore from my struggle with the fish and bore abrasions from its sandpapery teeth. I sought about for a bit of greenery with which to refresh myself. I had learned my gift could be used to draw energy from plants, and such a draw restored my vitality, both magically and in general.

I quickly located a creeper that had strayed out onto the roadway and set about peeling it up from the cobbles. As I tugged, its leaves shriveled and its vine withered away until naught remained but a trail of earthy compost. I was getting much better at this. Reassessing my magic center, I noted some small improvement, and the pain in my wrist had receded to but a dull ache.

Initially, Sholeena had observed this process with wide-eyed interest. But soon she shifted her focus to an indistinct chatter from down the road. Rising to my feet and following her frowning regard, I spotted a group of young men loitering just down the lane. They were making their lazy way along the walkway, coming from the direction we were headed.

On sighting us, there was a shift in the pitch of their banter, followed by a burst of boisterous laughter. I was hopeful, but based on prior experience of when young men clustered so, I had some few misgivings. They were finely dressed and approached us in a haughty strut. The one in the lead hailed me.

"Ho there. Am I right in thinking you're the new bloke from Westarbor, the one Royland's been telling us about?"

"That's me," I replied. "And you are?"

"Ellison Reznic, head of House Falcon. My friends call me Eli. *You* may call me Aspirant Reznic, at least for the next two weeks," he said with a self-righteous smile.

"With me are aspirants Scott McNair and Henry Sutherland," he continued, indicating each in turn. "Is it true you battled a witch and a goblin horde?"

"Sort of," I equivocated.

"Not the boastful sort, I see," said he. "What are you doing hanging about with this riff-raff? Did you anger your app-master somehow?"

I didn't care for the boy's disdainful tone and took an instant disliking to him. I sought about for some kind of innocuous reply. I'd found it was usually a mistake to confront a bully in front of his sycophants. Sholeena, too, remained silent, refusing to take the bait.

"Sholeena was showing me the lake," I said brightly, hoping to deflect his careless discourtesy. "We caught a fish for our dinner."

"Ribbit!" said the one called Scott, drawing a laugh from the two others.

Glancing over to Sholeena, I noted her skin had reddened.

"Oh look, it's blushing," remarked Henry. ""Hazh froggy got a new beau? Thinking to make some tadpoles are we? Showing the new kid your spawning ground?"

This impolite and ill-conceived attempt at jest nonetheless garnered grins all around. Content to let his underlings spearhead the attack, Eli just leaned back and smiled his approval. It was a toothy, mirthless, crocodile smile. My dislike of him deepened.

As to Sholeena, she had reddened another notch. Those who knew Paluda (as I was only just beginning to) wouldn't have made Henry's mistake. Far from being a blush, the reddening of her skin signaled rage to the more well-informed. Her hands shook, and I heard water slosh from our bucket over its rim to pool uneasily in the dirt beside the road.

Into this tense situation meandered my cousin.

"Ho, Royland," shouted Eli as Roy approached. "We were just greeting your countryman here and his ... housepet."

The others sniggered obligingly.

It was then that Sholeena finally lashed out. I don't believe she meant to do it. It was more likely an unconscious use of her magic fueled by her anger. The water on the ground seemed to crawl around, gathering dirt unto itself. Then it reared itself up and went hurtling toward Eli. The large roundish glob of muck struck him square in his midriff, spattering the uncivil martinet from neck to crotch (thus demonstrating most effectively that mud slinging could cut both ways).

Royland's blue shield went up a moment later, protecting him and his new cronies from a subsequent volley. Her anger spent, all color drained from Sholeena, and her face blended uncannily well with the background. Were I but a few paces farther away, I might have thought her headless. This reflexive camouflage, I was to learn, was an unconscious Paluda reaction to fright or embarrassment. Given the context, my bet was on the latter.

All stood in stunned silence as the reality of the sudden affront was absorbed. Thankfully, I was the first to recover. I, too, could work earth. And if I acted swiftly, perhaps I could salvage the situation. Calling on my inner hillock, I incanted 'pulver in ventis.' It was a dandy little spell Master Chadwick used to shed the mud from his boots back at Fowler Ranch. It loosely translated to 'dust in the wind.' The mud coating Eli's garments crumbled away and was soon jettisoned from his jacket.

"There you go, Aspirant," I swiftly supplied in a jolly tone. "Good as new and no harm done."

There was a pause as he considered.

"That doesn't atone for the insult," he pronounced. "I remain unsatisfied. There must be a penalty."

I turned to my cousin for support. Roy avoided my gaze; a game he was good at. When I gave him the stink-eye, he didn't even flinch.

"The conclave forbids the use of magic against the person of a fellow mage," Eli continued, a sloppy grin forming on his gloating face. "The penalties can be quite severe. I don't think you'll want to involve the seneschals. I hear you're on thin ice with the headmaster as it is. No. We'll just have to resolve this matter on our own."

Royland looked troubled for a moment, but then his false smile snapped back into place and he uttered not a word. Fumbling beneath her blouse, Sholeena fearfully drew forth a small knife. Women sometimes sported such as a last-ditch effort at self-defense. She began backing away.

"That'll do nicely, I think," said Eli. "Henry, if you please?"

At this, Aspirant Sutherland stepped forth and pursed his lips. An eerie sound emerged. I summoned my vines, preparing to do I know not what. The vibrations from Henry's whistling grew ever more intense, and I was struck with a severe case of vertigo.

I promptly lost focus on my magic and was having trouble maintaining my balance. As I dropped to one knee, I saw Sholeena's knife fall from boneless fingers. Before it struck the ground, Eli incanted 'levare conicere' and it went spinning off into the trees. The Paluda girl toppled to lie weeping upon the cobbles as the shrill whistling finally abated.

The world stopped spinning.

"You'll think twice before sullying a falcon again with your foul muck, Paluda," said Eli, tapping at his chin. "But I think we'll leave you now to reflect on the lesson. We've got an appointment with the butcher to keep. And we must get Royland here to Master Reinhardt for his work assignment."

With that, they strode off.

As he passed me by, Scott McNair gave me a final shove just as I was regaining my feet. I staggered and shot him a glare of hatred. Walking just behind them, my cousin had the good grace to look back and shake his head. But then he too moved on.

I moved over to Sholeena and helped her sit up. She was still quietly weeping. Her face had taken on a bluish tinge that I reasoned must denote sadness.

"Are you hurt?" I asked gently.

"It was my mother's," she moaned. "She gave it to me as a parting gift."

"The knife? It can't be that far in. I'll go fetch it for you," I offered.

"You can't," she sobbed, seizing my arm. "That's the Perilous Glade. Only masters can go in there safely. I'll ask Mistress Willoughby. Maybe she can find it."

My heart went out to the poor girl. Her tone told me she didn't hold high hopes for this prospect. Also, I understood her strong feelings for a memento of a loved one far away. Had that been my father's sword, I wouldn't want to wait.

"Relax," I urged her, "I have a special way with plants. I'll just duck in and retrieve it. I've got this."

So I tugged free of her grip (and her doubtful gaze) and headed into the brush beside the lane.

Not ten feet in, I grew concerned. The bramble was thick, and already I'd lost sight of the way back. I called upon my inner garden to part the thorny vines that barred my way and caught at my clothing. But they resisted. In fact, they seemed to be putting up a concerted effort to repel me. I dug deeper into my gift to penetrate the verdurous tangle, glad that the cold of winter had denuded most of their leaves.

I considered the trio Sholeena and I had encountered.

I prided myself in always seeking the good in people and trying to see things from their point of view. Others with whom I'd scuffled always had their reasons for pursuing the disputes. But I could see no excuse for the pointless cruelty the falcons had heaped upon Sholeena. Was it simply fear of someone different masquerading as disgust and loathing? And what was I to make of Royland's seeming indifference? Was he so eager to fit in as to cast aside our longtime kinship?

I was almost certain the knife had flown this way. Given the force with which it had been flung, it could be a good ways deeper in. And already I was growing fatigued. I opened a conduit to my inner hill. This added but a mere trickle to my magic. Earlier efforts at the lake had depleted much of my stored strength.

The surrounding vines rallied once more, and I saw them actually move to cage me in. Formerly clear zones into which I had carefully stepped were suddenly rife with brambles that caught at my ankles and with greenery heretofore unseen. The very trees seemed to press about me closer. I thought I should perhaps turn back.

But then I perceived a twinge of discomfort in the forest. It was like a stinging echo of distress at the edge of my awareness. I opted to continue onward. Redoubling my efforts, I parted the way ahead and made for its source. At the rate I was using my magic, I mayn't have the strength to return, but I was curious. I could always refresh my magic and clear a path by drawing the life from these plants. But I didn't wish to do so needlessly. In my ignorance, I might damage something the mages valued.

Fighting for every inch, I forged ahead. After what felt like an hour of straining, but was more likely just a few minutes, I saw it. Sticking out from the bole of a tree at about head height was Sholeena's pearl-handled knife. The stinging sensation emanated from the cut in the bark and grew more pronounced as I approached.

Cautiously, I reached up and wiggled the knife free. A drop of sap slowly welled up from the wound. That was peculiar. Sap shouldn't be freely flowing until spring was further along, but it was there, nonetheless. It may have been a maple tree. I could tell better if it had its leaves.

"Sorry tree," I muttered.

As an afterthought, I summoned my vines once more and dumped the rest of my inner garden's vitality to seal the cut. Immediately, the stinging sensation eased. There remained, however, a similar ache from much farther away. This one felt older and more profound. I was still intrigued, but I'd achieved my main aim and probably oughtn't to press my luck.

Now, to retrace my steps.

Turning, I was amazed to see a clear path running back the way I'd come. It hadn't been there before and wasn't straight by any means. But with each turning, I discovered to my delight an unobstructed trail that led toward the lane. I emerged to find Sholeena staring at me in astonishment.

"You *are* good with plants," she praised. "I'd shwear the treesh opened up and shpit you out!"

I nodded, accepting the undeserved compliment, and presented her with the knife.

On noting it, the girl's eyes sparkled, and she flung herself at me.

Parting from our embrace and shy once more she said simply, "Thank you."

And with that, we hefted our bucket and continued on our way.

CHAPTER TWO

The Scholar

"The more that you read, the more things you will know.
The more that you learn, the more places you'll go."

~ Dr. Seuss ~

I stood staring with wonder.

Before me stretched out the enormous chamber which housed the academy's collection of books. Free-standing shelves stood in neatly ordered rows, each laden with their precious codices, manuscripts, and tomes. Franklin had escorted me here and introduced me to its custodian before departing on business of his own. It was here I was to meet Madam Julia to discuss my work detail. As I'd arrived early, I thought I might have a look around but was at a loss as to where to begin. Compared to all this, the baron's library back in Westarbor Keep was but a dusty alcove.

The custodian was a peculiar chap named Edgar Englewood. He seemed rather young for a scholar. I supposed that white-bearded old scholars must perforce begin as younger men. Edgar was a journeyman mage, and this was his assigned duty - one he had requested. More curiously, with him was a bird, a raven he called Lenore. She sat perched on a crossbar atop a pole in a corner near the door. Her inky black feathers reflected the light of the chandelier above.

"In all this," I said, indicating the room at large, "where might I find a map of the academy and its grounds?"

"That one's easy," replied Edgar. "Lenore, show him to the scriptorium."

She cocked her head and peered at me from one coal black eye. Then the bird took wing and glided silently down a long aisle to alight upon a writing desk. That was a bit too blatant to be a mere animal trick. Lenore must be the young man's familiar animal. I'd read of such during my apprenticeship. Long had I suspected that Master Chadwick enjoyed a similar relationship with Sampson, the sheepdog back at Fowler Ranch. My app-master had always played it off as the result of training, hand gestures, and the dog's natural intelligence, but his explanations had grown ever less convincing over time.

Curious, I followed the bird.

The desk on which she had alighted sloped upward to meet a heavy wooden bookshelf. Housed thereupon were dozens of hefty volumes attached to their shelves by chains.

"Well done, Lenore," Edgar praised, ambling up beside me and reaching to the second highest shelf. "Here we are: 'The Anatomy of the Academy.'"

He gently lifted down a thick tome and lay it open upon the sloping boards of the desk. In it was depicted an overhead view of the academy building, drawn in precise lines of ink and neatly numbered. On the opposing page was a legend, labeling each numbered area with a concise description of its purpose. Each page portrayed a different floor of the academy. Some had broader views showing features of the grounds or drawings from other perspectives. I was familiar with such drawings from father's work with Javier Lewis, but never before had I seen architectural plans so exquisitely wrought.

Noting my expression, Edgar smiled.

"That's why it's chained up," he explained.

I thanked the man and then thanked Lenore for good measure. They soon left me in the throes of my new obsession. Edgar promised that when Mistress Julia arrived, he would direct her where to find me.

Tilting my head to better read one caption revived a disturbing, squelching in my inner ear. Since the early morning plunge into Lake Placid, both ears had been beset with this little reminder of my former soggy state. I'd earlier cleared the left side by canting my head and bouncing upon the heel of my left foot. Though this had dislodged the droplet from my left ear, it had also driven the other even deeper into my right. It didn't hurt exactly, nor did it interfere with hearing. It was, however, a most distracting and unsettling sensation.

Once again, I leaned to the right and began hopping on the heel of my right foot, hoping at last to ease the condition. It was thus she found me, hopping and hoping and looking like a loon.

"Harper? Aspirant Lucas Harper?" came a bemused voice from just to my rear.

I righted myself and whirled about.

"I am he," I casually confirmed, trying to conceal my startlement.

"It says here in Luther's notes you need lessons in comportment. There is no mention of a strange, one-legged dance."

The woman confronting me was slender of build and bore the Elven features so distinctive of her race. She carried herself with the grace of her kindred and was bedecked in flowing robes of a fine weave. I swiftly surmised she must be the master with whom I was to meet. She seemed youthful, but I knew that could be misleading. Elves had long lives and could retain a youthful aspect for centuries.

"You may call me Mistress Julia," she said by way of introduction.

She pronounced it differently than others had: 'Jo-LEE-yah.' Something tickled at the back of my mind. I had conversed at length with some Elven jugglers on the caravan's journey here.

"I take it your true name has ought to do with sunshine," I guessed.

She peered at me searchingly before replying: "I see you know something of the first people. My parents gifted me with *Puquabeth Chosha Julia*. It means 'daughter of the twilight sun.'"

Struggling to recall my earlier interactions, I exhausted nine-tenths of the Elven words I'd learned to say: "*jhivath shohvath batlaponia noba*."

At this, her pouty lips seemed to stiffen a notch.

"While I appreciate the effort, your diction is truly atrocious. We shall conduct the rest of this interview in Ostentinian standard speech. I doubt very much I do you humor with the gift of my nose."

The lady wasn't quite what I had expected. The Elves I'd met previously had been possessed of a carefree and playful attitude. From the stern set of her jaw to her high, starched collar, Mistress Julia seemed cut from a different cloth. Her manner bespoke of formidability with which one oughtn't trifle.

Gesturing toward a nearby table, Mistress Julia bade me be seated.

"Thank you for arriving early," she said. "Punctuality is a point in your favor, aspirant. I have much other business to conduct today. I have promises to keep and miles to go before I sleep."

"But the woods are lovely, dark and deep," I recited before I'd thought better of it.

Her entire demeanor seemed to soften a bit, and a hint of a smile played about the corners of her mouth.

"I do believe you could be just the fellow for the job," she said. "I must confess I was puzzled that Luther Prowd had recommended a male aspirant for this task. Teaching the young is considered a lowly task by men like Luther. As such, it is often deemed 'women's work' by those of your misogynist race. Among the first people, be assured the very opposite is true. Are not our young ones the hope for our future?"

I took the question as rhetorical and listened on.

"What has Luther told you?" she asked.

"Only that I am to teach young children and some of the newer apprentices their letters, Mistress."

"And how do you believe you will go about that?"

"I imagine I would arrange to meet with each and instruct them on the subject," I replied.

"No."

"No?"

"We are envisioning an entirely new way of teaching; at least it will be new to your people. Rather than a traditional private tutoring or apprenticeship, we will instead gather the students into one place where a single teacher will impart his knowledge to all at once."

That made no sense. When children gathered, all they wanted to do was play with one another (or squabble among themselves).

"I can see by your expression you doubt the efficacy of such a program," she continued, "but be assured it can work. Furthermore, you will find it is a superior way to impart both knowledge and social skills to the young once proper discipline is established."

"When would I start?" I asked, trying to wrap my mind around how to 'impart knowledge' to a dozen screaming brats.

"Lessons will be taught at the créche. You may meet your students in its small dining hall at their midday meal tomorrow. I would suggest you start slowly and get to know them. Discover their interests and work these into your lessons."

"Yes, Mistress," I replied, bowing my head low.

Squelch, added my right, inner ear.

She stood and made to depart.

"There are numerous rules at the créche. Mistress Meredith will review them before you begin. But additionally is this: under no circumstances are you to teach them magic. The council of masters was quite insistent on this point. That is a subject better left to their eventual app-masters."

I nodded my understanding.

"Oh, and Mistress?" I forestalled.

"Yes?"

"I meant to deliver this to headmaster Prowd, but I became distracted."

Reaching into my pocket, I fished out a folded piece of parchment and slid it across to her.

"It's a proposal for a griffin hostelry here at Conclave. Baron Westarbor has recently acquired a trio of tame griffins that can be ridden. He wishes to establish a network of stops for rapid delivery of packages and the like. I hoped you might convey this to the council."

"Westarbor is just full of surprises these days," she remarked, taking it up. "Very well, I'll see it is brought before the council of masters at our upcoming session."

After my letter vanished within the folds of her garments and with a final nod of dismissal, she turned and glided silently away. Happy to have that duty discharged, I made my way back to the scriptorium and its academy maps. I needed to discover where this créche could be found.

***

I was still at it when Franklin came to retrieve me. There were a thousand topics I wanted to review in this vast collection of books. I wished, not for the first time, that I'd brought along my Bob. Among its other treasures, it contained a quill and ink and some parchment for writing. I could have sketched a rude map and begun a list of things to investigate. Alas, the backpack the Cain's had gifted me sat out of reach back in my bedroom, neglected and unable to share its bounty. I vowed to come better prepared on my next outing.

"How did your interview go, Lucas?"

"Far better than the first, I think. I'm to meet my students tomorrow."

Franklin stared impatiently as I gently lifted the large tome and slid it back onto its shelf, careful not to tangle its jangling chain.

"I see you've found the means to better make your way about," said the older aspirant.

"Yes indeed," I replied. "I intend to haunt this place for as long as they let me."

"Well, there's something else you should see before we return home," he declared. "Follow me."

I nodded affably at Edgar and Lenore as we took our leave and slipped without. I followed Franklin as he led the way.

"Where are we going, Franklin?" I asked.

"The Hall of Masters," he replied. "They're not in session now. Elsewise we couldn't visit it uninvited. I thought you should see it because occasionally we are all summoned there for special announcements. When they toll the bell atop the steeple, here is where you must head."

We finally arrived at a grand hall. It was presently unlit, only a few distant votive candles shed an eerie glow wholly inadequate to brighten its cavernous interior. As we entered, I called upon my darksight, and the room resolved. Our booted footfalls returned multiple echoes, emphasizing the enormity of the stone room. Its vaulted ceilings were shrouded in a darkness that even my enhanced vision failed to penetrate. Polished wooden pews were arranged in orderly rows, all facing a tall lectern up near the front. Behind this rested another set of benches. These bore elaborate carvings on their high backs and cushions on their seats. Though I knew its purpose was like Lord Westarbor's audience chamber, the place put me more in mind of a church.

Rather than moving to the front, Franklin led me over toward the right side where hung a long row of oil paintings.

The first was a portrait of a man I recognized. Smiling out from its frame was the visage of Luther Prowd. It was not the old gentleman I had met in the headmaster's office. Rather, it was the younger version I'd seen angrily shouting amid a field of blossoms. My gut churned, and I was hard-pressed to quell the discomfort.

"A portrait is commissioned each time one of our mages arises to his mastery," Franklin explained. "Mark them well, for one of these will be your new master for years to come."

The next painting over to the left of the first was of Mistress Julia, looking just the same as I'd seen her today.

"You can forget that one," he said, shaking his head. "She takes only elves as apprentices or journeymen. We think that's why she remains here. There are usually around twenty masters present at the conclave at any given time. Another dozen or so are scattered about the kingdom. Most of these are stationed down near the southern border."

Embedded in the frame of each painting was a small bronze nameplate on which the name of the wizard depicted was engraved. As we picked our way down the long row of portraits, Franklin gave a running commentary on each, along with their current number of journeymen and the likelihood of their choosing another. The young man definitely did his research.

"Why are there two of this fellow?" I asked.

"Those two are twins," he replied, as I hastily scanned their confusing names.

'Redmond Peter Doyle,' said the one on the left. 'Peter Redmond Doyle,' proclaimed the other.

"They are two brothers, both found to possess the gift," he continued. "Only Master Redmond is in residence here at Conclave. Master Peter is stationed at one of the southern fortresses overseeing the war effort. They share a unique talent."

Like my winding, I thought, or Royland's sensing of emotions.

"Well, what is it?" I asked, intrigued.

"Since childhood, Redmond has been able to channel Peter's thoughts and words. No matter the distance, he can instantly convey what his brother is experiencing. The talent only runs in one direction, though. The conclave thought to use them to maintain a keener watch on the enemy's movements down south. Master Redmond lives here in the Hall of Meditation and gives a daily report of what's going on at the war front. Their names are a bit confusing, so most people just refer to them as 'Pete' and 'Re-Pete.'"

I waited expectantly for a chuckle, but Franklin's deadpan delivery lacked any hint of amusement. I decided then and there to make it my project to cause Franklin to laugh at something. The young man's perpetually morose disposition couldn't be healthy. From his parents' descriptions back at Barony Stein, Franklin had once been a happy child.

Moving on, I was taken aback once more. Staring out from the following frame was a young man with long sideburns. 'Elizar Chadwick,' was emblazoned on its plaque. His smooth, unlined face differed from that of the man I knew, but underneath, it was undeniably him. The likeness even captured the sheepishly amused expression I knew so well. Reluctantly, I moved on as Franklin began discussing the next master.

We soon approached a portrait that was covered by a black velvet cloth. To either side of it were the two votive candles I'd noted when we had entered. Only the bronze nameplate peeked out from beneath its veil. 'Denis Feininger,' it read. Franklin inclined his head and paused for a moment before remarking.

"Tragic, this one," he drawled. "This is how the masters honor the recently deceased. He died not two weeks ago, staving off another incursion by our enemies down in Eagle's Keep duchy. The dark druids' abominations were repelled, but not before Master Feininger here was swallowed whole by a frog-headed thing with tentacles. His portrait will remain here enshrouded until the time of the next choosing. Then it will be borne below to the vault of memory, there to dwell among the other past masters."

I had heard of a recent push by the enemy. Soldiers were being recruited back at the caravansary to reinforce the fortresses to the south. And wasn't Eagle's Keep where Taylor was driving that load of copper ingots from Westarbor? I hadn't realized the hostilities in the south had become so dire. Somehow, this shrouded frame with its vigil lights brought it home to me as mere words could not.

Just then, we began hearing something from up near the front of the auditorium. Footfalls not our own were rising in volume, accompanied by muted voices carrying on a discourse.

"Be still and silent, Lucas," whispered Franklin urgently. "Though it's not a hard and fast rule, we're discouraged from coming here without first getting permission."

Startled by this revelation, I quickly crouched down beside my fearful friend, as a faint light grew to bathe the raised area behind the lectern. I peeked over the pew that sheltered us from view. Two men emerged. The raised hand of the taller of the two was wreathed in a steady flame that licked lazily at the air above it, seeming to cause him no discomfort. I recognized him as Gunther Brubaker, father to that Victor chap I'd met. We'd discussed his portrait just a few frames back. According to Franklin, he was a pyromancer of some note. He worked in the foundry of Conclave, firing its smithies extra-hot to produce various enchanted weapons for the war effort. The other was unknown to me. Their voices became more distinct as they paced across the stage, sound being enhanced by the chamber's fine acoustic qualities.

"So, have you decided to see reason at last, Martin?" Gunther grumbled.

"I don't know," said the other. "It's all so confusing."

"What's so confusing about it? Are you with us or not?"

"I'd prefer to remain aloof from such squabbling," returned Martin.

Could this be Martin Bates, the newly minted master from Westarbor about whom Lloyd had spoken? Gunther's voice took on a menace that was practically a growl.

"Far from being mere squabbling," he said, "these matters represent a fundamental difference among the masters. Of course a balance must be struck, but if we listen to Balderas and his loyalist lapdogs, we'll soon be naught but chattel locked in eternal servitude to a crown that cares not a whit for our well-being."

"The *Elves* at least don't see it that way. Your words might be construed as treasonous. His majesty--"

"--Is not the man his grandfather was," Gunther supplied in a clipped tone. "The Northford uprisings demonstrated that. Think about it, Martin. Denis followed the loyalist line. And what was his reward? How many others must we sacrifice on the altar of an incompetent monarchy before we mages take up the reins of our own destiny? Your future and that of every mage of the conclave rests with the Autonomists. Our numbers are greater than you may imagine. We must have your answer by the ceremony. Join us, and we shall ease your way. Side with our detractors and things shall become... uncomfortable for you."

As if to emphasize his point, Gunther's flames rose higher for a moment, then receded to their former brightness.

"There's no need for threats, Gunther," Martin whined. "I won't work against you in any event. I had only hoped to remain neutral. Above the fray, as it were."

"Unacceptable. The time draws nigh when every mage must choose a side. You must cease your dithering and do so."

With that he withdrew, stalking toward the side of the platform and beyond our view. Hastening to remain in his cohort's dwindling light, Master Martin scuttled after.

I was reasonably certain we weren't meant to hear all that.

Franklin and I remained as still as statues. After a minute passed and my heart had stopped hammering, we crept back the way we'd come, careful to make no sound.

***

"Have you written home yet?" I asked as we trudged our way back toward House Blue Jay.

"No," Franklin replied, staring straight ahead. "Stop badgering me about it."

Despite the man's dismissal, I wasn't yet ready to let the matter drop.

"Your parents are concerned, Franklin. They miss you and haven't heard from you in a long while."

He halted and turned on me.

"And what am I to tell them?" the man exploded. "That I'm happy here? That things are well? Well, they're not. It's bad enough I've disappointed them by being an unfit heir. But now I

45

shan't even be able to aid the kingdom through my 'gift.' The masters don't allow me to so much as practice my 'unsavory art' outside the secure vault down in the bowels of the academy. If they have their way, I'll never be permitted to master it. House Stein will end with me, and it will all have been for nothing."

The young man had spoken with more passion than I'd yet heard from him. His cold gaze bore down on me as though he sought to break my resolve with the sheer force of his misery.

"All gifts have value," I gently returned. "They were given to us for a purpose, even if we can't see it as yet."

I hadn't meant to change his mind by spouting such platitudes. I'd done it more to express sympathy and to foster hope. But Franklin surprised me.

"Perhaps you're right," he whispered, twisting his lips as though considering.

Wetting those lips, he peered out over the gardens. His eyes became unfocused as he continued in a hushed tone.

"I'm working on something that will make them all sit up and take notice. I can't say more - not until I've succeeded. Should I do so, it will shake the conclave to its very foundations."

That didn't sound ominous at all. I thought this might be an apt time to change the subject.

"Speaking of shaking up the conclave, what do you make of that business Master Brubaker was popping off about to Master Martin?"

"Best not to speak of it," said Franklin, scuffing at the dirt with his boot.

We returned to walking down the lane. We entered the wooded stretch that passed through the gardens, the one where Sholeena and I had been accosted. Franklin had been furious when I'd related what had occurred with the falcons earlier that morning. An eerie silence had descended, and I had the feeling the forest was watching me.

After a time and heedless of his own advice, Franklin then began discussing the encounter we'd witnessed.

"The masters are always bickering over how best to run the conclave. It comes from too much democracy. You see, any important concerns of the conclave are subject to votes. Each master casts a ballot, then the headmaster tallies them up, and the majority wins the decision."

"I thought the headmaster was the one in charge," I put forth.

"He's the one who summons the council and determines which matters come to a vote."

That would be a very powerful position indeed, I thought. Something still bothered me, though.

"Don't they have to heed the king?"

"Oh, they do. The king's word is law on matters of the greatest import. His emissary is present each time the council is gathered. He reports on the decisions of the council and can overturn their judgment should his majesty so decree. The current dispute is over how much autonomy the conclave should have from the crown's authority when it comes to --"

Franklin reached over and seized my shoulder, hauling us to an abrupt halt. His brow was creased and his spine had stiffened.

"Death approaches from behind," he croaked, his eyes gone distant.

When a necromancer made such a pronouncement, I reasoned it was best to pay heed. So I began looking about for a place to hide. But then Franklin relaxed.

"Oh," he said. "Only that."

Swiveling about, he sighted down the lane and frowned, as though awaiting something.

Rounding a bend in the lane were two aspirants I recognized. In the lead was Henry Sutherland. He was stooped forward and lugging a pig upon his back. In each hand he held the hog's hind legs. From just such a scene, the term 'piggyback' may have found its origin. Trailing behind was Scott McNair.

Franklin remained in the center of the lane as the porcine procession approached.

"One side, Blue Jays," Henry grunted. "This fellow is heavy."

"Clear the road," added Scott McNair scornfully.

The dead pig did indeed look to be a considerable burden, but Franklin refused to budge. A frown of resolve graced his face, his wroth written plainly thereon.

"Let me help with that," he said instead.

And at this, the pig began to kick and flop about. Henry soon released it as though it had scorched him. Scott too was startled, backing away in wild-eyed panic.

"Here now," shouted Henry when he'd regained his wits. "What's the meaning of this, Franklin?"

His words were brash, but a hint of unease edged his voice. Upon encountering the road, the pig rolled up to its feet and stared at the two, its dead eyes unblinking.

"It's to do with an incident from earlier today," Franklin calmly returned. "Take a message to Eli. Tell him I don't appreciate my aspirants being tormented. Sholeena is to be left alone."

I saw Henry's jaw firm with defiance, and he pursed his lips in that odd fashion I'd witnessed before. This time, when the screeching sound emerged, I was ready. My special talent for winding had the unfortunate side-effect of messing about with my inner ear and adversely affecting my equilibrium. Constant practice had inured me to this condition, and I'd developed several reliable coping mechanisms to deal with such dizziness. Thus, when Henry unleashed his distressing sound, I simply matched the spin by winding in precise counterpoint to it. I folded my arms before me and stood firm.

Lacking such a defense, Franklin crumpled to the ground at once. The pig, however, launched into motion. Apparently, a dead creature's ears were less susceptible to such an attack. It butted Henry firmly in his midriff, knocking the wind from his bellows and the sound from his sneering lips.

I spotted Aspirant McNair gesticulating madly and muttering darkly. He was dabbling about with the shadows on the roadway and giving them form. At a loss as to how to counter this, I summoned my vines to prepare a defense.

Then without my willing it, several vines shot out from the Perilous Glade to wrap about Scott and lift him from his feet. One encircled his neck as well. His eyes grew large. The shadows he'd been conjuring splashed upon the roadway to shimmy and seep down between its cobbles.

And just like that, it was over. Henry lifted both hands in a gesture of surrender. The pig stood menacing the young man, holding him in its unnerving, lifeless gaze. It scraped one forehoof over the stones of the lane. Henry turned to Franklin, who was sitting back up.

"We didn't mean any harm by it, Franklin. We were just having a little fun for star's sake. Call this thing off."

Scott, too, had ceased his struggles. The vines ensnaring him lowered him gently back to the road and withdrew.

"Henceforth," my friend sternly declared, "such 'fun' will be conducted absent any members of House Blue Jay. Is that understood?"

"Yes, Franklin," Henry replied. "We'll pass the word."

As Franklin stood, the pig gave one final twitch and tumbled over on its side. The two falcons stared at it with distaste. Scott McNair prodded at it with his boot as though loath to touch it. Having said his piece, Franklin strode over to me and we stared silently as our erstwhile adversaries gathered their wits. I took no joy from the fearful glances they cast our way. Though perhaps it was a necessary thing, I thought Franklin might be mistaken to escalate matters so. Would Eli consider this a challenge? He didn't strike me as the type to shy from such.

"How are we supposed to eat this thing *now*?" complained Scott in a hushed whisper.

"I dunno," muttered Henry, taking it up once again.

And off they went, scurrying down the lane like rats.

"Was that wise?" I asked.

"Force is the only thing some people understand, Lucas."

That was true enough of bullies. My attempts at friendly outreach had garnered me little respect. Still, it rankled to solve a problem by becoming the very thing one despised. And it was a stopgap measure at best. I suspected the bad blood between our houses would erupt again at the flimsiest excuse.

"That was good work with the vines," Franklin remarked.

I shrugged. Those vines hadn't been acting at *my* direction. I peered into the Perilous Glade and again had the feeling of being watched. It was more than that. I sensed from the glade an invitation, as though the forest was urging me to step back within. It was compelling.

"I think Scott McNair actually wet himself," Franklin added.

He said it without smugness, as though merely noting a fact. I recalled my earlier vow to make Franklin laugh at something and decided to give it another go.

"Say rather," said I, "he went wee wee wee all the way home."

Nothing. Franklin merely cocked an eyebrow and nodded.

***

Well before the appointed hour, I entered the area the mages called their créche, eager to begin my first work detail. I'd been told that Mistress Meredith had already arrived and was expecting me within. Wife to Gunther Brubaker, she was a prominent figure at the conclave and a master in her own right. Prior to her nuptials, she'd been Meredith Sutherland. It was said that her voice could charm the birds from their nests. It was also reported that same voice could flay the hide from a goat should said goat have the misfortune of arousing her ire.

The place seemed familiar. Advancing down its polished wood floors stirred memories of some similar hallway from long ago. I paused and rested my boot on a board to the right. It creaked, just as I knew it would. The scent of wax tickled my nostrils and a sense of gloom settled upon me as the cold realization struck. *She* had lived here once.

Whether from careful study of the academy maps or from my newfound familiarity with the place, I had no difficulty finding my way directly to the créche's small dining hall. Within it I sighted four young maidens at one end of a long table spooning up porridge from wooden bowls and chatting amiably.

At the table's far end sat two more mature women speaking in hushed tones. The first was outfitted in the billowing robe of a master. It was a deep burgundy in hue and had lace embellishments at the collar and cuffs. A golden necklace and ring each set with sparkling rubies completed the ensemble. The other wore a plain white peasant's blouse beneath a tan skirt and jacket. There wasn't a doubt in my mind as to which was Mistress Meredith.

I cleared my throat to gain their attention.

"If it pleases my ladies," I began. "I am Journeyman Aspirant Lucas Harper. Mistress Julia bade me present myself here to take up my work assignment."

As the ladies' gazes swept over me, the four girls also quieted and peered at me assessingly.

"Come join us then, young man," said the lady in red. "I was just telling Miss Spencer here of our little experiment. The others will arrive shortly."

"As you wish, Mistress," I said with a nod, approaching and taking the offered seat.

"I am Meredith Brubaker, as I'm certain you've surmised," she stated in crisp, dignified tones. "I am the matron of this facility, and while you are here, you may address me as such."

She paused expectantly.

"Yes, matron," I dutifully responded.

"Miss Elissa Spencer here is its governess. She sees to the children's day-to-day needs and is responsible for their comportment and education."

"I'm pleased to make your acquaintance, Miss Spencer."

"I don't know what Julia has told you, but the créche is underutilized at the moment. As such, I believed it to be an ideal time to attempt her new learning program. Apparently, it's all the rage among the Elves. Our rules are simple..."

But they were not simple.

As she blathered on cheerfully and endlessly about all manner of tedious trivialities, I struggled to retain an expression of interest. The children had returned to their discourse, and the swelling babble of their conflicting chatter further hampered my comprehension. A few rules stood out. All disciplinary problems were to be referred to the governess. No children not in residence at the crèche were to remain on the premises were I to depart from it. These and some few other relevant rules somehow found their way into my beleaguered brain.

"Um, Matron...?" Elissa interrupted "Some others have arrived."

And sure enough, yet another source of sonancy had arisen to assault the calm of the modest room. A dark-haired lad was jabbering at a petite young woman as they passed into the hall.

"... on sighting the black flag, the captain shouted over at me. Boy! Go and fetch me my red shirt!"

Mistress Meredith called for quiet, then turned to me once more.

"Well, here they are. I shall just leave you all to get acquainted. I'm overdue at an essential function. Elissa can make the introductions."

Facing the newcomers, Miss Spencer stood to address them. Being a gentleman, I stood as well.

"As guests of the crèche, young people are expected to comport themselves with proper dignity. Please claim a seat and give Aspirant Harper your utmost attention."

As Mistress Meredith exited, she almost ran into my final student lurking in the hallway. Sholeena shuffled in to assume her place at the table.

Rounding on the four more junior girls, Miss Spencer made a beckoning gesture, and they all moved nearer.

"Girls, this young man is here to teach you your letters."

And thus it began.

In the days ahead, I would come to know these seven very well indeed. Of the four younger girls, only Susanna Feininger lived here at the créche. Hers was a sad case. Her father was the master who'd recently been slain down in Eagle's Keep duchy. Her mother had died previously, so she had dwelt here since Denis had been called to service. Now orphaned, she'd become the sole heir to a rich estate she wasn't even of age to claim. None doubted Susie would soon be declared a ward of one of the other mages, but it was too soon for all that. The girl was still grieving, as would *you* be had *your* father been swallowed by a frog-headed abomination.

The two older kids were apprentices given special leave by their respective masters to take part in our little experiment in education. The boy was Skyler Hendrix. He hailed from Farax Duchy far to the east. His father was first mate on a ship in the king's navy. He had briefly served beside his father as a cabin boy until the discovery of his gift. Skyler was a wind mage. He bragged he could read a map and navigate by the stars, but readily admitted to needing help with his letters. The young woman was Bella Gibson, a simple farm girl from a small village right here in Deerfield Duchy. She seemed to be overwhelmed by Conclave and was struggling to fit in. Bella called her magic center her 'inner glow.' She could perform miraculous acts of healing, but these sometimes went terribly wrong. She now travels to outlying farmsteads with her app-Master, Christopher Spencer, practicing on animals suffering from various maladies so that she might perfect her gift.

Then there was Sholeena. Although she had passed her apprenticeship in the Indigo Isles under Master Marcel Jordan, he had been woefully lax regarding the reading requirement. As citizens of the kingdom, he reasoned the Paludaria fell under the king's edict that anyone discovered to have the gift must serve the guild. But not only did her people speak a foreign tongue, they lacked even the concept of a written language. Master Jordan had every confidence that at Conclave Sholeena would eventually overcome the deficit.

I could see how any one of these seven might benefit from some private tutoring, but how on earth was I to tutor all seven at once? I shuddered as I considered an eight-way Socratic discourse among us. But that was for another day. Today we were just getting to know one another. And at least everyone seemed friendly.

***

My afternoon was spent back in the library. I didn't see Edgar upon first entering, but his bird was roosting watchfully on her perch.

Turning to her, I asked: "Lenore, I don't suppose you know where I might find books about the mages and their various gifts."

The raven regarded me fixedly. After a moment, she obliged and launched herself to glide down a long aisle to my left. Intrigued by the bird's uncanny acumen, I followed to find her resting atop a bookshelf midway down the row. I scanned its titles. There were several that seemed to fit the bill: "Common Wayes to View One's Magic Center" and "The Sutherland Gift, being a treatise on the study of sound." All were affixed securely in their niches, this time by a single long chain on each shelf that threaded through the rings of the books thereupon.

"I see Lenore's been giving you a tour," said Edgar, approaching from the other direction. "This is the masters' section. You would need written permission to inspect any of these."

"Hello, Edgar. I was hoping to learn a bit about the different magical gifts and especially how they're inherited down family lines."

"Ah. Research," he said cheerfully. "Our fees for that are quite steep. If the masters approve your proposal, we can locate some relevant tomes and make them available. Or for a few shillings more, a researcher can be assigned to do the digging and ferret out the facts you seek..."

I was crestfallen.

Despite my best attempts at thrift, my purse (never a heavy burden to begin with) had lightened considerably since setting out upon my journey here. Royland had earned additional coin with the minstrels of our caravan, but I'd had no such subsidy.

54

Something of this must have shown on my face, for Edgar's sales pitch trailed off haltingly.

"Oh dear me," declared the young man. "I suddenly recall this one is long overdue for an update."

Retrieving an oversized ring of keys from the hook on his belt, he sorted out a silver one. This he inserted into the lock at the end of the second shelf. He muttered an incantation, and the chain snaked its way through the rings to lay slack at the far end, loosing the tomes in its care. Edgar then slid a particularly heavy one out from its place of rest and cradled it in his arms.

"The masters have been at me for months to add their recent findings," muttered Edgar. "I shall place it in the scriptorium to remind me. Can you hold it for a moment?"

I accepted the weighty tome as Edgar worked the chain along the shelf to fasten the others securely back in place. I stole a glimpse at the tall golden letters of the title.

"Genealogy of the Gift," it read.

"Thanks," he said, relieving me of my burden.

Lenore hopped down to rest comfortably on the man's shoulder.

"Perhaps you'd like to continue your study of the academy maps," Edgar suggested. "If so, can I ask you a small favor?"

"Of course," I agreed as we made our way along the aisles.

"I need to gather my notes and attend to some other business. May I impose on you to keep an eye on this until I return? I'll not be more than an hour or so. I'd be ever so grateful..."

"It's no bother," I assured him as we arrived at the escritoire.

As Lenore lofted up to alight atop the shelves, and Edgar tethered the large volume to a fresh chain, I carefully slid "Anatomy of the Academy" from its slot and brought it down to lie beside it. I unslung my Bob from my shoulders and rested it on the floor nearby.

"I'll just be off then," declared Edgar. "I'll leave Lenore to keep you company."

After he'd gone, I quietly spread open "Genealogy of the Gift" and began carefully to leaf through its pages. The raven peered down reproachfully from atop her high perch.

"Don't look at me that way," I berated her. "It was clear he meant for me to peruse it."

There wasn't much in the way of text. The title page read simply: "Genealogy of the Gift: Being a Studie of the Bloodlines of Mages of Osten." After that it was all just annotated family trees with lines branching downward, naming people and noting their affinities. There were lengthy, convoluted listings for families such as Brubaker, Willoughby, and Sutherland. These dense entries were cross-referenced and overflowed onto additional pages. Near the back were pages with only a few names. I reckoned these were newly discovered apprentices without known magical ancestors.

My own page contained only four names. At its top was written 'Abigale Wagge' with the label: 'Geomancy (Lesser).' Alongside that entry was a question mark. Down from these, a line was drawn to join a new name: 'Isabel Wagge (likely latent - deceased).' Adjoined to this was my father, 'Elliot Harper (non-magical),' and from them, a line descended to yours truly with an unfamiliar label. 'Lucas Harper (Verdumancy),' it read. The rest of the page was left blank.

Unnoticed by me, Lenore had quietly taken her leave. I was startled when she came swooping down to land near my elbow, a dead mouse dangling from her beak. Regarding me with one obsidian eye, she bent and set this prize beside me, then winged her silent way to roost above once more. I nodded to her before returning to my reading.

I paged through more of the book, seeking any other reference to my own gift. The core gifts seemed to relate to the four elements or subcategories thereof. There were also references to light, animal mastery, life and death, and some rare ones I would need to look up later. There were even several instances of Royland's gift of entomancy. Most of these appeared on the Willoughby tree. But try as I might, I saw no other occurrence of verdumancy. The closest I found was Master Reinhardt's gift of dendromancy. My studies of the old tongue informed me this somehow related to wood. It was clear I would find no ready answers here to the mystery of my grandfather's identity.

With a sigh, I eased the volume shut and returned to reviewing the academy atlas. On a few of its broader maps, I surveyed the gardens. They were quite extensive, accounting for perhaps a third of the mage's quarter's acreage. They appeared equally divided between productive gardens and orchards and the Perilous Glade. The latter area was managed by Frida Willoughby, who I'd only just learned was Royland's grand aunt on his mother's side. I also located the standing stones formation Master Prowd had been going on about. I was still browsing through it when Edgar returned, shuffling up behind me bearing a bundle of loose parchments and sealed missives.

"Still plumbing the academy's secrets?" he asked. "Have you got them all unraveled?"

"Hardly," I replied. "Each answer seems to spawn several new questions."

Noting the dead mouse, Edgar looked up at Lenore.

"She must really like you," he asserted.

The young man smiled and set his notes on the edge of the long writing desk we now shared. He examined the topmost parchment and absentmindedly retrieved a quill and inkpot from an upper drawer of the escritoire. Setting these beside the missives, he opened and sought through the great tome from which I had so recently stolen a peek. Under the entry for Denis Feininger, he added the word: 'Deceased.'

I pretended to busy myself with my map, but my focus kept shifting to what Edgar was doing. On one of the Brubaker pages, I spotted some familiar names. He placed his index finger on the entry for my uncle Robert and muttered, 'scripturam vim extermina.' The ink labeling him as (non-magical) faded to blank parchment. Edgar dipped his quill and replaced this with (likely latent).

"That's handy," I remarked.

The young man looked over, shrugged, and returned to his task. I returned to my pretending. When he took up the next scribbled note, Edgar frowned. He flipped all the way to the back to begin a fresh, blank page. At its head, he wrote 'Ferdinand Cummings II,' and adjoining this: 'Joc--'

He eyed his empty inkpot and grimaced.

I'd heard that name before and fairly recently, I thought, struggling to recall just where. Then it came to me. Ferdinand Cummings was the lord with whom Taylor Allen had been so upset, the former Duke of our province. He and his family had been exiled to the Indigo Isles in disgrace years ago for fomenting the Northford uprising. It seemed likely this newly discovered mage was related. I bent and hastened to root about in my Bob.

"I have some ink," I offered, retrieving it.

Bemused, Edgar stared at me quizzically. Accepting the boon and nodding his thanks, he dipped his quill and continued. 'Jocelyn Cummings née Sanderson,' he wrote. Descending from these, a line connected to a new name: 'Galwell Cummings (Therianthrope).' What in the stars was that? I didn't have the nerve to ask outright, seeing as I wasn't supposed to be privy to the information at all. So I took it as yet another puzzle to solve later.

Eventually, Edgar completed his updates and I my pretense of studying the local landscape. I pocketed the dead mouse to avoid offending Lenore and made ready to depart. As he detached the refreshed reference from its tether, Edgar returned my inkpot along with his thanks. Evidently, Mistress Willoughby had recently delivered a batch of oak galls. He could readily grind these and combine them with other reagents to produce a fresh supply of ink.

There was one final matter I wished to take up. I was reluctant to discuss it, but Edgar had been most accommodating and had shown a willingness to bend the rules a bit. I felt I could confide in him and knew Lenore would keep mum.

"Edgar," I began, "I may wish to hire your services as a researcher after all."

"What's the topic?" he inquired.

"I lack the funds at present," I put forth. "But once I've earned enough, I should like you to find everything you can about how to purge a possessing spirit from a person."

"May I ask why?" he returned with a look of concern. "Such magics are dangerous, and a topic best left to the masters."

"Well, I don't have a master as yet, and am not likely to get one anytime soon. Let's just say the question is one of academic interest at the moment. It's not urgent as yet."

"I'll think on it," he promised. "Let me know when you're certain. In the meantime, I hope you'll visit us again soon. Feel free to study other topics or just browse around. We've many a quaint and curious volume of forgotten lore."

CHAPTER THREE

The Captive

"The history of the world is learn forgiveness and try to forget!"

~ Sweeney Todd ~

That night over dinner, discussion turned to our house's finances.

"Aw. Not fish again," Lloyd complained.

"If you want something more to your taste," Franklin returned, "perhaps you would be willing to toss an extra shilling into the house treasury. Otherwise, be thankful Sholeena is such a generous and efficacious provider."

"I think not," the boy returned, making his purse vanish even as Franklin reached for it.

On his return from the village, Franklin had visited the Lord Mayor's clerks at their counting house.

Each mage at the conclave received a weekly stipend from the crown to carry on our work providing superior weapons and armor for the soldiery. Master wizards received the lion's share, of course. They used it to run their estates and seemed to want for nothing. They, in turn, paid each of their journeymen a wage. Apprentices were unpaid, but as they were attached to a master's household, they had no real need for money and supped well at their app-master's table.

We aspirant journeymen dwelt in a limbo in between. We drew a small weekly stipend and were expected to live within its meager means. Franklin, as our head of house, had retrieved ours after his shift in town. It had taken him nearly an hour to explain to the Lord Mayor's clerks that our house now had an additional member. His patience was finally rewarded with the addition of my paltry, partial week's pay.

I was sore in need of such.

"What's this?" muttered Lorraine upon completing her count. "There's less than usual."

"Don't look at me like that," said Franklin. "As the clerk's explained it to me, taxes have been increased again - on everything."

"But that makes no sense," Lorraine sputtered. "Our stipend is given us by the king. How can he justify reducing it and call it a tax?"

"He doesn't need to justify it," declared Lloyd, waving his spoon about. "He's the king."

"Ah well," I sighed. "I suppose what the lord giveth the lord can taketh away."

Lorraine shot me an amused grin. Lloyd giggled. Sholeena just looked confused, and Franklin, alas, failed to laugh once more. He just raised one eyebrow and nodded grimly.

***

It was another clear morning when Lorraine and I set out. The sun's golden rays bathed the land, and the earthy odor unleashed from the thawing grounds foretold the onset of milder days. Dripping icicles hanging from our eaves wept in solemn assent. I steered the rickety handcart through the door of House Blue Jay. As I eased it down from the front stoop, a fresh trickle of these formerly frozen tears tickled the back of my neck.

Having recently received our weekly stipend, it was time for our house to restock on staples. Lorraine had promised to do so as she conducted her other weekly business. I'd gratefully accepted the offer to accompany her. The girl was conversant with the merchants in the trade quarter and knew the standard prices for most goods and services. On this, my first trip out, she would help assure I wasn't bilked overmuch.

"Be careful with that," said Lorraine.

I could understand her caution. The cart seemed sturdy enough, but it would certainly benefit from an overhaul by a wainwright. Its left wheel was slightly misaligned and emitted occasional squeaks as it wobbled along. Both wheels turned on their axle, independent of one another. This allowed the cart to swivel in place when not resting on its rear strut. For her official work detail, Lorraine had the task of retrieving purchases from town and delivering them to various estates in the mage's quarter. Some of the grander estates tipped her well for such efforts. Thus, the small, two-wheeled cart was essential to her livelihood.

The only gloom to eclipse the radiance of the fine day came from just across the way. Eli Reznic was scowling down upon us from the porch of House Falcon.

"What's *his* problem?" Lorraine sniffed.

"Don't ask," I replied, resting my eyes fixedly upon the road ahead. "So where are we going first?"

"I thought we'd start at the haberdashery."

This unexpected reply struck me as peculiar, but the explanation that followed made perfect sense.

"The merchants in town can mark a foreigner from a mile away, Lucas. That hat you wear isn't in the local style and practically shouts at them to increase their prices. Investing in some local attire at the outset will pay dividends all throughout your stay here. Besides, the family running the establishment could use the custom."

"If you say so," I returned, happy to defer to the lady's judgment on such matters.

As we approached the trade gate, the serenity of the mage's quarter was gradually overcome by the rising ruckus of the bustling streets beyond. Entering them, Lorraine led the way with surefooted grace past shops and stalls lining the lane, ignoring the barkers and their eye-catching wares. I trundled the cart behind, hard-pressed to match her nonchalance. My time with the caravan had taught me not to meet a merchant's eyes, lest he mark me as a likely source of income. So despite the intriguing odors of eateries and the colorful displays, I remained steadfast in following Lorraine in her nimble dance, and we wove our way through the crush of the milling throngs.

"This is the place," she announced as we came to a halt.

It was a small shoppe down a side street that seemed to specialize in apparel. Wedged between a clothier and a purveyor of handbags, its shingle was shaped like a conical hennin. 'Hightoppers,' its sign read. As Lorraine opened the door and strode within, a jingle of bells alerted the shop owner of our arrival. She was a merry little lady with a roundish face on which smile lines spread as she regarded us.

"Doña Lorraine!" she exclaimed. "To what do we owe the pleasure?"

"I've brought you some business, Madam Bridges," Lorry returned with a nod that was practically a curtsy. "I trust you are well?"

"Just the usual aches, my dear, but none to match the one in my heart. How's my little Lloyd?"

"He is well. In fact, he's just acquired a new roommate."

Indicating me with a wave of her hand, Lorraine said: "Goodwife Bridges, this is Aspirant Lucas Harper, newly arrived from Westarbor. Lucas, allow me to present Madam Maisie Bridges."

So this was Lloyd's mother, I thought. She stood smiling amid the many hats displayed in the small shoppe with her arm outstretched. I came around the cart to take her hand gently between my thumb and forefinger, saying "A pleasure, Goodwife."

She gave my hand a squeeze, and the joy left her eyes to be replaced by a nervous tension.

"I trust there have been no ... untoward incidents?"

"Indeed not," I hastened to assure her. "Lloyd and I have an agreement about how to handle any... inadvertent pilferage. He seems to have the situation well under control."

"Lucas here is in need of a proper hat, Goody," Lorraine chimed in. "I told him Hightoppers was the place to obtain something... adequate."

"Say, rather," the matron returned, "Hightoppers is the premier purveyor of superior headgear for all occasions."

And thus it began. I'd seen it many times on my trip south as the caravan's merchants dickered with their customers to arrive at a price. This game was much the same. Both women seemed well-versed in the verbal dance that was haggling. Without actually insulting the goods, Lorraine struck an indifferent air as she steered me toward the men's section and we examined the various styles to be had. For her part, Goody Bridges maintained a smug confidence as she emphasized the quality of each item we viewed.

I untied the chin strings and removed my coif that I might sample a few of these offerings. Men's fashions in Conclave ran chiefly toward wool felt berets of various hues and shapes. Lorraine fitted me with one she favored. Although its ear-flaps were warm, I feared they might make me look like a dolt. When I expressed these doubts, Lorraine paused in her dickering.

"Ut reflectum speculum," she incanted, making a palms-out polishing motion.

The air shimmered, and I was confronted by my own aspect staring out in startlement from a circular plane before me. This mirror made of nothing hung in mid-air and gave me an up-close view of my doltishness. From behind me, Lorraine's smiling reflection reached out to tuck the ear flaps up and into the beret. She then tugged it down, so its brim slanted a bit to the right. This resulted in a fit I found rather fetching.

We soon arrived at a price I was certain was fair, took our leave of Goody Bridges, and made our way back out into the market to continue on our errands. I followed Lorraine hither and yon about the busy streets as she collected all manner of oddments and stacked them upon our cart. I was introduced to many a merchant and was gaining a rough idea of all the trade district had to offer. As midday approached and with our cart nearly topped off, Lorraine told me it was time for her to depart to make her deliveries.

"I think I'd like to stay for a while," I demurred. "I've a few errands of my own to attend. Thank you for the tour. I'd have been quite lost had I started in cold. Can you manage the cart on your own, Lorry?"

"Of course," she returned. "I can manage my route quite well unattended. I'll see you at dinner."

And with that, we parted ways. The girl went squeaking off with her fully ladened cart.

I had some business at the apothecary I'd spotted earlier. On my way there, I would take in the sights. Now that I was alone, cartless, and no longer hustling after Lorraine, I found the barkers to be much more bold and insistent. Their gazes would alight on me like flies upon honey and their beseeching voices would soon follow, extolling the virtues of their various wares. I ignored them for the most part, but one caught my attention.

"You sir! You in the fine, new hat!" he cried. "I've not seen you here before! First time's free! Not a farthing will you spend! I wish only the chance to introduce myself, exhibit my skills, and benefit you thereby!"

He was probably a huckster, but I was hard-pressed to ignore the word 'free.' Whatever he was selling, his opening bid seemed to suit well the present state of my finances. I moved closer. The red and white striped pole on the building behind the man identified it as a barber shoppe and its sign proudly named its proprietor.

In small communities, there was little need for surnames. Everyone knew 'Harry' or 'Tom' and no more need be said. As towns grew, however, it had become problematic to distinguish among several men named Tom, so folks began referring to them as 'Tom the Smith' or 'Tom John's son.' These were later formalized and shortened to the surnames we use today. I imagine that somewhere back in time, one of my own ancestors played the harp; hence, I am now known as Lucas Harper. I could readily fathom how such surnames as 'Miller', 'Smith', or 'Johnson' were derived. I couldn't help but wonder, however, just what hijinks one's predecessors got up to to saddle him with a name like 'Simon Strangelove'.

"Ah, young sir. I see you can use a proper trim and a shave so subtle the angels will weep in jealousy at the smoothness of your chin."

It was true my hair had gotten a bit shaggy since it was last visited by scissors. Very well, I thought. I would see what the man intended. Nodding, I stepped nearer.

"Whom do I have the supreme honor of welcoming to my humble shoppe?" he asked, placing a hand on the crook of my back and steering me toward its door.

I felt like a fish that had just been netted.

"I am Lucas of Meadowfork." I answered.

"Meadowfork? I've not heard of such a town. It must be far away. Would you be one of the mages, then?"

"Yes," I confirmed. "I'm an aspirant, newly arrived."

I looked about the narrow room. Prominent in its center was a comfortable-looking chair. The periphery was littered with various accoutrements, ointments, and a large glass jar I was to learn contained leeches. We had no barber back in Meadowfork. I'd heard such men dabbled in dentistry and the treatment of minor cuts and wounds, as well as shaving a man's face. From my studies, I'd learned that 'barba' was the word for 'beard' in the old tongue. And the red stripes of the barber pole had been inspired by the bandages associated with bloodletting.

"Just a trim then," I said as he ushered me into the seat.

The man pressed his thumbs to my cheeks. Stretching my lower eyelids downward and tilting his head back, he peered into my eyes.

"Are you certain, aspirant?" he asked. "I can tell from your aspect the humors are unbalanced. You would do well to have a small reduction of sanguineous matter."

I'd read of Hippocrates and his theory of the four humors. But why was it always blood that savants of his teachings wanted to let? And why never their own? That was a bit too convenient and even a tad 'hippo-critical' if you asked me.

"I'm certain," I assured him.

Nor did I assent to the bowl cut he insisted was all the rage in Fairglen. Fashion aside, I didn't want to be mistaken for a monk. Disappointed, he took up a comb and some shears and set straight to work. The man was quick; I'd give him that. I soon felt the weight of four month's growth falling away, and my ears were once again exposed to the open air.

Next, he pressed a heated, damp cloth over the lower half of my face and neck. His straight razor sparkled and flashed in a regular rhythm as he stropped it back and forth across a wide leather belt attached to the arm of my chair. Lifting the cloth, Simon slathered my face with a foamy white substance. This he proceeded to remove with deft strokes from his blade.

Finally, he selected a scented oil from the bottles on a table nearby. He poured out a dollop, smeared it into both his palms and began working it into my scalp. It felt cool and refreshing and had a vaguely floral musk with just a hint of mint. He patted some onto my cheeks and neck as well before wiping his hands on his apron.

"Tell all your friends in the conclave. They will doubtless wish to know the source of your stylish coiffure. Tell them such comeliness can be theirs as well for the small price of two pence."

I felt awkward having gotten such fine service from the man as a free promotion. I knew that tips were welcome in such situations, or at least some small purchase to compensate the man for his efforts. I liked the pomade he'd put in my hair. It felt nice and had a pleasant fragrance. So I promptly purchased a bottle. I thanked the man, donned my hat and went my merry way.

My stomach rumbled, insisting it was time for a meal. I knew the smell of sweet meats wafting about the trade quarter's streets was to blame. I think the restauranteurs did it on purpose. I resisted the persistent urge to splurge on a midday treat and headed straight to my intended destination.

When I arrived at the apothecary, the adjoining street churned in chaos. There was a small contingent of the Lord Mayor's soldiers holding back the crowd. These must have been summoned by the shrill whistling I'd heard from a few streets over. A man was leaning in the doorframe holding a blood-soaked rag to one side of his head and jabbering away at their sergeant.

Most citizens veered around the congestion, intent only on making their way past. But some few others paused and clustered about to overhear what had occurred. I joined the latter and strained to make out what the man was saying.

"...He stank like sumpthin' done crawled up his arse and died. I felt sorry for the bloke; he looked to be in a bad way. When I asked what I could get for him, he started babbling some baby talk about spiders. I offered to take him to the physic cause he looked mighty unsteady on his legs. That's when he went berserk and struck me. Next thing I knew, he was breaking up the place and tossing things into his sack. I crawled under the counter to hide."

"And you'd ne'er seen this man before?" asked the sergeant.

"I can't say for sure," the victim replied. "He was wearing a heavy cloak with the hood pulled up."

"Sergeant!" exclaimed a soldier, shoving his way through the crowd. "Such a man was sighted entering a house in lowside near the north gate. We've cordoned off the area and sent word to the lord's knights."

"Come with us, goodman," said the sergeant. "We'll see to your injury. We may need you to identify the scoundrel and bear witness to his lawless misconduct."

Turning to the crowd, he proclaimed: "There's no need to fear, citizens. We'll soon have the culprit detained. The man must be crazed to think he can escape justice after committing such an act."

And with that, the soldiers moved out with the apothecary in tow. I supposed I would just have to wait and attend to my business later. I shuffled along as the crowd dispersed and headed for home once more.

***

The midday sun still blazed fiercely above, but its light failed intermittently as clouds swept by overhead. The western sky was darkening, and the scent of rain was on the breeze. At first refreshing, that breeze began to stiffen and bite, as the dying winter refused to surrender his feeble grip upon the land.

I picked up my pace and pulled my cloak tighter about me.

I wondered how the Lord Mayor's knights were faring against the mad malefactor who'd assaulted the apothecary.

As I entered the garden lane, the wind abated, impeded by the trees to either side. The light was further reduced by the canopy of branches that stretched above. It was the first time I'd trod this path alone, and I found the sudden stillness unsettling.

Again I approached the spot where I'd scuffled with the falcons - twice. And once again I felt a presence watching me, as though the very woods had eyes. I kept my own eyes on the stones of the lane ahead and trod warily on. Then I heard it, a sudden rustling sound just to my rear that caused me to jump and turn about. Was it perhaps the falcons laying in wait to exact their revenge?

But no figures sprang forth, and no ambush greeted my sight. Only the empty stretch of stillness that was the garden lane. On the left, however, where an unbroken bramble had been but moments before, was the unmistakable opening of a trailhead. It was like the one I'd used when I'd emerged from the Perilous Glade with Sholeena's knife. It seemed to beckon me thither.

Now I was intensely curious as to what this mysterious forest would have of me. But I knew I ought not to tempt fate a second time. No one knew where I was. Should I go missing, they wouldn't even know where to mount the search. No. I would take the path most traveled and keep in mind a saying of which Royland was fond: 'Prudence is the better part of wisdom.'

I turned and continued to make my way homeward. Suddenly, a vine shot out from the Perilous Glade and reached for me. It whipped out of the weeds so swiftly that I had no chance to dodge its wide, undulant grasp. I blinked and gasped aloud only to discover I was not caught. Retreating into the dense foliage, the vine slithered from view, its only victim, my new hat.

I was outraged. I'd only just purchased the thing. Moreover, after the haircut and in this biting wind, I was finally looking forward to those doltish ear flaps. And here some sorry excuse for an enchanted forest wanted to play keep away with my prized possession? I imagined I heard the forest laugh. This should have made me even more wary, but the childish prank roused me to show this forest what I was made of (figuratively, I hoped).

"Give that back," I commanded sternly.

I don't know what I expected. I could have been baying at the moon for all the good it did me.

So I mustered my courage, cast caution to the wind, and stepped onto the pathway. We would see where this trail led. The going was easy. The brambles behaved themselves as I followed the turnings and wended my way ever deeper in. I soon lost all sense of direction.

After a time, I came upon an open glen. I could see an oval patch of gray sky above, ringed by treetops swaying in the wind. At its center was a stone bench, whereupon rested my hat. I approached it warily.

"That's more like it," I said to the forest at large. "A man's hat is not to be trifled with."

At this, I heard actual laughter from over to my right. I spun about to spy a fair-haired young woman peering out from behind a tree. Her angelic face bore a grin of mirth and her emerald eyes shone forth undeterred by the overcast sky.

"Lucas, that other boy called you," she said. "The new bloke from Westarbor, the one Royland's been telling us about."

The words sounded unnatural on her tongue, as though she were just parroting the sounds bereft of any meaning. I vaguely recognized them as something Eli Reznic had spouted a few days prior. Still, her voice was as honey to my ears, and I wished she would say my name again. I struck a non-threatening stance and stood stock still.

"I take it you're the one managing the vines?" I said in a gentle voice lest it seem an accusation. "Who are you? And why did you aid me that day?"

"You may call me Hazel," she replied, emerging fully from her erstwhile place of concealment and slowly approaching.

She wore a diaphanous gown that swept low in front. It did little to conceal her graceful curves and struck me as most impractical. Such garb was ludicrously inadequate in the brisk chill of the afternoon. I noted this only in passing as my eyes remained riveted to hers, fascinated by their viridian depths. She approached nearer still with a dainty stride that scarcely disturbed the ground over which she glided.

"I helped you because you apologized."

"I... what?"

My mind grasped feebly at the loose threads of our conversation. I rarely had difficulty with elocution, but I found my tongue also was rapidly losing the ability to convey such few scattered thoughts as I retained.

"You apologized," she repeated. "To the tree. What's more, you made it right. In sooth it is the first time I've held out hope for your kind since first I came here."

The lady now stood within arm's reach, but this small distance seemed an insurmountable chasm. I stood as though rooted, unable to make the slightest movement. She was the epitome of feminine allure. I longed for her touch. My heart sang its rhythm in my ears. I yearned only to please her.

"I have a task for you, Lucas, the bloke from Westarbor. Will you grant me a small boon?"

I wanted to shout 'Yes! Anything!' so enraptured I'd become with those mesmerizing green eyes. But a part of my mind (a very small and presently out of favor part) rebelled. This wasn't the first time my psyche had been overwhelmed by another's will. Despite her heinous domination of my spirit, it seemed my experience with Abigale's mendacity had at least given me a fighting chance.

My vision swam. The green eyes seemed to waver and shift in hue. In my mind's eye, I was looking into blue eyes, a startling sapphire I knew I could trust. Other memories surfaced. A stern lecture; a playful punch on the shoulder; milk dribbling down from her nose; the wet tickle of an eyelash as her lips brushed my cheek in a chaste farewell.

I invoked my mage sight, and the figure before me shrank. Her size remained constant, but she no longer loomed as large. Her ethereal beauty diminished, and with it, her pull upon my will.

"I think not," I replied, emerging from my stupor. "Not unless you first tell me what it is," I amended.

"Oh poo," said the girl.

She stood poised to flee; her eyes grown large. Even lacking her potent charm, they were still beautiful eyes. I was curious, and though I'd broken free of the bewitching fascination, I still couldn't summon any anger over it. Perhaps sensing this, Hazel pouted.

"There's your hat, Lucas the Bloke," she said. "Take it and go."

Her mention of a 'boon' had put me in mind of the tragic tale of William Winkle, a tailor I'd met back at Sir Harrison's manor. It was the way the fey talked about exchanging favors. I had believed Hazel to be another aspirant or journeyman mage I hadn't met as yet, but could I be talking to a real live faerie?

"My kind," I returned. "You said you 'held out hope for my kind.' And just what is *your* nature if it differs so from mine? Mayhap, are you of the woodland fey?"

She seemed to wilt, and her eyes bespoke a sadness that stabbed at my soul.

"No longer," she sobbed. "For this is no proper woodland; tis merely my prison. As to my nature, you have guessed correctly. I am a dryad transplanted into this mockery of a forest by the cruel people of your conclave."

"Transplanted?" I exclaimed. "How was this possible? Surely the fey look after their own."

"It was a most dastardly trick of fate," the girl replied. "Since I've brought you here, I will share the tale. For long have I been lonely. Be seated in comfort, Lucas. My kind does not sit, but I've been told your folk find it restful."

"I will on one condition," said I. "It probably makes no difference to you, but would you please wrap yourself in some warmer clothing? I'm getting cold just looking at you."

I was glad when she agreed because quite the opposite was true. With a repentant look and a wave of her hand, Hazel became outfitted in attire more suitable for the season. As I seated myself on the stone bench, I heard the rumble of distant thunder. Treetops swayed more vigorously as they were buffeted by the rising wind. I knew I should seek shelter to escape the coming downpour, but I'd happily risk more than a drenching to hear *this* story.

"My first memories are of rising up from the forest floor. The urge to grow was a heady feeling brought on when rays of sunlight pierced the shade of leaves above to warm the earth where I rooted. Many acorns lay strewn about, but only I had the special élan that made me one of the fair folk. Squirrels and chipmunks snatched them up to carry off and eat. I wept for my little sisters who would never know of the bright sunlight nor the dribbling flow of sap beneath their bark.

"Mother stood nearby, tall and proud. When she'd been just such an acorn as that from which I'd hatched, she too had been carried off far from the grove of her sisters to lie here forgotten. For five years and twenty, she stood alone, and the seasons made her as many rings before bearing acorns of her own. I now grew beside her. We would start a new grove.

"The other fey would oft come to chat, for some had the mobility which we lacked. Pixies and sprites and all the others kept us abreast of the doings beyond our formative glade. Lamentably, none of these would stay for long. Mother had the misfortune of growing too near what your people call a 'road.' When men came along this road moving from one place to another, our brethren of the forest would flee. And even the will-o'-wisps couldn't lead such men astray.

"Then came the day a man entered our glade. He stopped at mother's trunk. Mother and I hid our aspects within our trees, waiting for him to go away. But before he did, he drove an iron spike into mother's side, using it to affix a parchment thereon. 'Mother!' I cried when the man had gone. But she was trapped, unable to respond or even to call for help. I was but a sapling, not able to do much of anything on my own.

"Several risings of the sun later, the bug lady came. She was of this place, the conclave. On spying the trail of sap dribbling down from mother's wound, she quickly surmised our nature. With mother powerless to intervene, the bug lady had me dug up and brought here. She has many cruel ideas for how to use the parts of a wood nymph. But first she would have my acorns. That was many years ago. I am recently come of age. Thus far, I have refused to blossom, but soon I will have no choice, for a hamadryad must spawn at least one daughter.

That was a horrific tale. And to think it all happened simply because a man hung a notice of some kind on a tree beside the road.

"You said you had a task for me. Name it, and I shall consider it."

"Since I've failed to compel you, what boon will you require of me in turn?

I recalled the cautionary tale of Wee Willie. He had told me the fey could: 'tell a true heart from that of a greedy bastard.'

"I will require nothing of you," I said. "I offer my friendship. Among my folk, friends do small favors for one another all the time, asking for nothing in return. If you like, you may offer me some small reward by way of thanks."

She paused to consider this. From the look on her face, such a concept was alien to her experience. Then she stiffened.

"The bug lady is coming," she whispered fearfully. "You must not be found here. Flee. I shall hide your tracks."

I trotted off, then returned, snatched up my hat, and set off once more. I had a pretty good idea who the bug lady was. Frida Willoughby, the master charged with the maintenance of these grounds, was, after all, an entomancer. Within the twisting trail of the Perilous Glade, I invoked my darksight. The sky had dimmed another notch, and I heard the sizzle of the first sheets of rain striking the canopy above.

I came out on a different stretch of the garden lane, one much closer to home. I emerged to be showered by the windblown rain. I knew I would soon return. Hazel was an interesting sort. And I could do with another friend.

***

I knelt by the walkway of House Blue Jay. The sun beat down on the back of my neck. The rains had moved on, but the slick mud which constituted our courtyard provided ample evidence of their recent passing. I took another weed between my thumb and forefinger and watched it decay as I tugged.

I thought of the dryad confined to her glen at the bug lady's mercy and fearing her ill intent. Of course, I'd only heard Hazel's side of the story. My father had once advised me that for every dispute there were two tales, and the truth lay somewhere in-between. I found it odd I was so ready to believe Hazel's version of events and to revile a woman I'd never met. Perhaps I was suffering the lingering effects of that compulsion she'd used on me, but Hazel had seemed quite tragically sincere. It was for this reason I'd decided to wait a day or two before returning to the glade.

I reached over to the wretched shrubbery that passed for a hedgerow at our house's frontage. Years of neglect and half-hearted attempts at care by aspirants soon to move on had reduced them to a sorry, bedraggled state. I played my fingertips across them and willed them to drink of my essence. For a short time last autumn, I labored beside the greenskeeper at Westarbor Keep. Zak was a genius with topiary and had shown me a trick or two. He told me the shapes he imparted to the hedges in his care were already present in the predictable path of growth. He just gave them a nudge and removed the other bits.

Tomorrow would be my first actual teaching session at the créche. I was still considering how best to introduce the kids to the noble art of reading. I couldn't remember exactly how I'd picked it up myself. To be sure, we must start with learning the letters, but that was tedious work and children were notorious for their short attention spans. Still, they must first learn to crawl ere they could toddle. What I did recall was sitting in father's lap

76

as he read to me. If only I could give them a taste of what real reading was, perhaps it would inspire them. Alas, my lap was inadequately broad for such a task.

It was with this in mind I had borrowed a book from Edgar earlier this morning. It was a newly written work, a set of adventurous tales which just might hold their interest. I'd also used my time there to investigate some facts about the fey, specifically dryads, and about oak trees in general. Useful things, books.

I returned to my weeding. It was a familiar and comforting task which allowed my mind to wander.

As honest sweat beaded upon my brow, I heard bells in the distance drawing ever nearer. I stood to peer down Aspie Rowe toward the source of the sound, and Lorraine came out from the house to stand at my side.

"Are those the harkers bells I hear?" I asked.

"Harkers? You mean the heralds?" she asked of me in turn.

"I suppose," I returned. "In Westarbor we refer to them as harkers."

The girl shot me an amused smirk.

"And what do you call the knights in your backwoods barony? Foe-stabbers?"

I was given no time for rebuttal because just then a man in the conclave's livery appeared. Upon reaching the fountain at the end of the lane, he turned our way and rang his bell once more.

"Hear ye all residents of the conclave," he bellowed. "There is to be a gathering this day in the master's hall. All mages must attend. Prepare. When next the steeple bell doth toll the hour, you are to present yourselves there forthwith."

So having said, he turned and marched on. The man obviously enjoyed his work. But honestly, who said 'doth' anymore? I spied several residents of House Falcon and a few from House Owl down the way, standing out in their respective yards. All hastened inside. Taking my queue from them, I gathered my few tools, hefted my Bob and did likewise. There was still time to clean up a bit and make myself presentable.

***

My housemates and I sat all in a row on the polished wood bench. Fully lit, the Hall of Masters seemed far grander than the darkened chamber Franklin and I had visited last week. Despite the many mages gathered here, there was seating for all and legroom aplenty. From the lofty heights of its vaulted ceilings hung three grandiose and intricately wrought brass chandeliers, each sporting hundreds of candles.

I puzzled over how they could afford so many, much less light them all. When I remarked on it, Lorry informed me these bore a permanent enchantment. The candles would ignite upon command, and each could burn for several months before being fully consumed and requiring replacement. The enchanted flames shed their brilliance down on a scene of austere elegance.

On the plush seats behind the lectern sat the masters draped in their flowing robes. Were this the cathedral it so resembled, they would be its choir. With no little amusement, I imagined them all bursting into a rousing hymn. The pews toward the front were occupied by journeymen, by far the most numerous of the congregation. Our lot sat more than midway back. Apprentices and some few other interested individuals were seated just to our rear. Behind these, rows of empty benches held a place in hopeful anticipation of an increase to our number. All told, I guessed that just over a hundred wizards graced this assembly. It was stunning to realize that so few represented most of the mages from throughout an entire kingdom. It was indeed a rare station to be a mage of Osten.

The indistinct murmuring of dozens of hushed conversations echoed about the hall. No one spoke aloud. Instead, a sense of reverence pervaded the chamber.

"I don't see Master Prowd," whispered Lloyd.

"He'll doubtless make his entrance soon," muttered Franklin.

But such was not the case.

Arising from her seat, Mistress Meredith approached the lectern in a dignified stride. She waited for the crowd to still, then addressed us.

"I am sad to report," she began, "that Master Prowd is feeling a bit under the weather today. I have been elected to address this assembly in his stead."

She took a moment to look about and survey the crowd's reaction.

"There is no need to panic, but we've had some rather distressing news and thought it prudent that all be informed the better that we might prepare."

I began to panic.

"Yesterday, the knights of our good lord mayor sought to apprehend a felon who had assaulted a citizen in town. There is some confusion as to exactly what has occurred, but the facts are thus. After his violent and lawless behavior, the fellow was tracked to a house in lowside. On entering the house, our good knights found the man dead upon the floor. Though there were no marks of violence upon him, apart from some bruising on his hands, his corpse was in an advanced state of decrepitude. Moreover... he bore symptoms of the plague."

The silence that followed was profound. Into it, a hundred horrified glares gave voice to a riot of unspoken questions. Mistress Meredith now had the complete attention of everyone present as all ears strained to hear the next words to fall from her lips.

"We suspect he may have escaped from one of the villages to the north under the duke's quarantine. The owner of the house, a fellow named Russell Moore, has gone missing. If you know aught of this man or his whereabouts, you are to notify the proper authorities at once.

"I'm certain you can all appreciate the severity of the situation. The plague cannot be permitted to find purchase in our community. Therefore, travel into and out of the mage's quarter is henceforth forbidden to all save for essential services."

That certainly cast a different light on the headmaster being 'under the weather,' a euphemism I'd never favored. Weren't all of us under the weather at all times, regardless? Was Master Prowd even now loading up a wagon and heading out of town? I took a deep breath to still my racing thoughts. Though it was natural at such times to become suspicious, rampant paranoia would serve no one.

You hear tales about it. You feel bad for the sorry wretches who've been quarantined. You feel angry when one tries to flee such an area, knowing this only allows the infection to spread. And then one day it's you. And it all starts with just such an incident and a proclamation just like this. In the days to come, I would often reflect on this speech and mark it as the moment our lives had changed. Our world had just become smaller.

"Know that those in charge are looking out for you," Mistress Meredith declared. "Decisive action is e'en now being taken on several fronts to assure the safety and welfare of all the people of Deerfield."

Such words did little to still my nagging doubts. For couched within the pontificating reassurance, her emphasis on 'all the people of Deerfield' betrayed her true thoughts. I knew well that 'those in charge' were quite capable of sacrificing some for the good of the healthy majority.

She tightened her lips and cast a glance over her shoulder to the other masters before turning back to face us.

"I shall now turn this meeting over to Master Redmond. As a special treat, you will all be privy to his daily report of conditions at the war front. Master Redmond?"

From among the masters arranged behind her, one stood up and stepped forth. He was one of the twins, the one they called Re-Pete. Though upset over her prior announcement, I was still fascinated by the strange and perplexing talent possessed by the brothers and was eager to see it in action. A timely distraction; said a more cynical part of my mind.

As Mistress Meredith reclaimed her seat, Redmond Peter Doyle spread his arms wide, closed his eyes and tilted his head back as though looking straight up. He stood poised in this manner for several seconds before abruptly lowering his arms and twisting to one side.

"Very well, sergeant," he said to the empty air beside him, "I shall include it in my report. Carry on."

He then paced nervously, looking downward from time to time. Just as my attention was beginning to wane, he looked up and smiled, facing just a little off to our left.

"Greetings Conclave. It's another clear day here in Eagle's Keep, and reckoning by the sundial it is time to commence my report. I hope my brother is receiving. I'm told I look rather silly standing on the battlement talking to the merlons.

"Lord Gaulle commends the conclave and instructs me to express his thanks for the recent shipment of enchanted spears. We are expecting new levies soon, and each will require an effective weapon that is not subject to the wood-warping tactic so favored by our foe.

"Although action along the front has been subdued for the most part this week, the enemy's strategy of quiet encroachment continues unabated. The latest examples are the one-eyed bat-things that harry our citizens by night. A sting from their barbed tails can cause a man to froth at the mouth and go into convulsions. Though most survive, it is unpleasant to say the least. We have christened these beasties Cyclo-Chiropteans. What the soldiers call them in private, I cannot repeat in mixed company.

"Though not overly aggressive, the Cyclos have become more numerous of late and will swarm to defend their nests. We finally found where they hide by day, and the news, I'm afraid, is most dire. They infest the fruit orchards. We've had to burn clear much of the acreage where they've been encountered in an effort to rid ourselves of the pests and halt their spread. As a result, many more farmers have become disenfranchised and are fleeing the region. Please inform the king he can expect more refugees seeking asylum in Fairglen.

"We need more of the following items..."

He then began listing various materials and provisions in short supply.

It struck me as a strange way to conduct a war. And yet it had been thus for decades since first the dark druids had begun their relentless northward advance. Efforts at diplomacy were met only with silence or an occasional terse demand that we withdraw from contested areas. Over the years, many tactics had been attempted. Various sorties into enemy-held territories might succeed at their outset, but were unsustainable. Eventually, our troops would be beaten back to our former borders, unable to retain a firm foothold in the marsh for very long.

All the while, one horrific creature after another would arise from the Black Plagued Marshes to challenge the doughty soldiery of Osten. And the tendrils of this fetid fen cast a pall upon our land.

One had to wonder how the dark druids commanded such creatures or even survived their depredations. The few enemy combatants we'd captured over the years had been human enough. They worshiped some strange swamp demon and our best efforts at interrogation shed no light on how we might dissuade them from further extending their influence. Their mages had proven most elusive and defiant.

Thus, the steady war of attrition had worn on. And most concurred that Osten was losing ground.

"...and so in conclusion, my brothers and sisters of the conclave, we shall use this most recent pause to regroup and prepare ourselves. He's not shared his battle plan with me, but I sense the duke is becoming impatient. When the fresh troops arrive, I suspect he might consider another push into the enemy's heartland. God willing, I shall report again tomorrow at this same time. Until then, be safe and pray for those who keep you thus. Peter Redmund Doyle."

With a nod and a wink, Peter concluded. Redmond then sagged and stared vacantly, blinking at us for a few moments before rounding on the other masters.

"Did he say anything exciting?" he asked.

***

"That's fine for us here," moaned Lloyd, "but what about the people in town?"

"We don't know there's a problem yet, said Lorraine. "It was just that one stranger and he's dead. I hear they burnt the body and then the house just to be certain."

We stood on the stone steps leading up to the academy's

imposing front doors. All except the masters themselves had been banished from the hall at the meeting's end. The journeymen and others clustered about commiserating with one another about the restrictions and speculating idly and pointlessly over what was to be done. Many worried about food, but I figured the lake would provide. Life would go on as normal, at least for a time. It was the Lord Mayor's problem at the moment.

I made up my mind. The events of the day had reminded me that life was short. It took me a while to disengage from Lloyd, who was afraid for his family and Lorraine, who was concerned for her livelihood. Was hers an 'essential service?' I just wanted to forget about it all for a while.

I expected Mistress Willoughby would be tied up with the other masters as they continued their meeting. So, casting caution to the wind, I set out for the Perilous Glade. I was reasonably certain my decision wasn't colored by Hazel's compulsion. I merely had a yen to know what she wanted of me and now seemed an auspicious time to find out.

When I arrived at the garden lane, I distanced myself from the others returning to their homes. Finding a suitable lapse in such foot traffic, I entered. Some distance in, I stepped to one side and summoned my gift to part the brambles and slip within. Once again, I felt the forest's welcome; a path of least resistance formed along which I was drawn. I slipped through the thickets and thorny growths as a duck glides across a pond. I soon found myself once again in the small clearing with its weathered stone bench. Hazel stood abreast of it, her hands clasped behind her back. From beneath an unlined brow, her eyes met mine, two deep pools viridian in hue.

"You've returned; I wondered if you would."

"How could I not?" I asked. "I promised to consider lending you my aid."

"Come then," she said, striding with a purpose to the edge of the forest and disappearing within the folds of its boughs.

I hastened to follow, finding the path readily enough and gliding behind as Hazel parted the way. Once again from up at the fore, I felt that ancient ache. It grew in my perception the nearer to it we drew. The dryad stopped and turned to me. Upon her sorrowful face, apology was writ plain.

"I dare go no further," she lamented. "But you who have the gift of green and yet still can bear the touch of iron; you may succeed where the fair folk fail."

Worried as to what I might find up ahead, nonetheless I passed her by. Though I no longer swam in a dryad's wake, by my own gift, I managed to forge ahead. The way to advance was clear enough. Delicately, I parted the final branch. I stood at the base of an ancient oak. It towered high above. Its limbs spread wide, bearing the unfolding leaves of early spring.

But from it, I sensed a sickness.

Attached to the young leaves were many small brown orbs. These tumorous growths hung like fruit from the tender new leaves. Around them buzzed gall wasps, harbingers of this well-known blight. Such were known to infest oak trees and lay their eggs thereon. A healthy tree could suffer a few galls, but this tree looked to be losing the battle.

All this was absolutely dreadful if one were a dryad, I'm sure. But this was not the source of the ache of the oak. Sticking out from its trunk was the head of an iron spike. This was no mere nail, but a great iron piton driven deep into its heartwood. Where it pierced the trunk, the bark was split and rent. The knot which bulged up around it gave a silent testament to the age of the wound. Who would do such a thing, and why?

I knew what Hazel wanted of me, and I wondered if I could do it. This was no simple knife to be wiggled free. I would have to rely on my gift. I placed my palm on the bole of the tree just to one side of the wound. I summoned my magic to penetrate its bark. Ring after ring, I wriggled within, matching my will to the grain. Until at last I encountered the rotten wood that lay up against the intruding barb.

'Gently now,' I told myself. 'Do as little harm as you may.' I wrapped my will around the barb and began to spread decay. It was like what I did when weeding, but it had to be done with surgical precision so as not to damage the entire tree. The deadwood around the spike began to loosen and crumble. But just as drawing energy from a living tree was far more refreshing to me than siphoning a mere vine, rotting dead wood required a great deal more than withering a weed. I left off when I felt my magic was nearly spent. I seized the head of the piton with my other hand and pulled, but found it to be still wedged in too tight.

"Spacium girabit," I murmured, invoking the mightiest tool in my arsenal.

With my mind I locked on to the head of the spike, I attuned myself to the turning force of the earth. Being a narrow little thing and not a proper large wheel, it was devilishly slippery to grip. Uncle Robert had once said that to a fool whose only tool was a hammer, everything looked like a nail. I suppose my talent for winding was much the same. Though the turning force couldn't be resisted by anything I'd encountered thus far, it was only useful in very limited situations. Nevertheless, I bore down.

With a sudden wrenching twist, the nail turned loose within its hole. I was able to drag it free at last. The surrounding forest seemed to spin about, and nausea arose in the aftermath of my talent's use. I took a moment to regain my balance.

I knew the hole shouldn't be left open. It would permit diseases and pests direct access to the heart of the tree. The hole would grow over time, hollowing out and weakening the oak. Since I was uncertain about how to proceed, I fell back on my old standby and rooted about in my Bob. Surely there must be something among my bric-à-brac to plug such an abscess. If nothing better presented itself, I still had that brick of clay. Ah. Just the thing. From Bob, I withdrew a set of corks, selected one of a suitable size, and pressed it firmly home in the empty socket. The rusty spike I entrusted to Bob as his reward.

"It's done," I called out, certain that Hazel was waiting nearby.

She emerged from the thicket, staring up at the oak in wonderment. Remnants of the ache that had emanated from the tree were receding. And if I could mark it, how much more poignant might this be to a dryad? She spared me not a glance as she all but danced up to my towering patient. Then, raising her arms skyward in supplication, she unleashed a torrent of magic that caused my mage sight to flare.

The magic of the fey was unlike my own. She had no magic center, or if she did, it rested in her tree far away. Instead, I felt a surge of supernatural energy traverse the ground at my feet. Belatedly, I shifted my focus to my inner hillock. Using its connection to the earth, I peered beneath the ground to better sense this new wonder. I saw roots. Both those of the oak and others that appeared as glowing green tendrils. The latter surged forth to intertwine with the former, which also began to shed a faint radiance. This collected at the base of the tree until all at once it flowed upward just beneath the bark.

My earth-sense failed me at this point, but I imagined the process continued on up because soon the budding leaves were opening before my eyes. Most of the galls were shed to the ground in a hail of jetsam that made me take a step back. A few clung stubbornly to the leaves, but these seemed of little consequence.

The oak now exuded vitality. Not so the dryad. Hazel had become pale and wan and swayed on her feet. I guessed her effort had been the dryad equivalent of a grand working, for it had clearly taxed her dearly. Finally, she turned to me.

"Long have I yearned to make that one whole," she said with a satisfied smile. "You will be remembered in this glade, Lucas the Bloke. But seek me not again until after the next full of the moon. I must sleep and regain my strength. Return to me then, for I have another friend-favor to ask of you."

Naught else need be said, I supposed, for she promptly turned and vanished into the undergrowth. I noted with wry amusement how quickly she'd latched on to the idea that friends did favors expecting nothing in return. I wondered whether she understood the obligation side of friendship or merely its benefits. With all the recent happenings over which I was powerless, it felt good to take action where I could make a difference. I was soon to learn that action alone was often useless unless coupled with understanding.

CHAPTER FOUR

The Teacher

"Time is the best teacher, but unfortunately, it kills all of
its students."

~ Robin Williams ~

"We shall begin with story time," I announced. My students
shifted in their seats, glancing at one another then back to me.

"I should have thought we'd start with letters," put in Skyler.
"I've stories aplenty from my time at sea."

Skyler was the eldest of my charges, save only for
Sholeena. As my sole male student, he fancied himself the cock
of the walk. The others seemed to concur and looked to him for
leadership. This made the brash young man prone to speaking
his thoughts. Therefore, gaining his good opinion might prove
instrumental in retaining the group's regard.

"I'm sure you have many fascinating tales," I allowed. "I'd
like to show you a way to tell them such that thousands of
people both now and far into the future can know of your
deeds."

His questioning gaze as he weighed my words bore more

than a hint of suspicion.

"I refer to reading, the reason you're here," said I with a gentle smile.

Reaching down within my Bob, I drew forth from it a book. No flaw marred the supple leather cover that stretched over its newly wrought bindings.

"In this," I began, holding it up, "are a set of tales recounted by men and women on a journey. One fellow among them thought to write them all down so that we might learn of their remarkable adventures. Reading can be fun as well as informative. Each day when we meet, we shall start with a tale before knuckling down to learn our letters. In this manner you may find the heart to persevere. One day, you shall all be able to enjoy such tales for yourselves at your leisure."

I thought it was a pretty good speech. I'd even practiced it a few times. The dubious stares that were the only applause told me it may have come off a bit preachy. Such suspicions, however, were laid to rest and interest returned once more when I began to read aloud.

Once on a time, as old stories tell to us,

There was a duke whose name was Theseus:

Of Athens he was lord and governor,

And in his time was such a conqueror

That greater was there not beneath the sun...

When I reckoned I'd read enough and it was time to move on to something else, I found a convenient place to stop and set a bookmark.

"We'll take a short recess," I informed my charges. "It's a fine day, and Susanna can show you to the recreational area out back."

"Hold Aspirant," demanded Skyler. "Will Palamon escape from his gaolers?"

"Will Arcita ever see his lady love again?" sobbed

Cassandra.

And from the rapt expressions on their upturned faces, I knew them to be properly hooked. I returned what I hoped was a mysterious smile as I packed the book back into my bob.

"We'll find out next time," I replied to both.

Outside, the weather was fair. and the area here behind this part of the academy was kept as grounds for children to play. I set them loose to enjoy the day in whatever manner they might.

Daisy Sutherland and Susanna Feininger immediately claimed the teeter-totter. The curious device consisted of a long plank of wood resting on a fulcrum. The girls sat at either end, alternately rising and descending, each borne briefly aloft by the weight of the other. Though quite pointless, I could see the attraction. Bella Gibson and the other younger girls were inspecting the May pole with some notion of organizing a game involving the long strips of colored canvas hanging down from atop it. Skyler held himself aloof from such frolics, merely overseeing their efforts as he stretched out languidly nearby.

And then there was Sholeena. My housemate sat morosely beside the sandbox, lost in thought as the grains of sand fell in a steady stream from her partially opened hand. I approached to sit beside her.

"How am I doing so far?" I asked.

"It wazh a nice shtory," she remarked. "When will we shtart learning the lettersh?"

"That depends," I replied. "Can you dampen this sand a bit, perchance?"

She peered at me quizzically, but then complied. Muttering 'praefundo harenae,' she waved her hand above the sand. The gritty grains promptly darkened several shades. I stood and took up the long, pointed stick I'd brought. The children had glared suspiciously when I'd first entered with it, wary it might be intended as an instrument of discipline.

Sholeena smiled when I used my gift to smooth out the dunes of her miniature beach. The damp sand now lay flat and even. Onto this blank slate, I inscribed the serpentine shape of the letter 'S.'

"Do you know this one?" I challenged.

"Of coursh," she replied at once. "My app-mashter showed me the shnake shymbol. It'sh the firsht letter of my name."

"She talks funny," said Cassandra, approaching us from behind.

I smoothed the sand once more. Onto it, I carved out a large letter 'C.'

"And how about you, Cassie," I inquired. "Have you seen this letter before?"

"No," she returned, blinking up at me blankly.

"Then study it well, for it is the letter that begins your own name. It's called a 'cee' and can make two different sounds. In your case, it makes a 'kah' sound."

After a moment, I erased the symbol and handed her the stick.

"Now you make it," I urged her.

With the tip of the stick, she did a credible job of rendering the rune in question. In time, the others drifted over to join us, attracted by the new game. Involving Sholeena at the outset had proven a blessing. For as the game caught on, I found she could use her own gift to smooth the sand. Moreover, she soon added her own innovation.

Rather than merely flattening out, the sand would erupt in a disturbance. A fin would emerge and travel along the letters, consuming them and leaving smoothness in its wake. The 'sand shark' apparently preferred his waters tranquil, so you had to call out the letters quickly so he could be appeased. It became clear to the children we weren't going back inside. The game was soon a hit, and we whiled away our afternoon in the leisurely pursuit of learning our letters.

"To pass this first lesson," I finally asserted, "each of you must step up and carve out the first letter of your name in the sand. Tomorrow we will move on to more worthy pursuits."

I caught a strange glimmer from my mage sight out of the corner of my eye. It came from the back where the yard was fenced off from a set of small garden plots. When I turned to look in that direction, it was gone. With a shrug, I returned to my teaching as my students lined up for their quiz. All passed. I dismissed them, well-pleased by our progress. The sand shark had fed well this day.

***

I approached House Blue Jay, well-satisfied with my teaching debut. The late afternoon sun shone down upon our house and smoke curled up from both chimneys. If the parlor hearth was lit, then comfort couldn't lie far beyond its threshold. I noted with approval the hedgerow in front and the courtyard it encompassed. Both had grown more lush since the infusion of my gift, and I perceived vague shapes taking form atop the former.

"Hail House Blue Jay!" I sang out with pride as I stepped up onto the stoop.

Upon entering, I was greeted by an unaccustomed sight. In the parlor were gathered all of my housemates around an unfamiliar young man sharing tea and conversing amiably.

"Well met," he said, arising and thrusting out his hand toward me. "You must be Lucas."

"He is indeed," remarked Franklin somewhat stiffly. "Lucas Harper, allow me to introduce Galwell Cummings, most recently of Fairglen. Galwell is an aspirant newly assigned to our house."

I closed the distance and clasped his hand, uncertain of just what to say. The typical phrases like 'well met' or 'tis an honor to meet you' seemed a bit premature given what I'd surmised of his past. I settled on humor to see where it went.

"Galwell met," I declared neutrally.

With a firm grip and a broad smile, he shook my hand. And was that a twinkle in his eye from my feeble jest?

"Well met, indeed," said he, releasing my hand and resuming his seat. "From what I've been told, you're an interesting chap and hail from the land of my family's origin. Pull up a cuppa and join us then. Your head of house here brews a most exquisite blend."

"I've heard something of your family as well," I returned.

His face became pinched.

"No doubt not all of it good," he put forth, understating the matter, I thought. "We've already gone over my family's past deeds ere you arrived. To catch you up to speed, I was but a swaddled babe at the time and share not the passions of my grandsire.

"As I have attested time and again, I was not suckled on resentment nor raised to seek vengeance for grandfather's chastisement by the crown. Lo, have I spent my last tedious months in Fairglen while the barristers bickered over whether my family's exile should take precedence over the king's edict regarding newly discovered mages. I now stand ready to take my place among my fellow aspirants only to find I've arrived just in time to be bottled up within a quarantine."

Having said his piece, he took up his teacup and sipped at it. His smile returned.

This earnest, factual, unapologetic summary smacked neither of resentment nor of pleading and even bore a hint of graceful forbearance. I found his pretentious manner of speech, however, most amusing. He would get on splendidly with the local herald. Who said 'Lo' anymore, after all? The 'sins of the father' argument played well with me, and I was inclined to give the man the benefit of the doubt.

"We're not precisely under quarantine as yet," put in Lloyd. "It's more like just a precaution. But we take your point."

"Alright," I said, accepting the man's account. "Just so we're clear about that. While we're all being forthcoming, what type of magic brought you to conclave? What is your magic center?"

I never had gotten around to looking up what a therianthrope was. Galwell grimaced.

"There remains some argument over whether those of my kind are proper mages at all," he said. "Our 'magic centers' are our entire bodies, and the reach of our magic is limited to workings within."

"You're a therianthrope?" prompted Franklin.

"Indeed," Galwell replied. "We can stretch our limbs, sprout claws, achieve heightened senses, increase our strength and so forth."

"Master Sheppard, the head of our seneschals, commands such magic," Franklin exclaimed. "At the pinnacle of his art, a therianthrope can take the form of his totem animal. Brayden Sheppard becomes a mighty gorilla. What, pray tell, is your totem?"

"Alas, that is uncertain as yet," Galwell returned. "Though he taught me the rudiments at Indigo Bay and passed me as his apprentice, Master Jordan is not well-schooled in the discipline. It remains for me to discover."

Sholeena perked up and stared at the man. He returned her gaze and smiled.

"Yes," he said in answer to her unvoiced remark. "He was my app-master just as he was your own. If this house is indeed where ne'er-do-wells are sent to languish, I must confess to curiosity as to what a beauteous Paluda is doing here. The Paludaria are brave and stalwart allies. I should think such would be given a place of honor within our guild. I've heard many a shipwrecked sailor was saved by the intervention of your people during the naval engagement at Rappa Sanguine. At grave personal peril, they delivered our countrymen from drowning. It was a far cry more loyal than those craven merfolk. Master Jordan sends his compliments and bids me write to him of your progress.

Unused to such lofty praise, Sholeena discolored in embarrassment.

Whatever else he was, Galwell seemed to be a most learned man. He was also a charmer. Already, he'd ingratiated himself to most of us. After some further discourse, it was determined that Galwell would bunk with Franklin, who had agreed to set aside their mutual familial antipathy. The Steins had remained staunch supporters of the king throughout the disastrous Northford rebellion. I was shooed away to prepare the meal of welcome. It was my first time cooking for the house. I'd nearly forgotten amid the excitement of the day's events. So, no pressure, I supposed.

Just as on the day I myself had first arrived at House Blue Jay, it began with a trip to the fountain. As I filled the pails, I considered the mermaids atop it. Galwell had spoken scornfully of such folk. Skyler, too, had mentioned mermaids in a negative fashion. When the topic had arisen, he'd cited something his father had said of them. 'I don't understand the fascination,' he'd remarked. 'Sure, the preening things are comely enough, but I think any sensible man should prefer his woman be properly bifurcated.'

Returning to the house, I set to work in its small scullery. Sholeena had already filleted the catch of the day. Her pearl-handled flensing knife had made short work of gutting and scaling the brace of tench she'd caught. It still amazed me the girl could reliably retrieve such bottom-feeders during their dormant season. I decided to pull out all the stops and prepare this feast Westarbor style.

I brought out the can of spices Gregor had gifted me. The Cain's 'secret family blend' that had so finely flavored frog legs could definitely do the same for our pan-fried meal. To go with it, I chose to attempt Tilda's savory sweet potatoes. She'd sworn me to secrecy on its recipe, though in truth it was mostly just baking them with a drizzle of honey.

We couldn't afford the good wheat bread. In Deerfield, however, the duke had established a set of price controls for bakers designed to allow even the meanest, unlanded serf to buy at least some quantity of bread for a penny. Each year the size of this bread was set according to the price of wheat and other grains. This was termed the 'assizing' of bread. Lorry never failed to get us our assizement and today had acquired a loaf of a wheat-rye blend called meslin.

For the pièce de résistance, I retrieved from my trunk the jar of Jenkins plum preserves I'd carried all the way from Meadowfork. I'd been saving it for a special occasion when I might truly savor a taste from back home.

When all was in readiness, I laid out the spread upon the boards of our table, Franklin said grace and we all tucked in. On sighting the jam, Lloyd wasted no time before reaching for it. He stuck in his thumb and pulled out a plum.

"Use a utensil, for star's sake," complained Lorraine. "Being a friend of your mother, I may know better, but Galwell might think you were raised in a barnyard."

Over dinner, Galwell spoke more of therianthropes. This special breed of shapeshifter was confined to working transformations within his or her own body. It had been discovered by studying them that similar transformations could be wrought upon others, willing or otherwise. This was accomplished by advanced use of enchantment over time. Changes thus wrought were permanent and inheritable once fully complete. In times past, such workings had given rise to the stories of evil enchanters transforming a fellow into a frog.

This practice was absolutely forbidden by the conclave since its founding. Nothing damaged the reputation of mages more than ill-advised and foolhardy tampering with the dictates of nature. It was speculated that such creatures as gryphons and perhaps even peoples like the Paludaria had originated in such a manner. But for every good and noble creature thus born, a hundred foul and wicked races were so spawned.

It was believed to be how our enemies were raising up the vile creatures that so beleaguered our southern border.

I considered the Cains and their curse. Grandma Abbey had violated a central tenet of the conclave in causing their metamorphosis into wild boars. It was very nearly the same sin as that of the sorceress Circe. Instead of holding Galwell's past against him, perhaps I should look to the beam in my own eye. My family tree had at least as many rotten fruits and much to answer for.

***

In the morning, I rose and stretched. Bob assured me he was ready to go. He'd earlier disgorged the rusty spike to rest on my dresser as a trophy of sorts. I dressed, and we left Lloyd dozing contentedly on his bed nearby. I found it pleasant to accomplish my morning ablutions absent the overloud snoring of my cousin. I was delighted that such sweet morning music would now be rendered for Falcons to cherish.

If my current roommate had a single flaw (or two, I suppose), it would be his feet. Having attained the age of adolescence, they put out a prodigious stink. He needed to launder and change his socks much more often if there were to be any semblance of peace between us. His malodorous miasma wafted about our shared room and seemed to permeate the very boards of the walls and floor. Ah well. Few things in life were ideal.

Plenty of time remained before I needed to meet with my students, but I wanted to visit the library beforehand. And so I hastened to prepare a bowl of porridge to break my fast. Upon entering the mud room to retrieve my boots, I was astonished to find it immaculate. Overcoats hung neatly upon their pegs sporting nary a nit or speck as though recently brushed clean of such. Boots stood in an orderly row, arranged by size and shining with such a luster that any of them might be used in place of a mirror. No hint of mud besmudged the floor, the boards of which gleamed as though from a fresh coat of wax.

It was a far cry better than the unruly mess that formerly was our mud room. Who could have arisen so early as to put this all in order? It could have been Lorraine. Her cart was gone already. She'd been well-pleased when informed that her work was deemed even more vital under the conclave's current restrictions. Under the bans, many who previously shopped for their own goods in town were now forbidden to do so. Thus, the embargo was in fact a boon to her business, and her dealings with the traders were to become a daily affair. I doubted it was she. Lorraine had never exhibited such domestic proclivities before. Perhaps Galwell was an insomniatic neat-freak. If so, that was all to the good. I retrieved my pristine boots and made ready to soil them once more.

The children at the créche sat attentively at story time and diligently pursued their lessons thereafter. At the outset, I was puzzled to find a capital letter 'T' carved into the sand of our lesson box. I was certain we'd left it blank the day before. I asked Susie whether she had done it, thinking to praise her initiative, but she disavowed any knowledge of such. It would remain a minor mystery; I supposed. None of my charges had a name beginning with 'T.'

There was only one disciplinary incident among them. This occurred when Daisy Sutherland referred to Sholeena as 'the teacher's pet.' Unfamiliar with the phrase in this context and recalling Henry Sutherland's taunts of the prior week, this had sent Sholeena into a red-faced pout which the other girls found amusing. I could understand the Paluda girl's angst, especially given Eli's rude comment about her being my 'housepet'. She refused to take part in the sandbox game and sat distant from the others. Her skin acquired a bluish tinge that set her even farther apart.

I considered sharing what Franklin had done to Henry with the dead pig to jolly her out of her bleak mood. But I thought better of it. There was enough cruelty in the world without adding to it with tales of vengeance. Instead, I drew her aside and explained the difference. 'Teacher's pet' simply meant that she was my favorite among them. It was a backhanded compliment of sorts. Eventually, she caught on. It helped that she trusted me so.

Before the third bell, the students could render their entire first names upon the sand. I explained how important it was to make such marks as it would enable them to sign for things. In truth, this was as far as most in my village ever progressed. And we had accomplished it in a mere two days. Only a few misspellings or backwards letters marred the perfection of our second quiz. I gave each a pass, assigning extra practice drills to those whose efforts had lacked definitude, and set out for home once more.

As I passed down the garden path, I peered over at the Perilous Glade. Absent its welcome, I probably ought not to intrude. On the other side, however, I noted a lone figure prodding at a tree in the orchard with a long pole. His face was familiar. He was one of the masters, but I couldn't recall his name. Stalking over toward him came another. *Her* I knew quite well, though we'd not officially met. It was Frida Willoughby, Royland's great aunt and Hazel's 'bug lady.' I'd marked her with interest when last I'd sat in the master's hall.

Her words were angry and loud enough to carry to where I stood unnoticed on the lane. I had a sudden urge to rest here a bit, perhaps in the shade of this tree. Though it's very impolite to eavesdrop, could I help it if I overheard her unguarded remarks?

"I know it was you, Jonathan!" she accused.

Leaning his pole against the tree, he turned to the woman

confronting him.

"What are you going on about, Frida?" he asked in annoyance.

"You know quite well, you scoundrel; the tree. And now that blasted dryad has gone and healed it - just what I was trying to prevent!"

"Calm yourself, woman. What tree are we talking about here?"

"I refer to the oak, of course. I finally solved the dilemma of the Fetid Fen Wetland Beetle, and that tree was crucial evidence of its solution. My experiment is ruined! We shall just have to proceed without the final proof. Though where I shall now obtain enough gall wasps, I cannot fathom."

"I warned you not to set those beetles loose in the glade. They devastated the hardwood groves in the south. You told me you could control them."

"I can," she replied absently, "but that's not the point. If I'm to release my modified galls to repel the blight, we need to be certain. The cure must proceed without my intervention. I promised the duke my answer by next week. Am I to take it you had no hand in removing the spike? Swear it to me."

With an exasperated sigh, the man raised his right hand and said formally: "I, Jonathan Reinhardt, master of the conclave of the second order, do solemnly swear I did not meddle in your experiment. Are you satisfied?"

The woman blinked and looked as if she'd eaten something sour.

"If not you, then who? Only a dendromancer such as yourself could have removed that spike so neatly. It was driven in rather deep. You don't suppose it could have been the autonomists; do you?"

"Not everything's an autonomist plot, my dear. What would they have to gain?"

"I wouldn't put it past them. They're zealots. Perhaps they seek to damage our reputations or weaken the king somehow."

"Well, it seems your tame dryad might know. Try asking

her."

The old woman sighed.

"She still doesn't trust me. And she's anything but tame. The ungrateful little thing will barely even speak to me, and then it's only to make impertinent demands. I haven't detected her aura all day."

"Well, don't take it too hard," Master Reinhardt consoled her. "You know the truth, even if she won't accept it. I remember how hard you fought to delay the duke's emergency measures as long as you did. Even if she'd somehow survived the clear-burning, the beetles would've made short work of her. It's a shame about the other one, though. Best not to dwell on it."

"You're right," Frida acknowledged, straightening. "We should look forward. Have you decided whether to take on a new journeyman?"

"Well, I considered it. But my dance card's pretty full right now. So as like as not, I won't. I can recommend that Royland fellow, though. You should see how he uses the Willoughby gift."

"Oh?"

"He's a sharp one. For his work detail, they lent him to me at the carpentry shop. I figured he'd be shaping wood and fire-hardening spears and axe handles and the like. But he managed to pick up 'inexsuperabilis permanens lignea' all on his own. Claimed he'd seen it done on a gate once. And he can knock out more than one of them in a row."

"Really," she said with interest. "I'll keep him in mind. Under whom did he apprentice?"

"The fellow's from Westarbor. His app-master was Chadwick."

"That old reprobate? I thought he stayed aloof from the conclave's affairs. Some kind of scandal."

"That may be," returned Master Reinhardt, "but he turns out a fine aspirant. Anyway, now that I've officially sworn my innocence, I hope you'll let me get back to my work. These apple trees aren't going to prune themselves. And if you do manage to get on better terms with little miss wilderness, send her on over. Maybe she can lend a hand."

I was dumbfounded. As Mistress Willoughby made to depart, I crept back from the tree and slunk down the shaded lane, lost in thought. Hazel must learn of what I had just heard. But it seemed she might already know it. The choosing was only a few days off, and I hadn't given it a single thought. It seemed that Royland already had some sterling reviews. Should I come clean about the spike? It would be the right thing to do, but should I wait until after the choosing? And what scandal had estranged Master Chadwick from the conclave? Was he an exile of sorts? I needed some time to think long and hard on these matters without all the hectic distractions that had become my life. I liked answers, but sometimes ignorance was more restful.

***

Though the recently overheard conversation had satisfied many questions, I was hard-pressed to quell the dozen others that swirled up in their wake. Remarks regarding Hazel's history had piqued my curiosity. It had sounded as though Mistress Willoughby was on a sanctioned mission to save the kingdom's forests. These Fetid Fen Wetland Beetles were doubtless yet another blight sent by our foemen. I had imagined she was inflicting the oak with galls merely to make ink for the conclave. Could her wasps actually be designed to prey on such pests and purge them from our land?

Was I wrong to have helped Hazel? My desire to conceal the deed warred with a troubled conscience that bade me to confess. I had brooded overlong on such matters and decided to put them from my mind for a time.

This time on approaching our house, I noted the hedgerow was getting shaggy. The abundant new growth would soon be ready for some additional guidance. I looked forward to pruning it back and seeing what shapes would emerge.

"Now!" shouted Franklin, bursting out from behind the hedge with a white flag of surrender in hand.

He was followed by Lloyd who also sprang forth, a glass jar hugged close to his chest. The pair nearly frightened me out of my boots, materializing as if from nowhere. They sprinted toward me with Franklin leading the charge. Not a flag, I realized. The stick Franklin bore had a ring on its end about which was woven a fine net of white threads. Its pointed end billowed behind. He nearly ran me over in his pursuit of a winged creature that arose from the shrubbery to flutter aloft.

With a great leap, Franklin managed to snag it from mid-air and swiftly pinched closed the net's near end.

"Hurry Lloyd, lest it damage its wings," cautioned Franklin.

I approached them to inspect their catch. Lloyd squinted at the struggling, netted creature. It promptly vanished to reappear a few seconds later inside the jar. Lloyd held it forth that we all might inspect the colorful creature within. It was a butterfly with a wingspan as large as my open hand. It was bedecked in vibrant hues with two large spots resembling eyes.

"This is the part I hate" complained Lloyd.

For as we watched, the insect began skittering up the jar's glass side only to fall and lie on its back, its abdomen squirming in distress. Its jointed legs worked franticly and a strange light like that of a firefly began to pulse feebly from its backside.

"Yes!" exclaimed Franklin, raising a fist in triumph. "At last my collection is complete."

"You collect butterflies?" I asked, surprised.

"I do," he confirmed. "Although technically this one is a moth. The Lorédonian Moon Moth to be more precise. Lepidoptera Lunam Agrotis."

"They're said to be a sign of fey presence," he added while closely observing the dying insect's feeble struggles. "What a fabulous find. Under a certain light the eyes on their wings glow eerily as if with light of their own. Their abdomens are possessed of an actual bioluminescence. They're sometimes called, 'Faerie Lanterns.'

"Why did it die so quickly?" I asked as the insect stilled.

"That spec of cottony substance in the bottom of the jar is a mothball," he replied. Some people find them handy to place in their wardrobes to keep common moths from eating holes in their doublets. I get them from the apothecary for a few farthings."

"You should save your coin," I said. "I should think one of Lloyd's socks would do the job."

"Hey!" Lloyd exclaimed with wounded overtones.

If Franklin thought this funny, he kept it to himself, still staring in fascination at his prize.

"It's done," he pronounced.

"Well you should launder them more often," I admonished. "Speaking of cleaning up, do you know who tidied up the mudroom?"

"I thought *you* might have done it the way you've been fixing up the yard," Franklin returned.

"*I* think we've got *brownies*," said Lloyd in a hushed whisper, his eyes gone round.

"Don't be ridiculous," said Franklin, taking the jar from the boy. "That only happens out in the countryside. None of the fair folk would be caught dead in a village, much less in the middle of a large town like Conclave."

"You might be surprised," I put in, thinking once again of the dryad held captive in the glade.

"Say nothing," said Lloyd, "or you'll jinx it."

It was at this time we spied Lorraine returning from her day's trek to town. Her cart was light but her shoulders drooped, her weariness plain on her face. Letting out a loud breath, she squeaked up beside us.

"I couldn't fill your order, Lucas," she said in a burst of disgruntlement.

"Well met, Lorraine, " I cheerfully returned. "I am well. Thanks for asking. And you?"

The girl rested her cart and her eyes flashed at me as her lips twisted in a wry smirk.

"In truth, I've had better days," she replied. "With talk of an outbreak, the townsfolk are panicked, and all are hoarding provisions. I had to stand in the breadlines for more than an hour, and the bakers were hard-pressed to provide us even our assizement which has been reduced by half."

"That's dreadful," said Franklin, returning to his more usual disposition.

"I scarcely filled half of my orders, and the estates were not very understanding. Try explaining to a master's majordomo that the market is fresh out of eggs and see what kind of tip *you* get. The traders are all overwhelmed and many fear the shortages will only grow worse.

"The apothecary was still putting his shop back in order whilst being deluged by demands for his medicines. I'm sorry I couldn't get you what you require."

"It's alright, Lorry," I soothed. "It can wait a bit. Go and get settled and put your feet up. We'll unload the cart for you."

"Sholeena's cooking dinner," added Lloyd. "At least we won't *starve*."

So as the girl stepped off, Lloyd and I lifted the cart up onto the porch and trundled it within. Franklin led the way bearing his new treasure.

"I must mount this at once," declared Franklin.

He invited us along. It was an unusual offer. I'd not seen the inside of Franklin's room before. So we followed and entered the largest room of the Blue Jays' nest, the one he now shared with Galwell. Spread out across one wall was an enormous display of butterflies each pierced through its middle to a board made of cork. He delicately retrieved his latest trophy from the jar and pinned it up amid the others. The display was magnificent, made more so by the neatly printed labels underlying each specimen.

With a satisfied sigh upon filling that final space, Franklin let his eyes grow distant. At once, all the insects, large and small, began flapping their wings slowly and in unison. The obscene mockery of movement was made more macabre by all of the pins sticking out. But it was, nonetheless, a wondrous spectacle. Franklin looked at peace staring vacantly at his animate yet unliving wall. Although it was a far cry from the laughter I'd vowed to invoke; it was nice to see that something at least could soothe his sorrowful soul.

Though disappointing, Lorraine's failure wasn't a total disaster. She'd delivered half her consignments and I was certain she would do her utmost to accomplish the rest as soon as she may. That night as I lay nestled in my bed I was to be rudely reminded of the risk inherent in half-measures.

***

"Fetch me a hairbrush, my sweet," I said to the girl who sat moping nearby.

"Yes, Miss Wagge," she sullenly returned.

Removing the pins that held them in place, I loosed my generous auburn locks from their ringlet to flow freely down my back. The girl sauntered off. She was a moody little thing. Having recently arrived at her womanhood, the girl was constantly fretting over showing no hint of the gift. Like her brother before her, it was likely she would remain ungifted. Only one in three children of the mages were so blessed. Upon her return, I would set her a task, for idle hands were the devil's playground, were they not?

The créche was rather empty of late, with only the Spencer girl in my care. In truth, I preferred it that way. Whatever had headmaster Sutherland been thinking when he'd assigned me the distasteful chore of serving as its governess? I was no elderly matron, fit only for domestic duties, and I despised children. I peered in the mirror and reveled in the beauteous countenance that gazed forth to regard me in turn. It was indeed a pleasing aspect, or so I had oft been told. Stars willing, it would remain so until I achieved my aim.

I heard the girl's scuffling footfalls echo hollowly from the hallway without. Soon I spied her reflection in the glass. With a slothful gait and downcast eyes, she approached, in her hand, the brush and comb.

"You may brush it out, Elissa,"

"Yes, Miss Wagge," she returned with a frown, her somber gaze drifting upward to meet my own.

I perceived in those eyes an ungrateful gloom as begrudgingly she complied. Nonetheless, the girl's hand was gentle as she separated the loose braids and softly stroked my mane. Today of all days, I must look my best. I had come later in life to the conclave than most, and though I carefully maintained my womanly charms, at nearly forty years of age it was becoming more difficult by the day.

"Your father is due to return soon from Eagle's Keep, Is he not?" I inquired.

"So I have been told, governess," the girl replied. "I understand his replacements will be setting off to keep watch over the lands to the south. There are rumors that a dark force is gathering again to test the kingdom's borders once more."

"Replacements?" said I, a frown gracing my reflection. "I thought it was to be just one, Elizar Chadwick."

"It was, governess," she hastened to confirm. "But Master Elizar has been reassigned. A banneret from Fairglen, Sir Vincent Arenson by name, has struck upon a bold plan to repel the army invading Downham. He rides north with several dozen lances to confront the horde and teach them the folly of assailing Osten. Master Chadwick is to join them to provide magical support."

'Master Elizar.' It still galled me that the boy who'd given me up to the guild had arisen so quickly in our ranks. The young water mage I knew from House Owl had made quite a name for himself of late. Unlike my own meager gift, his command of his element was notable. Whereas I would probably never rise higher than journeyman, Sweetcheeks had attained his mastery far more quickly than most. Well, we'd just see about that. There were more pathways to power in conclave than mere magery.

"How came you by this knowledge, child? And why wasn't I informed?"

"Twas by mere happenstance, governess," she replied meekly. "I overheard the matron discussing it with Master Hans and Mistress Gretta. They came this morning to make arrangements to enroll their son, Robert. He's to stay at the créche while both embark on a sojourn to the south. I'm certain the matron will fill you in once such arrangements are done."

"Eavesdropping is an impertinent sin, my child. I shall have to assess you a fee. I charge you to go to your room and remain there to contemplate your wickedness until the bell doth chime for the evening meal. Leave me now."

"Yes, Miss Wagge," she dejectedly replied, her eyes downcast once more.

I was glad for the excuse to banish the child. I was well rid of her, for I needed the time to advance my plans. Such plans were fast coming to fruition. I'd arranged to meet Luther Prowd in the field of blossoms where we conducted our covert trysts. My seduction of the man proceeded apace, and today might be the day I netted him at last.

It had better be soon in any event, for I could almost feel the child quickening within. Had I not been careful? Had I not regularly taken the herbs and prayed to the saints to be spared such an odious outcome? If I bore the child out of wedlock, my fate would be most dire. Harlot. Wanton. Adulteress. Such would be the least of the epithets to be hurled at me in mocking scorn. Worse than this would be the whispers and silent glances of derision. And all for the simple sin of taking my pleasure in a way that any man would readily do. No. Such would not be *my* future.

Before my trim and attractive waist became bloated and I sagged with the burden of maternity, I would give myself to one of power. For though Luther was not the handsomest fellow, and had thus not been among my erstwhile paramours, I could spot a rising star.

My hair now shone with a luster that put gold to shame. But was that a gray strand marring its perfection? I plucked it out with annoyance and let it drift to the floor. I would soon need to forego the habit, lest my crown grow sparse. On a man, such harbingers of decrepitude were viewed as a mark of wisdom and only enhanced attractiveness. Would that a woman be given such forbearance, but alas it was not so.

I completed my other preparations and headed out the door. As governess, I was supposed to remain in residence, but prior experience informed me the girl would remain brooding in her room until the appointed hour. I crossed the playground, slipped through the fence, and crept across the small set of gardens in the rear. The day was bright, and all was right; I convinced myself as I strolled in perfumed elegance down the lane. Ahead was the field where we'd agreed upon for our assignation.

Journeyman Prowd was almost ripe. I had given myself to him on more than one occasion now. Thus, it would be credible if the child came early. He was of a lofty line, nearly nobility as mages went. Sensing my imminent embarrassment, I had carefully cultivated the affair, eschewing all others. For his part, the lusty young gentleman was only too pleased to win the favors of a mature woman. His fumbling efforts were a testament to his poor luck with the ladies thus far. I pretended to dote upon him and applauded such efforts with doe-eyed innocence. Yes. It would be soon. It *must* be soon.

"Boo!" he shouted, leaping out from behind a tree.

I feigned startlement, then smiled and softly laughed, though inwardly unamused by such churlish tomfoolery.

"Luther," I chastised with just enough sass, then set to giggling once more. "You gave me a fright."

"I shall soon give my lady more than that," he said with a wink, leering smugly at his own poor attempt at licentious innuendo. "Come. Our love nest awaits."

He offered his arm, and I took it. He ushered me out upon the field. It was replete with daffodils and other wild blooms whose fragrances wafted about. He steered me back beyond a low-lying hill that concealed us entirely from the road. Here, he had spread out a blanket. He bade me recline, and I did. I readied myself to welcome his awkward embrace. But rather than joining me directly, the young man stood aloof and uncertain. His expression was suddenly serious, and I noted a crease in his brow.

"Dearest Abby," began Luther with an air of formality. "Fain have I enjoyed our time together and such frolics as we have had will ever be remembered with joy. It is, however, time to consider our futures, yours and mine."

Could this be it? Had he finally taken the hint? Was he

going to make an honest woman of me? Luther would soon arise to his mastery. I would govern a splendid estate with servants at my beck and call, who would see to my merest whim. Despite the other odious duties this would entail, the name Mistress Abigale Prowd had a nice ring to it. And speaking of rings, where might he be hiding such a bauble? I hoped it was suitably large.

"Today I was given consent," he said, "to court the lady Pritchard. Her father blessed the endeavor, and soon I will approach Penelope herself with the joyous news."

"You... what?" I sputtered.

"So you see," he continued. "Our little tête-à-têtes can no longer continue. I must put my bachelor days behind me. I thought I'd grant you one final amorous adventure to remember me by."

I was nearly blinded by rage.

"I would sooner lay with the pigs than share one more moment entwined with a faithless, unworthy lout like you." I sneered.

He laughed nervously. He *laughed!*

"I thought you'd be happy for me, my pet," he said reproachfully. "Surely you didn't imagine *you and I* had a future together? I thought you just enjoyed a bit of harmless fun. Men talk, you know. And after all, what did you imagine an older gal such as yourself had to offer a distinguished man of a reputable family. No. I must soon find a suitable match to honor the name of Prowd."

Gathering the tattered remnants of my dignity, I rose to my feet and spat back at him: "I have a great deal to offer to him whose heart is true."

I then descended into language so coarse as I'm sure he had never heard uttered. I was no filthy rag to be used so and discarded. Nor was I a blushing lady to accept such a slight with dignified grace. I railed at the man and threatened to expose him as the cad he was in terms so vulgar as to disgust the very devil himself.

It was then that young Luther at last found his spine. With

his eyes gone round and his face grown red, he berated me in turn.

"Trollop. Whore. None will believe you, for I shall deny it. If needs be, I'll confess the affair and denounce you as the vile seductress you are. You'll find a young man's indiscretions are easily forgiven. Not so the lecherous acts of a wanton woman of easy virtue. Since you desire not my comfort, let us part straightaway, and if I ever look upon you again, let it be from a distance!"

At this, he turned and stalked off.

Wearily as I trod along, my ire turned to gloom. Utterly my plans had failed; thus was sealed my doom. All hope had fled, or lay burnt and strewn as ashes at my feet. The baleful sun looked down upon me and the flowers mocked me in their gay array with colors too bright to suit my grim mood. There was no time left me to start anew. What shall I do now? Whatever shall I do?

***

"... Whatever shall I do?"

"Lucas? Lucas! Are you alright?"

I sat up in my bed, bumping my head into something hard. Hot tears spilled down my cheeks, tears of anger, and tears of unspeakable grief. It was dark.

I took a calming breath and tried to recall who I was. The recent exclamations helped. Slowly the visions receded and the memories of my last waking thoughts returned.

On the prior night at bedtime, I'd unstoppered my flask and assessed the remains of my draught. A teaspoon wasn't much - a trivial amount. But over time these added up. There could be no doubt. As with so much else of late, I would have to go on short rations, at least until such time as the apothecary could refill it. If I were careful, I could probably stretch my supply to last a few weeks more. I had dribbled out a half teaspoon and quaffed it. I'd licked the spoon as well. Then I lay me down beneath my blanket and stilled my thoughts, inviting the sandman to bear me away.

The dreams had returned. Those were *her* tears on my pillow.

I invoked my darksight. Lloyd was sitting on the edge of his bed, pressing a hand to the side of his head. My own forehead throbbed a bit, but I think the boy had taken the worst of it.

"You didn't have to hit me," he said sullenly.

"I'm sorry, Lloyd. I wasn't myself."

"It's just that you were thrashing about and yelling the most unwholesome things. Ma would wash my mouth out with soap for an entire week if I ever said half of those words. Maybe two weeks cause I didn't even understand the other half."

I lit the candle on the nightstand with a bit of forbidden fire magic I'd learned from Roy. Apprentices weren't taught fire spells for fear they'd set things aflame by accident in their sleep. I'd read ahead a bit on the topic. Evidently, journeymen were instructed to 'cultivate their inner homunculus.' This advanced technique partitioned off part of their brain into which they invested a portion of their magic. It could then govern their magic even while they were unconscious, making simple decisions like: 'don't set fire to the bedding.'

"Here. Let me see," I said, moving over to the wash basin.

The boy arose and hobbled over. I'd given him a good crack alright. It was already raising a lump. I wet a wash towel and bathed the area while Lloyd flinched and grimaced. Where was my bar of soap? The house had other soap, but that was Madam Pennington's lilac-scented soap all the way from Westarbor.

"Uh, Lloyd?"

"What."

"You didn't perchance take my soap, did you?"

"No, I... Oh!... I'll check, just a sec."

The boy's eyes became unfocused and his head tilted back. Then he met my gaze and replied: "Nope. The void is clean - and no soap residue is in sight."

"What time is it?" I asked.

"I don't know. It feels like I just laid down."

"Go on back to sleep. I'll be fine. It's just those old night terrors I was telling you about."

And with that, the boy returned to his bed, rolled to face away from the light and stilled. As his breathing slowed to a steady rhythm, I envied his tranquility. I knew from prior experience I couldn't simply resume my sleep. Perhaps a bit of reading would be pleasant. But my thoughts kept returning to the dream I'd had. At least I could strike Luther Prowd from my list of potential grandfathers, thank the stars. I'd not liked him beforetime, and his dream self's antics did nothing to further endear me to the man.

Still, I'd learned something this night. Perhaps rather than resisting the dreams, I should embrace them and glean all I could. Maybe confronting them was necessary. Letting them run their course might finally free me from the distressing condition and let me win through to find a lasting peace. I must strike a precarious balance. I'd use my remaining elixir to secure at least half a night's sleep, then let the dreams take me where they may. So resolved, I felt much better until I had a horrible thought. Would I be subjected to the pain of childbirth, a fate no man should be forced to endure? I shuddered as this notion sorely tested my recent resolve.

***

Having fretfully dozed a bit prior to the dawn's early light, I yawned and stretched to greet the new day. I retrieved a fresh cake of soap from our linen closet and scrubbed clean my tear-stained cheeks and gummy eyelids. I could use a shave, but would likely pass muster for one day more. Instead, I dribbled out a dollop of Simon Strangelove's scented pomade, combed it into my hair, and slapped some onto my cheeks and chin.

Spotting the rusty iron spike atop my dresser, I paused. It sat there prodding at my conscience. I still hadn't worked out whether I should confess pulling it from the tree. I considered but a moment more before sliding it into my bob to decide later. I then padded out to the kitchen to quell the rumblings of my stomach. I poked up the fire from its embers, set a kettle on to heat, and added some oats. Eyeing the array of mostly empty bottles that was our spice rack, I decided to give it a pass and opted for plain. As it came to a boil, I went to retrieve my boots from the mudroom.

And lo-and-behold they were clean once again. Moreover, the polished boards of the walls and floor gleamed in spotless glory and smelled suspiciously of lavender. I was perplexed, but decided to ignore it today. Perhaps Lloyd was right that we shouldn't question our good fortune. So, returning to the kitchen, I ladled out a portion of gruel, ate quickly, and set off for school.

I arrived earlier than was my usual wont and was rewarded by catching a culprit in the act. As I walked out the back door and onto the playground, I recalled Grandma Abby having done the same; but there, the similarities ended. Ellisa Spencer was now a grown woman and a governess in this place. Nor was the sun shining from on high or the flowers blooming in the fields beyond the back fence. And there by the sandbox, stood Susie Feininger holding my long stick and turning about to face me.

The girl stood silently as I approached and set down the stick upon the ground. The sand glistened faintly with the morning dew and within it had been carved a single word. 'TERWILLIGER' it read.

"That's very interesting," I said to the girl. "What does it mean?" I asked gently.

"It's his name," she replied.

"Whose name?"

"My invisible friend. He likes your stories and wants to learn to read."

I smiled. When I was young, I had no mother to look after me. As an only child, I was often lonesome and had invented an imaginary friend of my own. Dash was his name, for he could run like the wind. Many a summer day I spent with Dash playing at soldiers or just splashing merrily in the mill pond. Though at eight, Susie was getting a bit beyond the normal age for such fantasies, she too was an only child and still working through bereavement at the recent loss of her father.

"Well," I said, "you may tell your friend he's welcome in my class for as long as he keeps good marks and plays nicely with the other children."

Susie smiled and hugged me then. Some days it truly paid to drag my sorry arse out of bed in the morning.

The choosing ceremony would occur in just a few more days. Despite my many negatives, it occurred to me that working with the children might prove my salvation. They were from the families, after all. Even the new apprentices had app-masters. If I kept their good opinion, and my charges showed progress toward reading, those masters just might look on me with favor.

When the others arrived, we had story time, and I finished 'The Knight's Tale' at last. The next was 'The Miller's Tale,' but I skipped past it. It got a little racy for young ears near its end. Since I was skipping about anyway and my class was predominantly young women, I thought I really ought to do one from a female perspective. So I found 'The Prioress' Tale' and bookmarked it for the next time.

For today's sandbox game, we'd all learn to spell our last names. Sholeena's proved challenging. I had her spell 'Blorlafargalish' phonetically, just sounding out the name and deeming it correct. The discussion quickly digressed into who the Phoenicians were and why 'phonetically' didn't begin with an 'F.' It took a great effort of will to get them back on track. When I quizzed them, only half could spell their last names and some had forgotten their first. They were beginning to lose faith in the game as its novelty faded. I knew I must devise some new method to change the game and keep them encouraged. Sandshark was getting a bellyache from consuming all those misspelled words.

I had to wait as the children filed out, all save for Susie, my only charge who lived here at the créche. Miss Spencer was quite the stickler for the rules. So I bided. As I packed up and made ready to depart, there was one ray of sunshine. Evidently, Terwilliger now had a last name. 'BROWN' the sandbox read.

"Susie dear," said I. "You may inform your imaginary friend he has passed the day's assignment."

"You can tell him yourself, Aspirant Harper," she giggled. "And I didn't say he was imaginary - just invisible."

Turning around, I saw Susie sitting on the teeter-totter. On the other end sat no one, and yet the girl was rising and falling and grinning with joy. I peered with mage sight but still saw nothing from the girl. There was only a vague rippling from the other end of the board, as one might see wavering above the stones on a hot day.

"Terwilliger?" I uttered in consternation.

"Say my name and I must appear," chanted a sing-song male voice from nowhere.

And appear he did. Squatting opposite Susie was a small man. He'd stand no higher than my waist if he were indeed standing, and one were to discount the tall, pointed brown hat with a buckle resting atop his head.

"I trust ye won't be sharing that around. Twas a dastardly trick trapping my name in the sand, but a bonny fine puzzle to boot."

As Susie's end of the teeter-totter came gently to rest upon the ground, Terwilliger somersaulted from atop its far end to land in the yard with his arms outspread. He then doffed his hat and bowed his head toward me.

"You can't be here," I said in a daze.

"Here now, Lucas the Bloke. I've met your two conditions."

He held up his forefinger.

"I've completed every assignment you've given and passed today's lesson by your own word."

He raised his middle finger to join the other.

"And here I am. Playing as nicely as you please with Miss Susie, despite the strong temptation to do mischief on this strange device."

He had me there.

"More's the thing, laddie. Did I not pay my tuition right and proper by the honest sweat of my brow? Dinna you find clean boots every morning in that pig wallow you aptly name a mudroom? And nary a saucer of milk was I given to slake my thirst after such labors. All to discover how you trap those fancy words using oak excrement on sheep's skins bound between the hide of a cow?"

Susie giggled.

"You've been in my house?" I asked worriedly.

"Of course, lad. That's how it works. That's the deal. Don't they teach you proper manners in the land of Westarbor? Now, your welcome this morning was soft and well spoken, but I'm starting to get the feeling you disapprove of Terwilliger."

"Certainly not," I hastened to argue, uncertain where such an affront might lead. "It's just I wasn't feeling well this morning and neglected to mention the third rule."

"A third rule, you say? Speak it plainly then, and I'll judge whether it be a deal-breaker. But know that the fair folk take a dim view of him who breaks a bargain once struck."

The menace implied in the latter remark was unnerving, and the grinning leer that accompanied it emphasized his pointy teeth. I scrambled to collect my thoughts.

"Ah... You can't allow yourself to be seen by the others of my kind. Not even the children unless I give you leave to do so."

"Only that? Tis but a trifle, but one caveat have I. Ye must not speak my name aloud, or all such bets are off."

"I can and do agree to that," I solemnly concurred. "Susie, best you return within. You've had enough excitement, and Miss Spencer will be looking for you."

"Aye. Run along, my wee lass. We'll have more fun on the morrow."

As I belatedly tipped my hat in greeting to the brownie, he promptly vanished, and again I was astonished. I could detect no trace of him with mage sight. Whatever magic the fey used, it didn't seem to follow the standard rules. I hefted my bob and departed the créche. 'Lucas the Bloke' he'd called me. I guess I knew who'd sent him my way. If I didn't remember to correct that soon, it might become my name all throughout fairydom. Nope. Some days it just didn't pay to drag my sorry arse out of bed in the morning.

CHAPTER FIVE

The Journeyman

"Be careful what you wish for, you may receive it."

~ W. W. Jacobs ~
Author of "The Monkey's Paw"

"I'll just give you lot some time to sort it all out," I said with a laugh.

Sweeping the front door wide, I strode out upon the front porch of House Falcon.

It was exhausting keeping up a pretense of constant good cheer, but I couldn't let up now, not with my goal so clearly in sight. The current argument was especially tiresome. They always expected me to weigh in on such matters. As the newcomer, I was perceived as a neutral party. Winning my opinion was thus a way to settle old disputes. My solution to the trivial rivalries among the falcons was simple: read Eli's aura and side with whom he favored. Though sometimes unpalatable and never based upon reason, this had proven a formula for success, nonetheless.

I leaned on the porch railing and felt the sunshine on my face. A gentle breeze brought the aroma of new growth, and the trees in the distance gently swayed with the first stirrings of spring. If I closed my eyes, I could almost imagine being on the Wagge farm, preparing for a day of tending its animals and crops. Animals didn't judge you.

Across the way stood my cousin amid his plants. To all appearances, he had not a worry in the world. I knew better. Lucas weeded when he wanted to think through a problem. And though at this distance my talent to read emotions was thankfully quite subdued, the aura of gloom that surrounded my cousin was discernible by naked observation alone. Something was eating at him.

I considered walking over and greeting him, but once again I refrained from doing so. Best to stick with the program. Lucas had made his choice by... well... by being Lucas. Here in this new place, I was determined to avoid the pitfalls of becoming marked as odd, as different. Here I could fit in and even thrive. Yet upon our first arrival, Lucas had gotten in trouble with the headmaster, even after I'd won the man's trust and all but paved the way for him. He'd been assigned to the worst house possible, and his prospects for advancement were grim. No. I oughtn't to be seen consorting with him during this crucial time. Perhaps after the choosing I could reacquaint myself with my kinsman and see how he was getting on. For now, I had my own future to consider.

There. Another one. I'd noted a curious increase in a peculiar glowing moth of late. They seemed drawn to House Blue Jay. And although I could summon them, it took more effort than usual. They seemed somehow resistant to my affinity. What was Lucas doing to that hedgerow? It had begun to resemble a castle battlement. Quite clever and appealing. To either side of the gate and facing it, two tall avian forms were taking shape. I was impressed at how quickly he'd mastered this strange art of shaping shrubberies. But then again, it was a predictable and natural outcome of his gift.

Our own hedges were well-kept, chiefly due to the greensmen lent us from the Brubaker estate. But they still didn't quite match the lush greenery that was arising under my cousin's caring hand. The Brubakers favored House Falcon. They acted as quasi-sponsors of our group, providing us with cleaning and scullery maids and all manner of assistance.

I wonder what would become of us now that travel from town was banned. The hired servants could no longer cross into the mage's quarter, and the house was descending into disorder. Already Eli's popularity was plummeting. As our head of house, he'd been forced to dole out work assignments to the pampered members of his privileged crew. I was used to doing things for myself. But I made sure to moan and kvetch along with the rest of them to avoid standing out or being saddled with more than my share of such chores. Not that I'd have minded. But I had to keep up appearances or risk being looked down upon as common.

I had decided to retain the name Wagge, both to honor my father's decision and so as not to threaten those in power. If I understood aright, Hans Brubaker, my true grandfather, had been the eldest son of that line. Thus, I had a credible claim by primogeniture to the large inheritance that had resulted upon his demise. But I knew the reality. That ship had long ago sailed, and only misery would ensue were I to take it up. Still, just the threat of such served as leverage and made that influential family most eager to please me. That suited my aims quite nicely.

Tomorrow is the choosing, and I remain well positioned. I was certain I'd impressed Master Reinhardt, and he'd marked me as well-gifted. Once I was assigned to a proper house, Eli and his cronies will have served their purpose and none of the drama of House Falcon would matter anymore. I think Eli felt the same, doing only the minimum to hold it all together for another few days.

To one who was observant, the conclave writhed with conflicting social drama. Some struggled to advance themselves, while altruists pursuing their own goals paid the price. Political passions ran at cross purposes. And power was a coin minted in the scheming of the major estates. Well, when in Fairglen, do as the Fariglennians do. To paraphrase Aristotle, man is a social beast. That often meant making the greatest use of the feelings of others. Who better than I? For too long had I been on the receiving end of such manipulations. Using my talent, I could easily move on to grander pursuits. I wished my cousin well on the more difficult path he'd chosen.

***

I stood trembling on the dirt path before House Falcon. With me stood two others. One I knew quite well. Though the sun had fully set, the night was young as yet and quite bright despite the fading of twilight's last gleaming. The full moon perched high in the heavens, bathing us in its luminance. This quite set off the stark white, hooded robes that were the only apparel allowed to us this night. Lucas turned to the other chap who'd recently arrived, sparing me not a single glance. And the silence between us was awkward.

The two seemed to be at their ease despite our ceremonial attire. I felt exposed. The thin garments lacked the layers that ordinarily protected one from the night's chill and guarded one's modesty. I sensed a spell running over my cousin's youthful form. Snuggling close to his skin, a fine lattice of tendrils shed a gentle warmth within. This was new. The other one's whole body seemed possessed of a faint, eldritch energy whose workings were a mystery I'd not beheld before.

"Are you ready for this?" Lucas asked of his new housemate.

"Having had an entire day to prepare," the man wryly remarked, "I dare say I am not, but at least I've not had occasion to worry about it overmuch."

"What about you, Roy?" Lucas asked, still not turning to meet my gaze.

For this I was thankful. My cousin knew well of my talent. By touching another or meeting their gaze I was subjected in an instant to whatever they felt. He might be simply respecting my boundaries. Lucas was a charitable sort and kind in his way. But it could also be he was guarding his own emotions. Perhaps he still nursed a grudge. I knew I had let him down in recent days. Still, the olive branch he dangled before me was appreciated and deserved a response of like kind.

"I am ready, cousin. Who's your new friend?"

120

"Galwell Cummings at your service," the man said, thrusting a hand in my direction.

In keeping with my outgoing facade, I gripped it, disliking such contact but understanding the need to uphold the social niceties. Lucas grinned knowingly. I was about to say something clever and introduce myself in turn when I sighted a group of armored men bearing lit torches. They turned at the fountain and advanced toward us in a rigid formation.

"Royland Wagge," I returned hastily, extricating myself from Galwell's grip and turning to inspect the approaching procession.

In the lead marched Brayden Sheppard. I'd examined his portrait in the Hall of Masters. Indeed, I'd studied all the masters, the better to know whose favor I should court, but I'd yet to meet this man. He was the head of the conclave's seneschals, who were charged with enforcing its edicts. His portrait hadn't captured the size of the man or the brutally raw energy he exuded. He was armored in a breastplate and pauldrons, the weight of which would bow a lesser man. Upon his back was strapped an enormous blade, equally impressive in its mass. Its hilt thrust up above his shoulder, offering a grip intended for both hands. I believe the soldiers called it a 'claymore.' Behind him marched the men of his command.

They drew to a halt before we three. The torch-bearers lined the lane to either side, and their leader stepped up to loom above us. I was unaccustomed to craning my neck upward, being rather tall myself. And beside such a man, Lucas looked like a mere stripling of tender years.

"Hail seekers," he purred.

His voice, though deep, was surprisingly smooth and not overtly loud. The formal greeting dripped from his lips in oily resonance. His eyes locked upon us from beneath a protruding brow, his grizzled features at odds with his cordial tone.

"From this point on, aspirants are to proceed in silence," he said. "Come."

He led us back toward the fountain and we followed. The soles of my bare feet slapped at the dirt of the path as we padded between the rows of silent men. I followed Master

Sheppard closely and in turn was followed by Galwell and then by Lucas. The double row of our escort marched in lockstep just to our rear. And thus we were led to the spot by the lake where first our forbears met in times of old. Seven great wizards of the past did there agree on the rules of conclave (or so I'd been told).

Our procession had taken us up a winding ascent with several switchbacks. On the way up, I'd had occasion to curse the rough spots of the road. Only that Galwell fellow remained unperturbed by the pointy pebbles the devil seemed to place in our path. We arrived at the top of a hill that overlooked the tranquil, moonlit waters of the lake.

Atop this solemn rise stood the dolmens, a series of megalithic, upright stones atop several of which lay equally large, flat stones to form shelves of a sort. They were arranged in a rough circle, and even the Elves claimed no knowledge of their creation or original purpose. They were of ancient make, having arisen well before the conclave's founding, which in turn predated the kingdom of Osten itself. They sat brooding atop this rise.

The masters awaited us there. Our fellow aspirants stood nearby, waiting for the choosing that would immediately follow our induction. All had already trod this path and sworn their oaths to the conclave. Only we three stood in the milky white robes of neophytes.

Luther Prowd was present. No one had seen him for nearly a week, and there were persistent rumors regarding his status. I thought it was good he was out and about until I got a proper look at him. He sat in a high-backed chair that looked to have been recently brought up here from the Master's Hall. His left eye bulged from an overthin face and shifted restlessly in its socket. His skin was like dried parchment and his right eyelid drooped. In his hand, he held a kerchief which he frequently brought to dab at the corner of his mouth.

He seemed but a pale echo of the capable man who'd greeted me two weeks ago. He should be resting and recovering from whatever horrific malady was responsible for his condition. When his eye came to rest on me, I sensed an anger in him. This didn't seem directed at me specifically, but at fate or the creator above or whatever malaise had laid him low. There was also fear. Though frail of body, the headmaster's emotions were strong, and they almost made me withdraw within. Wouldn't that be a sight? What master would want a journeyman who could be cowed by an angry thought? I quickly shifted my gaze elsewhere.

"Masters of the conclave," announced the seneschal, "I present new aspirants who seek admittance to our ranks."

I immediately felt the pressure of the many eyes that came to lie upon us.

"Proceed with administering the oath," Luther commanded in a reedy voice.

Turning to us, Master Sheppard drew himself up and began.

"Repeat after me. I; state your name and titles."

"I Royland Wagge, Journeyman Aspirant mage."

"Do here solemnly swear fealty to the conclave of mages..."

"In service thereof, I shall seek to advance the cause of magic in the righteous pursuit of its goals in the enlightened spirit of our brotherhood..."

"And forswearing all other oaths, I shall abide by its dictates and conduct myself in accordance with its tenets as laid down by the mages of old..."

It was at this point that Lucas trailed off and went silent. Master Sheppard paused and stepped over to look down on him.

"Say the words, boy," he said sotto voce.

My cousin made a dour face as though pained. He looked down at his feet and shifted nervously. Naturally, I thought. He would embarrass me once again. As usual, it was all about Lucas.

"Must I be forsworn?" he finally asked in a tremulous voice.

"Explain," commanded the seneschal, louder this time. "Have you sworn fealty to some other lord or master?"

The masters looked on with curiosity, annoyance and suspicion in equal measure as my cousin squared his shoulders and delivered his reply.

"The oath of a protector is binding upon me. To the Lady Megan of Westarbor, I have so sworn. This oath is dear to me, and I would not set it aside lightly."

The seneschal loomed above my cousin, and his brow descended as threat poured out from his grizzled gaze. The moonlight gleamed from his pauldrons as he took a step closer.

"You are aware, are you not," he gently intoned, "that by the king's law none are permitted to work magic throughout the land of Osten but under the auspices of the guild. Should you remain unsworn, you will be proscribed from ever using your gift. And should you even once be discovered to have defied this edict, prison for life will be your fate. What good will you be to your lady then? You must choose."

"Of what value are my vows," Lucas argued meekly, "if they are so easily overturned. If needs be, I will return to my village and take up some other trade. And if prison is my destiny, I will sadly accept such captivity rather than break my word, which is my finest possession."

And the seneschal smiled.

He turned to Luther Prowd who sat dabbing at the corner of his lips.

"Well-spoken, young man," the headmaster pronounced. "It reveals the fidelity with which you will adhere to the solemn vows you will take here today. As a master of the conclave of the first order and one duly appointed with such powers, I grant you special dispensation to maintain this additional pledge. Seneschal, you may administer to him the modified oath."

"And forswearing all *lesser* oaths," Brayden recited with a broad grin, "I shall abide by its dictates and conduct myself in accordance with its tenets as laid down by the mages of old..."

A relieved Lucas repeated the words.

"So help me God."

***

"Royland Wagge," the herald sang out. "Approach the central menhir and lay your hand upon it that all may witness the sealing of your vow."

I did so. Eli and the others had been somewhat secretive about this part of the ceremony, saying only that they couldn't wait to see me do it. I knew they weren't just having me on, for my talent had confirmed that within them lay an eager expectation. I approached, paused, and then lay my hand upon the central stone.

At once, my sight was drawn within. From my inner hive my magic swirled and gathered, rising up in greater abundance than I had ever seen. The hive mites swarmed as though stirred by an unseen hand and whirled forth to wreath the megalith in cyclonic points of light. The hairs stood up on the back of my neck. This proceeded upward until each follicle atop my head likewise stood as though eager to leap free from my scalp.

The menhir took on a glow of its own to shine forth with a light far more dazzling than the moonlight warranted. It was a bluish light that danced and pulsed along its surface. I'd once read of an effect noted by sailors, which occurred betimes in a storm. Saint Elmo's Fire, they termed it. That is what this phenomenon resembled.

After a time the glow receded, and I stood fatigued in its aftermath. Never had my magic been so depleted. My talent, however, remained intact. I noted with satisfaction the admiration of the masters as they discussed the power I'd shown. They muttered among themselves with many a nod. And from their cheerful babble, I discerned approval. Weary, I stepped back to resume my place.

"Galwell Cummings," the herald cried, and then continued unimaginatively his formulaic command. "Approach the central menhir and lay your hand upon it that all may witness the sealing of your vow."

Galwell strode willingly forth with a dignified air. When he set his hand upon the stone, nothing happened for a moment. But then, to my astonishment, his form began to twist and writhe. As he grew in height, his neophyte robes seemed to shrink until his calves were fully exposed. The masters gasped as a coarse hair covered these and thickened to form a fetlock, and he stood upon cloven hooves.

The man grimaced in dolorous woe and his head lolled about as horns sprouted out from his temples. These swept back then recurved to point forward once more. Then his buttocks swelled to enormity and began to protrude. A rending sound ensued as the tight-stretched robe finally gave way, splitting asunder under the assault of his prodigious backside.

At this point a mysterious parting occurred, for the process lay hidden beneath the robe's tattered remnants. But in some fashion a division transpired, for rather than two legs, the man now stood upon four. At last the changes settled down. He lowered his hand and turned wearily to regard us, a strange centaur in a shredded, white shirt. He pawed at the ground and his stubby black tail he did swish. After a moment, he trotted back to join us with the awkward stride of a newborn foal.

Unflappable as though he had seen it all before, the herald spoke once more.

"Lucas Harper," he called, followed by all the rest, and my cousin stepped to the fore.

When he placed his hand upon the stone, I confess to having misgivings. What would be revealed of my cousin's gift? I peered intently with my mage sight fully engaged so as not to miss a moment of the show. As with me, Lucas' hair stood on end. I peered within at his magic center. As expected, spindly vines grew from his inner garden, which he braided and wove into larger vines with his talent. To my surprise, however, the 'inner hill' that represented his earth affinity was much larger than I had ever seen it. It was a veritable mountain. I supposed he'd been storing up the energy from his 'weeding' for days prior to his debut before the masters. Clever.

As I watched, he opened up a conduit to this 'inner tor' and his field became awash with bounteous vegetation. This twined down his arms as usual, but the back pressure built until several more large, ropy vines burst from the boy's back to curve out and embrace the menhir. These further multiplied until Lucas resembled a great spider spinning a fly in its cocoon. Once again, the stone began to glow and pulse with an unearthly light, brighter and brighter still. And I watched this grow in counterpoint to the shrinking of Lucas' hill.

I should be happy for my cousin, I knew, for his star now shone bright and clear, declaring to one and all that the mages of Westarbor oughtn't to be taken lightly. But a seed of envy took root within me. Did his star now outshine my own? I knew the secret. It would take my cousin many days of completely eschewing his gift to recover from such a use of his magic. Still, it was bound to impress the masters who hadn't yet figured it out. Once again, my cousin had surprised me.

This time, in the muttering among the masters, I perceived a discordant note. From their auras a strange reluctance to their accolade could be surmised. Some were indeed impressed by my cousin's feat. But some others were repulsed by the manner in which he'd accomplished it. And as Lucas staggered back to us, he did so through a circle of withered and blackened vegetation. The menhir had drawn forth the last vestiges of my cousin's power, sparing not a blade of grass.

"Well then," said Luther Prowd, with his eye agog, "Let us move on to the choo--"

"Aaaahhh!" moaned an elderly matron who stood among the masters.

She threw her head back and all but howled at the moon as she sank to her knees. Those to either side caught and steadied the old woman, holding her upright between them. It was Sybell Dunham, the conclave's resident clairvoyant. She lived in the tower of meditation and was rarely spotted outside its confines. I had gathered little intelligence about her, as it was known that she took no journeymen. Several rushed to her aid, asking whether she was alright and what they might do to assist.

"Quiet everyone!" snapped the headmaster. "Listen!"

As a hush descended on the other masters, the old woman took to rocking back and forth. Her mouth worked silently and her eyes grew vacant. It was a posture with which I was familiar. But after a few more gyrations she stilled and spoke in a voice that was eerie for its sudden clarity.

The dead will rise and seek for him.

The fey will choose him as their own.

A harbinger of tidings grim;

A plague to wither flesh from bone.

At this, she sagged, senseless. From what I'd heard, Mistress Dunham's talent was a tetchy one. The oracular visions came to her at times not of her choosing. They made sense only in the aftermath of the events described. The master's paid careful heed as they'd oft proven accurate. I knew it to be a true portent because my mage sight had throbbed with bursts of brilliance throughout. The ominous reference to the plague certainly put a damper on our ceremony. What could it mean? How could we prepare?

Again, Luther took charge. Turning to his seneschal, he commanded him.

"Have your men bear Sybell back to her quarters. When she recovers and has had time to consider, perhaps she can shed some further light upon this grim prophecy. The rest of us will proceed with the choosing. I grow tired, and we must complete the ceremony."

After all that, I thought the choosing would be anticlimactic. But there were still a few surprises yet to come.

Lucas, Centaur-Galwell and I were herded back to the other aspirants while the remaining masters began their deliberations. My cousin soon shrugged off the whispered attentions of his other housemates and strayed over to a stone at the head of the footpath. Lifting it and fishing about beneath, he unearthed a long, rusty iron spike.

Whatever was he up to now? He approached the masters, stepping with a purpose, and drew the attention of several standing over on the left. He offered the spike to Mistress Willoughby along with some brief explanation I couldn't make out. Her face showed surprise, then she narrowed her eyes and snatched the long nail from the boy. I didn't need ears to know what came next. I could recognize a scolding when I witnessed one.

I would never understand Lucas. Just when he emerged from the stew, he would find some new turmoil in which to become embroiled. Trouble and success seemed to find him in equal measure. I was tired of his shenanigans, but impressed, nonetheless. Lucas was in and out of hot water so often that were he a cake of soap naught would remain of him but suds and froth. Like that sword fight with Sir Eric, it seemed he could always wrest victory from the jaws of woe and come back up smiling. He wasn't smiling now. He returned to us looking rather forlorn.

"What was that all about?" muttered Galwell.

"Just making a clean breast of things," returned my cousin with chagrin.

The masters, having finished their discussion, turned to us as one. First Mistress Willoughby stood forth. We all knew she would choose today. She folded her arms and glared at Lucas. Then she looked angrily at me as well as though I were complicit by mere association.

"I choose Eleanor Fortescue of House Owl if she will have me as her master."

The aspirants of House Owl were all smiles and nods at this. Eleanor was well liked.

"I choose Royland Wagge," declared Gunther Brubaker. "By all accounts, he's strong in the Willoughby gift and would make a worthy addition to my household."

Eli Reznic looked surprised and glanced resentfully at Master Brubaker. Something passed between the two and Gunther shrugged.

This was far better than I'd hoped. Gunther and Meredith Brubaker were among the most influential members of our guild. Both were strongly gifted masters of founding families. Many opportunities would be available to a journeyman of the Brubakers, the conclave's foremost power-couple.

Selections continued. Eli's new master was Martin Bates. Most from House Falcon were placed, and several from House Owl, but none from House Blue Jay were chosen until the very last. Brayden Sheppard, the chief seneschal, stepped to the fore and cleared his throat.

"Galwell Cummings," he said. "I hadn't intended on taking on a new journeyman, but the lad is of my kind and will need an experienced shape shifter's guidance. I will choose the Cummings lad if he will accept me as his master. With a gazelle as his totem, I doubt very much he will come to be much of a warrior. But that centaur form shows some promise; he may do well as a courier. The seneschals are in need of such."

With the choosing complete, the gathering broke up. The few remaining seneschals helped Luther to stand and half-carried him back down the hill. They were followed by several more bearing his chair. Lucas and his friends were congratulating Galwell on his rapid rise from among their number. Most of my own housemates were speaking with their new masters, as so too very soon would I. Scott McNair was elected on the spot to be the new head of House Falcon. It took only a single vote to pass unanimously, in the truest sense of that word.

***

Sometimes misery doesn't love company. I sat in the austere, stone room deep beneath the academy, pondering the circumstances that had brought me to such a pass. Rising, I crossed over to the ceramic basin in which was provided my wash water and began my morning ritual. The choosing of the night before last had been an exciting time, as had been the hectic aftermath wherein I'd been introduced to my new master and borne off to his grand estate. My musings were interrupted by a commotion from out in the hall. I padded over to the door of my cell and opened it just a crack to peer out.

All the masters were tramping down the hall in their sables, bearing before them the shrouded painting of Denis Feininger. Of course. The image of the poor fellow was to be laid to rest among those of the many others who had passed. This procession was to afford the man full honors as it was consigned to the Vault of Memory. I only wished they could do it a little more quietly. Their prayers and sobs as they passed my door were quite a noisy distraction. Although I hadn't known the master, I nonetheless bowed my head and offered a short prayer of my own that he might find peace. He had, after all, died defending the kingdom. One day I might be called upon to do the same.

Easing closed the door and returning to my few furnishings, I laid out an outfit on the cot on which I slept. Fine of weave, it was burgundy and black, the colors of my new house. My mind drifted once more to my first encounter with my master and his wife. As expected, the Brubaker estate was large and well-appointed. Upon entering it I'd been struck by its opulence. Even the draperies that filtered the light from the smallest of its large, glass windows likely cost more than my entire wardrobe. The entry foyer was clean and welcoming and smelled of fresh spices. As my boot crunched upon the rush mat of the entryway, I was greeted.

"So," said the matron. "Gunther's new journeyman has arrived at last. It was quite an impressive showing you managed at the choosing, young man. Keep up that level of effort, and you might just meet our standards. Come attend us in the parlor then. Gunther should be along soon."

The lady's dress was the vivid burgundy in which the parlor was also themed, almost the color of blood. Her long skirt lay in flawless folds before her as she seated herself in a plush armchair fit for a bishop. I was afforded no similar comfort. The lady flashed me a half smile, revealing a set of even, white teeth.

"You have the Willoughby gift unless I am mistaken, and I am seldom wrong about such matters. How came you to dwell in the far-flung and barbarous reaches of Northford?"

I sensed by my talent she knew quite well my origins. A test then, to see whether I'd take offense or answer untruthfully. Before I could reply, a cat wandered in, its plume of a tail held proudly erect. It bunched up and leaped into Mistress Meredith's lap, needing no invitation to do so. It was mostly white with patches of black and tan on its long, silky fur. Surveying its new perch, it began kneading the lady's thigh in a flagrant demand for attention whilst waving its white banner under the lady's nose.

"My father was orphaned at a young age," I began carefully. "He was indeed descended from the Willoughby line, by his mother, Mistress Gretta. He was spirited away from the crèche by a disreputable woman who absconded with him into the wilderness, fleeing the wrath of the guild. Being ungifted, my father chose to take up a trade and make a new life among the humble folk of the village where I was reared."

"And yet you keep the name of Wagge," she noted while absently stroking the fluffy feline.

I made no reply to her veiled reference to my legitimacy as a Brubaker heir. The tense silence was broken by the sudden arrival of her husband.

"Ah. There you are, my dear. And I see you've wasted no time introducing our new journeyman to the true owner of our house. And what do you think of Contessa, Royland?"

The cat turned and flattened her ears, marking Gunther's approach. Her eyes were odd, one being as green as a pea and the other a bright, cerulean blue.

"I've only just met the lady," I said in reply. "She was just making her claim known. I daresay she's a colorful damsel."

It was exhausting making this 'small talk' that was anything but. How did Lucas do this day in and day out with barely a pause for breath? Still, it was expected. And as I knew some people doted on their pets, Contessa would get her fair share of praise from me. Perhaps it would smooth my way to more quickly gaining my new master's favor. It couldn't hurt.

It was then that Gunther took me aside and explained why I wouldn't be staying here.

"I sense you are ready to begin practicing real magic, my boy. By day you will work in the foundry, and I shall teach you the command of fire. *Real* fire spells, mind you, not the simple cantrips your housemates say you have learned."

So, someone had been speaking out of turn. I supposed Eli's machinations extended to reporting on the doings of his fellow aspirants. I shouldn't be surprised.

"But for this to happen," continued Gunther, "you will need to be sequestered by night until such time as Mistress Dunham deems your magic to be safely bound."

The crazy old oracle? What did she have to do with it?

"You will spend a portion of each day in the Hall of Meditation. There you will be instructed how to raise your homunculus and infuse it with enough magic to govern your unconscious will."

"For how long must I do this?" I had asked.

"For as long as it takes, my boy. I know it's depressing, but it's something we all had to go through. You'll come out the better for it. You'll see. Fairglen wasn't built in a day."

So here I sat languishing in a cell like a hermitic monk while an odd-eyed cat sat literally in the lap of luxury enjoying my house. Due to Denis Feininger's funerary rites, there would be no work at the foundry. I dressed quickly and prepared for the day.

***

Fully dressed now, I was considering how to spend my holiday when there came a knock upon my chamber door. Only this and nothing more. Then there was something more.

"Oy! Royland!" shouted a familiar voice.

"Go away, Eli. I'm sequestered."

He shoved the door inward and stood glaring at me from its threshold. No points for politeness.

"You and I need to have a talk," he declared. "Come. You can help me with something as we do so. We both know sequestration is only for when you're asleep."

"How do you know I wasn't planning on sleeping in?"

"What? Fully dressed like that?" he snorted.

As with most things Eli, reason didn't enter the equation. He couldn't have known the state of my attire *before* he came barging in. Eli must be made to understand our relationship had changed. He was no longer my head of house. We were full journeymen independent from one another. As such, I would heretofore be spared from participating in his wild-eyed scheming.

He turned and headed off, expecting me to follow. Reluctantly, I did so. Fortunately, the hall was still lit from the masters' recent parade. Candles flickered in sconces along their route, not yet snuffed by the chandler to preserve the duration of their enchantment.

133

"That was a sweet coup you pulled off at the choosing. Masterful. I didn't see it coming."

I made no reply as he led me farther down the stone hallway.

"You knew the script. Mistress Frida was to be your master, and Master Brubaker was to choose me. Interesting using your cousin to pull off a switch. What did he say to the old bat?"

"I had nothing to do with my cousin's shenanigans. Lucas finds trouble all on his own."

"Well, it was a right cock-up. It was supposed to be a clean sweep. Lucky for you and I, it could be salvaged - mostly. It's a shame about Scott McNair. He was to be selected by Master Martin. I guess he'll just have to wait his turn. Ah, well. Done is done, I suppose."

It was then I caught sight of another man. He was stooped slightly forward and lugging a bulging, bloodied canvas sack over one shoulder. I recognized him as the head of House Blue Jay, Franklin Stein by name. Our caravan had weathered a winter storm in his parents' castle just a scant few months ago. The Steins were most convivial hosts, and I could mark the man's similarity to his father. But physical features aside, the lad bore little resemblance to the congenial Lord Leopold when it came to matters within. There was an intensity to him and a sadness so deep and mournful that my talent forced me to look aside.

Scott and Henry had related to us the incident with the pig. It sounded hilarious to me. I could just picture it. I wished I'd been there. Eli, on the other hand, had taken the affront rather poorly, but had instructed us to steer clear of the man, nonetheless. Franklin occupied a private chamber just down from mine where the masters allowed him to commit unspeakable acts. Last night, I saw him leading a live goat into that room, and I doubt it had come out again. It's frantic bleating had been most disturbing, and I'd had to retreat to my pillow.

Eli briefly locked eyes with the man. After a moment, Eli stepped aside to make way.

"Franklin," he said, nodding stiffly.

Franklin merely scowled and grunted, voicing no words of greeting in return as he shuffled past. Looking back, I spotted a cloven hoof protruding from his sack. It was much larger than that of a goat. I shrugged mentally and put it from my mind as Eli resumed his trek down the hall.

I suppose I did owe Eli something for the pillow. Since early adolescence, I'd received complaints about my snoring. I had only the word of others on this, for I'd never heard it myself. On my first night at House Falcon, it became a source of embarrassment. Eli pronounced my condition intolerable over breakfast the following morn. He commanded Henry Sutherland to devise for them a reprieve. Henry, being a savant of sound owing to the Sutherland gift, was able to craft an enchantment to muffle all noise in a spherical area around it. With it, he imbued my pillowcase. At our celebration after the choosing, I was told I could keep it as a parting gift.

"Ah. Here we are," Eli announced. "Have you ever been to the Vault of Memory?"

I confessed I had not. Producing a key, he unlocked the large iron door. It creaked ajar to reveal a darkened, cavernous chamber that could have fit my meager cell within it many times over. Eli touched his finger to the wick of a lantern that hung from a hook nearby. With 'digitus flamma,' he invoked it to shed its steady radiance, brightening the near end of the long room. Shadows from the clutter danced up and down upon the far walls as Eli took up the lantern and raised it before him.

"Come on then. I think they're near the back."

To my right leaned a stack of framed portraits. Most were covered in dust and grime, discolored by the ravages of time. But the foremost was clean and unblemished. From it, a man's face stared out, his grinning aspect blissfully unaware of his eventual, horrific fate. It was the portrait of Denis Feininger, newly arrived here and unshrouded. He looked a little like Lucas. I noted in passing the fine quality of the artist's work. No errant brush stroke did I perceive.

We neared the back wall after passing by a plethora of unusual curios and items of note: a spinning wheel, a standing suit of armor, and many things odd and strange. The Vault of Memory, indeed. A highfalutin name for a storeroom, more like.

Eli drew up short and held the lantern high. Rolled up and leaning against a set of trunks were some long carpet remnants. They were filthy and doubtless infested with many vermin. This I confirmed with my gift. According to Eli, they'd once been red. They had formerly served as aisle runners in the masters' hall before the prior year's renovations.

When Eli bent and reached for one, I gripped his arm and hauled him back.

"A moment," I said, urging forbearance and suffering his frown of annoyance.

I called upon my inner hive, sending forth my magic specks to penetrate the festering layers of rolled cloth and rouse its tiny denizens. My efforts were rewarded first by a flutter of moths. Soon after, pill bugs and all manner of assorted insects came marching out under my command. These I directed to the room's far corner, having no better destination in mind. Eli clapped a hand upon my shoulder.

"I knew I was right to bring you along," he exclaimed. "Roy, I could kiss you."

"I'd prefer you restrain yourself," I returned. "But stay cautious. Spiders and centipedes could yet remain. I haven't quite got the knack for bugs with more than six legs."

"If you'll help me lug these up to Master Martin's estate," said Eli. "I shall forgive you for stealing my master away, and we can begin with a clean slate."

"Why don't you summon the porters?" I asked before thinking it carefully through.

"Perhaps because there *are* no porters," Eli returned with a scowl. "They can no longer enter the mage's quarter, thanks to that creepy bloke who roughed up the apothecary. No, my friend, journeymen are the new grunts of the conclave now. It's a whole new pyramid and we're starting at the bottom again."

***

We approached Master Martin's cozy villa atop the hill. Eli and I each shouldered one of the rolled up runners. They were heavier than they'd looked at first glance, and I was short of breath from my unaccustomed exertions. Our conversation, en route, had been perforce curtailed, consisting mostly of Eli grunting and cursing at the burdens we bore.

We found the master himself seated on a bench beneath a rose arbor bereft of its blooms. A small way back from him, stood a young lady before a canvas which rested on an easel. She was prodding at it gently with a narrow brush. In her other hand she balanced a mitten-shaped painter's palette through which her thumb protruded. It contained splotches of paint in various shades. And on her face she wore a frown of concentration.

On sighting us, Master Martin looked over.

"You found them. Good. Who's your friend, Journeyman Reznic?"

"Please sit still, Master Martin," said the woman distractedly. "This one's no practice piece."

"You should recognize him from the ceremony, master," answered Eli. "Tis Royland Wagge, my former fellow aspirant from House Falcon, now journeyman to Master Brubaker."

"Ah, yes. I couldn't tell with those beastly bundles draped across your backs. I'd rise to greet you, young man, but we're trying to finish today, and Jessica is most concerned about that cloud cover rolling in overhead. You're from Westarbor I'm told. Any relation to a scoundrel named Robert?"

Eli set his bundle down as, after a moment, did I.

"He's my father, Master," I replied. "Though I daresay he's more a farmer than a scoundrel."

"Well, you can tell him from me," returned Martin amiably, "that the masters here aren't all 'disreputable politicking do-nothings' as he makes us out to be. Not by half. Yes. I believe half is a fair assessment."

"You should explain to Royland what the *rugs* are for, master," spouted Eli. " He's already in the know."

"It's to do with my latest assignment," said Martin. "Griffin riders will soon be plying the skies all across the realm! The council has entrusted me with the task of preparing a hostelry of sorts. A layover where the beasts and their riders can rest for a day or so before setting out for their next destination. We live in exciting times."

As he spoke, I edged sideways to gain a better view of the portrait taking shape on the canvas. It appeared to be nearing completion. This 'Jessica' wasn't sweeping with the brush, as I'd seen other artists do. Instead, she would transfer a single drop of paint onto her canvas with the tip of her brush and would then smear it around using her magic. The droplet would flatten out and blend with other colors it overlay, resulting in a smooth, seamless finish that was remarkable for its realism and fidelity to the subject. As I watched, she added abundant greenery and budding flowers to the naked vines that entwined the arbor. It was in some ways more interesting even than talk of griffins. Nevertheless, I returned my attention to the discussion at hand.

"The Bates Estate is ideally suited in several ways," Master Martin was saying. "Being a bachelor, I have several available guest rooms, and the small barn out back can be easily converted to suitable stalls for the animals. Moreover, it sits atop a hill and very near the academy. In truth, I chose it over several larger estates for the sublime view."

"You need to refrain from speaking now, master, and attend," Jessica interrupted. "I'm done with the outer parts and need to complete your face. This one's for posterity. You don't want to be forever looking out upon the Hall of Masters with your mouth agape. Strike that wistful pose we practiced and hold perfectly still."

"In a moment, journeyman," he returned. "Take a break. I shall sit for you more properly once I've finished my discourse."

"As I was saying," he then continued. "Mother quite enjoys the view. She sits in her rocker, looking out over the estate from her window up on the second floor. I understand several of these griffin-riders are young maidens. With mother acting as chaperon, all proprieties shall be observed, and nothing untoward will ever occur at the Bates Hotel."

"I'm sure you're right," I agreed.

"Thank you for your help, Royland. I shall now strike my pose and remain still as a sleeping cat so that Journeyman Woodwindle here may capture my likeness upon her canvas. Eli, unroll those rugs in the back courtyard. They are to resemble a large letter 'X' when seen from high above. After that, go to the docks and place an order for a small barrel of mixed fish, preferably live. We shall need it by next week."

I left Eli to his labors and took my leave. Master Martin was certainly a chatty old thing. Demanding, too. Maybe we'd done Scott McNair a favor when we'd bumped him from the running. I headed back down the hill. I should just return to my cell.

I liked being alone. I had recently discovered this was often true of my grandma's folk, a downside of the Willoughby gift. It had a tendency to draw one within. The stronger the gift, the greater this inclination. Over time, the elders of my family would succumb. Many Willoughbys passed their final years in a near-catatonic state of introspection. Would that be my eventual fate? My gift was unusually strong, and I had nearly given in to the hive since childhood. In a way, it was unfortunate I *hadn't* been selected as Mistress Frida's journeyman. She may have provided some better insight on the matter.

***

The sessions with Mistress Dunham were relaxing, not at all what I'd feared. I spent my allotted hour each day in silent contemplation of my navel. She urged me to seek within and select just one speck from among the many hive-mites that dwelt in my magic center. 'Give it a difference,' she said. 'Pay it more attention than you do the others and listen; listen for its voice.' To the best of my ability, I tried to do as the woman bade me. At first, it seemed a mere exercise in futility, but over time I found her method to be sound. The mite in question took on a different shade, and I could find it more readily.

"You're making good progress," Sybell remarked as she rose from her mat on the floor. "I've taught many Willoughbys in my day. Yours is not an easy gift to manage. Come back tomorrow and we'll see what more we may accomplish."

"Thank you, Mistress. I shall."

I arose and departed, heading for my first day's work in the foundry. It was fortunate that the foundry and its workers had been deemed an essential service by the masters. How could it not? The weapons forged there were central to the conclaves mission. More than that; in the crown's estimation, it was the very point of our existence. When I approached the postern gate, the seneschals issued their challenge.

"Halt in the name of the Lord Mayor!"

They seemed a trifle overzealous today. And the wary eyes that met my gaze pricked at my talent. I presented the token granting me special dispensation to depart the conclave's grounds. As the men relaxed and passed me through, I sought the reason for their anxiety.

"What news today, good watchmen?"

"Tis all worse and worser still," bemoaned the younger of the pair.

His cohort frowned, but let the man speak on.

"The duke strengthened patrols to the north, and it was a good thing he did. They caught up to that Russell Moore fellow. The town's all abuzz about it."

"I should think that would be *good* news," I returned "Now we can finally get some answers."

"Would that it were so. They caught him trying to sneak out of Shanningham Village, toting a sack. Now I ask you, who would risk smuggling goods into or out of a village under lockdown? When they called for him to surrender himself, he made a run for it and they were forced to cut him down."

"Tell him the worse part, Arn," prodded the more senior guard.

"The bag he was carrying was full of dead rats. Dead plague-infested rats. They must not have been *all* dead, though, cause when they came spillin' out, one went scurrying off into the weeds."

I thanked the men and continued on my way. As I did, 'Arn' gave me a final piece of advice.

"Watch yourself, journeyman. These are some twisted times; they are."

The mood of the town was subdued. After the initial rush to hoard goods, those who still retained any coin found the merchants no longer stocked what they wanted. The outlying farms weren't carting their goods in, so milk, eggs and other staples were especially hard to come by. I strode down smithy row and approached a long stone building with multiple chimneys, the famous foundry of Conclave, a jewel in the hilt of the kingdom's defense.

The door was open, the better to dissipate the heat, I would imagine. But I knocked upon its frame to announce my entry. A man crawled out from a brick furnace just down the way. Disengaging himself from the unlit oven and stepping around the anvil before it, he turned my way and approached. Soot covered his face, streaked by runnels of sweat, and he wiped his hands and forehead with a filthy bit of cloth.

"Would you be Royland Wagge?" he asked.

"I am," I replied.

"Good. Master Brubaker said we should expect you by midday. You're a bit early, but the master should be along directly. I'm Roger, Roger Anderson. Come. I'll introduce you to our master smith."

Wasting no words, I followed the man. He led me past a row of workbenches to a larger station at the building's far end. There, a short man was hunched over a metal shield, scraping away at it with a burnishing tool. Roger called out to him as we drew near.

"Lefty. The new journeyman mage has arrived. Come and meet him, master."

"Aye," the man responded. "This can wait."

Setting down his file, the man turned. He was a dwarf. The top of his head barely came up to my chest when he straightened, but his stocky frame more than made up for it. He probably outweighed me by several stone. In truth, he was nearly my physical opposite. I studiously avoided lowering my gaze to the man's missing hand. I'd seen him once at the tavern where I was tossing back a pint of bitters with my caravan mates. Stories varied about how he had been injured. Some were quite fanciful. But 'Lefty' was an expert in metallurgy and had traveled all the way from his home in Echo Hills duchy to consult with the masters of the conclave.

My attempt to draw no attention to his maimed member was thwarted by the man himself as he thrust it at me. An iron smithing hammer had been affixed in its place.

"Lefty McHammerhand," he said.

His blond beard bristled, and he stared as though defying me to spout some clever remark. At this point, it was rude *not* to stare. I reached out tentatively, preparing to grip the head of the hammer in question. But then the dwarf rolled his eyes and chuckled.

"Among my people," he explained, "tis customary to greet a fellow by making a fist and knocking your knuckles to his, a 'fist bump,' we call it. I hope you'll indulge me in this practice, for I've no proper hand to shake and revel in my newfound advantage in such sport."

"I am Royland Wagge," I began with formality "and I find it unlikely your parents knew in advance the nature of your injury and its remedy. I would know the proper name of him whose 'fist' I bump.

"So it's to be like *that*, is it?" said the dwarf, with a jolly glimmer in his eyes. "Aye.Tis meet. I was born Thorbaldric Anvilthane, a fine young dwarf of a long and noble line. An accident involving a cauldron of molten iron deprived me of my hand about four years ago. So my kinsmen granted me a new name to mark the occasion. Shall I recite my full ancestry to you? Have you an hour or so?"

I bumped the man's 'fist.'

"Now don't get the wrong idea, journeyman. It's rare we at the foundry stand idly about wagging our tongues over long introductions. There's work aplenty and no time for such lolly-gagging. We're just on a bit of a break, waiting for your master to arrive. It's shameful he's left me here so long twiddling my thumb. Roger, how's furnace number two?"

"I wouldn't trust it, master. There's a lot of spalling on the bricks, and the ceiling is looking too unsteady now. I think we'll need to rebuild it from the ground up. I'll let the brick-makers know."

"Aye, tis just as I feared. Royland, Master Gunther may be a dainty little member of your unbearded lot, but he can fire a smithy hotter than the fires of perdition. I've had to ask the man to scale it back a mite lest he melt the anvil right out from under my nose. And all this without the aid of blackrock."

"It's unlike Master Brubaker to be late," Roger remarked. "I wonder what's delayed him. With the people so unsettled, perhaps the master's council meeting has run long."

"In these uncertain times," said Lefty solemnly, "I wouldn't doubt it. It doesn't help matters to have that daft barber running about claiming he can prevent the plague with a good leeching. It's bad enough the folks are on short rations without 'em getting all pasty-faced for lack of their vital fluids."

"So you don't recommend Goodman Strangelove's remedy?" Roger asked uncertainly. "Have you been to the barber, master?"

"No self-respecting dwarf would trust his beard to another man's hand. Much less to a mealy mouthed snake oil salesman such as Simon. No, lad, I'll trust in my hearty constitution and keep my blood in my veins where it rightly belongs. Why don't you take Royland here over to the sorting bins and instruct him in how to identify the base metals there? I'll return to detailing this shield until his master arrives."

With that, he turned back to burnishing the bronze shield, and I followed Roger back the way we'd come.

"Why is the shield made of bronze?" I asked as I hustled after the man.

"It's for the sorry grunts they're fielding for the next offensive into the swamp," he replied. "The dark druids command a nasty magic that heats iron hotter than a brick oven. The first troops we sent at them were well nigh stewed in their own juices. Most wear leather now, but we've found bronze is immune to the effect. It's a bit old-fashioned and not as sturdy as steel, but it affords the men at least some better protection. Ah, here we are. The sorting bins."

Roger introduced me to the various metals, extolling the virtues of each. I noted a curious lack of bronze and its constituent metals and a surfeit of iron. When I remarked on this, the man explained.

"That's where you and Master Gunther come in. Eagle's Keep has its own bronzeworks, having recently secured large shipments of copper and tin. They can outfit the soldiers well enough. For the nobles and commanders, though, there's no substitute for good steel. Master Brubaker has devised an enchantment that keeps iron ever cool to the touch. From what little I understand of such matters, the spell requires a great deal of effort. Therefore, he selects for his journeymen only those who are strongest in their gift."

The light from the open doorway diminished, and we turned expectantly to see whether it was my master. It was not.

"Who are *you*, then?" Roger asked of Franklin.

The man wore a heavy cloak. the hood of which was drawn up to shade his face. I'd almost failed to recognize him, but my talent revealed the aura of melancholy with which I was familiar.

"Just a buyer. I was told this was the place to acquire a bit of refined metal. A few ounces is all I need."

"What kind of metal? We've all sorts."

"I need something that will temper well, preferably with a low melting point, but not too soft."

"What shape?"

"Anything will do. I intend to melt it down for one of my experiments.

"Might I recommend brass? We've some recent shavings I can let you have for a groat."

"Done," replied the man, retrieving his coin purse and counting out four pence.

As Roger stepped over to the weighing station and measured out the powdered metal upon its scales, I peered at Franklin. I wondered how (or if) he'd gotten leave to cross into the trade district. Unlike the foundry, I'd heard the butchers had to let many of their workers go when the travel restrictions had gone into effect. It was no affair of mine in any event. So I returned to my sorting as the transaction concluded and Franklin went his unmerry way.

Not long after, Gunther Brubaker arrived toting a leather satchel and grinning cheerfully.

"It's about time," grumbled Lefty, leaving off from his make-work and approaching us. "What kept you?"

"Greetings, master," I added.

"Ah, good. You're here," said my master. "And to answer your question, master smith, I decided on a little side trip to one of the aspirant dwellings. I think you'll be most pleased."

He laid down the bag with a clunking sound, and several chunks of metal poured out from its mouth. Lefty quickly snatched one up and sniffed at it.

"This is nearly pure and needs no refinement, or I'm a beardless namby-pamby."

Gunther smiled.

"The girl can no longer deliver them to us, so I stopped by her residence to collect them."

"That lass is a gem," exclaimed the dwarf, "A veritable treasure, I tell you. The goose that lays the golden eggs. Already she's retrieved far more of the sky metal than your other teams of so-called divers have in all of last season. And you pay her only a pittance. I think you missed a bet by not snatching her up at the choosing."

"Nonsense, I find the current arrangement to be most gratifying. And besides, my wife was most insistent we oughtn't to take one of those people into our household. I'm certain Royland here possesses the proper traits to be of benefit, given his strong showing at the menhir."

"Ah. Wives can be most particular when it comes to matters of the hearth," the dwarf returned with a dour expression. "You certainly wouldn't want one of *those people* muddying up the floors of your fine manor."

Oblivious to the sarcastic undertone, Gunther then turned to me. He took up a lump of the shiny mineral and polished it with his sleeve.

"In case you were wondering, Royland, this is a special metal found only in the depths of Lake Placid. Mostly iron, it contains traces of some rare heavier metals and is ideal for forging enchanted armor. It's how we pay good Master Anvilthane. What else might tempt a doughty dwarf of Echo Hills out from his burrow to dwell among us lesser folk? We're hoping to amass enough for a full suit of armor for Prince Henry."

"Why do you call it sky metal?" I asked.

I'd heard some fanciful tales about it, but wanted to hear my master's opinion on the matter.

"It is said that long ago before even the Elves walked upon the face of the earth, a star fell from the heavens. It's impact formed the bowl that we now call Lake Placid. Whether or not this is true, fragments of this metal are found around the lake's rim and in no other locale. More are thought to lie in the depths beneath it."

"The mother lode," Lefty muttered, his eyes flashing with avarice.

"But that's neither here nor there at the moment," said Gunther. "Come, Royland. I'll show you how to light the furnaces. Roger, weigh out Master Anvilthane's share and place the rest under lock and key. We've almost enough to pour out several new ingots."

Gunther led me over to furnace number three, and I watched carefully as he imparted to it a magical flame.

"Calidus ignis ardentis," he incanted with both arms outstretched.

This magic came naturally to the man whose magic center was a searing ball of flame. I was hard-pressed to duplicate the feat with my inner hive. It took me most of the afternoon and many attempts before I was able to light a lesser fire in furnace four.

All the while, Lefty pounded at a rod of iron with his prosthetic fist, working it into a fine steel blade. The tongs in his left hand were nimble and precise. The crushed blackrock was used only sparingly to temper the metal. I thought the dwarf looked a bit silly. His beard was parted into two great masses and tied around the back of his neck lest they singe from the heat of the anvil over which he labored. Roger attended him, retrieving various tools and supplying him with sips of water that he absently swished around and spat back out.

When my master gave me leave to depart, I was more than ready for the cool relief of a quiet walk back to my humble cell.

CHAPTER SIX

The Bootblack

"Earth does not belong to us; we belong to earth. Take only memories, leave nothing but footprints."

~ Chief Seattle ~

With the excitement of the choosing behind us for another season, things began to settle down. Lorraine still made her daily trips into town, as did anyone working in the carpentry shop or the foundry. But for most of us, such travel was proscribed. Franklin had lost his job at the slaughterhouse. He claimed he didn't miss it and that this would allow him more time for his other pursuits. Lloyd too was mostly out of work. The boy had been tasked to assist with maintenance of the cobbled walkways that ran throughout Conclave. The ones in town needed more frequent attention than the few footpaths here in the mage's quarter. I sat between the two of them shelling peas for our dinner.

"What service does Sholeena provide for the conclave, anyway?" I asked.

"She works at the marina," said Lloyd. "Mostly, they have her swim down under and clean the hulls or remove the bilge. She doesn't mind. Claims it's way easier than scraping barnacles from saltwater craft."

Conclave's fishing fleet had become more important recently. With fewer goods arriving from the outlying farmsteads, the lakeside fisheries had to pick up the slack. Franklin pried open another shell, deposited its contents into the bowl, and discarded the pod.

"It still boggles my mind how quickly you grew this bumper crop, Lucas," he remarked.

"Just doing my part," I replied. "Spring peas come up pretty quickly, all on their own. I just helped them along with my affinity. When I pull up weeds, I can transfer some of their life force into other plants."

"The power to imbue with life force; I would kill for such a gift," said Franklin after a wistful pause.

"That would rather defeat the purpose, I should think," put in Lloyd. "Where'd you get all the wooden stakes for the plants to climb, Lucas?"

"One of my students works in the carpentry shop. Master Reinhardt is his app-master. He saved me some scraps and off-falls from their projects there."

In truth, the stakes were but a bonus. I had asked Skyler to obtain as many thin strips of wood as he may for a class project I had in mind. I'd set all the girls to gathering nettles. The spring festival was coming up in a week or so. And despite the depressing mood in town, I thought it would be nice for our group to add a bit of flair to what were sure to be its subdued festivities.

"Here comes Lightshow," announced Lloyd, discarding another husk.

Lorraine was returning from her day's deliveries, pushing her cart before her. She glanced over and waved at us but kept going on past. She stopped before the gate to House Owl and hustled up its walkway. Hannah Brownyng met her on the porch and the two got to talking.

"I hope she doesn't spend too long gossiping," the boy added. "It's her turn to fix dinner, and the void is feeling pretty empty."

We finished shelling all the peas, and I hauled the empty husks over to spread atop the compost heap. When Lorraine returned, she headed straight to the kitchen to unload her cart. We men joined Sholeena in the parlor where she was pouring over my book. She couldn't read it yet, but was making fine progress at sounding out some of the smaller words.

It was then we spotted a rare bird, a lone falcon, returning to his nest. Through the parlor window, we saw him trudging through his overgrown yard and up onto the stoop across the way. We had seen little of Scott McNair since the choosing. He spent much of his time moping about. His clothes were rumpled, and his face was sorely in need of a shave. We suspected the young man didn't know how to take proper care of himself. With no one around to tell him what to do, it was like he'd lost the will to even try. Being masterless was tough, but at least in House Blue Jay we had each other.

It turned out that Lorraine set a fine table. When I remarked on this, she flashed me a rare smile and explained that my Westarbor feast had inspired her to concoct a few dishes from her own homeland. This consisted chiefly of flat griddle cakes made from cornmeal. She called them 'tortillas.' She ladled a dollop of spicy fish chowder onto each and showed us how to fold them in half around this filling. To wash them down, she'd obtained a fruity red wine she called 'sangria.' To be fully traditional, she claimed this wine should be served in a bowl with a mix of fruits. But as access to fresh fruit was still half a season away, we contented ourselves to sipping it directly from our tin tankards. The meal was delicious, and all agreed the peas could wait for another night.

"It's really Sholeena you should be thanking. She tossed a few extra shillings into the household fund to make all this possible."

"Well, in that case," declared Franklin, "I will take the clean-up duty in her stead."

We rose from the unexpected feast and made for the parlor once more. I was certain 'the void' was suitably appeased because Lloyd had actually suffered some leftovers to remain.

"Did you get the milk, Lorry?" I asked.

"There's none to be had in town," she replied. "I did, however, make an arrangement. You know those two nanny goats House Owl keeps in their back yard? I've struck an agreement with their new head of house. If we supply them with some fresh fish, they'll share a portion of their milk. It won't be much, but we've all got to pull together in these trying times. Oh. And you have to grow their hedges to match ours."

While Franklin was clearing the table, I thought it an ideal time to conspire against him. The task I'd assigned myself was proving too onerous for just one man, so I enlisted the aid of my other housemates. Upon due consideration, they all agreed. When he rejoined us, we would each give it our best shot.

"Who's for a spot of tea?" asked Franklin, approaching with the kettle in hand.

No one declined, and Franklin poured all around. We settled ourselves before the crackling fire and gathered our wits. Because it was my game, the first salvo was to be mine. As Franklin was the son of a baron. I reasoned the cerebral approach might bear fruit.

"Say, Franklin," I asked, "did you hear about the dyslexic agnostic insomniac?"

"I confess I have not," Franklin returned.

"Do tell," prompted Lorraine, taking a sip of her tea and staring with interest.

"The wretched fellow was up all night wondering whether there was a dog."

"I shall pray for him," said Franklin.

We sat in silence for a time before Lloyd made his attempt.

"Yesterday," he began, "I saw Sholena and Re-Pete sitting on a boat out on the lake. Sholeena dove in. Guess who was left."

"I would imagine it was Master Redmond," said Franklin with a puzzled look.

"Ah... yes, that's right," said Lloyd, frustrated.

"Speaking of unusual happenings," Lorraine put in conversationally, "in the village last night, I heard a woman gave birth to a child having both male and female parts. The midwives were most distraught."

"Oh?" I supplied.

"Truly. The poor child was born with both a willy AND a brain."

Franklin only frowned, saying "Quite."

We all looked to Sholeena, who stared at us each in turn. Then suddenly, she made a silly face. Her wide eyes crossed and rolled about, and her tongue lolled out to one side. Her hands came up, clawing wildly at the air, and to top it off, her entire head turned orange.

Franklin stared at her in startlement. After a moment, his lips quirked upward. Then he threw back his head and roared with laughter. We all soon joined him in the throes of his delight. Though the manner in which we'd succeeded was strange, our work here was done. At last, I could relax, knowing that my troubled companion could still reap the healing benefits of mirth.

Before bedtime, I went up to the fountain to retrieve more water, so we'd have enough come morning. On my return, I spotted Sholeena crossing the lane with a tray. She crept up to the porch of House Falcon and knocked upon its door. After a long pause, the door opened, and Scott McNair stood framed therein. Sholeena handed him the tray without a word as he glared at her in stony silence. On the tray were the leftovers from our dinner and even a small carafe of wine.

As she turned to go, the young man suddenly looked repentant, saying: "Thank You."

Poised to step down from the stoop, the Paluda girl turned and stared back at him.

"Ribbit," she said with a broadening grin.

This one-word benediction caused the lad to first startle, then laugh. It seemed I'd created a monster.

As I lay down to sleep, I knew contentment. Times may be tough, but our community was rising to meet the challenges. Sholeena had especially impressed me. It was one thing to be kind to one's friends, but quite another to show charity to one who had wronged you. Galwell had been right. If Sholeena was any example, the Paludaria were indeed a noble folk. I smiled, recalling the strange look Lorraine had shot at me when I'd set out the saucer of milk atop her cart. I wanted to show my newest student that people from the land of Westarbor were indeed properly schooled in manners. The next move was his. Let's see what he'd make of it.

***

I awoke in the dead of night. The crèche was still as a tomb. With Elissa gone back to House Spencer, there was only the boy to worry about. Robert was a handful. He seemed possessed by an overabundance of vitality, and I could scarce keep up with the unruly child. Confining him to his room did no good, for it only added to his nervous energy when at last he was released. I'd found it best just to let him run wild and exhaust himself. Finally, the boy lay abed, and I had time once again to consider my plight.

And what a sticky wicket it was. My failed seduction of Luther Prowd left me few alternatives. The child within me must have legitimacy, if not for its own sake, then to uphold my own reputation. Yes. To secure my future, I must confront the child's true father and force him to pay the price for his dalliance. It was only right.

Denis was a journeyman at the Brubaker estate. I knew him to be a night owl, having planned our assignations to occur by the dark of night. Perchance he was even now stirring and wandering about the grounds, as was his wont. As Robert lay sleeping in his cot, what time would be more ideal to seek him out? I arose and dressed. I took up the pendant from a box on my dresser and opened its heart-shaped locket. Withdrawing from it a lock of his hair, I summoned the magic of my inner hill.

'Quaerite mihi amans,' I muttered softly while envisioning the man I sought. The black fibers seemed to singe and produced a wisp of smoke that gathered and swirled above my

152

outstretched palm. This whirling mass ignited and shed a dim glow from within. It slowly drifted off, and I followed, maintaining his image in my mind's eye. It led me out onto the lane with the flickering light of the fey. Not to the House of Brubaker it led, but quite the other way.

On and on my wanderings took me. Why had he strayed so far? Still, the night was quiet, and no fears shook me, until to the base of the hill I trod. What was he doing here? Although it was not the proper time for such, strange lights played above. Upward I crept dispelling my guide for only one destination was possible now. By the light of the stars alone did I tread the path leading up to the standing stones. What if he wasn't alone? Did he have some other dainty lass in his thrall? If so, I would send her packing. A claim such as mine had priority.

But no. As I stealthily crept over the final rise and crouched behind the stone at the head of the footpath, I could see the man stood alone. His hand was on the menhir. The strange light I had spied earlier played about the rim of an opening framed between two of the dolmens. As I watched, this light settled into a shimmering plane, and a monstrous face swam into view upon it. It was a horrid visage angular in shape with its mouth drawn down in a frown. It peered out, all covered in pustular boils, and on its head, a crown. A cloud of vapors rolled forth to spread across the hilltop, and I nearly retched at the feculent stench they emitted.

Releasing his hold upon the stone, Denis Feininger knelt and lowered his head nearly to the ground.

"Arise and report, wight!" the figure demanded.

"It progresses, my lord Orenob," said Denis. "They suspect not a thing. E'en from these ancient stones they have unearthed not a glimmer of truth. They use them in great ceremony, but tap not their power. This host is strong and unbridled, but I have worn him down. I walk among them undetected, growing in renown."

"Do not underestimate them. These men of Osten have surprised us before, as when they went to the aid of the Elves. Their lands are not yet ripe for conquest. But we are patient. If you do your job well, our child will rise among them, a viper held to their very bosom. When the verdant child comes of age, we shall see an end to their defiance."

"What of the two I warned you about?"

"The Brubaker's are no longer of concern. It was a bold plan they hatched in seeking me out but a futile one, ultimately doomed to failure. They succeeded in finding my haven, but their journey came there to an end. You'll not see that couple returning again."

"My lord is wise and his plans far-reaching. I humble myself at the foot of his teaching."

"Meanwhile, continue to sow discord among them. Play to their vanity and all other vices to which human hearts are prone. Drive a wedge between their monarch and his mages, the only real weapon they own."

And with that, the vision shattered and dispersed. I felt sick, and not merely from the malodorous effluvium that still ringed the hill. I crawled back from the stone and made ready to flee, my heart pounding rapidly in my chest. But as I arose, still woozy from the fumes, my unsteady legs betrayed me and I swooned.

And Denis looked over to where I sprawled.

"Abigale?" he said, his voice his own once more. "When did you arrive, my dear, and what do you think you heard?"

I blinked back tears because I knew my fate was sealed. Though I was a practiced liar, the man would have to be daft not to know I'd overheard it all. He stepped over swiftly and offered his hand. When I took it, he helped me to sit, peered into my eyes and smiled.

"Come," he whispered. "Let us talk."

He helped me to gain my feet but did not release my hand. His face then transformed. His gentle eyes now shone with wicked glee, but these rested above a scowl most perverse. He wrenched my arm behind me and up into the crook of my back. With his other hand, he sought my middle and fondled the slight bump thereupon.

"I see my master's seed has taken root," he exclaimed with sudden joy. "Be of good cheer, my dear, for I hear wedding bells in your future. And you shall live at least until you have done your part."

He marched me over to one of the dolmens, a peculiar, solitary one, and thrust me up against it. Pinning me there, he summoned his gift. By my mage sight, I saw it gather. And from the stone I felt oily tentacles of power pierce me through and bind me still further.

"Geas silentii," he intoned.

I felt his will enshroud my own, and the next words he spoke echoed down the corridors of my mind to fasten upon the very core of my being.

"You shall not speak of anything you have witnessed here this night. You shall not speak of the true parentage of the child within you. Nor shall you write of such things or convey by other means the topics so proscribed..."

I felt the enchantment taking hold and knew it was no use struggling. The words were seared into my soul. Then a boyish shout was heard from beyond the dolmens' ring, interrupting whatever he would have said next.

"Let her go," the boy commanded. "No proper man should treat a woman so, say I."

Robert? Had he awakened and followed me here? The boy was only eight. No rescuer he.

"Run!" I shouted. "Warn the conclave! Denis is not to be tr--"

It was then I first felt the enchantment's bite. Excruciating pain lanced through my head, and my tongue clove to the roof of my mouth. I sagged against the stone as Denis released me. For once, Robert must have heeded my command. I could hear his footfalls beating a hasty retreat. Denis then stalked to the edge of the circle and grew flummoxed.

"Levare!" he shouted, plucking the fleeing boy from the path.

"Her I need, boy, but you I do not. As a fellow named Jack once said to Jill, 'Tragic you broke your skinny neck tumbling down the hill.'"

Before he could carry out this dire threat, I knew I must act. My hands rested on a small round rock. It was a good fit for my hand. So I took it up. The man would regret discounting me as a threat. His attention was bent on destroying the boy who was scrabbling about in mid-air, I brought my makeshift mace down upon the back of his head, rendering him insensate.

I thought about killing him right there, but I sensed that would be wrong. Whatever 'wight' or 'wraith' possessed the man might just rise up and claim another. No. I should warn the conclave. Dropping the stone, I hoisted my skirts and made for where the boy lay on the path below. He was still alive, thank the stars. I scooped him up and fled.

"Why did Journeyman Feininger attack us?" he asked.

"He wanted to--" I replied in agony.

I realized the man's magic had taken hold, at least in so far as it went. Not a word could I utter of what had occurred on that grim rise this night. I could tell no one. I couldn't so much as nod or shake my head. Even if I managed to find someone to protect me, surely they would think me mad. And Denis could concoct whatever lies he liked to discredit me. I recalled Luther's words from but a week ago. 'No one shall believe you, for I shall deny it,' he had said. Was this any different?

I could imagine only one solution, and it was a slim hope at best. I must hie from this place and lose myself lest Denis capture me anew. And what of the boy? His parents were dead, and he would soon follow if I left him here unprotected.

"Robert," I said, "you were naughty to leave your bed at night, but I'm not cross with you, my sweet. You need fear no punishment from me. In fact, I've a bit of a treat for you. I was saving it to tell you in the morning. We're going on a special outing today. Oh, what an adventure we will have. Since we're both up early, we should set off straight away."

On arriving at the crèche, I wrote a quick note stating that young Robert in missing his parents had taken off down the south road to find them. I was going after to fetch him back. I found it most odd that although I couldn't speak or write the truth of the matter, I could lie about it quite blithely without consequence. I gathered up a travel bag and what few coins I had amassed. To these I added the governess' fund, which was set aside for food purchases and the like. I scoured every surface to gather every stray hair that might be used to locate me. I even crawled upon my hands and knees to retrieve any errant gray strand I may have plucked.

Just before the dawn, with Robert's hand in my own, I strolled down the lane toward town. With any luck, we could hire a horse and be gone before a pursuit could be organized. Gone where? North, I think. As far as we can go.

Robert turned to me and poked me in the chest.

"*What's* to the north?" he asked.

"Safety, a place for us to hide." I mumbled.

"Hide from *whom*?" asked the boy "You're not making any sense."

"From the--"

"From *who* now?" demanded Lloyd once again.

The lantern was lit at my bedside. I rubbed at my bleary eyes.

"It's alright, Lloyd. I'm awake now," I croaked. "Go back to sleep. I'll try not to disturb you again."

I needed some time to process all this.

***

Lorraine, Sholeena and I stepped into the small dining hall of the créche. We shook the droplets from our cloaks and hung them on pegs in the back. Miss Spencer and Susie were already seated at the long table. The governess frowned.

"What's this?" she challenged.

"Miss Spencer," I answered, nodding to Lorraine, "my housemate is here to assist with today's lessons. The rain has forced us indoors, and she's had to postpone her business in town."

After brooding half the night on the grim visions sent by my Grandma, I was in a bit of a bad mood. The rain wasn't helping. I began to understand being under the weather after all. When I'd made ready to go, I found Lorraine in the mudroom examining the empty saucer I had set atop her cart. The cart now rested upon freshly polished and well-aligned wheels and sparkled as if new.

"I don't know what you did," she had remarked, "but I feel I owe you my thanks."

"It's not me you should be thanking," I'd said, "but if you want to pay it back, perhaps you can help me tutor the kids today."

And here she was.

Miss Spencer soon took her leave, eager to enjoy the rare freedom from her responsibilities my daily lessons provided her. No sooner had she departed than Susie stepped over to the window and swung it open. Though the breeze was refreshing, some drops of rain slanted in to bespeckle the hardwood floor. After a moment, she closed the window once more. Lorraine looked at me curiously, confused by the girls strange behavior, but I merely smiled. Sholeena, however, was staring suspiciously at a suddenly damp chair near the back.

Our attention was drawn to the doorway where Bella Gibson and Skyler Hendrix were arriving. Her eyes were red-rimmed, and her expression of melancholy was plain for all to see.

"There, there," Skyler comforted. "She would've died, anyway. You tried your best."

"They still want me to try it," sobbed the girl. "But I can't; I'm not ready."

The others arrived in short order in various sodden states. Once again, Sholeena muttered her strange spell that caused moisture to be shed from their slight figures. The girls preened with delight at the small show of magic. Sholeena was making good headway toward full acceptance.

Once all were seated, I addressed the class.

"Did everyone bring their nettles?" I asked.

Most of the girls I'd charged with this duty had come bearing baskets filled with the plants in question. Within the cheerful chorus of 'Yes Aspirant Harper,' was one divergent response.

"I forgot," said Ariadna Balderas.

Susie hopped up and moved to the back, retrieving two baskets. She brought one to Ari saying: "You can have Willy's; he won't mind." The other girls looked at her strangely.

"That's a project for another day," I hastily averred. "This morning we will do something different. Because of the rain, there will be no story time. Instead, I've brought Doña Lorraine here to assist us with a spelling bee."

The children looked disappointed. And Cassie pouted.

"We don't want a spelling bee," she petulantly sobbed. "We want a story!"

Before I could respond, Lorraine stepped over to the girl to loom above her.

"Only naughty children speak out of turn," she said sternly. "And the penalty for that is... I got your nose!"

Reaching out, Lorraine tweaked the protuberance in question between the fore knuckles of her right hand and swiftly withdrew it into a closed fist. Then, opening her hand palms outward, she showed the class that she did indeed have the child's nose. The students gasped, and Cassie reached up urgently to confirm her horrible disfigurement, only to relax and giggle when it proved unnecessary. Fortunately, only Susie and I seemed to realize the clapping and piping laughter that ensued began from an empty chair at the back of the room.

"If you are well-behaved," continued Lorraine. "You may have it back when the lesson is done. Now attend. Spelling bee wants you to spell the word: 'cat.' Can anyone guess the first letter?"

"C!" Cassie exclaimed, "Like the start of my name."

And to the wonder of all, a large, black-and-yellow striped bee emerged from the girl's mouth. It buzzed about. It darted toward Skyler, causing him to flinch. Then it swirled lazily to the head of the class where it hovered in a graceful arc to form the letter 'C.' From its backside, it emitted a sparkling trail that hung in mid-air fizzing and popping.

"Okay," Lorraine decreed, "Spelling bee agrees. Can someone else guess the next letter in 'cat?'

"A!" shouted several voices in unison.

And so it went. Lorraine kept to simple and common words, her stern demeanor quite offset by spelling bee's playful antics. For my part, I lounged in the back near Terwilliger's chair and returned to my own bleak thoughts. If Denis Feininger was Susie's father, did that make her my half-aunt? Despite the disparity in our ages, it was certainly a possibility. I would have to find out exactly how her mother had died.

Finally, spelling bee was all spelled out. Outside, the drizzle had ceased, and the window was propped open once more. The day was sunny and smelled of freshness. Birdsong was heard. I thanked Lorraine, as did all the children. She trundled her spotless cart toward town with nary a squeak.

As I watched her go, I once again considered the prior evening's revelations. Who was this 'verdant child' of whom the swamp demon had spoken? Was it to have been my mother? Was it me? I would need to learn a great deal more about such matters before putting it before the masters. I could just imagine Luther Prowd's reaction if I told him: 'the conclave is in danger because I had a bad dream.' One place to start might be the library.

***

The conclave was rife with rumors and dire portents. From all the fanciful tales, one was confirmed by those in charge. Several cases of the plague had broken out in lowside. His grace, Lord Deerfield, had issued the order to place Conclave Village officially under quarantine. A full company of the duke's men were now encamped beyond the walls to enforce this edict. The order included lakeside, lowside, the trade district, and even highside, but excluded the mage's quarter itself. This made us an island within the quarantine. This could change at any moment, but for now, people could still pass into or out of our area by boat.

The masters were all in a private meeting with the king's emissary. There was talk of evacuating the conclave to the City of Deerfield. The mages could not be risked. But the logistics of such a move were daunting. All this I gleaned from the clusters of worried bystanders who stood loitering about in the hallways. They would accost me with 'Did you hear?' or 'Do you know ought of?' every time I rounded a new corner on my way to the library.

Edgar sat behind his desk with Lenore perched nearby. He was pouring through a manuscript, seemingly oblivious to the chaos taking place just beyond the door to his sanctuary.

"Lucas," he greeted me.

"Hello, Edgar," I greeted in return. "Things are getting grim out there. I won't bore you with the rumors. Do you perchance know where I might find any references to something called the verdant child?"

"I seem to recall mention of such. Unless I'm mistaken, it has to do with one of Mistress Dunham's prophecies. Her predictions are under restriction in the masters' section. You seem to have quite a penchant for seeking forbidden knowledge."

"Well, I don't want to be any trouble. Have you considered my earlier request? I have the funds now and should like you to proceed with it."

"Indeed? I'll place you on my list then. The means to purge a possessing spirit, I believe, was the topic. I shall glean all references to such and provide you with an annotated treatise on the topic. You must realize, however, that knowledge from books will in no way ready you to perform any practical magic. You would need to observe such spells with your mage sight to comprehend the underlying forces. But as a purely academic matter, this will prove quite interesting. Do you still wish to proceed?"

"Yes."

As Edgar returned to his scholarly pursuits, I considered the next items on my agenda, when I spied two of my housemates on a fast approach. On sighting me, they drew up short and exchanged a brief glance with one another. Lloyd bent to retie his bootlace, as Franklin stepped up to Lenore.

"Lenore," he said, "I'm looking for more information on butterflies. There's a fish head in it for you if you'll show me the way."

After considering, the bird took flight and winged off with Franklin trailing after.

"Strange," muttered Edgar. "You'd think he'd know the way by now."

It was then that Lloyd approached.

"Hey, Lucas," he said sheepishly. "Fancy meeting you here."

"I take it you've a request," Edgar inquired.

"I'm just waiting on Franklin," said Lloyd, shifting nervously. "But now that you mention it, there's a book I've been wanting to study. I can't remember its name, but I know where it is. The problem is, its up on the top shelf and I can't reach it. Can you come and help me fetch it down?"

Edgar sighed and closed his manuscript.

"Lead the way," he replied.

The two trudged off and I headed to the shelves containing books about how to construct simple mechanical devices. It lay in the same general direction that Lloyd had headed.

"The one with the stamped bindings," the boy announced, pointing high above.

Edgar retrieved a ladder on a triangular frame and wheeled it over.

"This one?" Edgar asked, after climbing to the top.

My mage sight twitched.

"No," Lloyd replied, working his hands nervously in his pockets. "The one three over. Yes, that one."

From atop the ladder, Edgar retrieved the tome and began climbing back down.

My mage sight twitched again.

"One of these days," remarked the scholar, "you're going to need to get much better at levitation so you can fetch these down for yourself. I haven't had to use the ladder in months. I'd have levitated it down if you could've told me precisely which one you wanted. 'St Cuthbert's Gospel,' next time ask for it by name. You may peruse it while you wait for your friend, but it's not to leave the premises."

"Alright. Thanks Edgar."

Lloyd hustled off, and after scanning the titles on the shelf before me, I found the volume I sought. I ambled off with it hoping to find where Lloyd had gone. I discovered him at a table, flipping idly through his book and glancing up from time to time. He jumped when I dropped my own tome on the table beside him and drew back a chair.

"Oh. Hey Lucas."

"What have you got there, Lloyd? I didn't take you for the religious sort."

"Oh. I promised Ma I would keep up on my studies," he said, reddening. "What are *you* reading?"

I turned the book so he could make out its title. "Making Things Wondrous and Strange," it read.

"Just a project I'm working on for my class," I said. "You wouldn't have access to any cloth scraps from your parent's shoppe, would you?"

"Maybe I would have a week ago, but the trade district is off-limits now. I doubt even Lorraine can go there anymore. They're talking about setting up a station at the postern gate so they can pass supplies in and out, but it's all up in the air."

"Well, talk to Lorraine," I urged him, "I haven't much of a budget, but I'll take any off-falls you can acquire. I might be able to scrape up a shilling for some larger pieces."

"Lloyd, a word," interrupted Franklin.

He was standing impatiently between two bookshelves and beckoning the boy thither. I started to rise, then thought better of it. It appeared to be a private matter. As Lloyd arose, I sank back into my seat to examine my find. Lloyd never returned. So when I arose to depart, I took up his scripture along with my own book to return to Edgar at the front desk. As I exited, I spotted Lenore contentedly munching an eyeball she'd plucked from the fish head laying nearby.

Dinner that night was sub-par. It was Franklin's turn as chef. He served us each a bowl of peas along with the heated leftovers from several prior meals. He had fired the oven too hot, and an oily smoke with an acrid, metallic tang wafted about as we enjoyed his burnt offerings. I went to bed early after taking a half-measure of my nightly tonic, dreading what dreams may come.

***

I awoke in the stillness of my room. No dreams had troubled my rest, and I still lay swaddled in the drowsiness of the apothecary's brew. By this I knew the night could not be too far advanced. The rays of the gibbous moon shone through our solitary window, and Lloyd lay unmoving upon his cot. What could have awakened me?

Then I felt it again. Something was jabbing me in the side.

"Wha...?" I whispered from my dreamlike haze.

Then a hand clasped my lips. It was a small hand, but none too gentle for its size. I snapped awake and half sat up, only to fall back with my head spinning.

"Softly, young human," whispered the voice of the unseen hand. "Ye wouldna wanna wake yon sleeping lad."

"Terwilliger?" I muttered through the side of my mouth.

"Say my name and I must appear!" the brownie all but shouted.

Lloyd moaned and stirred restlessly in his sleep.

"Must you do that?" I hissed.

"Sadly, I must," muttered the sprite with an apologetic nod.

Fully visible now, the brownie stood crouched above me with his pointed boots dimpling my mattress and a walking stick poking into my ribs. I invoked my wakefulness spell to counter the effects of the medicine.

"What are you doing here?"

"In case yer mind be so addled by the deathly stillness you people style sleep, I'll remind ye then. I work here."

"No, I mean, why are you in my bed?" I asked, struggling to keep my voice lowered.

"There be mischief afoot in House Blue Jay this night. I thought you might wish to join in the frolic."

I was still a trifle uneasy over the faerie's familiarity with my home. But as my heartbeat slowed, my thoughts quickened. Terwilliger had done us no harm. Quite the opposite. And his discreet approach to this matter told me it was unlikely to be something dangerous or urgent. I rubbed my bleary eyes and sat up.

"Well, what is it then?"

"Fill your boots as I make ye the wiser," he said, hopping down to the floor.

I invoked my darksight and quietly slipped from beneath my blankets. Terwilliger tottered out into the hall. His soft footfalls made no sound. I stumbled after, hastily donning my daytime attire. He led me over to the mudroom where I collected my boots.

He leaned up against a wheel of Lorraine's cart.

"You'll note that two of the boots in my care are missing. Scarcely was I finished with my cleaning and polishing when the tall lad who keeps dead bugs crucified on his wall came creeping out from his room. Most cunningly did he tread the halls in silence not a quarter turning of the glass ago. Before covertly creeping off, he withdrew from his pocket a key made of brass. Examining it, he smiled and thrust it back from sight ere stalking off into the night."

"Franklin smiled?" I asked.

"That be your first take away? Anyway, I thought to follow him to find what mischief he might be about. Then I thought to myself perhaps Lucas the Bloke might be interested in these goings on. Tis a fine night for a frolic I trow, and the rest of the tale ye already know."

By this time I had laced up my boots and retrieved my cloak from its peg. Franklin had been acting rather suspiciously of late. My interest was piqued. Perhaps I should respect the man's privacy, but could I help it if I ran across him during my own nighttime stroll? By a 'quarter turn of the glass,' Terwilliger must be referring to the hourglass we used in the kitchen to time what little baking we attempted.

"Alright," I said, "I'm in. But which way do you think he went? He could be anyplace by now."

"Trust in yer bootblack and the wily wits of the fey," said my capricious friend.

After we had exited the house, Terwilliger brought two tiny fingers to the sides of his mouth and let out a high-pitched whistle. Several sets of glowing eyes soon appeared. I fretted when they closed in upon us from the surrounding darkness. But such fears abated when these were revealed to be Lorédonian moon moths, their abdomens aglow. And where their light fell, I perceived dimly glowing footprints.

"Foxfire fungus is one of my best polishing agents," said Terwilliger with a smug grin. "I may have taken the liberty of coating the soles of his boots with it. Yon lantern flies can lead us on, and soon we'll ken where the lad has gone."

It was slow going. I walked beside the tiny man with the moths fluttering out ahead of us. Franklin's faint tracks headed us up past the fountain, then along the cobbled lane and to the academy. As we passed inside, one of the beautiful creatures came to alight on Terwilliger's wrist as though it were his hunting falcon. The others he released to drift off into the night. Terwilliger then faded from view, and the moth looked strange drifting down the hallway ahead of me with its wings upright and unmoving.

We came at last to the doors to the library. Normally secured, one was open a crack. I eased it wider on silent hinges, then back to nearly closed after I had passed within. The boot prints now ran all over the place in a riot of directions, the order of which I couldn't unwind. They were also much fainter than before, just a scuff mark here and there. But two things were instantly apparent.

First, the unlit chandelier was nearly at the level of the floor. It hung from a rope which looped over a beam above. The rope's other end was loosely lashed to some hooks on the wall. These had been uncoiled to lower it, and a candle was missing. Second, a trail of scuff marks, the faintest of them all, led off in a line to my left. In the distance, I saw a dim radiance.

The drifting moth made for the light in the distance. Terwilliger was on the move. Then it stopped and fluttered its wings, rising up and coming to rest on a bookshelf nearby. Its glow subsided. The library was an ominous place by night, all silent and seeming to brood. With a cautious step, I crept toward the light as silently as I could. I passed by the master's section. One of its chains lay slack on the floor at the shelf's far end.

And there was Franklin, hunched over a tome and studying it most intently by the light of a single candle. His fingers were splayed out on the table before him, and he was frowning in deep concentration.

"So Franklin," I said, causing the man to jump and whirl about. "Have you read any good books lately?"

He glared at me and narrowed his eyes. I had never once been afraid of Franklin until I saw that look. Then the moment passed. The tension eased from his frame and he stared at me with a measuring gaze.

"Couldn't sleep?" I continued. "Cat got your tongue?"

"I don't know why you followed me here, Lucas, but I would appreciate it if you would just step away and forget you saw this. Failing that, at least cease your annoying attempts at humorous banter."

"I was worried for you. I still am. You're supposed to request permission to peruse books in the master's section."

"And what master would grant me permission to pursue my unsavory art?" he shot back. "They won't even allow me to advance to journeyman."

I felt sorry for Franklin. I knew what he was saying was true. Should I turn him in?

According to Edgar, one couldn't learn a spell from books. Surely, bending the rules a bit in pursuit of knowledge could cause little harm. Perhaps I was blinded by my own thwarted need for information. Though it felt like a justification, I was inclined to let it go.

"Lucas," he entreated, "I seek only to use my gift in service to the kingdom. What I'm doing here could make a real difference in the stalemate that has gone on in the south for far too long."

"Alright," I said, "Give me the key. Since we're here anyway, there's something I need to find."

"How do you know about the key?" he asked.

"Lloyd talks in his sleep," I fibbed.

With a disgusted look, Franklin reached in his pocket and handed me the bauble. Maybe now Franklin would be less inclined to enlist the boy's aid in future misbehavior. I walked back to the master's section and worked the key in the lock to its third shelf. I only had to slip the chain through four rings to retrieve the volume that had been calling to me.

'Glimpses of the Future,' its title read, 'by Sybell Dunham.'

I brought it over to the table and stood beside Franklin. Darksight was good for sensing one's surroundings, but was all but useless for reading. By candlelight, we stood shoulder to elbow in the empty library; each engrossed in the pursuit of forbidden knowledge. Mistress Sybell's prophecies were baffling. Each began with a heroic couplet vaguely referencing some supposed future event. These were followed by rambling discourse of impressions and suppositions about what they might mean. There were indeed several references to a 'verdant child.' But they either made no sense whatsoever or were so cryptic that one should forego even trying to sort them out. Prophecy was an exasperating and inexact science.

The enemy doth spread his seed, the northern lands to ravage.

The verdant child, in time of need, must go confront the savage.

Let all beware the verdant child, by whose power the land doth drown.

A kingdom shall be reconciled, and none shall wear its thorny crown.

What could it mean? The first part reminded me of the enemy to our south, but was it? There seemed to be a sequence of events and a call to action. It was stubbornly non specific and contained some strange imagery one would recognize only afterward. Useless. Or what about this one?

Tiny traitors of the skin on small rodents ridden

Grim malady doth place within and foster death unbidden.

Beset by awful scurrying of foemen unsuspected,

We stand alone and worrying by barber's brew protected.

What was anyone to do with that bit of nonsense? Go to the local barber and ask him to share a pint? When? Frustrated, I closed the tome. Franklin was looking over at me. His own manuscript lay closed upon the table. I glimpsed its title before he took it up. 'Invoking the Dead,' it read.

"Are you done, Lucas?" he asked. "If so, let's put things back in order before anyone else comes wandering by."

We re-shelved the books and restored the chains. While Franklin snuffed the candle and was hoisting the chandelier back up, I wondered where Terwilliger had gone. Most likely, he'd been bored by our cerebral pursuits and had wandered elsewhere. I couldn't blame him. Our 'frolic' hadn't been the lively escapade he'd obviously been expecting.

***

Still worn out by my nighttime excursion, I stood sleepily before my abecedarians. I had explained to my students that this rare and delightful word had been invented to refer to those first learning their ABCs. The kids sat assembled in the crèche's triclinium, another charming word from times of old which once meant: 'dining room.'

"You're weird," Daisy had announced to the tittering of all.

"Like we'd ever need to know that," Skyler had confirmed.

All were present, but some were of a most grumpy disposition. Bella sat beside Skyler, all but sobbing aloud, and

Sholeena's skin had a distinctly reddish tinge. They looked like something the cat dragged in (an appallingly cruel and sinister cat). I sought about for something to lighten the mood and set a more convivial tone for our upcoming project.

"Today, we will learn to fly," I began.

This caused a stir of excitement for a moment. But one by one, their faces lapsed into baleful glares of suspicion, prepared for my inevitable betrayal. Under my tutelage, they had lost much of their childlike innocence and gullibility. If this kept up, they would soon be a hardened band of mistrustful skeptics. Good.

"...a kite," I concluded, to the expected groans.

But I sensed from them a new eagerness as they considered my proposal.

"The spring festival is next week," I added, "and the matron has requested we provide a display of our newfound skills. She has blessed the project and even provided a small purse with which we may purchase supplies. With conditions in town being what they are, the folks need some cheering up. I feel certain that if we all pull together, we can show our newfound knowledge and uplift their spirits. Sky-writing, we shall call it."

"We take your meaning, aspirant," said Skyler. "No need to go on so about it. Tell us how we shall start."

I had Skyler retrieve the slats of wood he'd earlier provided. They were stacked in the créche's supply closet, and Miss Spencer was only too glad to be rid of them. He also fetched the partial bolts and scraps of colored cloth Lorraine had begged from Lloyd's mother. The girls retrieved their baskets of nettles and we all retired to the playground. Before we left, Susie closed and secured the window she'd propped open earlier. She rejoined us with a frown.

Outside, I spied a brief message carved in the sand with the stick propped up nearby. 'BORING.' It read. Apparently, Terwilliger hadn't yet forgiven me for disappointing him last night, or perhaps he was angry about not learning to fly. Whatever the cause, it seemed the brownie was to be my first truant. As a voluntary participant in our endeavors, I suppose it was his right to scamper off in a snit.

I directed the class, and we each settled down to our appointed tasks. I taught Sholeena the spell Master Chadwick had used to dry out Tilda's herbs. She was surprised I knew ought of water magic and set right to dehydrating the weeds. Skyler was crafting the main bodies of the kites. Five great crosses were to be assembled for their frameworks. Bella was marking and measuring the cloth that would be their sails. The other four girls drew the lettering on these and other scraps, preparing to embroider them with brightly colored threads.

For my part, I sped up the fussy and lengthy process of retting, scutching, and hackling the plants. I used my gift to wither the weeds. Their dried husks then shredded and peeled back with ease to free the fluffy white fibers within. Each brief burst of life force bolstered my magic minutely and instantly soothed the minor wounds inflicted by their thorn-like stinging hairs.

We soon had a basket of fluff with more on the way. Several of the girls left off from their embroidery to sit with distaffs high, whirling their spindles to fashion this into string. We would need a lot of it.

Mayhap Terwilliger had been foresightful. After a time, the repetitive activity descended into monotony. To fill this entertainment vacuum, a smattering of comforting gossip soon arose.

"Why so glum, Bella?" Cassandra Reinhardt asked. "You've hardly said a word all morning."

Skyler glanced over with a grimace, then returned to his task.

"I'm worried is all," Bella returned. "Dreadfully worried."

In silence, she completed a long cut along the cloth with her scissors before continuing in a nervous whisper.

"Last night, they took me to Headmaster Prowd and bade me to lay upon him a healing. I told them I wasn't yet ready, but they insisted something must be done for him at once. He lay in his bed all sallow and feeble, and his breath came out barely at all. Delving within, I found troubles aplenty and scarce knew where to begin.

"Apart from the decreased blood flow which had seized up the right side of his body, there was a vile blackness all throughout his squishy parts, a toxic malaise I was hard-pressed to purge. When I left him, he seemed better, and some color had returned to his cheeks. His chest rose and fell more vigorously, and the beat of his heart had steadied."

"That's good news, I should think," I put forth. "Well done."

Skyler pursed his lips and sighed. "Tell him about the cow, Bella."

The girl lowered her head and lay down her scissors.

"Last week," she said, "Master Spencer took me on his route to several of the outlying farms. This was just before the restrictions bottled us all up in here. At the Knowlton farm there was a cow stricken with murrain. She lay at death's very door, and the farmer implored me to do what I could for her. It was thought that if I could overcome the malady, mayhap I could do the same for those poor wretches suffering from the plague. It was a kind hope.

"I set to work and defeated the murrain most soundly. The cow stood to her feet and was soon lowing contentedly and munching at her feed. Though tired, I was so proud to have been of such service. As we left the happy farmer, we thought that all was well. Alas, we were mistaken in this.

"Word came not three days later that the cow was off her feed again. This time, it was consumption of a most fast-acting sort. A few days after, the cow lay dead. They couldn't even chance eating its meat. When they tried to butcher her, they noted numerous tumorous growths had spread throughout her innards. Tis this I fear for the headmaster. Betimes my healing overstimulates the body and can cause parts of it to grow too rapidly."

That was a grizzly tale, and the girl now sat openly weeping for all to see.

"Well, let's all pray for the headmaster then," I breathed. "If it's of any help, when I heal plants, I seek not to mend them completely. I feel it's better merely to fortify them a bit and encourage them to overcome their challenges on their own."

"That is precisely what Douglas Weil advised," she whimpered. "He's the physic attending Master Prowd. I tried to restrain my gift and gentle its touch, but I know not whether I succeeded in such."

"It would be a marvelous thing if the headmaster recovers," observed Susie wistfully. "It would mean hope for the people with the plague."

It would indeed. In most communities stricken by the plague, barely half survived it. Many were bereaved.

"What I don't understand," groused Skyler, "is why this sickness is spreading so fast. Already there are a dozen reported cases in lowside alone, and even highside has seen a case or two. They still let me into town, but only to the carpentry shop and back. They've got that and the foundry roped off from the rest, deeming them essential to the war.

"But I can see the poor buggers lined up down the street every day to get leeched. I don't see how that can help, but a man frightened for his life will snatch at any hope. Who knows? Maybe the practice has merit. Doctor Strangelove keeps running on about how none who've received his treatment have yet seen symptoms, and no one's denying it either."

"What about you, Sholeena?" I asked, hoping to change the topic. "What's got your knickers in a knot?"

She frowned as she puzzled through the alliterated idiom to divine its meaning.

"It'sh nothing so dreadful ash all that," she said at last. "I'm just worried for the fish."

"The fish?" I prompted. "What about them?"

"With no meat coming into town, more and more people from conclave are overfishing the lake. It'sh shpawning sheashon, and taking all the fish now means no more for next year."

I hadn't thought about it, nor, apparently, had anyone else apart from the Paluda girl.

"I recommend you take your concerns to Mistress Julia," I said. "The Elves have a tradition of looking ahead to the future and limiting their footprint on the land to preserve its resources. They even have professionals dedicated to this calling. They call them *puachoqua*. I'm certain Mistress Julia will consider the matter and make suitable recommendations to the council of masters."

Sholeena's skin returned to a normal hue, and her mouth widened a bit.

"Thanks, Lucas," she said. "You're shtill weird, but it'sh a good kind of weird."

Yup. Sholeena was definitely beginning to fit in with my other gentle critics.

As we worked on in companionable silence, my mind turned to other topics. We'd made a good start today, and stars willing would have the skywriting ready by next week. It had been quiet on the garden lane each day when I passed the Perilous Glade. The full moon had come and gone, but I hadn't seen bark nor hair of Hazel. Perhaps healing the tree had taken more out of her than she'd imagined it would. When next I saw the tree sprite, I'd be sure to put in a good word for Mistress Willoughby. I had become convinced the bug lady meant Hazel no harm.

CHAPTER SEVEN

The Unfairy Godfather

"Knowledge is power."

~ Unknown ~
(just kidding; it was Francis Bacon)

The days wore on, and still there was no sign of Hazel. I was becoming concerned. One considerable stir occurred when a boat docked to the lone peer that connected to the mage's quarter. It arrived in the middle of the night, and Sholeena alerted us to its presence on the following morning. The masters were all aroused and convened a closed council to discuss the matter. By the time we were given the official word, the rumormongers had had plenty of time to grind out a dozen disturbing and scandalous conjectures from their ever-churning mill.

They say truth is stranger than fiction. Here, the citation held true. After a brutal spring offensive into the southern lands, Osten's soldiers had encountered a camp of hostages being held as slaves by the enemy. Master Pete had related the tale just eight days past. What he hadn't mentioned was that among them, one of our mages had been discovered. It was Mistress Gretta, missing these last twenty-five years. Filthy and emaciated, none had recognized the old woman. But Harland Reznic (Eli's dad) who'd accompanied the liberating force, had marked her magic center and recognized the Willoughby gift.

The woman was completely withdrawn and unresponsive. After returning her to Eagle's Keep, they cleaned her up and conveyed her in all haste to Conclave. Here she was identified by her sister, Mistress *Frida* Willoughby. Of her husband, Master Hans, there had been no sign.

Gretta was placed in a cell below the academy. She was made comfortable and was being looked after by her sister while she recuperated. The masters thought this prudent because who could guess what she might do in her strange state of mind if left to wander freely the conclave's grounds? Might she bear one of the strange illnesses known to thrive in the southern marshes? Could she be a Trojan horse with instructions imprinted on her addled mind to carry out some vile misdeed? For these reasons she was to remain cloistered.

Bella Gibson had been missing from my class for the past seven days. Luther Prowd was back in charge of the conclave and growing stronger by the day. His healing having been declared a smashing success, Bella had been conscripted to cure all those afflicted by the plague. The girl proved able to lessen the affliction, and none had died as yet. But she was fast becoming overwhelmed. New cases were arising at an astonishing pace. Every day there were more reports of fever and chills among the townsfolk, and the buboes continued to stiffen their necks, groins and armpits. Priority was given the very young or old, but we feared the girl was becoming outmatched. When last I'd seen Bella, she'd been pale, and dark circles had ringed her sorrowful eyes.

One saving grace was the barber. He worked at a furious pace, leeching blood from those not yet affected. For it seemed to be true that his treatment offered some protection from the dread affliction. None who went regularly to Simon's shop had as yet contracted the ailment, though some were made dizzy or nauseous from loss of blood. Conclave's economy lay in ruins, and its people were underfed. It was said that only the barbers leeches and his purse had gained any weight in recent days.

It was into this woeful climate that time for the spring faire came at last. The people in town made a half-hearted effort at best. There simply wasn't much cheer to go around. But my class and I still adhered to our plan, having almost finished our project. We would fly a hopeful message above the town expressing our good wishes.

Our kites all lay in gay array practically complete. The day was fine. We could have wished for a bit more breeze to launch the affair. But Skyler informed me there was wind aplenty higher up if we could first achieve the needed altitude. I didn't doubt the boy, for as a wind mage he could sense such things.

Skyler had assured me he could get them aloft. He told me of the time last year when his gift had been first discovered. He and the crew of HMS Resolute were all praying for safety after the galleon was becalmed in the waters off the Phantom Wyrm Atoll. Although the sailors were rowing hard, the current was dragging them ever nearer to a sargasso wherein other craft were ensnared. Gulls rested atop the weathered masts of many sunken ships sticking up like bones from its shallow waters. Then, like a miracle, the sails had filled, the current was overcome, and the Resolute had glided back to safe waters. Skyler stood at his captain's side by the ship's helm directing the wind to the wonderment of all. Captain Olaf granted all the crew an extra ration of grog that night to toast the boy's health and their own good fortune. They steered straight to the nearest port on the mainland and docked there that Skyler might set out for Conclave. Whether or not the story was true, the boy could certainly spin an exciting yarn.

Mistress Julia herself had come to bless our effort. I hadn't seen the Elven lady since our first interview, but she now stood with Miss Spencer beside us on the gentle rise that overlooked the town below. Mistress Julia, too, was a wind mage. Perhaps she would assist us should Skyler's bragging prove to be 'overblown.'

The kites were all assembled with large letters brightly embroidered thereon. Smaller letters were embedded in their tails. These were laid out but not yet affixed to their respective kites.

"Is everything spelled out correctly?" I asked.

"Yes, teacher," sang Skyler and the girls.

"Tie them together then," I proclaimed.

"Trust a sailor to tie a knot, aspirant," replied Skyler, setting to work at once.

It had all come together quite nicely. When all was prepared, Daisy Sutherland hefted the first large kite and held it erect by its crossbar, the ball of string clenched firmly in her other hand. Skyler summoned a breeze, and as its sail snapped taut, she released it to dip and bob away. Higher it rose as she let out more string, its tail finally loosed from the ground. On its sail a large letter 'O' arose above the town. And trailing below from its tail hung the lesser letters, all in good order. The other girls let out a whoop, and Susanna rushed to take up the next kite and hold it up in readiness.

One by one, the girls stepped forth and took up their kites. To each, Skyler imparted a breeze sufficient to send it soaring into the sky. There the westerly wind would take hold of each and keep it gently and steadily bobbing above. Daisy's 'O' was joined by Susie's 'S'. This was followed by another, then two more. Our message would soon be complete.

Calamity ensued when a cross-draft sent Daisy's kite dipping and slewing to the left. This sudden gust nearly pulled the girl from her feet, but she wrestled her string back to her will even as it became entangled with another, then another. The final two kites also collided transposing the letters thereon. Our full fleet now flew, but its message was all ajumble and askew.

'S T O N E,' the message read. 'Sickness Triumph Over Now Even.'

I stood frowning up, uncertain how to rectify the sorry mess. It was just like my father always warned me: 'Man plans; God laughs.'

Fortunately, we stood in the presence of a recognized master of air. As Skyler sat down, fatigued from his recent efforts. Mistress Julia looked over at me, her laughing eyes alight with mirth.

"Almost," she consoled, "but such blunders can be remedied."

She unfolded her arms and waved them about in a complex set of whirling gestures.

"Personalis zephyris spirantibus," she incanted.

A tremendous wind arose with a whooshing noise to envelope the smiling master. But no stray gust disturbed the children, so precisely did she channel it. Her billowing robes snapped taut at once. And I noticed the corners of her long cloak were tied tightly around her ankles. With a few short hops followed by a great leap, she rode the wind into the sky. Swooping about, she gained in height and shrank in our sight to join the lofty letters we had flown.

The children stared up in amazement, clinging fiercely to their strings. My own jaw hung wide, flabbergasted at the sight of the gliding Elf. I thought she might aid us by calling a wind, not going up there herself. She approached the letter 'O' and casually plucked it from the sky. About the other strings, she did pirouette and fly. Whirling back up as on an unseen eddy, she righted the 'E' and the 'N', then softly glided off to settle back to earth again.

All had been guided back to its proper place. And there stood Mistress Julia, resting her hands upon her thighs, for she'd been winded in fact as well as truth. But her formerly stern eyes twinkled with the playfulness of youth.

While high above the town of Conclave, the righted message read:

O - ver

S - ickness

T - triumph

E - ven

N - Now

Skyler and I walked over to join Mistress Julia and Miss Spencer. We sat in the grass and watched as the girls managed the display.

"I can't wait until I can fly as you just did," exclaimed Skyler to the master.

"Tell me that in ten or twenty years, apprentice," she returned. "It took me at least that long ere I could rise from the ground without the risk of breaking my neck or causing some other disaster. I haven't flown in years. It's a joy few ever experience, but it's quite a finicky and demanding discipline."

"Is it something any can achieve?" I asked hopefully. "Or must one have the air affinity?"

"I've known a few others to master it over time," she replied, cupping her hands in the grass and uplifting them gently, "but all were of the first people. Without the proper affinity, the necessary finesse takes significantly longer to train."

Noting my disappointment, she continued.

"Take heart, aspirant, there's more than one way to peel an onion. Each gift bestows its advantages. We of the first people find our inspiration in nature. Personal movement can take many enjoyable forms."

She spread her hands to reveal a daddy long-legs standing in her palm. It scuttled over her thumb to hang from the back of her hand. She overturned her hand so the creature was upright once more, then gently blew it off to land back in the grass below.

Elves are weird.

I was proud of my class and proud of our town and the message we'd cobbled and tethered to a few scraps of wood and cloth and string with ingenuity we'd worked together. For more than an hour, the steady breeze held our skywriting aloft until the winds, ever fickle allies, failed us. And as all good things must come to an end, our hopeful message at last did descend.

We retired to the dining hall of the crèche where Miss Spencer served warm milk and tea cakes.

"Do you think they liked it?" asked Cassie.

"Hard to say," remarked Skyler around a mouthful. "I suppose it depends on how many of them can read."

I noted Miss Spencer failed to scold him for his poor manners. I made sure to spill some warm milk over my teacup's rim and onto my saucer. This I promptly set aside on the sill of the open window. Susie grinned at me and nodded.

"I'm certain the townsfolk were suitably impressed," pronounced the Elven master. "We can only hope it gave them an uplifting if brief distraction from their worries. I shall report to the masters' council the exceptional success of this class. Keep at your studies. I'm certain Aspirant Harper has much more to teach you in whatever time remains to us."

***

As I was leaving the academy, I ran into Edgar. I wouldn't have run into him had he been watching where he was headed.

"Scraaaaw," said Lenore, who had been roosting on the man's shoulder but was now fluttering aloft.

It was the first sound I'd ever heard her make.

"I beg your pardon," said Edgar distractedly as he bent to retrieve a sheaf of pages which he'd dropped during our collision. "Oh. Lucas. Just the man I was looking for."

"Hello, Edgar," I greeted.

Lenore settled onto the back of a nearby wooden bench and set to preening herself, indignantly sorting out her ruffled feathers.

"I've finished with the research you requested," he said, indicating the rumpled heap of parchments which now lay sandwiched between his palms. "Give me a minute and I'll have them all back in their proper order."

"It looks like you found quite a lot."

"Indeed," he agreed. "Lenore and I left no page unturned. There is quite a variety of folklore on the topic of spiritual possession, but I just summarized the references to all that, citing only a few of the most relevant. I assumed you meant for me to stick chiefly to the means employed by mages within our guild. I've listed those from the simplest to the more complex."

"I really should have numbered these pages."

"The type of possession in which I'm most interested," I clarified, "was accomplished using 'miscere cogitata' on a permanently enchanted item."

"Someone's been playing you for a fool then. The power requirements for such an enchantment would be phenomenal, quite beyond the means of any but the greatest of masters."

"Humor me."

"Well, it's all in my notes here," he said, shuffling them about and straightening the stack. "But I daresay that narrows the field down to just two viable counterspells. 'Cogitationes liberare' is the more standard of the two, strengthening the possessed mind and allowing it to liberate itself from possession."

"And the other?" I inquired.

"The other, 'Exorcizo spiritus,' is much more involved. It is usually employed by a circle of masters, to cast out the possessing spirit and banish it entirely. Again, the power requirements are preclusive of casual use."

Edgar looked at me assessingly before passing me the stack.

"If you had any notion of dabbling with these magics, I would hope the cautionary notes I've included will dissuade you from such. You could cook your own brain. And a mind is a terrible thing to baste."

"Thanks, Edgar," I replied. "You too, Lenore. Maybe I'll bump into you again sometime."

As the raven reclaimed her human perch, the man hustled off.

"Let's get you something to eat, miss," said another man emerging from the academy.

Before him was Bella Gibson looking forlorn as he marched her along.

"Bella," I intoned as they passed by.

She looked up and smiled wanly.

"Good evening, teacher," she greeted me. "I saw your message from town this morning. I was afraid it had gone awry."

"It very nearly did, but Mistress Julia set it to rights."

"That was the Elven master? How I wish I could have met her. She was quite a sight, soaring through the sky."

The man looked down at Bella.

"Oh. Where are my manners?" she exclaimed. "Teacher, this is Douglas Weil, the conclave's most learned physic. Master Weil, this is Aspirant Lucas Harper, a man of letters."

"We really oughtn't to dally, miss," he said after giving me a dismissive look. "Several new cases have been reported in highside, and the Lord Mayor is most distraught."

"I can do no more today, Master Weil. I am beyond exhaustion. If I could just sit for a bit, Aspirant Harper can see me home, if that's alright?"

The latter remark was accompanied by a pleading gaze directed my way. I shrugged and nodded.

"Get some sleep then," the physic groaned. "I'll go and examine them myself. I'll fetch you early tomorrow. You know it will only grow more difficult if you put off giving treatments."

The man looked disgruntled. Moreover, from the set of his shoulders as he stalked off, it looked as though it would take quite a lot to re-gruntle him.

Bella slid unhappily onto the bench Lenore had just vacated, a look of relief etched across her weary face.

"I'm sorry to impose, teacher, but I needed a moment to rest. This past week has been a nightmare."

"I can relate," said I. "Take your time and collect your thoughts. And here outside of class you may simply call me Lucas."

The girl leaned back and let out a calming breath. Then, her lips twisted, and it all came out in a rush.

"For the past several days, I've been seeing spots before my eyes. At first I thought it was merely fatigue catching up with me, but as I gained more experience, I came to recognize it as a precursor to the illness. People having these little specks on and about their person would soon fall ill. There's something we're all missing here. If the press of new cases would just let up for a moment, perhaps I could figure it out."

"What does Master Weil say?" I inquired.

"Stick to the established triage," she intoned in a deep voice while clucking her tongue. "We've enough people showing symptoms without wasting our time on the healthy."

"He thinks I'm just imagining things. The worst part is I see ever more people sporting spots, some even here in the mage's quarter, which I'm told is most unlikely."

"Are there any on *me*?" I asked.

She paused and examined me from head to toe.

"No, you're clean, as are most hereabouts. I really do need to get some food and rest. Master Spencer's estate is only a few doors down."

Pleased by her verdict, I took her arm and escorted her there.

***

"Are you ready?" whispered Franklin.

"Almost," I replied as I crept from my room.

We headed down the hall, through the parlor, and into the mudroom. Taking up my boots, I ran a damp rag over their soles. Franklin stared at me curiously as I sat and pulled them on. Earlier this evening I had confronted the man about just what project was worth breaking all the rules.

"You can't learn a new spell by reading about it," I had insisted.

Franklin had leveled his gaze upon me and murmured: "There's another way."

I'm told I can be... persistent is the nice way to put it. Over the last several days, I had cornered Franklin at every opportunity until I'd finally pried it out of him what he intended. I knew he secretly yearned for someone in whom to confide.

"There hasn't been a necromancer in the conclave for decades, Lucas," he had explained. How do you think the masters preserve the knowledge of mages who've passed?"

I had imagined they passed on their learnings to their journeyman and told him so.

Shaking his head sadly, Franklin had explained one of the standing stones was called the Stone of Recall. Upon mastering a new spell, a wizard would commune with the stone to record its inner workings. The key was knowing the spell's name. Invoking the stone with the name of the spell, present masters could summon echoes of its casting. Thus, they could observe its inner workings closely with their mage sight. I should have guessed they had something like that. Had they not, much knowledge would have been lost over the ages.

"Are you ready *now*?" whispered Franklin more urgently.

"One last thing," I forestalled then whispered: "Terwilliger."

In the short pause that followed, Franklin narrowed his eyes, saying: "Ter-what now?"

"Nevermind. C'mon. Let's go."

We hiked up Aspie Rowe by the light of the half-moon above. The path we trod stirred recollections of when Galwell, Royland and I had last come this way in nothing but our neophyte robes. The night had warmed considerably since then, and spring was well underway. The glorious season of rebirth was overshadowed by the grim tidings we'd had of late and overlooked by many whose worries blinded them to the beauty all around. But still the vernal season sent us its comfort and regard in the fresh scent of budding plants and the joyous chorus of the night insects.

"I sense you are pensive about this... undertaking," said Franklin with a mortician's turn of phrase. "I find it restful. If Lloyd were coming with me on this trip, I would scarcely have a moment's peace from his ebullient jabbering."

"Leave Lloyd *out* of it. I've grown fond of the boy. He has enough troubles of his own without getting involved in *yours*."

"Lucas," Franklin asked hesitantly, "why were you so ...insistent on coming along?"

"Don't honeycoat it," I admonished. "By all means, tell me how you *really* feel about it."

"Very well then, 'pestersome' is how I would characterize your behavior of late."

"If it's as you say, then I have some business of my own with that stone. What will you do if we can't invoke it?"

"I thought I might enact my backup plan. Your cousin occupies a cell just down the corridor from my laboratory. Perhaps I can enlist his aid. He commands a powerful gift. You once told me his snoring could wake the dead."

Was that a joke? From Franklin? This finally confirmed my earlier suspicions. His air of quiet reserve was a mere affectation, a mechanism of defense. Having been scorned and hurt repeatedly by the opinions of others, the man had erected a barrier to shield his emotions. And now that we were thick as thieves, he'd opened it the merest crack. It was so funny that I forgot to laugh. And I meant that in the most sincere and least sarcastic manner possible. I'd always found that humor made a better shield than indifference, and it seemed I'd convinced Franklin to at least give it a try. Mayhap the young man would at last throw open his cellar of anguish and share its contents with those around him who cared. Alright. I'd play.

"You don't know the half of it," I returned. "The mages of Osten have been inbreeding for generations. Though primarily of Brubaker and Willoughby descent, I suspect from his caterwauling Royland might have more than a hint of the Sutherland gift."

We stalked on in silence, having staked out our respective comedic territories, until we came to the base of the hill. Despite the hour, there was activity atop it. Flickering lights could be seen and quiet voices could be heard. Could someone else even now be communing with the stones? We hid ourselves and waited to see who might be up there.

We didn't wait long. Just long enough to reconsider the consequences of getting caught. We both knew the rules. Non-masters were to be supervised on visits to the stones. Though it was considered only a minor infraction, it did conflict with the vows I'd taken just ten days prior. And I'd made such a big stink about my word being my most precious possession. Well, every rule had its exceptions (which, of course, meant by its very nature that some did not).

Speaking of big stinks, rolling down from the hilltop was a thin cloud of mist. I caught a whiff of it, and it was foul. Not only that, it was familiar somehow. Where had I encountered such an unpleasant smell before? Then it struck me like a thunderbolt. In my dream, Grandma Abbey had climbed this very hill to confront my true grandfather, only to find him consorting with some foul apparition and plotting against Osten. Could someone yet be in league with the enemy after all this time had passed?

"Whatever happens," I whispered to Franklin. "Don't be seen."

He shot me an exasperated look as though I'd just stated the obvious, but then he sobered and nodded, having doubtless noticed the look of fright my eyes conveyed.

When the lights had died down and the voices had stilled, we spied a lone figure creeping down from the hill. His clothing was dark, and the hood of his cloak cast a shadow upon his features. He wasn't over-tall, a mere slip of a man, but he carried himself as one accustomed to command. And as he navigated a switchback on his descent, a moonbeam revealed his countenance.

It was Atticus Skinner, a master we'd studied in hopes he might take us at the choosing. The man had only a single journeyman and was long overdue for another. Unmarried and heirless, he kept a large estate on a hill near the lake. Our hopes had been dashed when the man failed again to make a selection. Looking warily about, the man passed us by while silent as stones we sat, scarcely daring to draw breath.

Master Skinner was one of the few mages who sported facial hair. His thin black goatee was kept tidy and trim. It stretched but an inch past the base of his chin. He was a fairly handsome fellow, as the ladies reckoned such things, but he kept to himself, eschewing the company of others, and many thought him haughty. After he'd gone, we tarried a bit, lest he come back or others descend. For more than one voice we'd heard from that hill. But all remained quiet and still, with only the stars to witness our struggle to bolster our flagging nerves.

"Well, we won't find out anything hiding down here," Franklin remarked.

"You're right," I said. "Time is limited."

We arose from where we squatted and crept up the path.

"What gave you such a fright?" Franklin whispered.

"Just some bad dreams I've been having," I replied. "But I'm here to put an end to all that."

I couldn't put my finger on it, but I had a strange reticence about sharing my knowledge of the dark entity that I'd seen in my dream. But that was unworthy. Here I'd been demanding that Franklin come clean about his mysterious project whilst keeping important facts about my own doings private. Trust had to begin somewhere.

"You see, I once visited this place in a dream, a lucid dream which I suspect arose from the shattered remnants of my grandmother's consciousness. When she went up on the hill, she--. I--. My tongue clove to the roof of my mouth and a sharp pain struck me dumb. I was momentarily staggered, and my right knee gave out beneath me.

"It's alright, Lucas. You don't have to tell me if you don't want to."

I was gobsmacked; or spellbound, more like. Could the enchantment Denis Feininger had wrought upon Abigale have rooted so deep into her twisted soul as to apply to the things she'd witnessed in my dream? If so, I suspected I couldn't even relate my mother's true parentage to anyone. A test, then. *No!* Screamed my aching head. Yes, my stubborn will replied.

"You see, Denis Feininger is my--"

Ouch.

Franklin was looking down from above me, concern written on his pale face.

"Denis is dead, Lucas. We discussed that on your second day here. Come on. No more talking. We're almost to the top."

He offered his hand and hauled me back up to my feet. What had that vile traitor done to Grandma Abbey? To me? I settled down and crafted a semblance of calm, but within I was seething. It would do no good to alienate others or give them cause to doubt my sanity. *Lies.* Grandma had discovered she could still *lie* about the events she'd witnessed. Could that be helpful? Could an ancient and powerful enchantment perceive sarcasm? Perhaps it was a thing to try, but 'convey by any other means' covered a lot of ground. I'd have to convince myself I was attempting to deceive, else I suspected punishment would swiftly follow.

We topped the rise and found the circle empty. Well, at least there was that. The stench was all around us. Remnants of the same miasma that had laid granny low assailed my nostrils.

"Phew," said Franklin, "What's that smell?"

Try it. Believe it. Hope that Franklin is clever enough.

"Definitely not a side effect from having a conversation with some kind of demon," I quipped.

Just a bad joke. Surely nothing worthy of swift and painful retribution.

Franklin looked at me strangely.

"It's this one over here, Lucas. The one with the three white lines."

He placed his hand on the stone, but nothing happened.

"I think one of us has to feed power into the menhir while the other searches," he continued. "Give it some of your vines to chew on."

I did as the man asked. I could feel the menhir drawing the power out of me, but at a much less reckless pace than on the night of my initiation. I wondered where all the magic had gone that night. I would just have to chalk it up as another mystery of the dolmens, I supposed.

Franklin's eyes had gone glassy, and he stood as though frozen with his right palm pressed to the Stone of Recall. I heard from him a strange muttering. It made no sense to me and yet it made perfect sense. I felt linked to it somehow. Though its meaning was pure gibberish, it called to my soul. Suddenly, my soul answered. The draw on my magic intensified, and my vines thickened to be eagerly devoured by the menhir. A short time later, Franklin sagged back. His vacant expression transformed to a countenance brimming with transcendent joy. He looked like Archimedes having his eureka moment. The menhir released me.

"Did you find what you needed?" I asked.

"What? Yes. *Oh yes!*"

"It's my turn, then. I *do* get a turn," I explained as though to a dimwitted child.

"What? *Oh!* Sorry, Lucas. Of course you may seek your answer."

As we swapped places, I studiously avoided glancing at the two dolmen between which the visage had appeared. Another large, flat stone rested atop them to make a *pi* symbol or doorway of sorts. I wanted no truck with what lay on the other side of that door. I felt that brushing against it while Franklin was feeding the menhir would be a seriously bad idea. My hand came to rest upon the rounded stone with the three white marks.

At first there was an icy chill that crept up my arm and spread out to suffuse my being. Then came the murmuring. It was as though a thousand voices were all speaking at once in a crowded hall with poor acoustics. The voices were muffled, but they seemed to call to me. As I focused on the words of the first spell: 'Cogitationes liberare,' several of the voices became more distinct, and disjointed scenes of old men and a few women passed before my eyes only to be stretched out and replaced by others. My lips were moving, and I suspected Franklin was hearing the babble to which I'd been privy during his sojourn within. But I only had ears for the masters of the past.

For I sensed from their droning incantations the impetus that underlay the spell of liberation, and my mage sight drank it in. It was like trying to drink the contents of an ale barrel that had been overturned all at once, and yet somehow I managed. I felt that with thought and perhaps a bit of practice I could recite this spell. I wondered how Franklin was getting on. I could feel his dark energies roiling all around, permeating and energizing my life within the stone.

Now for that other spell. 'Exorcizo spiritus,' I thought. The world seemed to tilt, and the voices lifted anew. But something was wrong; terribly wrong. Instead of a gentle muttering, there arose a harsh jabbering as of men arguing or shouting to one another over a storm-tossed sea. Rather than individual faces, circles of men would appear. One after another these rings of jabbering men would be replaced by another spinning ring of them gesticulating madly and raising their shrill voices to the four winds. I glimpsed in the eye of this cyclonic storm of images and voices the underlying principle of exorcism, just before all was replaced by blackness.

I awoke with Franklin bending over me wearing a mask of rage. It felt like some time may have passed.

"What did you *do?*" he demanded.

"Only what we came to do, Franklin. I learned the spells I need."

"*Spells?*" he asked indignantly. "As in, more than *one?* You crazy idiot. You could've been killed. You could've gotten *me* killed. This process isn't all that safe, Lucas. Thats why the masters prefer traditional learning: master to student. They only use this technique in *extremis*. As a safety precaution, they're required to wait at least a month before using this method again."

I was still working through the knowledge on which I'd been force fed. And Franklin's tone was too much akin to the shouting voices from the second spell I'd summoned. It got my dander up.

"Well, you could have told me all that beforehand instead of *hoarding* all your secrets! I didn't know. Are you alright?"

"Getting there. You?"

"I'll be fine."

I had said this before I tried sitting up. Afterword my opinion on the matter had been renegotiated by my aching everything. I felt like the quintain after jousting practice was done. Edgar had spoken truly; a mind was a terrible thing to baste. But from my spinning thoughts, another notion emerged. I reviewed my two new spells. I felt certain I could manage the first. The second one, less so. I understood how to invoke the dire invocation that could banish a spirit whence it came, but sensed the power required to fuel it might lie beyond my reach. Nonetheless, I thought with a spreading grin, Sholeena had also spoken true; a good meal of catfish was worth a few scratches.

With the moon now high above, we headed down the hill.

"I wonder what Master Skinner was doing up there alone," Franklin remarked.

Time to try again.

"Nothing untoward, I'm sure," said I in honeyed tones. "An upstanding man like Atticus Skinner would certainly never consort with Osten's enemies to plot its downfall."

I was straining the bounds of the enchantment's credibility, for I felt my tongue begin to cease up, and a dark echo of torment to come hovered above my bruised psyche.

"Tis only a jest, Franklin. I *certainly* wouldn't want you to take the *opposite* of my words for the truth."

"There's an awful lot of... certainty drifting about in your oddly specific ramblings," said Franklin, flummoxed. "And since when do you say 'tis?' Are you trying to tell me something obliquely, my friend?"

"*Certainly* not" I hastily replied.

Come on, Franklin. Put it all together.

Roy would've solved it at once. Sadly, I was estranged from my cousin of late. I had to rely on others to convey my grim warning. Franklin lapsed into silence as he considered. I observed his face contorting this way and that as he mulled over my strange behavior. Once again, I felt sorry for grandma Abbey, for she'd had no good friends to lie to.

"I think I take your meaning. Tis a strange game, but I'm certain you have your reasons. Speak on."

And as we walked side by side down the lane, I began to lie like I had never lied before. I lied about my true origins. I lied about Denis Feininger's betrayal, and I uncarefully hid my suspicions regarding the purpose and prophecy of the verdant child. Franklin listened with a cynic's ear to all I had not to say. An occasional twinge would furrow my brow when too near the truth I drifted. But I was getting much better at falsehood by now; thus, my burden of silence was lifted. When near to the Perilous Glade we arrived, my entire tale was untold.

"Franklin," I said regretfully, "You go on ahead and consider well what I have not said."

For the glade was calling to me once again.

***

Franklin reluctantly departed down the garden lane. I itched to enter the glade, but I waited impatiently for the man to pass from view. Both in body and in mind, I was fatigued from the reckless adventure we had shared, but my spirits soared on my suspicion that Hazel had returned. Though it was night, I felt no unease when I parted the bramble and strayed from the path.

I followed the will of the woods, well familiar with its turnings, until the open glen I spied. And there she stood, bathed in moonlight as beauteous as I remembered, and more. For in her silent stance, I perceived a new confidence along with a joy she hadn't had before. What a difference a fortnight of rest had wrought.

"I mark you peeping from the forest's edge. Not much occurs in this parody of a woodland of which I am unaware. Come, then. Approach. For I've a new favor to task thee with."

Oh. So I'm a 'thee' now, am I?

"Well met, Hazel. How fares the oak?"

"He is mending well, Lucas the Bloke."

This was getting out of hand, I thought as I approached.

"It's just Lucas," I corrected her, "and I'm still amazed at how you healed and fortified the tree, delivering him from the sickness that had beset him."

She smiled demurely on receiving the compliment.

"Nonsense," she said, "yours was the greater challenge. His bark was much worse than his blight."

Her piercing green eyes stared at me in solemn sincerity, and I was hard-pressed to suppress the laughter that bubbled up and threatened to burst forth into the lady's face at the clever wordplay she had unconsciously wrought. As I clamped down on it, my expression grew pained and tears dribbled down from the corners of my eyes.

A sadness overtook Hazel's face. She bent toward me, and a consoling kindness fell from her down-turned lips.

"You really *do* care," she soothed. "Fear not. The oak recovers nicely. As a reward, I shall grant you the appellation you've requested. And seeing your devoted heart makes my next request all the easier."

I was still speechless. I writhed in the throes of laughter denied as the dryad girl continued.

"From all my years observing those who wander by, I've learned. Rightly it is said among your folk that friendship must be earned. Although your deed has won my favor, the friendship of the fey is not so cheaply bought. I will ask of you a boon this night. I perceive you as a man whose word is dear to him, and only if you give it, will I entrust to you a task I require. Swear to me by all you hold dear that you will not betray my trust."

Her words freed me from the paroxysms of mirth in which I'd been ensnared, and I considered them most carefully. It was gravely urgent that one pay full attention when dealing with the fey. According to all the stories, one must adhere to the letter of bargains struck with them. I could detect no hidden meaning or consequence of the vow she would have me make.

"I so swear."

Her smile was like the sun rising to warm the day.

"There is aught I must check up on first," she declared. "Terwilliger."

"Say my name and I must appear!"

"I thought so," said she. "Tis as I did fear. Is no matter safe from your prying ear?"

He was standing beside the stone bench, not three paces distant, leaning upon his walking stick.

"Yer baseless suspicion's a wound to my pride. I'm just passing by. Have ye something to hide?"

"Be that as it may," said Hazel. "your footfalls have betrayed your intrusion, for I can detect e'en a leaf's gentle falling upon the forest floor."

"Good to know, dear lady. Your chastisement doth have merit. A dryad's power within her woods - henceforth, I will beware it.

"Speak plainly, then. Why are you here?"

The brownie removed his hat and stared at the ground.

"Here and I had just finished up my nightly labors and consumed my milk when I noticed my teacher was out of his bed. Strange, I thought, perhaps he be traipsin' off to the library at night as he and that other are wont to do. I thought for a laugh I'd take myself there to see whether it be true. On my way there, I spotted a trail leading off from the garden lane. Curious, I followed it. It led into your domain. I had no thought to disturb ye. I swear by the hem of my cloak. But here by your side I found him, big as life, Lucas the Bloke.

"Name him not so," returned Hazel "He's requested a new title: 'Lucas the Just.' And to this I agreed. So call him this. You must."

"I didn't mean..." my budding objection trailed off.

The two stared over, blinking at my interruption of their poetry contest. Never mind. I'd best quit while I was ahead.

"Since you're here," declared Hazel, "you may as well be of some use. Will you bear witness to a bargain struck?"

"I will," the brownie replied.

That sounded ominous. But I decided in the spirit of friendship to believe in Hazel.

"Lucas," she said, turning toward me once more, "you know I've been imprisoned here these five and twenty summers. Condemned by fate to stand alone in a false grove far from my people."

"And what am *I* then?" Terwilliger sputtered in indignation.

Ignoring him, she continued.

"I would spare my daughter from such a fate. After resting from the healing of the oak, I contrived to blossom and breathed life into the first of these to bear fruit. The bug lady shan't suspect it, for such rarely occurs until the heat of the summer has passed. It was my service to this goal that kept me away for so long. Her acorn now hangs ready, awaiting only rich soil in which to root and the touch of the sun's rays. It will leave me lonely, but I'll bear it, knowing my daughter will live wild and free amid the cavorting of her kind. I beseech you, Lucas the Just, to bear her acorn to a grove acknowledged by my folk. Plant her there. Will you do this for me?"

Again her eyes bore into mine, but no compulsion accompanied her sorrowful gaze. This was to be a task freely undertaken.

"I am most honored by your faith in me, Hazel. When would this need to be done?"

"Most acorns can sprout for as many as four moons after their falling. Those having the élan of a hamadryad can last for years beyond that."

"I will see it done, Lady Hazel, fair dryad of the conclave. You have my word."

"So witnessed!" exclaimed Terwilliger, as Hazel shed a tear.

It was a tear of joy, but also one of sadness. Joy for her daughter's freedom, but sadness that she would never see her. I expect the former outweighed the latter, for such was a mother's love, be she made of flesh or wood. Some things were universal.

"Kneel before me then," she commanded, "and receive the mark of the fey, so my sisters will not shun you and scatter when you approach. I would fain kiss your lips, but I sense your love is for another. Your hand will do quite nicely in their stead."

I what then again? My stomach flip-flopped. I knelt before the young tree sprite and she took up my hand gently in both of her own. She pressed her lips to the back of my hand and from where they touched a tingling warmth was felt. From the back of my hand to my wrist, then my arm, the magical blessing trickled.

This must be what it's like to have sap running through your veins, I thought.

When it rounded my shoulder, it exploded outward, traveling hither and yon. My heart nearly leaped from my chest with the joy of it, and still the sensation rolled on. When the lady withdrew, echoes of her benison still rebounded within my body. I knelt before her, red-faced and reluctant to stand, for it had lingered too long in my loins. That was some kiss. Had she given it on my lips; no natural woman could ever again have compared.

Save perhaps for one.

"By the queen's green booties and her tall, silk hat," said Terwilliger, dancing a merry little jig, "I wish someone would kiss *me* like that!"

"Be still cheeky hob," said the dryad, "and swear not by our queen. Besides, I doubt you'd survive a kiss such as mine."

I was inclined very much to agree. Judging from Terwilliger's repentant frown, so was he. I used the distraction to rise to my feet and straighten out my doublet. On the back of my hand where her lips had touched, a glimmering stain caught my eye. It was shaped vaguely like an oak leaf. I held it up to see it more clearly.

"That's the mark of the fey, Lucas" she said. "It is visible only by moonlight, but all faeries can perceive it. It lets us know to treat its bearer with respect, for only rarely is it ever awarded to a mortal man. We dryads make them to send with our proxies to wherever the Seelie Court may be called. We cannot stray far from our trees. It has the added benefit of letting you know when pests are around. Like *these*."

She directed that final remark toward Terwilliger, who crossed his arms and made a haughty frown of defiance.

"Come and stand ready. Terwilliger bide."

She turned and glided to the edge of the glen wherein we stood. She approached a tree, embraced its trunk and dissolved into its bark. Ah. So that was her tree. It made sense. The stone bench oversaw it directly. Mistress Willoughby doubtless arranged it in that fashion so they might converse.

Remembering my pledge, I thought to say a word on her behalf.

"Hazel, I hope you can still hear me. I think you have nothing to fear from Mistress Willoughby. I overheard her speaking about it with another. She's sorry your mother couldn't be saved. She was holding back tears as she spoke of it. I get the impression her work with the wasps is meant to protect the kingdom's forests from the very fiends that were responsible. You should talk to her. I think she moved you here only to protect you from harm."

I heard a creaking sound from high above and stepped back when I sighted a branch plummeting to the earth. It bounced and twirled when it struck before coming to rest on the forest floor. From it hung a golden-brown acorn nearly as large as an apple. My mage sight throbbed as I looked upon it, and the mark of the fey began to itch. I approached it for a closer look.

Just then, Hazel emerged from her tree. We were standing nose to nose.

"Your words have touched me as hers could not. For your sake, I will try to suspend my passions on the matter and let her plead her case."

She threw her arms about my neck, then hugged me close and wept.

Dryads were moody little things.

After a time we parted. She retrieved the stick and its passenger from the ground where it lay. With a twisting motion and a cracking sound, she separated the two. She kissed the acorn in a fashion similar to how she had my hand, whose sympathetic throbbing made me wish I was that nut.

"Every dryad has a true name," she explained. "You must whisper it to her when she's planted in the ground. Ordinarily, the fairy godmothers are given this duty, but I reckon you'll do in a pinch. Say it not aloud until the time is ripe for rooting."

Then she leaned in once again and her lips found my ear. She softly whispered the child's true name therein.

"You told me once," she continued with her eyes gone distant, "I could offer you some small reward by way of thanks."

She handed me the stick.

"This is the umbilicus of a dryad's first birthing. It is no mere stick and contains much power. I offer it to you in friendship. I've little else to give. I'm an oak, not a giving tree. Mayhap it will be of use."

"Now truly I can call you friend for all the conditions have been met. I have done you a small favor by agreeing to listen to the bug lady and asked you for nothing in return. It may be several days before we can speak more, my friend. My birthing labors have tired me, and I must sleep again. I know few words of parting, for I never before had a friend of your sort. But I once heard the tree chopper say to the bug lady: 'Don't let the door hit you where the good lord split you.'"

Hazel pivoted and 'lumbered' back into her trunk, 'leaving' me again in stitches.

I carefully entrusted my new treasures to my bob, then ambled back to where Terwilliger sat stewing on the bench.

"Hob indeed," he grumbled to himself. "As though I were a lowly hearth sprite bound to some simpleton's shack. 'Bide Terwilliger,' as if such a sorry stack of lumber-yet-to-be could ever command as fine an example of browniehood as..."

"Yet here you sit," I inserted "meek as the devil on Christmas."

"Ye could have been a mite more supportive," he complained.

"Sorry. I was busy being blindsided, kissed, and becoming an unfairy godfather."

He smiled at this.

"Ye did appear to have yer hands full at that, and damn near yer britches as well."

"Speaking of filling my britches," I said, "have you ever heard of a warty-faced demon named Orenob?"

"Don't say that name aloud," the brownie hissed. "His minions could be anywhere. And though that be not his true name, tis near enough to conjure by, not that any would dare. Where did you hear tell of *that* one?"

"Well, I saw--. Well, I can't say. But he might be or is most certainly not speaking to one or more of the mages and urging them toward dark acts."

"Well, now. That be most interestin'. If *that one* is mucking about in mortal affairs, it would explain a lot of recent events. The queen must be notified at once. I'll do it myself, there being no other in the ken. Tis a shame ye reneged on yer promise to teach Terwilliger to fly. That would've made it a much simpler matter. As it is, I'll need to be taking leave from my duties for a couple of days."

"That's alright," I allowed. "Classes have been suspended for the duration of the spring festival, such as it is. And the boots can wait."

"I'll make sure to share the tidings and tale of Lucas the Just," he said, flashing once more his pointy teeth.

The tiny man vanished, and I blundered my way back to the garden lane. When at last I collapsed onto my bed, I didn't even bother to undress. With school not in session, I could sleep till noon if I liked. I'd definitely earned it. Tomorrow would be just another humdrum day. Franklin had invited me to visit his laboratory in the academy's basement. Yep, things were finally settling down.

CHAPTER EIGHT

The Monster

"Only one soul was to be seen, and that was Madame Defarge-- who leaned against the door-post, knitting, and saw nothing."

~ Charles Dickens ~

Abandoned.

Close. So close I'd come to a solution.

Only Sebastian had stayed with me. The pitiful excuse for a man who craved mistreatment was the only one to remain loyal.

I looked into the mirror.

The years had not been kind.

I'd suppressed the girl's power, and the boy's as well; I was fairly certain of it. They had quit eating the gingerbread after a time, but my special ingredients had done their work. Their magic centers had dwindled to the point where I could no longer even detect them.

I was foolish to trust the boy.

He had called me 'mother.' I thought he understood. Isabel is a danger to us all. Her father mustn't find her, mustn't even suspect she yet lives. But I couldn't tell him that. I couldn't ever tell him why. You would think with the power at my command I might overcome that geas the wight had placed on me. All my attempts to mitigate it had failed. Such was the cunning of the makers of those ancient stones. And each time I avoided answering the boy, he grew ever more mistrustful. I think he was the one who poisoned the servants against me.

They were coming for me.

After all these years.

I suppose I could go west and try my luck with the seven clans. But no, I could think of few worse ways to spend my final years than dwelling among goblins. If I were younger, perhaps I would have attempted it.

I could fight.

I'd probably win.

But what good would that do? I'd still be a lonely old crone in an empty castle. And the Ostenians would never stop coming. Furthermore, each time I dipped into the power of the ley line, I left a little more of my humanity behind. I suspect that was another reason I'd lost the boy's love.

Then there was the witch's heart.

I picked it up and rested it in my palm.

It was meant for Isabel, but could it be activated without a host? In the presence of the ley line, I shouldn't want for the power necessary to endure. And one day, surely, a suitable host could be found. It had taken me long enough to craft it. Why should all that effort go to waste? Had I not been selfless? I had spared the kingdom from the contemptible scourge Orenob planned to unleash upon it with his vile demon seed. And it had cost me dearly. Why shouldn't I be permitted to begin life anew and enjoy fully the life that was stolen from me?

"Sebastian! Attend me. We've work to do."

Suddenly, I felt a splitting head ache. My vision swam. No, it was only my reflection doing so while all around it remained steady. The face in the mirror was no longer my own. It was that of a dark-haired boy with a sad expression. This was not among the enchantments I'd placed upon it. Where was my own reflection?

I reached for the ley line and was surprised to find it absent.

"You can't work your magic here because you didn't do so at the time," said the boy. "You're but a memory."

"Begone foul spirit!" I said, spearing him on my narrowed gaze. "And spare me your riddles. You don't know who you're dealing with."

"I know all too well," he replied. "I'm taking back my own life, the one *you* tried to steal from *me*."

"I would never--"

"Don't try to deny it. We just now decided to do so. I thought I was rid of you when I crushed the witch's heart, but ever since then, the memories of your life have been playing over and over in my dreams."

I glanced at the crystal in my palm. It glistened there. But a shadow fell over it. In my mind's eye, it lay broken into pieces. There was a window behind the boy. A window with a starry sky. But I was deep underground. On his side of the glass, everything was so sharp and clear. My side appeared indistinct by comparison.

"I've spent the night systematically expunging you from my psyche with a new spell I've learned."

"An intriguing tale," I said archly. "Have you any proof?"

The boy considered.

"Not that it's going to matter, but what did you have for breakfast this morning?"

"I... I don't recall."

"Nor can you," declared the boy, nodding. "I erased that a few minutes ago. For the record, Sebastian made you sausages and eggs. You thought the eggs were underdone, so you made him eat them from off the floor."

Was I losing my mind? According to this boy, such was precisely the case.

"This is the very last bit of you that remains," the boy continued relentlessly. "I saved it for last. It's the moment you decided your life was more important than that of your grandson. The moment you decided to overlay his will with your own."

"Now see here. Perhaps we can come to an arrangement. There is much I could teach you --"

"If it's any consolation," he interrupted, "you succeeded for a time."

There was a drifting sensation and then I...

***

I followed Franklin down the steps. On arriving at the dark landing, he clapped his hands twice saying: 'lumina in.' All down the corridor, the ensconced candles ignited two by two, illuminating the way forward. Neat trick, that. My housemate was in a rare mood. His normally glum expression was absent, and I marked an eagerness in his long strides. Lagging behind, I trailed after, staring curiously about.

We passed a room from which a rhythmic clicking sound emerged. Its door was slightly ajar, and I spied Mistress Willoughby seated within. Beside her sat an elderly woman bundled up in a shawl. That must be her sister who was found down in the war zone. She stared vacantly as though blind, and in her hands she worked two long, slender needles. From these descended a length of cloth she wove from several drab balls of yarn in a basket nearby.

Click. Click. Click.

The door opposite this room creaked open slightly, and an eye peered out. Then it eased back shut.

"Are you coming, Lucas?" prompted Franklin, who stood several doors down looking back.

"On my way," I replied, hustling along.

Franklin inserted a key into the reinforced door and opened it to reveal the workplace he'd invited me to visit. Franklin ushered me inside and then closed and secured the door.

Prominent in the room's center was a stone slab nearly nine feet in length. It was covered by a cloth beneath which odd bulges and protrusions outlined a shape like that of an ogre. To one side was a table filled with accoutrements and glassware of

204

various sorts. I recognized a butchers axe and bone saws, several large needles and spools of coarse thread, an alembic, and many stoppered flasks and bottles. Across from this stood a tall set of standing shelves. On these rested glass jars containing all manner of fleshy organs floating suspended in fluid. From one, an eyeball peered out. At the chamber's far end, I saw what appeared to be a blood-stained altar.

The odor of the place was difficult to describe. It had the astringent tang of cleaning solutions overlaying an effluvium akin to that of rancid meat.

I could tell Franklin was quite proud of this setup and was awaiting my reaction. I wanted to be encouraging. I did. But suitable, honest words of praise escaped me at that moment.

"It's remarkable," I said.

"Isn't it, though?" Franklin preened, gazing fondly about the disturbing surroundings. "Here is where I shall bring necromancy back into the mainstream."

He moved to the slab and shot me a final assessing glance before drawing back the cloth. I was wholly unprepared for the macabre sight this revealed. On the slab lay a gigantic parody of a man stitched together from parts of various animals. Its legs were the hindquarters of a bull or cow, but they were affixed to its torso in a bipedal fashion. Oversized shoulders bulged out from the main body. The 'arms' appeared to be the forelegs of some other large animal, but instead of hands, they ended in a hook and an axe, respectively. To top this all off, to his sinewy neck was attached the head of a swine.

"Lucas, meet Adam, the very first of his kind."

May he also be the last, I prayed silently.

"I've been replacing his blood with a substance I've infused with my gift. He's brimming with necromantic energies. I've spelled these fluids to refresh themselves by absorbing the life of other creatures who die nearby."

"Um. That's nice?"

"Don't you see, Lucas? He'll be the perfect warrior. Immune to all but the most debilitating of wounds, he'll fight on re-energized by the death of the foes he fells."

"Will he recognize friend from foe?"

"That's the best part, Lucas. He won't need to. You'll note I crafted him all out of animal parts. This was to forestall any objections the masters might have about the sanctity of human remains. Elsewise, hands would have been nice, but we make do. I figure people are repelled by necromancy because of their own fear of death and therefore the dead. But Adam here will actually save lives."

Franklin turned and stalked over to the shelves. I'd rarely seen him so excited. From a high shelf, he plucked a pair of steel helmets and returned to his beastly creation.

"With these," he explained, his eyes alight with glee. "Anyone will be able to practice necromancy. No longer will our soldiers need risk themselves against the enemy's abominations."

He placed one helm on the creature's head, fastening it there securely by a chin strap.

"Once I empower these with the proper spell of linkage, donning the other helm will let one peer out through Adam's eyes and control his movements. The soldiers of Osten can sit protected and secure behind the lines while my creations carry the battle to the enemy. Think of it as donning a suit of armor. None object to tanning the hide of a cow and fashioning it into leather armor to protect soldiers in the field. Surely you can see that this is no different?"

I sensed that Franklin was using me to practice arguments he would set before the masters. But though he presented a good case, I was still uneasy about 'Adam' and using the walking dead to butcher our foes. It seemed ignoble somehow.

"Why a boar's head?" I asked.

"An excellent question, my friend," he praised. "Initially, I thought to use a bull and make of him a mighty minotaur of sorts. But I found the horns interfered with the helm. Moreover, a hog is one of the more intelligent of God's creatures. It is more capable of carrying out complex commands."

"It seems you've thought of everything," I said. "When will you present your idea to the masters?

"I only just learned the spell to link the helmets. I will attempt it tonight. Tomorrow I will seek an audience before the council. They have a great backlog of business and many urgent matters to attend to of late, so it may take some time. I feel confident they will see the benefit."

"Well then, good luck with that. I mark you've been working very hard on this. I hope it pans out for you."

"You don't know the half of it, Lucas," replied Franklin with a sigh. "I can't tell you how many night's sleep I've missed pouring over anatomy texts. But before long, it will all pay off."

He bent and lifted the cloth from the floor. I helped him to spread it once again across the hulking figure on its slab, thankfully removing the misbegotten monstrosity from view.

"Can you see yourself out, Lucas? There are a few things I need to work on here."

On the way out, I again approached the room in which Mistress Gretta had been cloistered.

Click. Click. Click.

Across the hall, the door was once more open a slit. This time, I recognized the owner of the eye which peered without. I stepped over and knocked on the door. It eased open further to reveal Royland wearing a frown of annoyance.

"I'd heard you'd been sequestered," I said. "So this is where they've been keeping you."

"Won't you come in, cousin?" he said with a slight shrug.

I had a lot to say to Royland, but I was pretty sure he wasn't ready to hear it. I did want to know how he was getting on as a journeyman, though. I was composing a letter for my father and would like to include a bit about Royland he could share with uncle Robert. I crossed the threshold into my cousin's dingy cell and smiled over at him.

"Why were you peeking out into the hallway?" I asked.

"I can feel her," he replied.

"Her? You mean Mistress Gretta?"

Royland nodded somberly.

"She's trapped. Her inner hive has her mesmerized. I sense she could come out if she wanted, but she's unwilling to confront the sorrow that would bring."

"Why is she knitting?"

"She finds it comforting. Her sister brought her those things. They're the only items from her past to which she's reacted."

"Well, I hope she gets better," I declared. "How about you?

"Mistress Dunham claims I'm making good progress. I'll be out of here in a week. Already I've identified my homunculus and invested her with a portion of my power."

"Her?"

"I envision her as the queen bee of my inner hive. She has a bit of a personality and can exert control over my magic as I sleep. We're in the process of negotiating rules of behavior and areas of responsibility."

"And then it'll be all extravagant comfort at the Brubaker estate, I suppose."

"I suppose."

"You don't sound too certain, Roy."

"Lucas... They're not nice people. It's difficult to be around them."

"Like it's hard to be around me?" I asked, meeting his gaze squarely.

Royland flinched and turned aside, but then turned his brown eyes back to lock upon mine.

"Yes, quite frankly," he returned.

"I've only ever been nice to you, Roy--"

"-- You felt *sorry* for me!" he exploded. "It's not the same thing as treating me as a person. It's more about *you, your* goodness, and how *kind* you are to your *poor, peculiar* cousin. Well, guess what? Here I've made a new start, earned respect, and cut ties with the ghosts of my past. I'm a full journeyman now, and you're a what? A creepy little spawn of a faithless witch."

I held his gaze, shocked that he might feel that way but glad to hear him give voice to it. It rang false somehow.

"That's not what's truly bothering you, Roy," I argued. "You've been acting strangely ever since we left Westarbor. I think you've been fooling yourself about why. Very well. If you feel you must push me away, then I'll oblige you. You can *have* your fine new friends who care so much for the person you're not."

And with that, I turned on my heel and left him there. Franklin Stein's monster wasn't the only thing down here that was pigheaded.

***

Back at Aspie Rowe, I was surprised to find a new project underway. A gang of aspirants from all three houses were working with picks and shovels, digging at the footpath that ran down between them.

"What's all this?" I asked as I approached.

Lorraine looked up from her digging.

"Hey Lucas," she greeted, wiping at her nose with the back of her wrist. "We're cobbling the path from the fountain all the way down to House Owl. We're tired of muddy boots. It was Lloyd's idea."

Just then, the boy in question arrived with a wheelbarrow full of round pavers accompanied by Scott McNair.

"Pull up a shovel and join in the fun, Lucas," he said. "Everybody's pitching in. Sholeena's fishing up suitable rocks from the lakebed. We should be done by suppertime."

I grinned and began unlacing my boots. Rarely had I seen such a prime opportunity to practice 'ambulare interitus', my withering stride. Barefooted, I walked down the pathway withering the grass and weeds that lay beside the trail. Every few steps, I would pause and churn up the hard-packed dirt into a frothy loam making it easy work for the shovels of my neighbors. When I arrived at House Owl, I turned and retraced my steps back to our own home.

"Show off," muttered Lloyd as I passed him by.

But he was smiling, nonetheless, as were many others. I waved to them before retreating indoors.

With Terwilliger away and granny laid finally to rest. I looked forward to a proper nap untainted by dreadful dreams or meddlesome fey. Alas, it was not to be. For no sooner had I struck up and stoked the parlor hearth than I heard the chiming of the steeple bell from off in the distance. Peering out the front window, I saw all of my neighbors engaging in sudden, heated conversations. They were collecting their tools, stripping off grimy aprons, and heading for their respective houses.

Lloyd came bursting in followed by Lorraine. I understood we were being summoned to an assembly at the Hall of Masters, but I was mystified by their grim expressions and fretful behavior.

"What's the matter?" I asked, pulling my boots back on.

"Someone's died," returned Lloyd dolefully.

"They toll the bell thus when there's been a death," confirmed Lorraine.

The two cleaned up, and I dismantled the logs of my abortive fire.

When we arrived at the master's hall, it swirled with the whispered babble of angry speculation. Franklin was already there, holding our seats for us, and Sholeena arrived not long after. I slid onto the bench. I felt a tug at the shoulder of my cloak. Turning, I spied Skyler seated with some other apprentices.

"Do you know who it was, teacher?" he muttered in a concerned whisper.

I set my mouth in a tight line and shook my head, then returned my attention to the platform whereon the masters gathered. Once again, I failed to spot Luther Prowd among them. Mistress Meredith soon separated herself from the others and stood before the podium.

"I am aggrieved to announce," she said into the sudden hush, "that Luther Prowd is no longer among the living."

This set off a babble among us she was hard pressed to quell.

"Silence!" she demanded, bringing her hand down hard upon the lectern.

There was a quality to her shout that demanded we pay heed, and a sullen stillness engulfed the chamber once more as its ringing echoes subsided.

"He passed only this afternoon. He was found in his office, slumped over his desk. Master Weil is attempting e'en now to determine the cause of his untimely demise. The plague has been ruled out, for he bears not its mark upon him.

She paused, considering her next words.

"If any of you saw or spoke with Luther today, you are to report to Master Sheppard immediately following this assembly. We will carry on as before. The council has appointed Clement Brownyng to serve as headmaster *pro tem*. Any matters you would have brought to Luther, you may instead entrust to him. I believe Master Brownyng has a few words for the assembly."

As the man arose to take center stage, the masters shifted restlessly. Despite their uniformly solemn faces, some seemed more pleased than others. I guessed his appointment had been a divisive matter.

"Mages of the conclave," he began. "We face challenging times. All four grim horsemen have been stalking the town of Conclave. Do not our citizens want for food? Has not war taken its toll? Is there not a pestilence spreading among our people? And now death has raised his bony fist to strike at our very heart."

He lowered his head and was silent for a moment, then raised it to stare at us again, his jaw set in resolve.

"Fear not. The conclave has suffered worse. All is presently quiet on the war front. Our spring offensive has gained us a bridgehead in the enemy's land, and fresh troops are even now being outfitted by our efforts here. Your efforts. One of our own has been returned to us. Good progress is being made against the advance of the disease, which God willing will soon have run its course.

"Though Luther's death is a staggering blow, it is not a fatal one. We shall recover. I shall do my best to minimize any lapse in leadership until a new headmaster can be elected. In the meantime, be of good heart and keep to your efforts. It is crucial we continue making brave strides to defy our enemies both abroad and here at home. We shall emerge the stronger for it. In unity we shall prevail.

"Services for Headmaster Prowd will be held beside the lake, tomorrow night. All are invited to attend. The herald will announce the time. Pall bearers will see his remains borne off by boat to be interred among his ancestors. They will lie in the family crypt of quiet repose across the lake. Seneschals if you will."

At his signal, a procession of men entered from the chamber's rear door. The man in the lead beat upon a drum. It was a single beat repeated once every few seconds. Behind him marched two men in their sables bearing a black cloth. The steeple bell began to toll once more as the procession turned as one and proceeded to the portraits on the hall's right side.

At the portrait of Luther Prowd, they arrived, whereupon they stepped forth and hung the shroud upon its frame. Two candles were set, one to each side of it, and lit.

"Sic transit gloria mundi," intoned Master Brownyng, at which point the drumbeats ceased.

"This assembly is adjourned."

"Lumina quell," added the headmaster *pro tem*, clapping twice.

The light from the chandeliers above diminished to half their former brightness, and we all arose to depart. The ringing of the steeple's bell had ceased, leaving only its echoes in our minds. As I shuffled toward the exit amid the press of my brethren, I heard the herald shout from behind me.

"Harper! Lucas Harper!"

I turned, surprised to be directly addressed. Others nearby turned to witness the event as the man caught me up.

"You are to report at once to the headmaster's office. Master Brownyng would have words with you."

Me? I nodded to the man to signify my understanding. Franklin, Lloyd and several others shot me questioning glances.

I shrugged my response and waited for all to clear the hall. Then I hefted my bob and headed off toward the foyer where it had all begun.

***

I sat in the foyer attempting to still the turmoil of my thoughts. Had they discovered my trespass at the library or my unsanctioned use of the standing stones? If so, Franklin would also be here. Would he berate me for my intrusion into the Perilous Glade? I thought that matter had been settled on the night of my initiation. Perhaps I was to be commended for my class' successful project at the spring festival. But I shouldn't think so trivial a matter would be worth the master's time. Surely, he had many more pressing concerns on his docket. No, I would just have to wait and see what the man had on his mind. Waiting would've been a lot easier with a clear conscience to keep me company.

When Master Browning arrived, he glanced down at me and uttered only a single word before stepping briskly over to his office door.

"Come," he said.

I followed him into the office. I was uncertain how to address the man. An irreverent part of my mind put forth that 'Preeminence' was more appropriate than ever, but I decided that simply 'headmaster' would be fitting.

"Have a seat, young man."

He indicated a cozy set of chairs at a small table near the window. I sat in one, and he eased into the other across from me.

"I've had good reports about your work here at the conclave. And your showing at the choosing was... interesting, to say the least. Tell me, Lucas, have you ever heard of the Autonomists?"

"Of course, headmaster. I believe it is a faction among the masters who want the guild to enjoy greater freedom to decide matters of consequence."

"Freedom. Yes. And freedom is a good thing; is it not?"

I felt he was prodding me to answer how he wanted. I sighed.

"It's not so simple as all that, master. We all want to be free to do as we please, but without the righteous rules of society, the strong will inevitably prey upon the weak, thus curtailing *their* freedom. Conversely, should governments grow *too* strong, the rights of individuals suffer because of tyrants with corrupt motives. Philosophers have been arguing about it throughout recorded history, and most agree a balance must be struck."

"You surprise me, young man. Most men twice your age can't string together so cogent an argument."

"I read a lot."

So, in your *opinion*, are the Autonomists good or bad?"

"I wouldn't presume to judge them as either, headmaster. I lack the knowledge of what they intend and the context in which it's intended. I only just got here a month ago."

Where was this all leading? I was certain Master Browning hadn't asked me here for a philosophical debate. Was he one of these Autonomists? Or was he embarked upon a program to root them out?

"I like you, Lucas," he said, steepling his fingers before him. "I had wondered why Master Chadwick had done it, but now I'm getting a glimmer. You're just *like* him in many ways: intelligent; a bit naïve; and committed to the status quo. I take it you are unaware that he granted you his proxy."

What?

"No, headmaster. He never discussed it with me. What does that *mean*?"

"It means, my boy, that if his proxy application is approved, you can vote on his behalf on any matters that come before the council. It was in your letter of introduction. I'm sure Luther would have gotten around to it in time. Likely, he was giving you a chance to settle in before he became troubled by his illness."

"What do you mean by 'if it is approved?'"

"Usually, proxies are offered to other masters or a trusted senior journeyman. Although the bylaws technically permit anyone who has been initiated at the menhir to hold a proxy, appointing a new aspirant is highly unorthodox. Elizar always was a bit of a renegade. You can expect it will be challenged, but our laws are literally chiseled in stone. I don't imagine we can do aught but uphold it. Let me be the first to say: 'welcome to the affray.'

"The next meeting of the master's council will be tomorrow at the seventh bell. I'll introduce Master Chadwick's proxy as the first item of its agenda. There are some rather urgent votes coming up, and several of them will be close. I'm certain there will be many who will offer to get you up to speed and help you decide how to vote."

I think I understood what the man was not saying.

A part of me felt honored by Master Chadwick's charge. But another part wanted to rail at the old man. He *hated* politics. I could almost hear him laughing from two duchies over. Shepherds were supposed to protect against wolves; not throw people to them. Had he made me the butt of his joke upon the conclave? But no. Whatever else he was, Master Elizar was a responsible sort. He always had good reasons for what he did. It is possible he simply didn't know whom else he could trust. Alright. I'd play.

I was just coming to grips with it when there came an urgent knock upon the door.

"Come," said Master Browning, reverting to his one-word vocabulary.

The door swung open to reveal Douglas Weil. Behind him stood Bella Gibson with a look of excitement upon her face.

"You told me to come and inform you the moment I had news," said the physic.

"Tell me then," said the headmaster. "What killed Luther? Is it as we suspected?"

Master Weil hesitated and glanced pointedly in my direction.

"You may speak in front of Lucas," stated the headmaster. "He'll need to know of it soon enough. Come in and report, I say; you too miss."

"The man was strangled, headmaster," said Douglas after entering and easing the door shut. "That bruising about his neck wasn't there at his previous check up. Bella assures me his crushed windpipe was caused by a sustained force and could not have resulted from a fall."

"This means that on top of all else we have a murderer running about. Any indication as to who?"

"None." The physic replied. "We've some good news to report as well."

"I could use some good news," said Master Brownyng, running a hand through his hair. "What is it?"

"Best I let the young lady explain. It was her insight."

Bella stepped up beside the physic. There were still dark circles beneath the girl's eyes, and her face was a bit pale, but some color rose to her cheeks as she began.

"I think I grasp how the sickness is spreading, your preeminence."

"Spare me the title, but speak on girl. What do you mean?"

"I can see them. Itty-bitty plague carriers get on people. It took me a while to understand what I was seeing. But they're fleas. The spots I've been seeing are fleas that have gotten on people. It all came together last night in lowside when I saw a rat slinking around a rubbish heap. It was just infested with them."

"Fleas, you say? Are you certain?"

"Yes, pre... yes, master. There's more. We trapped the rat. When we poured some of the barber's hair tonic on it, the fleas all leaped away. It wasn't the leeches at all!"

"Master," Douglas Weil added, "I believe your entomancers might be of some service here."

"So ordered," returned the headmaster with glee. "Round up everyone with the Willoughby gift and have them do a sweep of the town. Purge every vermin from the populace. And send Master Guthrie to me at once. I'm putting him in charge of banishing all the rats. Finally, some progress!"

Turning to me, he said, "Lucas, you're dismissed. I'll see you tomorrow."

As I exited, I found Franklin moping in the foyer. He looked even more forlorn than usual and wouldn't meet my gaze. I held back when Master Weil left with an energized stride, followed meekly by Bella.

"If you're seeking the headmaster," I said, "I believe he's available now. What's wrong?"

"Everything," Franklin moaned. "Adam's missing."

***

I stood pruning at the hedges of House Owl. Aspie Rowe was looking sharper than ever; what with its new cobbled walkway and stylish topiary. The owls wanted me to sculpt two of their signature nocturnal avians facing their gate to match the blue jays I'd managed for my own house. My heart wasn't in it.

Franklin now languished in a cell beneath the academy, waiting for this mess to be sorted out. The gigantic monstrosity he'd constructed was more than just 'missing.' His laboratory lay in ruins, its stout door shattered from within. It was surprising that no one had heard the commotion. Roy had been at the foundry. The only possible witness was Mistress Gretta, and she wasn't talking. How the overgrown thing had made its way out of the academy's basement unobserved was a mystery that one could scarcely credit. Yet it was nowhere to be found. It spoke of cunning and intent. Franklin stubbornly insisted that his creation had no volition of its own, and he'd never gotten around to spelling the helmets he had intended to command it.

It got on everyone's nerves to think that Adam was stomping around out there and would never run down so long as he could kill or be near dying things. On Franklin's advice, the Lord Mayor's soldiers were staking out the slaughterhouse and other venues that might attract the creature. Meanwhile, Master Guthrie and all savants of the Willoughby gift were making a sweep of highside to drive out all the rats and the fleas they carried. Even Royland had gotten roped into it.

"Ho teacher! Ahoy there!"

I looked back to see Skyler walking down the cobbled lane.

"Hey, Skyler. What can I do for you?"

He ambled up and crossed his arms, looking my sculptures up and down.

"Nice chickens," he remarked.

217

"They're meant to be owls," I returned.

"Oh. I see it now. Maybe if the eyes were a bit larger... Anyway, I had an idea for tomorrow's class and thought I'd run it up the mast."

"I forgot we were to resume our studies tomorrow," I admitted. "I think I need to put it off for one more day. There's a special meeting of the masters' council, and I have to attend it."

The boy looked surprised.

"What? Are they skipping you right past journeyman?"

"No. I remain a lowly aspirant. I just... It's complicated. Would you go and find Miss Spencer and tell her I need to cancel tomorrow's class?"

"Aye, aye, teacher. I'll let her know. Maybe she'll let us meet anyway. Susie could use the company."

"That would be great. Do you think you can manage without me?"

"Anyone can hold the helm when the sea is calm," said the lad.

"Anyone who can quote Publilius Syrus deserves a chance to try," I returned thoughtfully. "Perhaps I'll stop by after that council meeting."

The boy blushed.

"I don't know about any publicus serious, teach," said Skyler over his shoulder as he ambled off. "It's just something my captain used to say."

I picked up my tools. *Damn it*. They did look like chickens. I decided to leave off for the day as my muse had obviously abandoned me. I returned to house Blue Jay intent on getting in some good moping time before heading off to my first council meeting. Working with the plants was a failed balm for my frazzled nerves. I needed some other distraction. Once again, I considered how best to thank my former master for the unwanted responsibility.

I sat in the parlor reorganizing my bob. There came a knock at the door. I glared over to Lorraine, who was closer, albeit only by a couple steps. She returned my glare and arched her brows, then rolled her eyes and silently arose. She lay down her book and marched to the door unhurriedly to greet the unexpected visitor. From around the corner, I overheard a muttered exchange. When Lorraine returned, she was smiling coyly.

"There's a harker here to see you," she announced.

"You mean a herald?" I inquired.

"No. This one's a harker, I think."

I was up on my feet in a trice and striding toward the door. Lorraine's catty tone aside, I hastened to see what she meant.

"Thanks," I mumbled as I brushed past her.

And there at our doorstep stood a red-haired lad whose face was bespotted by freckles. His curly hair had a windblown look, and he smiled as I approached. Beneath his cloak he sported an azure tabard bearing the symbol of the dove, the livery of Westarbor.

"Drew? Drew Cunningham?"

"Well met, countryman," the lad replied, acknowledging my identification with a nod.

"Be welcome in House Blue Jay! Come in and tell me how fares the barony since I departed from it. I'll hang a kettle and brew some tea. Come to our parlor so we can share news."

"Alright," he agreed, "but I can only stay a short while. I've other duties to discharge."

I grimaced, recalling my own responsibilities, then guided him to a comfortable seat by the fire. The boy had grown quite a bit from the young rapscallion who ran about the Cunningham dairy farm. I'd met his sister at barony Stein. She'd saved us from an awful pickle. I knew from her tale the boy rode a griffin of his own. One named Todd, if I remembered correctly.

As we sat, Lorraine poured us tea. From Drew's pocket, a strange movement was seen and a hairy, pointed snout soon emerged. Out scampered a long white ferret, sniffing all about.

"I hope you don't mind," said the boy sheepishly. "Dillon loves to explore new places, and he's been rather pent up of late."

"Not at all, Drew. He's most welcome as well," I offered.

As Dillon scurried and frolicked around the room, Lorraine's forbearance seemed strained. But her pensive regard was soon replaced by merriment at the playful creature's antics.

"I heard of your adventures at the House of Straw and could scarcely credit how you managed all that. I see by your livery you've been accepted into the baron's service. How's that going?"

"This?" said Drew, plucking at his tabard. "I'm proud to wear it and to bear the bell as well. They're right useful. They let people know not to shoot the messenger. Griffins are still quite new."

"Please tell us of my father and the baron and all the others. What news?"

"Alright. But first, these are for you."

From out of his side-satchel, Drew produced several packages and letters. They were from my father and Megan and some few others. I was ecstatic and could scarcely wait to tear them open, but I bided, first wanting to show hospitality to our guest. He spoke of my home and the doings there. A smiling Lorraine tossed in an occasional question when matters touched on aught we two already knew about. Our chortles rang about House Blue Jay when I recounted tales from the baron's feast and my journey south and all that had transpired.

A somber mood overtook us when we spoke of the plague and other dark concerns we faced. I tried to minimize the danger I suspected from such so as not to worry my loved ones when Drew brought the news home to them. Finally, leaning back, our tales all told, Drew stated he must soon be on his way.

"Lloyd will be inconsolable he missed this," said Lorraine.

"Send him up to the Bates Estate," Drew offered. "Dillon and I will introduce him to Todd. Speaking of which, where has Dillon gotten?"

Drew brought his fingers to the corners of his mouth and let out a sharp whistle. This was answered only by the silence of the house. Drew's brow furrowed, and he whistled again and stood to his feet with concern. Lorraine and I arose as well, looking all about.

When suddenly there came a scrabbling sound and several loud clatterings to boot. They came from the room I shared with Lloyd. And out from its door emerged a hideous sight, a scruffy rodent, black as night It was near as large as a cat. It scurried out, trailing behind it a worm-like tail. On its back was a long white rider whose jaws were clamped to the base of its neck. It was Dillon who rode the beast, his anfractuous form whipping about in its wake. The rat twisted and writhed as he sought to cast him off. Like yin and yang they spun.

I'd never seen it truly happen before; I thought it merely a cliché. Lorraine leaped up onto a chair, screaming in dismay. Drew and I moved to corner the rat. Its movements were erratic and most difficult to predict.

"Why isn't it dead?" asked the boy aloud. "Dillon can kill a rabbit in three seconds flat."

The answer was soon to be revealed, but was not at all to our liking.

A ferret, I'm told, can lock onto its prey with a bite so strong it can never be dislodged. Moreover, hunting ferrets like Dillon were so cunning in targeting a kill that the rodent's swift and certain demise was almost a mercy. Nonetheless, the confused ferret opted to shift his grip. Releasing the rat, the ferret rolled, encountering the wall limbs akimbo. He bounced right back into the fight. He puffed up like a bottle brush to nearly twice his normal size, with his fore-section reared up like a cobra ready to strike.

This failed to intimidate the rat, who backed into the corner and bared wicked, yellow teeth. Before the ferret could strike again, a mop came down from above. It struck with such force that the rat lay broken, leaking black fluid on the boards of the floor. Still it twitched, and the mop came down again and once more. Lorraine stood breathlessly wielding the mop, and the rat carcass lay with its innards oozing out.

"There's no blood," declared Drew, bewildered. "There should be a messy lot of the red stuff."

Dillon moved forward with his tongue lolling out to sniff at the untidy corpse, but Drew hauled him back by his tail.

"Wait here, harker," I said with sudden dread. "The rats hereabouts are infested with fleas. We've discovered these spread the plague."

I dashed to my room, retrieving the barber's tonic.

"Rub this pomade all over yourself. Work it into your hair and Dillon's fur. This should drive the fleas away, but the damage may've already been wrought. I'm told it can take up to a week for the symptoms to show. You wouldn't want to spread the infection all throughout Osten. You must return to the hostelry and sequester yourself there until cleared by our healer. Until then, my friend, you and Dillon are on the no fly list."

"What about my deliveries?" asked the agitated boy. "I've several other missives for your cousin Roy."

"I'll take them to him," I offered. "Just do as I've asked."

"Very well," Drew agreed, handing me his satchel. "Neither snow nor rain nor gloom of night doesn't cover dead rats and pestilence."

After Lloyd had gone, I went to my room. I noticed my flask of sleeping tonic lay on the floor unstoppered. Half of its contents had dribbled out. It must've been knocked down in the scuffle. It was a good thing I had no further need for the stuff. But wait. Nearby it lay a smaller vial affixed to a loop of leather. This one was empty. Had that rat been tampering with my medicine? I returned to the parlor and scraped up the dead rat's remains and bound them tightly in cheesecloth I'd retrieved from my bob. I placed this grizzly lump in a leather bag, the drawstrings of which I pulled tight. Franklin must see this, I thought.

CHAPTER NINE

The Proxy

"The greatest sign of success for a teacher is to be able to say, 'The children are now working as if I did not exist.'"

~ *Maria Montessori* ~

"All will come to order!"

The masters seated before me stilled their conversations and directed their attention to the man who stood at the podium. Unlike the grander assemblies I'd attended, the masters now sat in the audience portion of the hall, rather than the high-backed seats on its raised stage. Only Clement Brownyng stood up at the lectern.

To one side, seated almost in shadow, was the king's emissary. He silently sat observing the proceedings. Cassius McClure was the man's name. He had a parchment at the ready and would occasionally jot down a note.

"Some of you may have noticed a new face among us and wondered," began Master Brownyng.

Several of the seated masters turned to glance back my

way, but most remained attentive to the speaker.

"It would seem that Master Chadwick of Arborvale has at long last deigned to enter the fray, albeit only by proxy. I have here a missive introducing the young man who is to serve in this capacity. I will make it our first order of business to confirm this appointment."

"Objection!" cried Frida Willoughby.

Master Brownyng slowly turned to face her as she stood.

"For what purpose does the gentlewoman rise?" he drawled.

"I move we disqualify this boy from holding a proxy. He lacks the competence and maturity to have a voice in governing the conclave."

I noticed that all the masters seated to my right seemed to agree with her, while those to the left wore sneers and scowls. There seemed to be roughly an equal number of each.

"Denied," said Master Brownyng. "I'll have you know I have personally *voir dired* the lad and find him perfectly capable, You all know the bylaws. Master Chadwick may have taken an unprecedented step in appointing an unproven aspirant, but he is well within his rights to do so. It may even be refreshing to have someone look upon our issues with unbiased eyes. We will proceed directly to a vote."

Passions were running rather high on the right. Amid other murmurings, I heard Jonathan Reinhardt muttering to Frida: 'I'll just bet. Autonomist stooge, more like. They know what's coming next and figure this'll muddy the waters.'

"All those in favor of upholding the proxy application, signify it by a show of hands."

The masters on my left, who I grasped were the autonomists, all raised their hands, as, surprisingly, did several to my right. Among the latter was Mistress Julia. I was later to learn that some hands were more important than others. Just as I was to be entrusted to vote on Master Chadwick's behalf, Mistress Julia held the proxies of the three other Elven masters who lived in Lorédon. That gave her effectively four votes. Similarly, several others on both sides held proxies for absent masters serving at the war front or elsewhere. Needless to say, the motion passed.

"The motion passes," said Master Brownyng, needlessly. "Let us move to the second item on the agenda."

"Good of the order!" proclaimed Jonathan Reinhardt, standing to his feet.

"For what purpose does the gentleman rise?" asked Clement.

"Since we're on the topic of proxy applications," he said, "why isn't Frida's request to reinstate her sister's proxy on the agenda? Surely you'll agree that Gretta Brubaker is alive and thus deserves a voice in the urgent matters before us."

The headmaster raised his voice above the muttering that followed.

"This has already been explained to the good lady. Proxies are for members who are absent from the conclave. Gretta Brubaker is not, in fact, absent. Nor has she yet been deemed incompetent to serve. We remain hopeful for her recovery. Failing that, Mistress Frida will need to formally petition the council to act as her sister's guardian, a process that will not be resolved here today."

"As I was saying," he continued, "we will next have Master Guthrie's report on his progress in ridding us of our rat problem. Master Guthrie will be given the speaker's staff, and we shall attend him while he reports on this topic."

Zaid Guthrie accepted the staff from the chief seneschal and ascended to the podium.

"It progresses," he began. "With the help of the entomancers and others, I think we've swept all the infected bugs from the citizens of highside and the trade district. We've rounded up hundreds of rats and humanely put them out of *our* misery. Some of the rats have proven strangely resistant to my charms, but I'm told we're to discuss that during the third topic on the agenda. We're currently completing a sweep of lakeside. Tomorrow we begin with lowside. I suspect this might require several days as it's the biggest sore spot."

"Thank you, Master Guthrie. Unless there are any

questions, you may return to your seat."

"I have one," shouted Dorothy Stanwix.

Dorothy Stanwix was a large woman in charge of Conclave's fire brigade. I was told that as a water mage, she was quite proficient at quelling an errant blaze.

"The masters recognize Mistress Stanwix."

"There's been some talk of burning down some areas where the infection is the worst. Any truth to that?"

"We won't know until we address the problem," Zaid returned. "I wouldn't rule it out as a possibility. You should probably stand by, and we'll let you know before commencing with any such."

There were no more questions for Master Guthrie. Master Brownyng gave us a brief recess to use the necessarium or otherwise refresh ourselves. Some masters tried to catch my eye or corner me during this break, but I shunned their company like a Willoughby, caught up in my own thoughts. Third up was to be Franklin.

When we reconvened, Franklin was seated on the front bench directly before the lectern. A table had been brought in and rested in front of him.

He had the entire bench to himself. The masters sat to either side or several benches back from him. He looked ill-rested. His hair was disheveled, and he stared about wild-eyed. From the set of his shoulders, I could tell this wasn't the audience before the masters he'd craved.

"We will begin with the seneschal's report," the headmaster announced, with a look of disdain as he gripped the sides of the podium.

At this, Brayden Sheppard stepped up to the platform bearing the speaker's staff. He cleared his throat and looked sternly about before beginning in his deep, silky voice. Once again, I was struck by the fine acoustics of the chamber. For despite his gentle tones, we could hear each word with a clarity that defied distance, almost as if the man were whispering directly into our ears.

"Upon receiving word of the monster's escape, I set my

trackers the task of locating and detaining it. We circled the academy until we found evidence of the creature's passing. As some of you may be aware, the creature carries itself upon the hind legs of a cow. We followed its trail to the eastern orchards, whereupon it wound about. Most cunningly it made use of cover and confused its tracks, circling back many times.

"I became convinced this was no mere animal. Thankfully, some of us are blessed by our gift with keen senses and could track it by its scent. It slipped from the orchard into lowside. Lumbering through the back alleys, it made its way north. Skirting the north gate, the creature took itself instead to a culvert where we presume it hid until the fall of night. Several animals were found butchered nearby. But apart from the cuts and piercings that dispatched them, their carcasses were left untouched.

"The city's walls are not so high and are more for show than for true fortification. We followed the vile beast's trail to where one of these had been breached and out into the countryside. A nearby shepherd reported seeing a large monstrous form running hard to the north. From the spacing of its hoofprints, the creature must have been moving faster than e'en a horse can gallop.

"It was then we encountered the duke's men, intent on enforcing the quarantine. We informed them of the grim horror we'd unleashed and begged permission to follow it and see to its ending. But their orders were clear, and we stood in violation of their jurisdiction. The knights of Duke Deerfield have now taken up the pursuit. We wished them good hunting and returned here."

Master Sheppard leaned the speaker's staff on the lectern and quietly stepped down to rejoin the other masters. The headmaster resumed his place, rubbing at his chin and staring out into the silent chamber.

"Franklin Stein," he said, "how do you answer the charge of practicing necromancy outside the confines of the conclave's dictates?"

Franklin looked outraged, then slumped in resignation.

"I am not guilty of such," he pleaded. "I can't explain Adam's bizarre behavior. He has no volition of his own, nor did I imbue him with such. I can only assume he was somehow overtaken by the will of another."

"And yet you are the only necromancer here," said Clement. "Moreover, by your own word, your creature craves death. And his escape coincided with the murder of Luther Prowd. Are we to believe there were two murderers stalking the academy's halls that afternoon? Occam's Razor would suggest your creature and the murderer were one and the same."

Franklin sat bolt upright.

"Also, there is this."

The headmaster produced from behind the lectern the leather bag I'd given him earlier. He tossed it down to flop on the table before which Franklin sat.

"Yesterday, a rat was discovered in one of the aspirant dwellings, your own house to be exact. It had no blood and stank of the grave, yet it put up quite a fight ere it was laid low. What say you to that?"

Franklin stared at the bag with his expression gone slack for a time before he answered. Had my own evidence condemned my friend?

"I can confirm by my gift that this creature was raised up and hard used by necromancy, but such was not of my doing."

Master Brownyng's gaze swept up, and he scanned the other masters in the hall.

"You will recall Master Guthrie's mention of unnatural rats he encountered while purging the town of pests. I think there are more of these spreading the sickness. Franklin cannot be commanding them as he was sequestered in a cell while this was occurring. Furthermore, I had the Wagge boy present when Aspirant Stein was first questioned on the matter. That one is possessed of a truth-sense, and he vouched for this man. Unless he is lying as well, and Occam's Razor aside, it does indeed appear we have another necromancer mucking about in Conclave."

I sat transfixed, as round-eyed as all the other masters at Clements revelations.

"It is my recommendation that we free this young man and task him with assisting us in rounding up the undead rats. It may actually be fortunate we have a necromancer of our own. I suggest we dispense with debate and maneuverings and call it to an immediate vote... For what reason does the gentleman rise?"

Atticus Skinner stood among the frowns of his fellows.

"I believe a committee should be assigned to investigate this matter more thoroughly. I do so move."

"A motion has been made. Will any second it?"

The other masters sat in stony silence.

"Then we shall proceed to the vote. All those in favor of absolving Franklin Stein, signify by raising your hand."

All but Atticus did so. I was overjoyed to see justice done for Franklin. My housemate had been truly brave to admit the rat was undead with all the other evidence piling up against him. And the truth had set him free. Belatedly, I realized that I too could now cast a ballot. I hastily lifted my hand to join those of the others.

"The ayes have it."

As Franklin was led out of the hall, the agenda descended into the minutia of managing matters of the conclave. It put me in mind of the brief time I had served on Baron Westarbor's council of war. The masters remained fractious and disagreed on many things, but would eventually move on to the next matter.

Simon Strangelove had petitioned for remuneration for his ointment. His entire supply had been seized to be used by mages repelling the vermin from lowside. This request was unanimously denied. The barber was very nearly charged with price-gouging. His most recent fee of two groats for a haircut and leeching was seen as highway robbery in this time of emergency. He should be thankful he was even permitted to keep his blood money.

***

Smoke was rising over lowside. Most of the seneschals were seeing to crowd control. The citizens of lowside were understandably concerned for their homes as large bonfires were lit in the streets. As Zaid Guthrie coaxed out the living rats, many of which were covered in buboes and lesions, the mages dispatched them and burned the carcasses. The entomancers made certain the infected fleas also found their way into the fire pits.

Of course, I couldn't see any of this from up here on the overlook. But I had overheard the plans and had a very healthy imagination. Word had come that Franklin was moving in their wake, dominating the dead rats and marching them one by one into the flames. These had all gone quiescent several hours ago and showed no further signs of unlife.

Most of the masters not engaged in the purge were at the docks where a small contingent of seneschals was seeing to Luther Prowd's remains. I hadn't known Luther all that well (at least not as Lucas). And from what I recalled of him as Abigale, I hadn't liked the man. So I looked out over the town and prayed it would soon return to normalcy and that all would be safe and secure once more.

Tomorrow there would be a special meeting of the mage's council. I suspected this would launch the election of a new headmaster. Clement Brownyng was well-positioned for the post. He'd seemed fair-minded in his dealings during his interim appointment, but it was a sure bet the loyalists would select someone to oppose him. If Gretta's proxy were reinstated, the loyalists would own fourteen votes to the autonomist's thirteen.

And then there was me. I could either decide the matter in the loyalists' favor or split the vote. In the latter case, I assumed Master Brownyng would continue on as headmaster. It was no wonder the loyalists had opposed Master Chadwick's proxy application.

I could scarcely think on the matter anymore. My thoughts kept drifting in circles when I did. No one could even explain to me the essential difference between the two factions. Each time I asked, I was answered either by stale rhetoric or a list of grudges that one faction had against the other. It seemed they would govern much the same, but had become invested and entrenched in their labels. It seemed a Bigendian dispute. Each group was certain that ruination would follow if the other rose to power.

More important to me was the prospect that Atticus Skinner had revived the practice of contacting that demon thing in the standing stones. Terwilliger had spoken like it was something that threatened even the woodland fey. During Abigale's encounter in my dream, Orenob had called Denis Feininger his 'wight,' and Abigale had the distinct impression this was a fey creature that could inhabit another. If this were also the case with Atticus, perhaps I could free the man with 'cogitationes liberare.' But I needed to be certain. The man could simply be a traitor or could have just been doing some other harmless, smelly thing atop the hill that night.

I needed help.

I knew who I needed. He was busy just now, but tomorrow I would swallow my pride and seek his aid.

***

"All will come to order!"

The masters quieted. There was a tension, a closeness in the air which filled the suddenly still chamber.

"Today we shall consider the matter of succession for the post of headmaster," Clement Brownyng announced.

I could see it on all their faces. It was a call to arms.

"As is our custom, I have drawn a circle up here on the platform. Any who would seek the office may step up and toss his hat into the ring. There will follow eight days of debate during which time each candidate will be afforded an hour each day to present his case before the council. The matter will proceed to a vote on the twentieth day of March."

"I shall begin," he added, removing his hat and dropping it onto the floor.

Not an autonomist stirred. From among the loyalists, a single figure arose. It was Alonso Balderas, Ariadna's dad. I'd met him once when he was dropping off his daughter at the créche. He and his wife, Carmen, had come here from Freemark. I understood him to be a geomancer of some sort who had sculpted the fountain at the end of Aspie Rowe.

He paced over to the steps leading up to the stage and glared defiantly at Master Brownyng. The masters sat silent as he ascended to the platform and slowly removed his hat. Both groups had obviously gone through their preliminary processes and now stood ready to get behind their respective champions. Alonso extended forth his arm and with much deliberation dropped his hat to rest directly atop that of his opponent.

Unperturbed by this aggressive display, Clement turned to the council and asked: "Is there any other who seeks consideration?"

In silence, the wizards sat, presenting a distinctly disunited front.

"Point of order," came a voice from the side of the hall. It was Cassius McClure, the king's emissary, sitting all but forgotten on the side of the loyalists.

Clement arched his brows and regarded the man.

"All will heed the king's representative," he said with a servile bow.

"I have been in contact with his majesty since the prior meeting of this council."

Reviewing his notes, he continued.

"In the matter of Margaretta Brubaker, his majesty is of the opinion that she is indeed *non compos mentis* and should therefore have her proxy reinstated to her closest known relative, Frida Willoughby. The crown asks that this matter be taken to an immediate vote that her wishes may receive due consideration in the weighty issues facing us."

It was a severe but not wholly unexpected blow to the autonomists. While their adversaries all but crowed in delight, they sat scowling and considering their next move. When the vote was taken, all turned to await my choice. Had I not been granted a proxy, ties would be decided by the headmaster *pro tem*. Unfortunately for him, I was of the opinion that Mistress Gretta deserved to be represented and not to have her vote suppressed merely for political expediency.

I made quite a few friends with that one vote, but just as

many enemies. The king's emissary stared over at me assessingly, but then returned his attention to the papers he was shuffling before him when I met his eyes. Before we could return to regular business, there came a commotion from the rear of the hall. The herald at the door hastily bellowed an announcement even as two soldiers marched up the center aisle. Between them was a man who was sopping wet whom I vaguely recognized as another of conclave's seneschals.

"Journeyman Arnold Clark bears urgent tidings!" sang the herald.

"What is it, man?" shouted Master Brownyng. "Report!"

"We were attacked," exclaimed the man, gripping his right shoulder with his left hand. "All who set out on Luther Prowd's funeral barge are dead or worse!"

The announcement set off a blaze of exclamations and oaths among the masters, some of whom rose to their feet with expressions of incredulity.

"Order! Let the man speak," shouted Master Brownyng above the ruckus.

"Slow down, Arnold," he then cajoled, "Give us the entire story. Leave nothing out. And what on earth do you mean by worse?"

The soldier sucked in a deep breath, but this did little to still the panic evident in his haunted eyes. Then he began anew in crisp, even tones.

"We weighed anchor at dawn to bear the former headmaster's remains to his family crypt across the lake. The lake was tranquil, and the sky was clear. When we arrived, the pall bearers departed with their sorry load. Nor had they only just opened the crypt when emerged from it a group of knights wearing the livery of Duke Deerfield. The knights were bloodied and walked with a shambling gait. They fell upon the pall bearers with sword and mace and slew them to a man.

"Why? I bethought me. We had violated no laws and posed no threat. But these were not the duke's men, or were no longer so. For as they turned to board our barge, we spied the deathly pallor of their slack faces, emotionless from the slaughter they'd wrought. And behind them emerged as foul a demon as ever I saw. It stood ten feet tall if it was an inch on the hairy hindquarters of a bull. With the head of a pig and with blades in place of its hands, it stared at me with demented glee as its minions hacked my shipmates to bits.

"I was back at the helm. Twas only this that saved me, for there was no combating the creatures. Some tried, but they seemed oblivious to wounds that would lay low e'en an ox. Worse still, the pall bearers began to rise and join this awful host. Some of them rose to shamble forth e'en despite the spilling of their entrails upon the ground. I feared the same for my shipmates. Although none had yet arisen, I suspect the baleful monster had that power.

"Now I am no coward, but nor do I cast away my life needlessly when fighting would serve no purpose. I threw myself over the railing and swam for Conclave. Several of the creatures dove after. One even caught me by my shoulder and nearly dragged me down, but I managed to thrust him away. The monstrous knights in their armor sank, and I swiftly outdistanced the others."

"Do you mean to say that you swam all the way across the lake?" asked Clement in astonishment.

"Arnold is of my kind," said Brayden Sheppard with pride evident in his eyes despite the grim set of his jaw. "No doubt, he undertook some aquatic adaptations during his journey here."

"Just so, master," confirmed Journeyman Clark. "Though my totem is a cat, my training in mastering other forms served me well this day."

"These creatures have spilled our blood," Master Sheppard continued. "I beg the council's leave to organize a pursuit force at once to put an end to this threat."

He didn't raise his voice, but the promise of retribution was plainly written on his face for anyone with eyes to see.

"I think no vote is needed to grant you such leave," Master Browning growled. "Select your men and be about the gruesome business. And damned be any man or woman who dissents."

Whatever other business remained on the docket was swiftly set aside. The meeting broke up as Master Sheppard, our chief seneschal, hand-picked a group of masters to accompany the soldiers to the site of the attack. I was surprised that Mistress Julia was to be among them. The dainty elf hadn't struck me as a warrior. I think there was some plan for her to manage the winds to sail there faster. Nor, I suppose, would it hurt to have some aerial reconnaissance.

At a loss for what else to do, I considered dropping in at the créche to see how Skyler and the others were getting on. I had something else on my mind, but I wasn't quite ready to face that yet. No. Best to check in on the children first.

***

I found the créche's dining hall empty, but through its window I espied the children playing out in the yard. Well, when the cat's away, the mice can neglect their schoolwork, I suppose. As I stepped out into the yard, however, I found Miss Spencer reading aloud to them. It wasn't a story. Instead, it was a familiar set of aphorisms by a fellow I'd recently mentioned.

"Here's another good one," she exclaimed. "A rolling stone gathers no moss. I've heard it tossed about before, but I never knew it was this fellow who said it first. And to think he was a slave at the time."

"Actually," said I, "Publilius was manumitted by his master for his wit and talent. He was a free man by the time he wrote all that."

"Oh. There you are, Lucas. It's about time you got here. Now you can take over watching this sorry lot while I put my feet up for a bit."

Skyler and most of the girls were playing at the Maypole. Susie was off by herself with a basket plucking tulips. I suspected she might have invisible company, for I caught an occasional glimmer from my mage sight near her. Hold on. Terwilliger had said he'd be gone for days. Had he returned from his mission so soon?

"I suppose I can oversee the remainder of the class, but please stay nearby. There are terrible things happening in Conclave, and the masters may need me to attend them again

235

soon. I'll dismiss everyone if I'm summoned, but Susie will require supervision."

"Well aren't you the important one these days? I only let them meet today because Skyler begged me to read him this book. Something about things his old captain used to say. You've really got *that* one fired up to learn things."

"We try."

I had accepted the book from Miss Spencer before she scuttled off. Skyler sidled up to me, and we watched her depart.

"I think she liked it," he remarked. "I went looking for it after our talk the other day. Edgar helped me to find it. I used to think book learning was all hoi polloi, but there's some sound wisdom in this one."

"I think you mean 'hoity-toity,'" I returned. "'Hoi polloi' is Greek for 'the many' meaning 'of the common folk.'"

"See," said Skyler. "There you *go* again. How do you *know* all that?"

"I read a lot," I replied.

"Well," said the lad, "I mayn't read very well now, but I intend doing so a lot too one day. In the meantime, I do know about a few things. Our friend Publilius says, 'It is better to learn late than never' and also 'Practice is the best of all instructors.' Come see what we're working on."

I put up no resistance as he tugged me along.

Over at the maypole, the girls were winding or braiding some heavy twine into a rope. Skyler informed me they'd spent all morning twisting the kite strings into twine and were now counter-turning it to form a heavier length of rope. I asked what this had to do with learning their letters.

"You'll see, teacher," he said with the mysterious grin that I thought I owned the patent on.

I may have mentioned that patience was never my strong suit.

"Stand back, girls," I directed, beckoning to them.

Daisy, Cassie, Ari and Sholeena laid down the ends of the twine they'd been turning and stepped over to where Skyler and I stood.

I touched my magic center and whispered, 'spacium gyrabit.' Their respective lengths of twine began to whirl and... well... twine about one another. Their other ends had been affixed to the maypole's top. Within seconds, a twenty-foot length of rope was thus formed. I twisted it tighter still, gave it a final yank, then left it to dangle freely from the pole, its end nearly scraping the ground.

Smiling, Skyler shinnied up the maypole with the grace of a squirrel. Having ascended to the crow's nest of his ship to act as lookout on more than one occasion, he claimed our 'stubby little stick' was no challenge compared to the galleon's swaying main mast. When he slid back down, the rope lay in a tangled heap at its base.

"Alright now girls, it's time to spell," Skyler declared, "Sholeena and Daisy will turn it first and I shall have the first go at it."

The two took up the ends of the rope and separated until it was almost taut between them. Then, making large circles with their arms, they whirled it about. The rope would arc high, then come down to slap lightly upon the ground.

There was a rhythmic sound akin to that of a metronome. Slap... slap... slap.

Bobbing his head to the rhythm of the rope, Skyler soon launched himself into the space within its turning, ducking under the rope when it achieved its apex and hopping over it at its nadir.

"Sky-ler Hen-drix is my name" Slap... slap... slap.

"S K Y - L E R - H E N - D R I - and X! Slap... slap... slap.

When he leapt clear, Cassandra and Ariadna took their turns, eventually getting it right after several attempts each.

"That's quite clever, Skyler," I praised. "What made you think of it?"

"I took a page from your book, teach," he returned with a devilish grin. "On our first day you told us, 'Reading can be fun as well as informative,' or some such thing."

There was a great deal of laughter when Sholeena ran out of breath trying to spell, 'Blorlafargalish'. She also had a penchant for jumping too high and getting roped on the side of her head. Before she could get too frustrated, Skyler and I gave her a pass for the good effort.

Susie had come over and taken her turn, but then had returned to her flower gathering. I approached her while the others were still at their game and asked, "Is our friend, mister 'T', visiting today?"

"No aspirant, he hasn't been whispering to me."

"What are you doing?"

"Collecting flowers," she said. "They want to open. I'm going to give them to Miss Spencer for her room."

Stretching out her hand, she touched a tulip bud, and before my eyes it enlarged and spread its petals open to form a cup. There was a momentary glimmer from my mage sight. Looking deeper, I had the impression of a blotch of green. It was small but fraught with possibility and potential. When Susie touched the next bud, the patch of green sprouted a thin vine-like tendril which traversed her arm to her fingertip. The masters must be informed of this, I thought with wonder.

***

Would Master Brownyng be in his office? Surely, the discovery of a new mage was in the headmaster's purview. I entered his foyer only to find it empty. Susie Feininger's gift was exactly like mine, or at least like mine had first begun. What could it mean? After losing track of Abigale, did Denis merely start anew? Was *Susie* the verdant child of prophecy?

I stumbled back out into the hallway. Mistress Meredith was heading toward me. As she was the matron overseeing the créche, perhaps she was the one I should inform. But I hesitated.

"Aspirant Harper," she crooned as she drew near. "If you're looking for Clement, he's fretting in the dovecote awaiting word from the pursuit squad."

"Thank you, matron."

"A moment, aspirant."

"Yes?"

"With all the grim goings-on, we haven't had a proper chance to talk of late. Elissa keeps me well informed on matters of the créche, of course. But I wish to discuss your recent role as Elizar's proxy. Are you having any trouble following what's going on at council?"

"I think I'm keeping up with the general ebb and flow."

"Ebb and flow," she tittered. "What a delightful way of phrasing it. And you a proxy for a water mage. Quite witty."

Was she trying to flatter me? She was all but batting her eyelashes, and her smile had too many teeth to be natural.

"Who, by the way, do you support for headmaster?" she asked as if it were an afterthought rather than the main course.

"I haven't decided. I thought I'd listen to the debates."

"Gunther is certain you foolishly favor Balderas, the way you tossed the loyalists an extra vote on the matter. I stuck up for you, though. I told him you were merely naïve."

Alright. She could be catty as well as coquettish.

"The matron is entitled to her opinion, but if you'll recall, it was the king's representative who broached the issue. I only voted for what I saw as the right of the matter."

"As I said, naïve. But you have a chance to make it right. Consider well your position, young man. Choose wisely and rewards will follow. Other choices might lead to consequences you'll regret."

And there they were. The carrot and the stick. I'd been waiting for someone to come courting my swing vote. Amid her vague generalities and mood swings, I sensed a calculating mind. I'd been given to understand I had a very... expressive face. I think the matron was just testing the waters to see under what form of persuasion I might most easily buckle. As these and other mixed up metaphors swirled about my skull, I almost forgot to make a polite response.

"I shall, matron. I thank you for your candor. I will give your words the consideration they are due."

I considered seeking out Master Brownyng at the dovecote, but decided I had more urgent matters to attend. Susie's status could simmer and marinate for a while. Though I couldn't directly tell anyone about the treachery of Dennis Feininger at the standing stones, I needed to figure it out. It felt personal to me. I could put it off no longer. I headed for Roy's cell in the basement.

On arriving, I found the clicking had ceased. Peeking into her room across the way, I saw the old woman asleep on her cot, and Mistress Frida was nowhere in sight. I knocked on the door to Royland's cell. He should be in there, for there was no work at the foundry today. I knocked again, more urgently this time. Impatient, I turned the handle, finding the door unsecured. I swung it open and peered within. My cousin lay still upon his mattress. His mouth hung open, but no snoring could I discern. Was he dead? I moved quickly to his side and shook him by his shoulder to rouse him.

"Roy? Roy, are you alright?"

His eyes snapped open, and he stared at me in sudden fright. Then ire painted his face and his lips moved soundlessly as he sat up. Glancing to one side in annoyance, he reached down, snatched up his pillow, and hurled it into the room's far corner.

".... should know better than to come waltzing into a man's room without so much as a 'by your leave!'"

"I was frightened, Roy. You weren't answering and nor were you snoring."

He looked up at me and blinked. Then he stretched and yawned. He looked at me again with annoyance. I don't think my explanation had warmed him to my presence.

"Well, I've solved that problem now. My pillowcase muffles all sound near to it. What brought you here in the first place?"

"Some letters arrived for you from home," I replied, digging them out from my bob. "Why are you asleep in the middle of the day, anyway?"

"So would you be if you'd been up half the night purging rats and fleas in lowside. I doubt I'll ever get the stink of burning rats out of my clothing - or my memory. Well, you've made your deliveries. These came by griffin, I take it. Where's the harker?"

"He's indisposed and sequestered up at Master Martin's estate."

"Thank you for bringing them safely here," Roy said quietly, setting them on the floor beside his cot. "I'm surprised you didn't send another. I thought you were done with me when last we spoke."

"I need your help," I admitted.

My cousin once again tightened his lips, and his eyes narrowed.

"Go on," he said, his tone betraying no hint of encouragement.

"You have my permission," I said.

"Your permission?"

"Do you recall when I once told you to: 'never invade my mind again without my express permission?'"

"I do," he replied, "you told me I was weird."

"I believe I actually said '*It's* too weird,' but setting that aside for the moment, you now have my permission."

"To what end would you have me do this?"

I took in a deep breath and stared directly into my cousin's distrustful brown eyes. I had no practiced answer with which to mollify his disaffectation. Royland's gaze could pierce through verbal pretenses and perceive a person's true heart.

"You claim I don't love you and that I am only kind to bolster my own self-image. I am appalled and dreadfully sorry if I ever gave you cause to feel that way. Since we were very young, you have been a part of my life, and despite whatever you may think, I have always valued your friendship and your company.

"In these past several months when we have been estranged, I have missed you. You were always the one who knew how I felt and could offer advice or console me as no other could. I don't know why you have turned from me, but I beg you to reconsider. We were always stronger together, as when we fought the goblins at the gate.

"Things are happening at the conclave, Roy, terrible things. Of some you are aware, but there are other plots in motion. These you will ken if you do as I ask and join minds with me again. You would scarcely believe it otherwise. I know you are more than capable of standing on your own. You are intelligent, kind, and I have always envied the ease with which you readily excel at any endeavor you attempt. You have always aided me when I needed it. Please help me now, cousin, in my struggle against forces seeking to harm us all."

I knew it was enough when he wet his lips and nodded. "Sit then," was all he said.

Side by side on my cousin's cot we sat. I quivered with unease when Royland's hand sought my forehead.

"Miscere cogitata," he intoned.

Just as on the day of our first, desperate joining, I detected his presence in the corridors of my mind. Unlike on that day and despite the tumultuous jumbling of our thoughts, I felt a modicum of control. By this time, my mind had been so often violated by Abigale's practiced touch, her dreams, and even the compulsion of the fey, that I knew it was possible to protect some of my thoughts. Nonetheless, I allowed the doors of my mind to fly open wide that Roy might prowl freely through even my most private thoughts, hopes, and memories. I let him plainly see my affection for him was genuine and sensed in turn that he already knew it.

I guided him gently to the place in my mind where my dreams of Abigale rested. Then more specifically to the night of her confrontation with Denis Feininger and the demon he served. The scene replayed in our conjoined minds, and I winced with him to hear of the plight of his grandparents from long ago. I experienced his fright when the boy named Robert bravely stepped into the fray. Though we knew the child would survive, it was still hard to watch our father threatened so. I felt Roy's anger, and he felt my joy that another now knew of Denis' misdeeds. The two entwined until we arose from the scene to fly across our mindscape in a joyous anger the like of which only the angels knew.

We sensed Roy beginning to withdraw, but we held him firmly in the link. For in the corridors of Royland's mind, one door remained stubbornly closed. We circled it, both wanting and dreading to see what lay inside. Curiosity and shame won out. We stood before that dread portal and gently pried it open. In a rush poured out a river of emotion, as though a dam had burst at last. It was a river of guilty feelings and sly glances that guarded a truth one of us wished forever obscured.

"It was here we first saw her," we announced joyously in our inner voice.

"We were attending the spring flower festival in Westarbor, our family and I. She was crowned, *Reyna de las Flores*, with a garland of daisies. *We* were moping in the back with our nose in a book. *She* was being paraded down the lane atop a decorated wagon. When she passed us by, we looked up and her eyes touched ours. An echoing resonance ensued. As always when my eyes beheld those of another, I felt what she felt, but to my wonder and hers alike, the reverse was also true. I felt what she felt I felt and on and on it went.

"In that moment, besides merely being 'queen of the flowers,' she became the queen of my heart. Finally, we thought. Here is another who knows the burden of being made to feel as others do. I will love her forever and one day we shall be as one. And she felt exactly the same, or so I mistakenly thought. Peeling back Megan's feelings from my own was difficult as the two were so entwined. When we'd succeeded, we found kindness, friendship, and sympathy. But the only love was my own reflected back at me.

"We were crushed by the sudden loss. The girl felt not the same kinship and ardor. And her wagon rolled on. And the moment passed. For years we lived on, I on my farm, and she in her castle. I always hoped that one day my feelings for her would be returned, but from within her heart and not as a mere reflection. Then came the day I saw you in the stocks... "

We ambled down to another door to witness the event.

Within Lucas stooped, shirtless and bound. We were

outraged by the mistreatment of our cousin and confused that he seemed to be laughing inside. Whatever did he find so amusing? Then she appeared betwixt two other maids, more lovely to my eye than ever before. She tossed a bloom to lie at Lucas' feet. And as she smiled and turned, her eyes met mine, oh so brief. But in that single glance at last I saw the spark for which I'd longed.

I have ever since suffered in silence. I see it in her, and I see it in you. You are kind to one another. Your acquaintance slowly grew and blossomed into a friendship. Not a sudden and explosive passion, but rather a mutual kinship with always a 'perhaps.' Perhaps one day... When I look into Megan's eyes, I too see friendship, but there is no 'perhaps.' I envy your 'perhaps,' I've known other women since and basked in their affection. But I found physical love a poor substitute for the oneness I crave. I've since eschewed it and buried my feelings deep within. I've channeled my energies to more productive pursuits. And now you've come and dug it all up once again.

"Enough."

I was sitting beside my cousin on his cot. He was staring blankly at the far wall.

"Now you know," he whispered.

I said nothing. I knew Roy would appreciate that. I waited in silence until, after a time, he spoke again.

"I will help," he said.

"If it's any consolation," I remarked, "as a noble, Megan is beyond *my* aspirations. She'll likely be drawn into a marriage of convenience to secure an alliance between the Arensons and some other noble line. Even now, she's being courted by the heir of Downham."

"You can't let *that* happen, Lucas," Roy said sternly. "They're monsters. And your 'perhaps' has grown too strong. It's nearly a 'certainly' by now, I should think."

"Fear not," I returned. "According to her missive, Megan finds Eric Downham to be 'a very lovely person.' But she smudged the 'l' in lovely."

My cousin grinned. From this, I knew he had perused the

Arenson's secret code when he'd been traipsing about in my mind.

"Who will you support for headmaster?" he asked.

"Are you familiar with ternary logic?" I asked in turn, never doubting his answer.

"Of course," Roy replied. "I had mastered the trivium before I was six."

"Then you know it makes no difference. I'm damned if I do and damned if I don't, but maybe not damned if I do neither."

"Ah. I suppose this has aught to do with your monster on the hill -- *aaah!*"

Roy winced and brought both hands to his temples.

"Yep," I put in. "We can't talk about it. *Annoying*, isn't it? It helps if you lie about it."

"Lie?"

"So," said I, "there's no monster on the hill. He's certainly *not* been consorting with mages at the conclave, *none* of whom were my grandfather."

"Ah." returned Roy, nodding. "And do you think none of his or her minions are unseelie wights which would, in no event, ever possess any of our mages?"

"Definitely not. We can most certainly trust everyone here at the conclave."

"I sense you have a plan."

"I do. I swear on my mother's grave to never expose the culprit and will *definitely* keep his secret from all the other masters!"

***

My knowledge of Roy's unrequited love for Megan sat between us like an unwanted dinner guest. But the boil had been lanced. It was still tender if you rubbed at it, but I sensed it would heal nicely given time. I told Roy there would be one more person joining our conspiracy. I nipped down the hall to retrieve Franklin. The man was tidying up his laboratory and taking stock of all that was broken or missing. I bade him come to Royland's room, for my cousin had some questions for him. Soon we three sat hatching our plans.

"You claim the helmets were to animate the beast," said Roy, "but could a necromancer do so without them? Could *you?*"

"Most definitely," said Franklin. "Adam was assembled for just such control."

Roy rubbed at his chin and directed his next remarks also to Franklin.

"Lucas and I encountered a man in a town not a half days trek to the north. He was an undisclosed mage fleeing the king's justice and that of our Lord Westarbor. We thought him dead, having witnessed him breaking his neck. But as the life ebbed from him, a dog who also lay dead nearby rose to its feet and dashed out the door. Now I ask you, is it possible for a necromancer to survive his own demise?"

I hadn't thought of Truman Huber in months. It struck me as awful that such horrific happenings could be set aside so easily. My cousin was suggesting that Truman was the other necromancer, the one who'd released the rats. It made sense. The man seemed to have a grievance against the Harpers. He'd attacked my father once with a zombie thrall. When we encountered him in Buntingworth Village, he tried to poison me. I eagerly awaited Franklin's response.

"There are... stories," Franklin whispered, turning his head aside. "But possessing the dead requires energy, and most bodies would run down after a few days. Lacking a living body, one would have to kill almost constantly to renew one's life force."

"What if one had access to an area where a plague was running rampant?" Roy pressed.

"It's possible *that* could sustain one who has passed beyond death's veil. More so, if he's taken Adam. What have I done?" sobbed Franklin. "If such a fiend possessed my Adam, I... The fluids I used were of my own invention. They preserve the corpse and keep it supple even while collecting necromantic energy from deaths nearby. He would need only recline near to a slaughterhouse to recharge his magic center."

"Don't fret so, Franklin," I said. "You couldn't have known. The conclave is wise to him now. I wouldn't want to be Truman Huber when the seneschals catch up to him. I don't care how big he is. I'll bet Brayden Sheppard in his gorilla form will prove more than his match."

This reminded me that it was time to check up on the status of the hunt. All masters (and upstart aspirants with proxies) were to remain available in case any votes needed to be taken upon their return. I left Roy and Franklin deliberating our various challenges and returned above.

"There you are, aspirant," scolded the herald. "The masters have been called back to order. Word arrived not twenty minutes ago that the others are returning. Best you get inside."

He was a venerable gentleman with a distinguished white mustache upturned at its ends. These practically quivered with impatience as he glared at me and indicated the yawning double doors. I couldn't recall the man's name.

"Thank you, goodman."

Once inside, I walked down to my accustomed seat to the rear of the masters and ignored several of them on both sides who beckoned me to move nearer. Master Brownyng was up behind the podium pacing back and forth, oblivious to the babble that echoed all around. A few minutes later, he moved to the lectern and signaled for silence.

"I suppose we've enough present to outline the essential facts while we wait," he announced. Not quite a half hour ago, the pursuit squad sent the following message by pigeon, which I shall read to you aloud."

"All peaceful at crypt. Subject not acquired. Returning with remains."

"I take this to mean that the malefactors were not present when our force arrived. Master Sheppard has doubtless dispatched trackers. But because he indicates the force is returning, I see little hope for a swift resolution of this fiasco. We shall have his full report anon."

Anon turned out to be twenty-five uncomfortable minutes wherein I was accosted by half the masters present in ones and twos. As with Mistress Meredith, these were sounding me out about my vote for headmaster thinly veiled by offers of assistance in various forms. I stuck to my non-committal responses and insisted I wanted to first hear the debates before making any firm decision. I had a heart-stopping moment when Atticus Skinner approached. I tried to keep my face neutral and think pleasant thoughts as he made his offer, hinting he might need a new journeyman. I was certain he sensed something was off about my nervous responses, but I hoped he would attribute it to the general climate of panic over our recently fallen brethren.

When Brayden Sheppard and the other masters arrived, all took their seats and became attentive at once. Master Sheppard was given the speaker's staff, and the others rejoined their colleagues while he ascended to the stage.

"We set out across the lake in a light single-masted trawler we commandeered from the fishing fleet, our own vessel being unavailable. Mistress Julia put the winds in our favor, and we soon arrived at Quiet Repose only to find the site abandoned. Our barge lay sunken and disabled, and there was no sign of the enemy. The dead lay strewn about, but none of them showed any inclination to rise up and threaten us.

"The monstrous beast known as Adam had fled. His tracks led south. We've scouts in pursuit with instructions to turn back before the fall of night. Based on the spacing of its tracks, the beast was running at a pretty good clip, and we'll likely never catch him up. The dukes men and the lord mayor are being informed even as we speak."

He paused and shook his head sadly before resuming his report. The seneschal looked truly disheartened.

"On entering the crypt, we found Luther's remains. His head and forearms were missing. Resting atop them was the head of a pig."

No voting was required. Instead, the assembly was dismissed. The masters separated into small groups, muttering to one another, and I wandered off in a daze. I'd have to ask Franklin about it, but I had a fairly strong notion of what had happened to Luther Prowd's head.

CHAPTER TEN

The Exorcist

"Only a fool fights in a burning house!"

~ Kang, son of K'naiah ~

Wrap me in waxed paper and call me taffy. Between my classes with the children, and the many meetings of the masters, my housemates, and my conspiracy circle, I was being pulled every which direction. Despite the dreams having ceased, I managed to snatch little sleep and became once again over-reliant on my wakefulness spell. Skyler was picking up the slack with my abecedarians, and I came to rely on him ever more to drill the others after I'd introduced a new topic.

Bella was still tied up in treating victims of the plague, but these were tapering off since the main cause had been addressed. The young woman occasionally graced our class with her presence. She was getting some color back in her cheeks, and the dark circles beneath her eyes had become less pronounced. Terwilliger had returned as evinced by the clean boots that greeted me each morning, but he hadn't sought me out or left me any new messages in the sand.

Franklin, Royland and I took it upon ourselves to mount a near-continuous watch on the garden lane which led from Atticus Skinner's estate near the lake to the rise which led up to the standing stones. We needed to catch the culprit in the act that we might confirm and bear witness to his perfidies. At our direction, Lloyd began a pretense of maintaining the cobbles of this pathway. Roy and I assisted to lend credibility to our frequent presence there. We felt, however, that should the creature masquerading as Master Skinner again visit his demonic liege, he would likely do so at night. For this reason, Franklin had concealed a jar containing the brain and eyeballs of a goat overlooking the trail. With his gift, he could observe the path by peering out through these eyes. He slept by day and kept a vigilant watch all throughout the night. Being otherwise unemployed, he was only too happy to take the graveyard shift.

And so on it went, day after day. The daily debates between Clement Brownyng and Alonso Balderas were heated. Clement accused Alonso of being a 'loyalist lapdog' and a 'sock-puppet of the powers that be.' Alonso, in turn, referred to Clement and his supporters as 'wild-eyed radicals,' claiming they would overturn all that was good about the conclave. Each insisted that the election of the other would bring swift ruin upon us.

There was time allotted at the end of each debate when the masters could ask questions of the candidates. Alas, this did little to reveal how either would govern. They consisted either of thinly veiled praise offered by masters to the candidate they favored, or abrasive insults hurled at the candidate they did not. I yearned to pose some substantive questions of my own. Alas, although my proxy allowed me a vote, it didn't confer on me the right to otherwise participate. It was ridiculous. I think the entire farce was being played out for my benefit alone, there being few others who maintained even the semblance of an open mind.

We were winding down from yet another of these tedious question-and-answer sessions. Gunther Brubaker arose to pose his query.

"My question is for Clement," he announced. "I am struck by how swiftly you surmised the cause of the plague and halted it's spread. Tell us again of how on your first day as headmaster *pro tem* you handled the mess left to you by your predecessor."

Clement smiled and nodded, taking up the speaker's staff. I had learned that in addition to the fine acoustics of the master's hall in general, the staff provided even more clarity to the voice of him who held it. It had been enchanted by someone with the Sutherland gift to amplify and enhance speech.

"I thank you for the question and would be delighted to relate..."

Just then, the steeple bell tolled the hour.

"... Ah. But I sense our time is up. Master Pete's report from Eagle's Keep is scheduled to begin. Suffice it to say, this and other such judicious management of difficult crises will be the hallmark of my administration should you choose my leadership."

With that, he leaned the speaker's staff on the podium and headed for the central seat to the rear. As his sour-faced opponent descended and returned to his seat among the masters, Brayden Sheppard, as seneschal, guided Master Redmond up onto the platform to prepare for his daily report. Brayden retrieved the speaker's staff and retreated to one side as Re-Pete spread his arms and stood squinting upward in concentration.

"Greetings Conclave. It's somewhat overcast here at Eagle's Keep, and the sundial is, therefore, a bit hazy. Nonetheless, I mark it is time to commence. In case I'm a bit off, I'll allow for some slippage by stating the boring bits first before we get into the meat of it; not that there's all that much going on just now.

"As I reported yesterday, we're receiving daily reports from the troops out in the Black Plagued Marshes. Despite cases of dysentery and other odd illnesses cropping up among them, nothing noteworthy has yet occurred. Tis as wartime always is: 'hurry up and wait.'"

There was a pause.

"Yesterday, I received a missive from my brother. In it, he outlined some of the problems facing the conclave and beseeched me to reconsider my proxy. After some deep thought and soul searching, I have done so. I would like to take this opportunity to revoke the proxy I granted to Felix Wells. Instead, I want my brother, Redmond, to cast my ballots while I'm away."

The masters sat stunned in the silence that followed this pronouncement. It was nearly the eleventh hour. The vote would take place in just a few more days. And this change, if allowed, would rewrite the balance of power entirely. Unlike his brother, Peter Doyle had always been a devoted loyalist. Part of me felt relieved. No longer would I hold the critical swing vote. Perhaps now I would be left alone. My cajoling by the various masters had intensified lately and had nearly achieved the level of overt threats. And now, all in an instant, my vote was rendered moot.

"That's all I have for now, my brothers and sisters of the conclave. Take it as you will. I shall report again tomorrow at this same time. Until then, be safe and pray for those who keep you thus. Peter..."

As he was concluding, Brayden Sheppard whistled sharply, then threw the speaker's staff forcefully at the man. Wincing, Peter turned and caught it. Brayden stepped swiftly forward to grip the man by his shoulder, relieving him of the staff.

"Point of order," Brayden brayed, nearly shaking the hall with his raised voice.

"For what reason does the gentleman bellow?" asked Clement whose ashen face projected gloom despite his jocular turn of phrase.

"I ask for permission to revise and extend some remarks about the codswallop this foul weasel would have us swallow."

Clement Brownyng looked stricken, but bowed to the inevitable. There was already an angry muttering among the masters on both sides.

"The masters recognize Brayden Sheppard for five minutes if he will lower his tone and resume proper etiquette," he decreed.

"Very well," began Brayden, leaning the staff on the lectern once again. "In flagrant abuse of his gift and our trust, this 'fine gentleman' would have us believe that his brother suddenly up and changed his mind. You'll note when I tossed him the staff, he caught it with his left hand. Peter and Redmond are mirror twins. Peter is right-handed. Redmond is the southpaw; the twin sinister if you will. What say you to that, sirrah?"

Redmond squirmed within his grasp, but then shrugged and looked confused.

"What's going on?" he asked. "Did Peter say something exciting?"

"Don't play dumb, Redmond. Although it suits you well, you needn't play at it. Your fatal mistake was catching the staff at all. We all know your brother can't see or hear us when you're channeling him."

***

I awoke to the clangor of an old tin cowbell. I invoked my darksight. I nearly tripped over Lloyd as I rushed to the window and signaled. The boy was sitting up and looking about with alarm.

"Go back to sleep," I told him as I silenced the bell, detaching the string that ran out over our window's sill.

"What's going on?" he whispered.

"I've no time to explain. I must go somewhere. Don't even think of following me."

Lloyd looked dubious, but he lay back down as I shucked off my nightshirt and hastily dressed. Once outside, I hustled up the freshly laid cobbles of Aspie Row. I hadn't gotten very far when the back of my hand began to itch. Looking down at it, I could vaguely discern the oak leaf-shaped mark where it reflected the moonlight.

"If someone were thinking of tagging along," I said aloud, "I'd advise against it."

"Well now," said the brownie, fading into view beside the fountain, "if it isn't Lucas the Just out for his evening constitutional."

"If you're seeking an adventure," I said, "you mayn't find this one to your taste. It has to do with a certain warty-faced fellow you once warned me not to name."

The brownie startled and rocked back on his heels.

"Ye mustn't seek out the *unseelie*, lad. Especially not *that one*. Misfortune follows in his wake."

"It's something I must do," I said. "His minions are meddling in conclave, and only I can stop them."

"One day ye must tell Terwilliger," he said, "why a dead squirrel was ringing your window bell. But curious as I am of this matter, with *that one* I'll have no truck. I'll heed your word of warning and wish you no ill luck."

At this, he hopped up to sit upon the lip of the fountain and watched me out of sight.

Though frightened by what we intended, I was relieved Atticus Skinner was at long last on the move. I'd begun to despair of him returning to the standing stones before tomorrow's election. After the final debate this afternoon, the masters had been more insistent than ever to know which candidate I favored. I feared for my very safety should I voice a preference for either side, such was the vehemence with which their respective beliefs were held. The gentle courtship of my vote was fast becoming a betrothal by force.

Master Redmond had been censured by the conclave for his blatant attempt to skew the vote. He was made to stand in the well before the lectern as each of the masters castigated him and spoke at length of their displeasure at his perfidies. Although the man seemed repentant, I thought it a rather light punishment for his malfeasance. This mere slap on the wrist would do little to deter imitators from attempting similar wrongdoing were they of a mind to do so. All that aside, the heat was back on me. I clung stubbornly to my neutrality.

I was almost to the base of the hill. I slowed my pace and scanned about for the trail leading off to the right. We had scouted it out on previous days. The hollow was secluded and wasn't visible from the top of the rise. Royland was to have been alerted first and should have gotten here before me.

"Pssst! Lucas."

I slipped over the lip and down the slope to arrive at the site between the two men.

"Is he up there?" I asked.

"Yeah," Franklin replied. "He went up about five minutes ago. No strange lights as yet."

"Well then," I said, "It's time for Roy to do his thing."

My cousin stared at me, and I drew no insight into his mood from his blank, neutral expression. He sat and settled himself with his back to a tree. I sat close by, facing him. With my mage sight, I could see a stream of his hive mites drifting off into the night and scattering into the nearby trees. After a few minutes, they came drifting back in ones and twos, each with a gray moth miller flapping in its wake. These he gathered on the bark of a tree just across from us. Franklin stared at them, bemused.

"Let us know when you see the lights," my cousin whispered.

Franklin crawled up the slope to comply. After a tense few minutes, he looked down at us and nodded. Pursing his lips, Royland placed his hand on my forehead muttering 'miscere cogitata.' As before, our minds merged. Unlike then, I felt a third presence. When Royland's inner hive came slamming down to nestle amid the vines of our inner garden, the buzzing was much less contentious. As our thoughts combined to form the entity that was Roy/Lucas, we quickly recognized this was because our homunculus was governing the hive and keeping it subdued.

"Tell your workers," we said to her, "to guide the moths aloft to the crest of the hill."

"*So let it be*," said she.

At once, our viewpoint was fractured into a thousand slices of moonlit perception as the swarm of moths lifted from the tree and separated. It took us a moment to comprehend what we were seeing. Through the multifaceted eyes of Roy's insects, we could see in every direction at once. But slowly, through the kaleidoscope of images, an overall picture assembled. Though new to the Lucas part of our personae, as a combined entity, we were well accustomed to seeing through the eyes of a swarm.

Upward our viewpoint drifted, heading for the lights playing atop the hill. We liked the light and wished we could be one with it. We saw a ring of stones and separated further to be less noticeable. A bearded man was standing near the central stone with his hand upon it. It was strange seeing him from almost every conceivable angle. The light that was calling to us played between two of the stones that Lucas informed us was where the horrible visage of Orenob had appeared in our dream. We resisted the urge to approach and flap against it.

When the ripples of light coalesced to form an enormous face, there was a sudden outward pressure that tore at our wings, dislodging many of us from the stones on which we rested. Our vision darkened as many of our insect thralls flapped about on their backs, writhing with sudden agony in a foul green mist that emerged to enshroud the ground. Only those still aloft or clinging to perches high on the stones continued to report. Others thrashed about, struggling to draw breath. We released these.

Atticus removed his hand from the menhir and assumed a supine posture before the cruel visage framed between the stones.

"Arise, wight!" Orenob thundered. "Tell us of the chaos you have wrought in the world of men."

"They are leaderless, my lord Orenob, and their council is nearly riven. Foul deeds have been done, not so easily forgiven. The one called Prowd lays dead by my own hand. Though I confess it occurred not precisely as we planned."

"How so?" boomed the demon. "Was the poison ineffective?"

"It was working, my liege. The man was quite ill. But a healer has arisen among them, one of surpassing skill. She was undoing all my good work. I felt it meet to finish the deed by cruder means."

"Do not let suspicion fall upon you. Remember your primary task. Become the Feininger girl's guardian. Do whatever you must. When her gift becomes active, you must be the one to nurture it toward fulfillment of the prophecy. I must have the verdant queen by my side that my rule may sweep across the continent. Too long have I been thwarted by false starts and setbacks. Your predecessor is e'en now learning the fate of those who displease me."

"Fear not, my lord," Atticus hastily assured. "Serendipity has smiled upon us. A renegade necromancer has run amok among the mages. Twas he who brought that tasty plague to liven things up. Most ingeniously did he infest the town with his rats. I sensed an opportunity, so I acted. The mages of the conclave seek this monster, so you see, Luther's death will never be attributed to me."

"It is good then, Kieranos, most faithful of my wights. Keep building resentment among them. Let me know when the child has been properly secured. I look forward to adding her power to mine once it has matured."

The gigantic warty face with its crown of thorny vines gave a final leer before dissipating in another burst of foul effluvium. In the sudden darkness, we released our remaining moths and recalled our hive mites lest they be seen by the enemy's mage sight. Though each individual spec would be difficult to perceive in the presence of greater magic, in its absence we feared detection. As each mite returned to our hive, the queen welcomed them and grew in prominence.

"Return. Be at peace," she gently commanded.

It was the last thing I heard as Roy withdrew his hand from my forehead. Franklin sat across from us, his eyes agog, but none of us spoke. Though we were well off the trail, voices carried up on quiet nights such as this. And we wanted to allow Atticus or Kieranos or whoever he was, plenty of time to conclude his business and depart. Roy even produced and activated his pillowcase with a quiet utterance of 'silentium'. He'd brought it along in case further stealth was required. At once, the soft murmuring of the night insects was stilled, and we sat in silence until Franklin signaled that the man had gone.

Roy shook out his pillowcase and deactivated it. As he was folding it and stuffing it back into his pocket, a sudden gust snatched at it. It fluttered beyond my cousin's reach, snagged on a shrub, then tumbled to lie in a muddy ditch nearby.

"That's just great," grumbled Roy with annoyance, reaching down to retrieve the soiled bit of cloth. "How am I supposed to clean this? My cell lacks amenities to wash ought but my face in the morning, and the scullery staff still can't enter the mage's quarter."

"I can attend to it," I offered. "We've a washtub, and tomorrow's laundry day at House Blue Jay."

He handed me the damp, soiled linen with an appreciative nod. I wrung it out and placed it carefully within my bob.

Eventually, I returned to the path with my two subdued companions. Franklin was the first to remark on the dire event we'd witnessed.

"I wouldn't have believed all this had I not seen it myself from a squirrel's eye view."

"The masters must learn of this," I returned, "but I doubt they'll believe it either unless we can show them in no uncertain terms. To begin with, I think it's time we put a few others in the know..."

So we hatched our plans as we strolled along, then separated, each returning to our respective beds to lie fretting and anxious over what the morning would bring.

***

This was it, I thought as the headmaster called the hall to order. He stood at the podium as the other masters shuffled into their seats and waited expectantly. There was a tension in the room that belied the silence that had suddenly descended. The vote, however, was the last thing on my mind. I spied Atticus Skinner seated among the autonomists looking for all the world like just another of our solemn brethren. Even with mage sight, I could detect no hint of the fiend that possessed the man. The magic of the fey seemed proof against casual detection.

He turned to briefly meet my gaze. Did he suspect I knew? But no, I thought. He was not alone in casting me assessing glances or baleful glares. All the masters wished to know how I would choose in the upcoming, critical vote.

"As is our custom," said Clement, "we will cast our ballots in descending order of age. Rather than a hand count, I ask that each master or proxy rise as I call on you and clearly voice your choice for headmaster."

The hall had been cleared of all save for the masters, the king's emissary and myself. A crowd of other wizards had gathered out in front of the academy, waiting to hear the results and to witness the investment ceremony that was to follow.

"Puquabeth Chosha Julia," Clement called out in a ringing tone. "Please state for the record the name of the candidate whom you support for this exalted office."

The Elven lady stood from among her fellow loyalists. Taking up the speaker's staff, she announced her choice.

"I favor Alonso Balderas. I cast my ballot for him. In addition, I hold proxies for three absent masters: Bey Cholith Depa Shon, Baqua Lipo Sithia, and Qenga Taliha Shunje Qua, known to this assembly as Master Shon, Mistress Sithia, and Mistress Talia, respectively. They likewise would have their ballots cast in favor of good Master Balderas."

She passed Mistress Dunham the speaker's staff and reseated herself.

"That's four for my worthy opponent," announced Master Brownyng. "Sybil Dunham, what say you?"

And so it went. As each master was named, he or she would arise, take up the speaker's staff, and announce their selections. There were no surprises. The loyalists to a man chose Balderas, while the autonomists cast their ballots in favor of the headmaster *pro tem*. As the youngest present, my vote would be the last to be registered. And I was the subject of many a curious glance, while the masters speculated on whom I might select.

The tally stood XI to IX In favor of the challenger, when at last Atticus Skinner was called. I braced myself for the chaos to come. As he stood among his fellow autonomists, I stood as well, unnoticed by most. Before he could make his selection known, I took a calming breath and reached for my magic.

'Cogitationes liberare!' I cried, sending forth my vines to wrap around the man's head.

With a surge I felt my energies rush down the connection, bolstering the mage's will from where it lay enshrouded beneath the oily essence of his captor. With a startled shout, he cast the fey creature out, looking wild-eyed all about. As expected, the hall was immediately plunged into turmoil. The masters were rising to their feet. Most were watching Atticus from whose head a roiling black mist was emerging and gathering itself into a swirling dark mass. Several stared over at me, stunned. Among these was Gunther Brubaker, whose startled brow soon descended into a frown of ire.

Once the dark entity had wholly separated itself from the man, Atticus promptly crumpled to the floor. A babble arose as masters all throughout the hall began uttering oaths and various warding spells.

"Treachery!" cried Gunther, leaping over the back of the bench on which he'd sat. He made swiftly for the aisle in my direction hampered by the benches and their former occupants alike. Winning clear, he approached me with his hands held menacingly before him declaring, "Move not a muscle, boy, or I'll burn you down where you stand!"

As passions grew inflamed, the wight was not idle. It descended like a dervish to enshroud Mistress Meredith who took to screaming her dismay. Several masters who stepped up to help were beaten back by buffeting winds and flung every which way. Gunther paused. Suddenly uncertain, his attention was drawn to the spectacle of his wife's distress. She rose from the floor disheveled, her garments and hair in disarray. In her hands she clutched the speaker's staff. She narrowed her eyes with malice and directed her gaze my way.

"So I am discovered. You've caught me out at last. But I'll give you cause to regret the deed; the master's plans will yet succeed!"

At this, she lifted the speaker's staff in both hands above her head. Her mouth opened to release a wailing screech the like of which I was at a loss to describe. It was caught midway between a musical note and a scream. Amplified by the staff, it rebounded from the chamber's far walls to echo and throb, rising ever in intensity. It put me in mind of Henry's whistling, for at once I felt the vertiginous nausea take hold.

I saw the masters all stagger and stumble about. Some clutched at their ears, as did I. But these efforts were to no avail. The sonic vibrations pierced through my skull and despite my best efforts to counter the room's spinning, blackness was encroaching on the edges of my vision. I tried summoning the will to liberate the matron. If only I could have a moment's reprieve from her distressing banshee wail, I might succeed a second time. Alas, I lacked the concentration necessary to employ my own magic.

Then, as the masters began falling one by one, an idea arose from my agonized, failing mind.

"Silentium!" I shouted above the rising din.

I couldn't hear my own words, but the enchantment must've worked, for nor could I hear anything at all. Thank the fates all above for reminding me to pack my cousin's pillowcase, freshly laundered, in my bob. Just before me, Gunther Brubaker sagged to his knees, but on his face I marked a look of relief. He looked back and forth between Mistress Meredith and me, the only two in the hall still standing.

I braced myself as my equilibrium returned and I squared off with the devil once again.

'Cogitationes liberare!' I cried silently.

Sound wasn't necessary, only intent. Having practiced the spell repeatedly on my own mind throughout that long night when I'd purged grandma Abbey, it came easily to my bidding. My vines slithered forth to seize the foul spirit once again and drag it out of the newly fortified mind of its host. Mistress Meredith slumped to the floor insensate.

Joy found my heart to have beaten the spirit once more. Such joy lasted but a moment to be replaced by terror. The roiling mass of misty vapors was rapidly drifting toward *me!* And my heart knew fear. How could I resist such a fiend? I'd been relying on the other masters to overcome the enemy in their midst. I hadn't counted on the clever spirit disabling them all in one fell stroke! I leapt into the aisle and ran for the doors. I doubted the thing could outpace me. Sound returned to my still-ringing ears. My bob, containing Roy's sleeping aid, remained back on the bench.

At the broad double doors, I paused to peer back, my heart hammering within my chest. The creature was whirling where I had only just been, and in its grip lay Gunther. Still on his knees, the pyromancer twisted this way and that as he resisted, but the foul thing won out in the end. Gripping the back of the bench, he hauled himself erect and scowled.

"The mages of Osten are a pestersome lot," he declared, "but this one with fire doth abound. Where subtlety fails, mayhap force can prevail. I shall burn this place to the ground."

Menace dripped from his lips with every word. Had I any doubts about the creature's fey origins, its penchant for rhyme had laid them to rest. Whereas it was quaint coming from Terwilliger and adorable from Hazel, on this fellow it came off as downright creepy. I couldn't let him set the place ablaze; not with all these helpless mages trapped inside. I had to lure him outdoors somehow. I still had a few allies awaiting me there. I hated doing so, but I'd have to offer Susie up as bait. It was the only imperative I knew this 'Kieranos' to possess.

"You do that," I taunted. "I'll just go and snatch the girl away to safety. The Feininger child will never be found, and you can go out in a blaze of glory after telling your master the tale."

Gunther howled his fury as I eased the door open and slipped without. A burst of crimson flame caught it and fanned out from its frame. I felt the heat of it where I pressed my back against the door to hold it shut. The old herald looked down at me with his mustache aquiver, tilting his head and questioning me with his eyes.

"Run," I told him.

He didn't need me to repeat the command. He heeded at once and ran. Down the hallway and out through the front, our mad dash took us. Glancing back, I spied Gunther in hot pursuit. He ran pretty quickly for an older gentleman, but we had a good lead on him. He paused once to hurl more fire, but this only let me pull farther ahead as his spell flew wide. It occurred to me he may have missed on purpose. Was he counting on me to lead him to Susie? My singed elbow stung where the bolt had passed by. It had been too close a thing for comfort.

***

I blinked in the glaring sunlight as I stumbled down the steps; the herald wheezing at my side. A crowd of onlookers

262

stared at us wide-eyed. I'd nearly forgotten the folks had gathered to celebrate the election.

"Run! Flee!" I cried in alarm, windmilling my arms in panic.

Then I took my own good advice and sprinted for the trees, determined to outrace the grim horror that stalked me. Up ahead in the distance, near the edge of the wood, my friends stood gathered to lend me their aid. I had hoped it wouldn't come to this. Hope now lay in our final contingency, but I reckoned it a slim one at best. There stood Royland and Franklin with Lloyd by their side and Lorraine holding Susie by the hand. Sholeena, too, stood among them, her face shaded green with worry.

"Susie!" I shouted. "Run for the trees! There's a coach awaiting to take you far from harm!"

The girl looked affrighted as she released Lorraine's hand and sped away. She pelted toward the garden lane with all the speed her small legs could summon. Admittedly, this was not very fast. Gunther veered off from his pursuit of me, spying his prize at long last. His long strides ate up the distance that separated him from the fleeing child. I almost laughed when he caught her up and snatched at his prey only to pass right through. The illusion of Susie stuttered and blinked out.

I sucked in a deep breath and joined the circle of my friends. According to Edgar's notes, the spell of exorcism required the power of no fewer than six masters acting in concert. And though we had the required number, none of us had earned our masteries. Moreover, it took years to learn the balance of communal magic, years of practice that we sorely lacked. As I said, a slim hope at best. But we had no time for doubt. We would attempt it. There were no others to stand against this fiend.

"Exorcizo spiritus," I softly incanted as I bound the circle with my vines.

I felt the joining commence even as Kieranos whirled about in fury at the trick he'd been played. I heard the buzzing of Royland's hive. I saw the bright light that shone from Lorraine. I sensed the roiling dark energies from Franklin and felt the cool, refreshing waters of Sholeena's pond. From Lloyd I felt nothing, but perhaps that is simply what his void felt like. It was my task as conductor to bind these energies and guide them forth to their target. I took a step back, then another, and turned to face our foe.

I stretched forth my arm and sent my vines to encircle him and drive out the sprite. But as my gaze met his baleful glare, my perception was drawn within. My master had once told me battles between mages almost inevitably devolved to an inner struggle. Apparently, this one was to be no exception. I stood at the edge of my inner garden atop my small hill of earth. Before me, perched atop a writhing ball of terrible flame, was an imp with a pointed chin. He stared down at me with hatred, then began raining fire down upon the vines connecting me to my fellows.

I felt the heat and smelled the scorched earth where my vines began to parch and burn.

I recalled the time I was first assailed by magic. It was Shastageheggin, the goblin shaman who had scorched my inner field that day. My master had provided the perfect remedy, being a water mage. Just as I knew the answer, I also comprehended the means. In a flash, I drew from Sholeena's pond the substance that was needed.

"Tenera pluviam," I pronounced, causing the skies above my inner realm to open and release a gentle patter of cooling rain.

The rain swept across my inner fields and past them to the imp on his throne of fire. He sizzled and fumed and withdrew.

My vision swam, and I stood once more at the edge of the woods several paces to the fore. I stepped even closer to where Gunther stood scowling, a thrall to the dread wight that rode within him. It seemed I could call upon all the gifts comprising my circle of friends. Rather than merely reaching for my vines, I drew from each and wound them together to send forth in a stream of blended energies. This I played against Gunther, but it felt wrong somehow. Though each of my cohorts was strongly gifted, save for Lloyd who I felt not at all, the stream of power was oddly unbalanced and emerged as barely a trickle. Nonetheless, I bore down.

At first flinching, Gunther grinned and straightened, crossing his arms before him in taunting ridicule of my effort.

"That tickles," he jeered, leering smugly. "Is that the best you can summon? You're getting the idea, you hapless fool; but you'll need more than that to take *me* to school."

His name, I thought.

I'd heard once that the faeries' true names held some power over them. Worth a try.

"Exorcizo spiritus," I said once again. "By our circle's combined might, we banish Kieranos, the unseelie wight!"

Again, I summoned forth the surge of force. It was weaker this time, and the blending more off kilter.

Gunther cringed momentarily, but again stood tall.

"Closer and closer still," cackled the imp "but you lack both the strength and the skill. Your feeble effort will soon fall apart. Then I'll do with you just as I will."

He was right. I could feel it. Though my friends tried their best, the circle was weakening as each element sought its release from my binding. The power was there, far more than was needed. The fault lay in our inelegant orchestration. Soon exhaustion would claim us, and the imp would run amok. Through the despair descending upon us, we buckled down and held to our joining. For how much longer could we endure?

Then a voice was heard. From the woodland it came. It rung out loud and clear.

"Take heart my sweets and discount not the friendship of the fey. Against this dark, unseelie wight, ye'll have our aid this day!"

From out of the thicket sprang a small figure brandishing a stick before him. I didn't know what the brownie meant to do against the horrible demon we fought. But at this point, any help at all was much more than welcome, I thought. Then, to my wonder, I perceived a shifting. It came from beneath my feet. A familiar surge of magic was unleashed. Within this groundswell I saw once more the glowing green tendrils of the dryad's roots. Not toward our enemy did they slither, but rather to me and my comrade's boots. They gripped us one by one, twining up our ankles and holding us fast.

They bestowed no power that we could perceive, for the magic of the fey was alien to our ken. But as each member of our circle became thus rooted, I felt in the intricate network below an increased connection to one another, forging at last the alliance we'd sought. Taking the final few steps toward our foe until I could advance no farther, I gathered our remaining might and hurled it forth to enshroud the wicked wight. Perfectly blended, our energies wrapped him tight. I could see the dark fumes leaking out from Gunther's ears to gather above his head. His body went rigid, but his arms arose and his final venom he spat.

"You may have found your stride, young mage, with treacherous seelie aid. But know I'll not go gently into the final night. For e'en in death I shall claim my price! I'll take as many with me as I might."

With this, a great ball of flame formed above Gunther's outstretched arms. It whirled and seethed, growing both in size and intensity. I felt the tremendous heat from it lick at my face even as the dark cloud trailing from his ears twisted and shrank. Lowering his arms, he heaved it forth, shouting: 'sphera de incineratio!'

The twisting spirit collapsed at last. With a deafening roar, it imploded. But that miniature sun soared above me to land directly atop my friends. As it smote them, it brightened intolerably. Even from eight paces off, it set my clothing ablaze and scorched me nearly to the bone. I feared for my life in that instant, but I mourned for my friends even more. Our connection was severed clean, and Hazel's roots had been burned to the level of the ground where formerly they'd protruded.

Nearby, Gunther lay facedown, his hat on fire as well from the blast. Only he and I and Terwilliger remained. The brownie lifted himself up from the ground where he lay, all scorched and covered in soot. With an angry scowl, he brought his stick down on the back of Gunther's foot. The unseelie wight had been beaten, but oh what a terrible cost! I lay myself down on the sere earth and wept for my loved ones lost.

Some people approached from the academy, too late to be of any use. Water mages bathed the ground, and a murmuring was heard all around. Gunther was put out then given succor. I felt their hands upon me and sharp questions rained down. Why had we assaulted a master? What happened to the other masters? And even: 'Who won the election?' I paid them no heed and threw my arms about my knees, gathering them close.

Then, as I lay on my side, my bleary eyes began playing tricks on me. I sensed a flicker of motion from the field nearby where the grass lay blackened and shriveled. A finger crept into view, hanging in midair about a foot above the ground. The finger became a hand followed by an arm, then two. Then a familiar face swam into view. It was Lorraine, choking and gasping and gulping deep breaths, crawling out from nothingness. Behind her, Roy soon emerged. He reached back to haul out Lloyd. Franklin and Sholeena were the last to appear, gasping as Lorraine had done. It was nice to have such fantasies.

***

"I'm certain you recognize the need to uphold decorum," said Headmaster Balderas.

I sat in his office amid the boxes. In them, books and other possessions of two prior headmasters were packed up and ready to move out. I shifted in my seat. Although most of my skin had grown back, it was still pink and tender where the worst of the blisters had sloughed off, making it hard to get comfortable. I almost regretted my earlier advice to Bella not to mend wounds entirely. I chafed at 'overcoming my challenges on my own.'

"I still think expulsion is a rather extreme reaction," I put forth. "The colleague in question was colluding with our enemies. I believe I was right to expose him."

"Nonetheless," the new headmaster chided, "our rules are quite explicit. Attacking another master while in council is a breach of etiquette and quite frowned upon. Mere censure wouldn't set the desired tone for my administration. If such were to be tolerated, we would surely descend into anarchy. I will inform Master Chadwick that he must select a new proxy to represent him to our august body."

"In your letter to my app-master," I sighed, "I hope you will notify him of that other matter."

"I will. He shall receive a sealed missive by griffin. I'll expect his acknowledgment by pigeon within a few days. Miss Spencer is seeing to the travel arrangements as we speak."

I was most relieved to hear it. None yet suspected that Susie's gift had manifested, and only a few shared the secret of its dire import. She needed to be as far away from our enemy in the south as possible at an undisclosed location. Who would think to look for her at a sheep ranch in the northern wilds? It had worked once before. Besides, what better way to repay my old master for the unwanted responsibility of his proxy than by foisting upon him an eight-year-old girl for his new apprentice?

"Well," Master Balderas continued, "if that is all, you may depart, aspirant. I've some unpacking to do. And tell Victor I wish to see him. You should find him waiting in the foyer. There are some matters I wish to discuss regarding his management of the Brubaker estate."

"Yes, Eminence," I said, rising to depart.

"And try to look suitably chastened," he called after me.

I didn't know what kind of headmaster Alonso Balderas would be, but I liked the man. With Atticus Skinner exposed and the Brubakers *non compos mentis*, the loyalists had no trouble securing him the position. My vote wasn't even needed. Time would tell whether the autonomists' dire predictions would come to pass, but I suspected the conclave wouldn't fall immediately into ruination.

After sending Victor in to see his eminence, I went to the basement to find Roy. My cousin had been abruptly cleared from sequestration. The conclave had repurposed his cell. The beds were needed for three new recuperating residents. After possession by the wight, Gunther and Meredith Brubaker hadn't yet recovered their wits. Evidently, being wight-ridden left one befuddled. The couple could barely put two words together between them. Mistress Dunham was in charge of their rehabilitation and predicted their eventual full recovery. As she was an oracle, one tended to take her predictions as reliable. They were to share Royland's cell and were given soothing music and small, comforting tasks to occupy their days. Victor had even brought Contessa to warm their laps and demand their affection.

Atticus Skinner was a more tragic case. No one knew for how long he'd been under the wight's influence. It could have been years. The man lay catatonic in a cell nearby. Mistress Dunham cared for him as well, but was far less sanguine about the hopes for his recovery. So, along with Mistress Gretta, four masters now languished in the academy's cellar.

"Thank you for coming, Lucas."

Roy arose and stretched. He'd been seated in the hall outside his former cell with his duffel all packed and ready to go.

"Are you sure you want to attempt this?" I asked again.

"I have to, cousin. She's family."

"Well, I'm here. I'll watch and pull you out if you're overcome. Are you certain Mistress Frida wouldn't be a better choice?"

"I think she's too close to it. She'd be apt to be drawn in as well. No. I trust you to do the right thing."

He turned to face the door across the hallway. Stepping over, he eased it open. Mistress Gretta sat bundled in her shawl, staring vacantly ahead. Her needles were still. They were sticking out from her basket of yarn, well within her reach. Royland crouched down facing her and met that vacant stare.

At once, my cousin's eyes grew distant, and his shoulders eased lower. Looking within, I saw the mites swarming out to ring the old woman's head, swirling ever closer. Where they touched, they were absorbed by Gretta's skin to work their way within. More and more of Royland's swirling mites adhered to her temples to promptly still and vanish.

Then Royland began rocking back and forth on his heels. His lips moved silently. I hadn't seen him do that for ages. Before long, he was doing something else that I'd *never* seen him do. Tears welled up in my cousin's eyes to dribble freely down his cheeks. Should I pull him away? No. Best to let him have his moment. I'd do so if he became more distressed. A sob emerged from Royland, followed by a cough and some muttered words.

"... Hans. Oh my Hans. How could they? How can I go on without you?... I wish they'd come for me as well... But no. I shall do as you bade me. It was your dying wish. I saw it in your eyes. I shall do nothing to provoke them. One day I shall win free of this place. I'll live on to honor your memory. I shall be strong."

Roy became agitated and tore at his shirt, then leaned forward weeping and lay his head in the old woman's lap, his shoulders rising and falling with his sobs. Once again, I considered dragging him away, but instead I stood transfixed as the old woman lifted her scrawny arm and raised her bony hand to stroke my cousin's hair. From her temples the hive mites were reemerging to return to Roy. And on her face I spied a pinched expression.

As Royland arose to resume his crouch, the light still glistened from his tear-streaked face. And a kerchief wouldn't have gone amiss to attend to the untidy secretions of his nostrils. But when his eyes met hers again, she smiled. It was a sight not unlike watching a flower burst into bloom all in a moment. Her entire face was transformed. The wrinkles deepened in a way that signaled the quiet bliss that only a grandmother with a secret could convey.

She said not a word as she reached over to her sewing basket and withdrew from it a long, knitted scarf. It was all shades of green and brown and blue, arranged in a haphazard pattern with occasional spots of red. In truth, it was an ugly thing. In this, it contrasted sharply with the beauty of her beatific smile as she placed it over Roy's shoulders to hang loosely about his skinny neck.

Then, just as quickly as her transformation had been wrought, Gretta lapsed back to a state of quietude. Her gaze went distant and her face fell slack. Her eyes narrowed once more to mere slits as her head tilted back to rest against the back of the chair in which she sat. The tension eased out of her body once more. Her jaw hung open and from it emerged a vigorous snore. I shouldn't have been surprised. I supposed my cousin had to have gotten it from somewhere, after all.

I crept quietly back into the hall. I wanted to allow Roy some privacy to collect himself. It was at least ten minutes later before he joined me there, still wearing his scarf. He met my gaze squarely and nodded once.

***

"Do you think she'll wake up now?" I asked as we ambled along.

Uncertain of his status, Royland was moving his things back to House Falcon. Although technically he could have stayed at the Brubaker estate, Roy didn't want to impose while his erstwhile master and his wife convalesced. Their son, Victor, had taken up management of the estate, and Roy didn't want to be underfoot or be seen as an interloper.

I felt like we were just drifting along. The warmth of sunshine and the scent of orchards in full bloom that wafted to us on the gentle breeze barely penetrated my sense of ennui. My mind kept turning to the old woman trapped within her grief.

"I don't know, Lucas. She's still processing all that happened to her. Twenty-five years is a long time. I suspect she'll emerge , eventually. She's healing, and her will is strong. I think her sister's visits help."

"I thought she'd broken free when she gave you the scarf."

"No. That was just a onetime moment of clarity. She recognized me. She might have me confused with my father, but that's alright. She said she wanted me to have the scarf to make up for all the birthdays she'd missed."

The way abruptly darkened, and the breeze stilled as we passed into the shade of leafy boughs. The light dappling of the sun's rays played upon the cobbles as the wind stirred the canopy above.

"Um, Roy? She never actually *said* anything."

"She *felt* it at me. Her eyes said it."

As we passed through the garden lane, the glade remained muted and forlorn. When I'd checked earlier, I found Hazel uncommunicative. She'd doubtless withdrawn into her tree. I

271

hoped the flames hadn't singed her roots too badly. Perhaps she just needed more time to rest from her efforts. We certainly owed her a large debt of gratitude.

Roy turned down Aspie Row, and I followed.

"This place is certainly looking spiffy," Roy remarked.

"Yep. All the neighbors pitched in. It helps that most of them can't go into town. They're bored silly. Have you any plans for dinner tonight?"

"I'll have to see what's in the falcon's larder. I imagine I can scrounge something up."

As we approached our respective houses, Scott McNair stepped out onto the porch of House Falcon. The young man had cleaned himself up considerably. He appeared to be clean-shaven and was dressed impeccably if one were to ignore the frilly white apron he wore over his doublet. The man was gripping a soup ladle.

"Oy! Royland!" he hollered. "I suppose this means I'll be cooking for three tonight."

"Three?" said Roy, his brow furrowing.

"Yeah. The headmaster called me in this morning and assigned us a new aspirant."

Out onto the porch swaggered Skyler. He stepped up beside Scott to lean on the porch railing.

"Hiya teach," he greeted me.

"It's about time," said Royland. "So Reinhardt finally passed you as an apprentice. Congratulations."

I'd nearly forgotten that Roy had worked for Skyler's app-master.

"Yep," returned the boy. "He said he would've passed me months ago but for the reading requirement. I finally managed to squeak by, thanks to your cousin there."

"Well done, Skyler," I praised.

"What did Balderas give you for a work assignment?" asked Roy.

"His eminence suggested the marina, but I told him I wanted to teach at the créche once Lucas becomes a journeyman. He said he'd think about it."

"But Skyler," I objected, "you're only just learning to read yourself."

"That's what *he* said *too*. I told him I only needed to stay one lesson ahead of the others. He has a nice laugh."

"Well, I'd best go and see what my own housemates are up to. You three enjoy your feast. I'll see you soon."

House Blue Jay was unusually still. I discovered that Lloyd was napping, and the others were still out and about. It amazed me that none of them had suffered so much as a scratch from the horrific battle we'd fought. According to Franklin, in the final instant before the flames could claim them, Lloyd had pulled the entire circle into his void, including himself. They held their breaths for as long as they dared to ensure that the danger had passed. Before blacking out from the effort, Lloyd had opened a hole through which they could reemerge. My mind reeled as I pondered tearing a hole in nothing.

Unfortunately for me, I had been too distant to sit out the blast in asphyxiated comfort. It had scorched me all up and down the left side of my body. I didn't know exactly what happened to vengeful wights when they were dispelled, but I fervently hoped it was a suitably nasty fate.

CHAPTER ELEVEN

The Envoy

"To attain the impossible, one must attempt the absurd."

~ Miguel de Cervantes ~

Ahhh. Leisure time at last. I lay stretched out on my mattress with my back braced up against the headboard cushioned by two pillows. By the light of our lantern, I was enjoying the book that lay open in my lap. No council meetings awaited me on the morrow, nor were any hectic events brewing that I could foresee. What bliss to simply enjoy the quiet evening. The window was propped open, and a refreshing breeze wafted in, bearing the sweet scents of the first evening of spring. The night insects were in excellent voice, their chirping chorus rising and falling in a soothing rhythm that would soon bear me off to dreamland. It was a country I no longer need fear. Lloyd had already set off for that sublime destination as evinced by his peaceful countenance where he lay abed.

Those insects were really getting into it, weren't they? There was the high-pitched chirping of the katydids arising at even intervals. Between these spikes, the steady voices of the crickets hummed a chattering lower counterpoint. The croaks of bullfrogs produced occasional deep, percussive intrusions, almost as though the whole were being orchestrated. Above these cascading and ever more rhythmic vibrations, I heard an owl. Who-hoo! Who-hoo! That was just too much. The nocturnal avian was timing his hoots to occur in perfect sync with the surrounding noise.

This could be no random occurrence. Moreover, the back of my hand had begun to itch. I set my book aside and listened. Then I heard it. It was an eerie chorus of voices from just outside my window. There were no words at first. I arose from my cot and crept over to my window to peer without. Dim lights I suspected were faerie lanterns bobbed about some few yards distant. The mark of the fey began to tingle and throb more urgently as the rays of the half-moon above fell upon it.

I flinched as a slight figure leaped up onto my windowsill. It was a tiny grig, no larger than my hat. His hindquarters resembled the body of a winged grasshopper, but in the front, a minuscule human torso and head arose. He peered at me curiously as he raised a tiny vielle to his chin. An atonal scratching was heard as the bug tuned up. And soon this tiny faerie fiddler was reeling off a delightful melody perfectly attuned to the chorus of the night.

Outside, I spotted another fey creature emerging from the surrounding darkness to stand exposed beneath the window of my room. He was larger. He stood about as tall as Terwilliger. With the hind legs of a goat and horns protruding from his head, he lifted a set of panpipes to his lips and blew. Lastly, from among the moon moths flitting hither and thither, yet another tiny figure fluttered forth. She was bedecked in a gauzy gown that quite set off her trim figure. The perfectly formed woman was no bigger than the grig. Sporting the glittering wings of a dragonfly, she opened her tiny mouth, and her words joined the melodious tune of the faerie orchestra.

When the night comes creepin'

While the folks are sleepin'

And the moths come flappin' at your win-dows

With the crickets singin'
and the night owl wingin'
And that old man moon is in the sky.

When the fish are flappin'
You can FEEL it happen.
Fair folk harken to my cryyyyy.

That's when Seelie
Court will come to pass.
Gather one and aaaaaalll.

As the dewdrops glisten
You need ONLY listen.
Fair folk harken to the caaaaall.

My fey mark throbbed and burned, and the words pulsed in my ears, compelling me to come forth into the night to join the remarkable creatures. I glanced at Lloyd, who still lay insensate. How could the boy sleep through all this? Backing away from the window, I drifted toward the door in a daze. I retained the presence of mind to resist stepping directly out through the window, but it was a near thing. The music continued weaving its compelling spell upon my psyche as I ambled out the door, down the hall, and into the parlor. Before the parlor hearth sat Franklin and Lorraine, quietly sharing their evening tea.

"Care to join us, Lucas?" asked Franklin.

"What? No thanks," I said distractedly. "Don't you hear it?"

The music was louder than ever, and I was at a loss as to why neither of the two had remarked on it.

"Hear what?" asked Lorraine with a puzzled look. "Have you been dreaming again?"

"Maybe," I cautiously replied. "I think a walk will clear my head."

"Perhaps we should join you," said Franklin worriedly, "You don't seem quite yourself. With all that's happened recently, it's no wonder. Give me a minute, and I'll accompany you on your stroll."

The music was calling. And if they couldn't hear it, I suspected the invitation was personal.

"No need," I said cheerfully as I hastened to the front door. "I need some alone time to mull over a few things. Enjoy your tea."

And with that, I stepped out, leaving my two befuddled friends to exchange worried glances. I didn't see the faerie fiddler or his cohorts in the pale, moonlit landscape. But I could still hear their summons from down the lane where the light of the Lorédonian moths marked a clear trail into the distance.

Be ye Brownie, Dryad

Or a river Nyad.

Be ye Pixie, Sprite or Leprechaun

With the fireflies flittin'

We will all be sittin',

At the toadstool circle in the glade

As the leaf tips tremble

We shall ALL assemble

To the Seelie Court we maaaaade.

When the queen comes

Fairest of us all

Heed HER words withaaaaal.

So then come ye hither

Dally NOT nor dither

Fair folk harken to the caaaaall.

Hazel had mentioned the mark of the fey made one a proxy for the immobile dryads. Thus, they could have a voice when this 'Seelie Court' was called. Mayhap that was why only I could perceive the summons. For all that, she had neglected to inform me of the frequency or purpose of such councils. And I was woefully ignorant of what protocols or behavior was expected from its attendees. This was nothing new to me, having been thrust unprepared into the councils of nobles and wizards repeatedly over the prior year or so. I would follow these fey equivalents of heralds to wherever I need go and be as polite as possible to avoid giving offense. One day, I'd have to have a long talk with the tree sprite about manners among the fey. Until then, I'd just have to manage as best I could.

And as the music guided me into the Perilous Glade, I felt a rising excitement at the prospect of meeting more of Hazel's good folk. Little did I suspect the conundrum that awaited me there.

***

As I slipped through the leafy undergrowth, I sensed my destination was drawing nigh. The music arose to its crescendo and sounded as though it emanated from but a few paces ahead. The rhythm of its final chorus trilled upward and rang about its melody line in a stuttering conclusion.

Come and WE'LL wel-come ye

If your heart be good and TRUE

And our heads we're scratchin'

whilst our PLANS be hatchin'

Seelie court doth wel-come YOU!

Parting the boughs and entering the glade, I stared about in wonder. It scarcely seemed the same as the clearing where

Hazel and I had hitherto met, but there sat the old stone bench amid a flurry of activity. Pixies and sprites flitted about in a dazzling display of aerial acrobatics while numerous creatures of every description reclined on a ring of toadstools which had sprung up literally overnight. By the light of the faerie lanterns dancing above, I noted a frog-like creature smoking a long pipe, a watery being enveloped in a cascading cloak of blue, and tiny maidens wearing flowers for hats cavorting about the small glen. And these were but a few examples of the fey creatures I beheld.

Looking about, I spotted Terwilliger standing amid a cluster of other brownies at the base of Hazel's tree. He met my eyes but briefly, then shrugged, grimaced, and turned aside. I wondered what that guilty look was all about. Of Hazel, there was no sign, apart from the obvious.

A great shriek sounded, stilling the frolic. It came from a low-hanging branch of a hickory tree that bordered the glen. Perched atop it, a bespectacled owl creature glared down from just above the height of my head. The menagerie of strange folk came slowly to order, coming to rest on the toadstools or just resting on their haunches once all of these were filled. Without preamble, the owl-man addressed the crowd in a reedy male voice.

"To the court ye be summoned, with the equinox nigh and the half-moon riding in the clear night sky. Tis time all the seelie are gathered to meet. Grim matters await us, some bittersweet."

Not a cricket sang in the pause that followed. Then the owl-man stared directly at me and indicated the empty stone bench with a wave of his wing.

"Join us, young human, we saved ye a seat."

I tiptoed across the glen, careful not to tread upon some unwary fey, and settled myself on the bench. Though some of the faeries were large, the majority were so tiny they made me feel like a giant in their midst.

"When is the queen coming, Fengári?" boomed the deep voice of a furry-faced fellow near the back.

The owl-man's feathers bristled as the question was taken up and echoed by a myriad of tiny voices. When all was silent once more, he answered.

"This venue be special. The queen isn't coming, despite that it's here we are found. For her graceful bootprint mayn't fall on such unhallowed ground."

This was followed by bleats and blats and hoots of derision as the disappointed faeries jeered.

"Be still!" screeched Fengári.

With his wing, he pointed out Terwilliger, standing modest and silent just before the bole of Hazel's tree.

"This one," Fengári began, "brought us news most dire. By the given word of this humble brownie's mouth, the unseelie king allies himself with mages of the south. His minions stalk the mortal realm. The foul one sends them forth, to spread his swampy mire into our lands here in the north. How can we hope to counter this? Will all become thralls to the unseelie throne? Nay. I say! We must ally with humans of our own!"

The hoots and gibbers arose once more, and pixies swirled aloft, their small voices chiming in alarm. Some stamped their feet and others cried aloud or squabbled with one another. I got the general sense that allying with humans was deemed a bad idea. Opposition to Fengári's proposal seemed to solidify around the pipe-smoking amphibian. He drew himself up and puffed out his throat. He then voiced his objection in a slow, resonant, guttural voice dripping with scorn.

"That solution is preposterous. Your idea is absurd. Such allies do the fey abhor. Humans rarely keep their word."

The owl-man winced, but puffed out his own feathers.

"Your objection has been noted, Bogalump, the grudge. But be fair-minded. You will find that one among us sits. He has, unlike the others you would hasten to prejudge, beaten an unseelie wight with naught more than his wits. Let us hear from this one, whom some among us trust. I'm told he's known both far and wide as Lucas - the Just!"

All eyes turned to me. My face heated, and I suddenly felt more conspicuous than a baby deer amid a pack of wolves.

Was I being called upon to defend my race? That would be no mean feat in the best of circumstances. Certainly, it made sense to ally against our common foe in the south, but how had I gotten appointed to be the spokesperson for all of humanity? I'd noted the fey's formal speech was fraught with rhymes. I was no poet, but I'd have to try to work a few in. I ignored the panoply of strange beings who sat circumjacent and focused only on Hazel's tree. I pretended I was speaking only to the tree sprite. This calmed my jittery nerves and freed my tongue from its torpor.

"An alliance twixt your folk and mine could prove most beneficial..." I began, thoughtfully. "...But among my people I am not a leader or official," I hastened to add. "I'll take this proposal to those of my kindred responsible for such things. Such grave concerns are matters for our councilmen and kings."

"Not so fast, Lucas the unauthorized," Bogalump sneered. "There be another matter in this glen to resolve ere we could even consider such a proposal. One thing that distinguishes seelie from unseelie is we do not snatch children from their cribs. Yet here in our midst a dryad stands who was taken from her mother's side and brought here in shame to reside. Yer folk stole this child with premeditation; this be a hostage negotiation. My fellow fey and I will never agree, to deal with hostage takers till the hostage be set free!"

And with little prim nods of their wee little heads, the fairies clustering around him all seemed to agree.

"But how could that happen?" I asked, eyes wide. "She's too large to move. Uprooting her now would be the death of her!"

"Not my problem," declared Bogalump with his arms crossed before him. "Ye've heard my condition, scurry back to yer folk and seek their permission."

"But be swift," declared Fengári, the owl-man from his perch. "If you can meet this challenge somehow, it must be done ere the court doth disperse. Ere the moon to the treeline doth traverse."

Though outwardly calm, I fumed and raged as I exited the glen. Could the mages somehow move Hazel to a 'free' location? I suspected she was rooted too deep. I think this Bogalump character was only using her as an excuse to prevent an alliance with the men of Osten. I'd never heard or read ought of grudges before, but if Bogalump were any example, they seemed aptly named. I hustled toward the academy. It was the middle of the night. If I rang the steeple bell, would the masters come in time? And if they did, would they even listen to me? Maybe I should start with just one master. If anyone would know whether a full-grown tree could be moved, it would be Jonathan Reinhardt. But no, I hadn't the time to go down that route. I knew just one man the council would heed in a timely enough fashion. As I entered the academy, I made for his suite.

***

My knock on the door went unanswered for a time. This was understandable. The hour was late and all reasonable folk were nestled snugly in their beds. But after a minute, I was hailed from within.

"Who is it?" asked the emissary.

Despite the unaccustomed hour, I could detect no hint of annoyance in his flat, even tone.

"It's Lucas Harper, sir. I've come on a matter of utmost urgency."

The door creaked open the merest crack, and I saw a brief reflection from a bauble of metal and glass from the eye which peered without. After a moment, the door swung wide. Cassius McClure stood barefooted in his nightgown, holding a peculiar crystal to his right eye. It put me in mind of a jeweler's lens. In his left hand he held a short blade that gleamed wickedly with the reflected light of a lantern nearby. Dropping the crystal into a pocket, he stepped back and silently bade me enter. He sheathed his blade in a loose baldric that hung from a hook near the door.

"Speak then," he said. "I'm curious what matter could be so pressing."

He would hear me out. Good. I'd been worried he might toss me out on my ear rather than lending me one of his. As I quickly explained that the woodland fey were all gathered in the

Perilous Glade, offering an alliance with Osten but demanding we release the 'hostage' we'd taken, he listened patiently. From the way his cheek twitched throughout, I could tell this was difficult for the man. When I'd finished, he steepled his fingers over his lips and began pacing back and forth. Every so often, he would ask a question about the fey and my relationship to them. He seemed already to know quite a lot more about me than I would have credited.

"And this 'Bogalump' represents a faction opposed to an alliance?" he asked sharply.

"That was my impression of the matter, sir."

"I smell a golden opportunity, Lucas. I can't tell you for how long the king has desired diplomatic ties with the fey. And now the chance to achieve it has practically landed in our laps. For centuries the fair folk have refused to acknowledge our kingdom in any way, keeping to themselves and their own strange hierarchy. The fey would be powerful allies, especially given that some of their kind are in league with our enemies."

"I agree," said I, "but the task they have set us is impossible."

"You're right, of course," said Cassius, nodding. "I imagine if the dryad were harmed in the attempt, the consequences would be just as dire as if we do nothing. We're damned if we do and damned if we don't."

The phrase triggered a chain of thought, the links of which had been forged by long contemplation of ironic situations and impossible contradictions.

"Emissary!" I exclaimed. "Have you ever read the essays of Sir Francis Bacon?"

His lips twisted at the seeming non sequitur.

"Perhaps," I continued, "the mountain need not go to Muhammad..."

As I explained my idea, Emissary McClure became excited. He made his way over to a writing desk and began assembling a packet of parchments. He scribbled furiously as we added provisions and struck out others that didn't seem to apply.

Finally, he flashed me a smile and stuffed the stack of parchments into a slim leather valise.

"If we can pull this off, Lucas," he declared, "you and I will become legends. Of course, there is no time to consult the masters. They will just have to accept it."

He wrote out a brief note for Headmaster Balderas and summoned a seneschal. He instructed the man to waken the headmaster and see that he received it immediately. Then we set off. Time was fleeting, and I feared we might have already outrun our luck. As we hustled down the lane, I couldn't help but try to satisfy some questions that I had.

"Why do you so readily trust me?" I asked.

"A jester of our mutual acquaintance once told me I should keep an eye on you. And I have done so. He said that you have a good heart and are quite resourceful, but you're a lodestone for trouble as well. Thus far, I have found no reason to dispute this assessment."

"What was that strange ocular you examined me with at the door?"

"Being a prototype and somewhat of a state secret, I oughtn't to say. But seeing as you were responsible for its creation, I'll tell you."

The man explained that after the infiltration by unseelie wights had been exposed, the mages had set straight to work. It required a rare crystal, a geomancer to shape it and a tricky bit of enchantment by a light mage. But in a fashion similar to how our mage sight worked, peering through the ocular would now reveal fey energies. It could thus detect when a person's mind was enshrouded by a wight. According to Cassius, all the masters had been cleared save for 'those poor devils recuperating in the cellar.' They still bore a residual taint, but it was fading.

"Can I have one?" I asked.

This elicited a short bark of laughter from the man.

"I had to pull rank to get mine," he said. "Only the chief seneschal and I have working models at the moment. An expedition has been sent to the Iron Mountains to obtain more of the crystals. At a minimum, the king's court and the southern ducal strongholds must be protected. So... No."

It was just as well. My fey mark would likely accomplish the same thing. And I was certain Terwilliger would grow to hate those oculars. After a moment of silence, Cassius continued.

"Though you are clear of mental intrusion, I did note several interestingly strong emanations from your backpack. Care to explain?"

"A private matter, emissary," I hedged.

I'd have to find a more secure way to hide Hazel's acorn; I supposed.

As we reached the edge of the Perilous Glade, I wasted no time and dove right in, shamelessly using my gift to clear the way. I'd also have to give Cassius some credit for the way he followed me in without a second thought. Were we in time?

***

We emerged into the open glen swarming with fey. The mark of the fey on the back of my hand had set to tingling on our approach. By now it was pulsing with a steady throb that sent chills all up and down my arm whereon gooseflesh had arisen. As before, the pixies flitted about and all manner of unusual creatures stood in clusters conversing and drinking from small cups, some of which may have been tulip blossoms. I spotted Terwilliger among his folk at the base of Hazel's tree. To my delight, Hazel now stood among them, having at last been coaxed out to join the frolic. The moon had reached the treeline to the west and soon would be completely lost from view. This boded ill for our timing.

To the fore of his brethren, did Bogalump hop, the spokesman for our detractors.

"I'm surprised you even bothered to return, child of man," he croaked. "As all can plainly see by the moon, the Seelie Court is now closed. The child you wronged now stands among us - your villainy exposed."

"Look ye again," said Terwilliger, pointing with his stick. "The moon still be plain in the western sky and be not obscured by the forest. The Seelie Court still be open thereby to such matters as might come before us."

I looked up, and to my wonder, the moon was indeed clear of the treeline. I could have sworn it was half set but moments before. It took me a moment to suss out what had happened. The upper canopy of all the trees had bent as though bowed low by a mighty wind. The dryad standing across from me caught my eye and smiled wanly.

Bless you, Hazel, I thought.

So as not to squander the opportunity this afforded, I quickly declared, "We bring an offer for your consideration. The men of Osten wish to form an alliance with the fair folk to stand against the unseelie threat from the south!"

Fengári the owl man then spoke as Bogalump blinked up in confusion at the still-risen moon.

"A motion has been made before the gathering," he decreed, "by one with the mark of the fey. We must hear him out before we conclude our work here this day, I say."

As the fairies reseated themselves on the circle of toadstools they'd grown about the glade, Bogalump recovered his wits and bowed his acceptance. He then renewed his argument.

"Little will it serve you, boy, for just as earlier agreed, alliance is impossible till the hostage sprite be freed. I see you've brought another our forbearance to entreat, but you chose unwisely your accomplice. He's no mage and cannot help accomplish such a feat."

"In this you're mistaken," I hastily put forth. "A wise Elven lady recently told me that there's more than one way to peel an onion. Though he may lack the gifts with which our mages are blessed, his stature among us is great. Here's the thing - Cassius McClure has the power and right to speak for Osten's king!"

A muttering arose among the assembled faeries, who eyed Cassius with a new respect. A hush descended to be broken by their leader from his perch.

"Speak on then," said Fengári. "Bring forward your proposal."

Cassius cleared his throat and stepped to the center of the glade.

"In the Kingdom of Osten, all land is owned by our rightful king," he began.

This was ill-received. The faeries shifted about and began a discordant chorus of gasps and oaths that rapidly descended into a dark muttering.

"Be still and hear the man out." hooted Fengári. "Let us see what the fellow's about!"

Into the ensuing stillness, Cassius continued.

"To protect and manage his lands, our king raises up noblemen who swear fealty to him and take other sacred oaths to defend and govern their respective parcels by his auspices. Thus, the Duke of Deerfield holds title to this entire region. He, in turn, gathers barons unto his service, one of whom is the Lord Mayor of Conclave wherein we stand. Such men and the knights sworn to serve them keep the peace and would never suffer our lands to fall to a foreign power, land being the essential cornerstone of our kingdom."

Cassius paused to peer at the squinted eyes of the members of his audience, whose forbearance seemed to be growing rather strained.

"There is, however, one notable exception to this right of our monarch, which I would like to explore with you today. Betimes, when dealing with another kingdom, the crown finds it meet to grant such folk an embassy within our borders. Such lands are considered to be their sovereign territory wherein all of their laws apply. It is no longer owned by the men of Osten. An embassy is a place where diplomats of the respective kingdoms can meet in peace to discuss any differences that might arise."

The fey seemed confused and dubious. From the stillness following Cassius' speech, a quiet babble arose. And the faeries exchanged sidelong glances, many looking to Fengári to respond. The owl man sat on his branch pondering. Recalling that the fey seemed to assign more importance to words couched in rhyme, I took it upon myself to inject a note of clarity.

"Don't you see," said I, In summary. "The men of Osten and the woodland fey, by a treaty united can be this day. The glade within which the dryad stands will be duly acknowledged as seelie lands. By accepting our monarch's gesture of goodwill, the hostage can be freed by the stroke of a quill!"

I don't know whether it was my feeble attempt at poetic verse or the mark of the fey that made the difference. The faeries all perked up. The pixies chattered agreeably, and even Bogalump seemed to catch the spirit.

"A clever reply to the problem I assigned," he said with a spreading grin. "Lucas the Just has a cunning mind."

"Lucas the... Just?" muttered Cassius.

"It's what they call me," I whispered back. "Just go with it."

At last Fengári spoke.

"In principle, let's say we agree to your plan. How do we seal this treaty with man?"

Cassius held up the valise wherein we'd placed the written treaty. He opened his mouth to respond, but then hesitated, looking to me with a questioning glance. I knew he'd prefer I explain it. I thought furiously on how to best answer Fengári. I took a step forward and raised my hands in supplication to stall for time. I hoped the fey would think I was just honoring the gravity of the situation. Rhyming under pressure was no easy task.

"Owing to our shorter lives, we find it most regretful; just as you have pointed out, as a race, we can be forgetful. Whereas verbal bargains struck may work quite well among the fey (and we humans keep our personal word as faithfully as we may), humans find it works the best to write our bargains down. On parchment and in ink all our agreements can be found."

At this, Cassius produced the document and unrolled it.

"What does it say? What does it say?" sounded off the sprites.

Their eyes were wide and curious, with interest alight. And since the faeries save but one were unfamiliar with the marks set down by man, Cassius began to read the treaty, outlining the terms of the plan. All was well as the fair folk nodded in agreement point by point until the emissary was interrupted in his discourse by a mighty croak.

"Do you seek to play us false?" said Bogalump with sudden suspicion. "We all know you name this place 'Conclave,' but I've heard an incongruity. Your treaty states that we will own these lands 'in Perpetuity!'"

Rather than give affront to the influential grudge, we thought it best to halt right there and scratch out the offending phrase. We replaced it with the word 'forever.' This solution seemed to mollify the faeries in the glen who complimented the grudge for his sage wisdom and attention to detail.

"If we are all in agreement," said Cassius "all that remains is the signing. I shall make my mark on behalf of the Kingdom of Osten. Who will sign for the fey?"

The faeries glanced among themselves staring blankly and growing agitated. Then a chuckle was heard from the side of the glade where the brownie contingent stood. And a lone, small figure ambled forth from the edge of the darkened wood. It was Terwilliger, grinning ear to ear and surveying his brethren with delight.

"Long have ye scorned and denigrated the brownies as lesser sprites. But I say with great pride if no other stand forth, one will prove his worth this night. I have studied how men capture words on their dried-out sheepskins to lay. Give me the quill, and I'll sign on behalf of all the woodland fey."

And thus the treaty was sealed at last, a written bargain struck. At its end, two signatures graced the landmark agreement between two kingdoms existing side by side:

Cassius McClure, Emissary of King Raymond Osten III

Terwilliger Brown, for Kween Tinatia, the Fair

"If I understand aright," hooted Fengári, "Then this glade now be subject to faerie law. And as such, I hereby decree in the name of our queen that all must drink and cavort and celebrate all throughout the night!"

The faeries didn't need to be told twice. All leaped up with whoops and cheers, and drinks were served all around. Cassius and I sipped from tiny cups a liqueur that was at once fruity and potent. It crept up on one quite swiftly and would soon have rendered me insensate had I not slowed down almost at once. I still felt relaxed, giddy and besotted.

The fairy band took up their tune and Cassius and I cavorted with our new allies long into the night, taking care to avoid treading on some unwary fairy. The moon had set long ago, and the stars shone down, unblinking. By the light of faerie moths, we stayed there all night drinking. And although hamadryads neither bent nor sat, I found to my delight that Hazel proved most agile as we danced away the night.

***

The bright, pearlescent light which haloed the young woman slowly receded, and her angelic aspect faded. She was again but a frail girl, slight of frame standing barefoot in a plain white smock before the menhir. As Bella withdrew from the circle and returned to her housemates waiting at its edge, the herald cried out once more.

"Skyler Hendrix," he commanded. "Approach the central menhir and lay your hand upon it that all may witness the sealing of your vow."

The ceremony was a lot more fun to watch from the sidelines. As my erstwhile student placed his hand upon the stone, a great whirlwind arose to circle around it. This caused his neophyte robe to flap about and threatened to expose his unmentionables. I chuckled as he clutched his garment tight with his other hand while a bright blue light ringed the menhir and pulsed up along its length. He rejoined his fellows, looking weary and chagrined.

The masters began their deliberation. It had been weeks since the treaty with the fey had been signed, and Conclave Village was recovering nicely from the worries that had wracked it throughout the spring. The quarantine had been lifted, and the people were returning to their ordinary pursuits. Before long, the plague would be naught but a fading memory.

So too was the novelty of the fey presence beginning to fade. At first, the masters had been appalled that a third of the acreage of the mage's quarter had been given over to the fair folk. It had to 'gall' Mistress Willoughby that her wasps were now property of the fairies, shepherded by the sprites among them. Henceforth, the conclave would need to barter for such products as oak galls, rare herbs, and enchanted wood. Though for some of these the cost would be most dear, it was soon discovered that many of the fey could be bought off for as little as a drop of honey or a saucer of milk.

It was now an everyday event to witness a pixie buzzing above the marketplace or a satyr playing his flute for tips at the tavern. The people of Conclave soon learned to step cautiously. The fair folk did nothing overtly hostile, but they might bedevil you with flies or sour your milk if you displeased them.

Mistress Willoughby stepped out to stand before the other masters. To mollify her for yielding her management of the Perilous Glade, she'd been appointed ambassador to the fey. I didn't envy her the job. Hazel was now the 'Mistress of the Glade,' some title of significance among her folk. But it was felt the dryad lacked the experience and maturity to serve as ambassador. Perhaps in another hundred years or so she might be considered for such a post. No. Frida's counterpart was to be Ambassador Bogalump the Grudge. It was deemed that the crusty old sot would keep the humans honest in their dealings and better represent fey interests in the area.

And then there was me. After our extraordinary success in securing the alliance, I was commended by the king himself, or rather by a few terse words delivered by his pigeon. In a private ceremony conducted by Cassius McClure, I was granted a new title: 'Lucas the Just, Envoy Plenipotentiary to the Fey.' It was a nice gesture. Almost as amusing was the letter from Master Chadwick wherein he suggested my wizard name should be 'the wizard who wallops wights.' But I'd had my fill of accolades and pretentious titles. They were naught but a magnet for troubles. I didn't fancy every dark entity from throughout Osten seeking me out to make a name for themselves. I would rather just stick with 'the wizard who winds wool' and bugger all the rest.

Frida chose for her journeyman one of Gunther's former adepts, and the selection moved on. The masters had all been encouraged to take on more journeyman than was their usual wont. According to Headmaster Balderas, they needed to pick up the slack for the three masters who had recently been debilitated.

I was unsurprised to see Brayden Sheppard step up and announce his selection of Franklin. Our head of house had decided to enlist in the seneschals and make it his personal mission to hunt down and put an end to Adam/Truman/whoever-he-was-now. It was reasoned that having a necromancer on the task force would be an essential addition. By choosing him as his journeyman, Brayden cemented this relationship rather nicely.

Selections rolled on and I cheered with all the others when Bella, who'd recently been assigned to House Owl, was chosen by Flynn Campbell. The conclave had been charged by Duke Deerfield to send forth its new miracle worker to eradicate the plague from the areas of his duchy where it still festered. Shanningham Village was a lost cause, having been all but emptied by the depredations of the necromancer, but there were other areas that could be saved. Surprisingly, Simon Strangelove had offered to go along as well. Armed with his 'miracle pomade,' Simon would help repel the pests who spread the affliction, charging only a modest fee for such efforts. His leeches he left behind. Though he still touted their medicinal benefits, they would cease to be the focus of his aid.

Our ranks were thinning, but many yet remained unchosen when Mistress Julia stepped to the fore. I confess to some surprise for there were no Elves among us.

"It is known to all that my purpose here is to oversee matters that relate to the first people," she began, slowly scanning the aspirants assembled. "In times past, I have chosen only my kindred to shepherd forth to their masteries. The headmaster urged me to forego this proclivity and accept into my service some worthy candidates from more diverse origins. In these dangerous days, I fear we have not the luxury of time, so I agreed. Therefore, If they would learn in the Elven way and accept me as their master, I offer my humble teachings to the following:

"Lucas Harper."

Me?

"Royland Wagge."

Joy!

"Sholeena Blorla... Sholena of the Paludaria," she finished with a stumble.

And as the stunned expressions of our housemates and the others slowly transformed into cheery smiles and gladsome applause, I experienced once again Sholeena's double-armed squeeze of affection. Orange must be her happy color, I thought as I briefly returned the embrace. Roy took a careful step back to be spared such attentions. My cousin wasn't much of a one for hugs.

Epilogue

"Poems are made by fools like me, But only God can make a tree."

~ *Joyce Kilmer* ~

Bogalump dwelt in a mud-daubed hut next to the not-so-perilous glade. Its wattled brown walls blended into the surroundings. Apart from the single round opening at its front, it resembled a natural hill rising from the forest floor. The great toad sat before it as I approached, and his wide gaze took me in.

"Good day, journeyman," he croaked. "Have you some official business for the embassy today? Mayhap have the nymphs been running indecently down the streets again?"

A purplish plume of smoke curled up from the bowl of his long-stemmed meerschaum pipe. It had a pleasant fragrance.

"No, ambassador," I replied. "I've just come to visit with Hazel."

The grudge looked disappointed.

Just off to our left sat Mistress Willoughby and her sister on their stone bench. Gretta was still withdrawn, but Frida often brought her here for some fresh air and sunlight. Occasionally, she would look about and smile at the antics of the pixies. The fey had wasted no time in putting the glade back in proper disorder. They buzzed about shepherding the bees to pollinate the rare blooms which they traded for various things they desired. Frida was even now bargaining with a group of them.

"... If you complete this mission for the duke, he promises to send you a quarter cask of mead. The wasps are to be released in the Schiffner fief."

"But that's miles and *miles* south of here," whined the tiny shepherdess as she hovered before the matron's nose. "For that, we should get a whole *hogshead*."

Her voice was so high-pitched as to be almost inaudible, but her body language was most expressive. She emphasized her complaint by crossing her arms before her, zipping back and forth, and flouncing up and down.

"Nevertheless," Frida wheedled in honeyed tones, "it's a quarter cask that's been offered. Do it for the trees. The enemy's bugs are infesting them. They shall *die* if we don't halt the spread."

At this, the other pixies swirled up. Their leader lost her haughty manner at once as her sisters reproached her in their tinkling voices, their faces forlorn. Then they all wheeled about and were gone. I thought it a dirty trick to play on their feelings like that. Diplomacy was one thing, but this bordered on emotional blackmail. Perhaps it was for the best. A hogshead of mead would likely turn the pixies of the grove into a group of besotted pranksters for an entire season. It was good to see Mistress Willoughby finding her stride at negotiation.

We'd better all sharpen our skills, I thought. The war was heating up again. According to Master Pete's latest report, our toehold in the marsh had grown far more tenuous. The soldiers at the redoubt there were beset by gigantic shambling mounds of vegetation that walked about like men. Stabbing them with a sword seemed to do them little harm, and slashing with axes took too long to make a significant dent. They could engulf a man and bind him within to scream out his strangled last. Our mages were able to drive them off with fire, but the creatures were growing more numerous and aggressive.

Spotting Hazel, I wished Bogalump a good day and headed for the forest's edge. She stood serenely amid a group of garden gnomes. They were seated before the sapling, their red pointed hats all in a row. Their gravelly voices struck me as odd, coming from beings so small. They cheerfully chatted as they waited expectantly.

"Will it be today, do you think?" I asked.

Hazel smiled.

"Hello, Lucas. Well met, as you say. Be welcome in the glade of the fey."

Her warm, ritual greeting reminded me of her new role as Mistress of the Glade, and her serene demeanor reflected well the inner peace her new freedom had conferred. She glided over nearer.

"The winds only know when the clouds will part. Your query will find its reply, from the temperamental whimsy of a maiden's heart, and the spirit that moves her thereby."

Someone had been giving her lessons in elocution, I thought. Still, this aura of mystery and quiet wisdom suited her well, and I admired her new poise. I took my seat beside the chattering gnomes and stared at the sapling I'd planted.

In a quiet ceremony just after the seelie court departed, I had fulfilled my vow to the tree sprite. Since one dryad did not a proper glade make, and since this grove was now acknowledged by the faire folk, I'd planted Hazel's acorn and given her her name. Recently I'd sensed from within the sapling a stirring. It was a wondrous feeling that caused my mark to tingle and vibrate in resonance with her joyous absorption of the sun's rays. Her roots wriggled deep into the cool, sustaining earth to drink of the waters therein. Very soon now the child would find her aspect and shyly peep out from her tree, gracing us with her first blinking smile. I looked forward to the event.

And I doubted I would ever see anything as lovely as that tree. Mother and daughter growing side by side, just as it was meant to be.

Author's Afterword

Greetings, readers of Conclave!

It's another clear day here in Cincinnati, and reckoning by my iPhone, it's time to commence my author's afterword. I'm told I look rather silly sitting before my computer screen typing away at its keyboard...

A plague running loose in the land? A contentious election with accusations of voter suppression and fraud? High officials suspected of colluding with the enemy to work us harm? This may sound all too familiar. And though I confess my writing may have been influenced by recent events, I wish to set the record straight.

The storyline of "Calamity at Conclave" was conceived years ago, long before the first sniffle was reported in Wuhan. Believe it or not, any resemblance to people living or otherwise is merely a hilarious coincidence. As far as the politics go, I think you'll all agree my 'Loyalist' and 'Autonomist' factions represent no modern-day political entities. They do, however, represent the unwarranted divisiveness that permeates our society. In true Swiftian fashion, I wanted to present a bit of satire to shed light on how ridiculous it is for people to become entrenched so thoroughly in their political parties that they overlook civility and respect. As Shakespeare once put it: "A pox on both your houses."

No. I am most sincerely glad that hindsight is 2020 at last.

You may have noticed this novel is dedicated to Anthony Muñoz. Anthony was a celebrated offensive lineman for my hometown Cincinnati Bengals for 13 seasons. Although I have never been much of a football fan, I came to know him through the charitable work of his foundation. I have met the man on several occasions. My wife, Luanne, and I have for years volunteered to tutor children just learning to read in an after-school reading program he sponsors. Perhaps this sounds familiar?

When dedicating a novel, I like to think about my sources of inspiration. In writing Calamity, I borrowed heavily from my experiences tutoring the kids at Roberts Academy. Not only that, people like Mr. Muñoz who, having achieved their success, seek to give back and encourage others are the template for characters like Lucas who are kindhearted. And a special shout out to the children of Roberts Academy for helping me add some realism to how the kids in my novel behave!

I thank my readers for hanging with me through my three novels thus far. Presently, I'm envisioning a five-volume series. What's next for Lucas Harper and his no-longer-estranged cousin, Roy? Alright. Here's a teaser. The fourth novel is being envisioned under the working title: "Depravities of the Dark Druids." Following that, the series concludes with "A Royal Mess." Does this whet your appetites?

...and so in conclusion, my brothers and sisters of the written word, we shall use this most recent pause to regroup and prepare ourselves. I've shared my battle plan with you, and I sense my readers are becoming impatient. When the fresh chapters arrive, I'll tell you all about it on my website at www.thormans.org.. God willing, I shall publish again next year at this same time.

Until then, be safe and pray for those who keep you thus,

Daniel Bernard Thorman

Appendix I

(Dramatis Personae)

To help you keep track of the many characters populating this novel, I've provided the following reference. This is a short summary of characters directly mentioned or encountered. Reference with care and only at need. A few of these passages may contain spoilers. Otherwise, enjoy them with my compliments.

<u>Narrators</u>

Lucas Harper - Our reluctant hero. Known variously as Lucas the Bloke, Lucas the Just, and by other, more well-deserved titles, he arrives at Conclave to seek his new master and thus become a journeyman mage.

Abigale Wagge - Though deceased, Lucas' grandmother has a lot to do and say in this tale. She narrates several passages. Pretty impressive for a dead gal.

Royland Wagge - Cousin to Lucas and also an aspirant journeyman mage from Westarbor, Royland is going through a rough patch. He's determined to fit in and avoid the pitfalls of being marked as strange.

<u>Folks mentioned or encountered who reside outside of Conclave</u>

Lady Megan Arenson - Daughter of Baron Westarbor. Lucas has sworn a vow to protect and serve her. Megan shares her father's wild talent to perceive a person's true feelings by touching them or meeting their gaze. Roy once claimed Lucas was 'smitten' with her. Time will tell.

Drew Cunningham - Brother of Marjery who also rides a griffin and became a herald of Baron Westarbor. He owns a ferret named Dillon.

Marjery Cunningham - A former milkmaid who tamed a griffin.

Elliot Harper - Father to Lucas who runs a mill back in Meadowfork.

Truman Huber - Truman is a sociopath who first appeared in book one as an equerry. In the second novel, he used the alias: Mortimer Wilkinson. He died trying to kill Lucas, but it seems you just can't keep a bad man down. His gift of necromancy has allowed him to arise once more to wreak more havoc upon the beleaguered folk of Osten.

Madam Pennington - A soap maker back in Meadowfork.

Robert Wagge - Royland's father was abducted by Abigale decades ago and became her 'adopted' son. Lucas often repeats his 'Uncle' Robert's witticisms and folk wisdom.

Baron Westarbor - Born Vincent Arenson, knighted, and later raised up to baron, he governs Westarbor Barony and sponsored Lucas and Royland to the conclave of mages.

Journeyman Aspirants

House Blue Jay - The aspirant dwelling to which Lucas was assigned.

Franklin Stein - Head of House Blue Jay. As a necromancer, Franklin has been passed over four years running when journeymen were selected. He is often in a gloomy mood. Franklin works at the slaughterhouse and collects butterflies and builds monsters in his spare time.

Doña Lorraine Cordova of Alamendra - Lorraine is a photomancer, specializing in tricks of light. For her day job, she plies her handcart throughout Conclave Village, obtaining supplies and running errands for the mages. Lorraine is from Freemark Duchy, a southeastern region of Osten.

Lloyd "The Void" Bridges - An innocent young man born and raised in Conclave. His gift enables him to make objects vanish and reappear elsewhere.

Sholeena Blorlafargalish - Sholeena comes from a tribe of people called the Paludaria, marsh dwellers of Indigo Bay.

Her race is semi-aquatic, having webbed feet. Her skin can change color to reflect her mood or reflexively camouflage her when frightened. New to the written word, she studies among Lucas' abecedarians.

Galwell Cummings - Grandson of the former Duke of Northford, whose rebellion many years ago saw him and his family exiled to the Indigo Isles. Having been discovered to possess the gift of therianthropy, Galwell was remanded to the conclave to serve the kingdom as a mage.

Some Aspirants of House Falcon

Ellison Reznic - His friends call him Eli. He is the son of Harland Reznic, presently deployed at the battle front near Eagle's Keep. Eli is the head of House Falcon at the novel's start. According to Royland, there is little of logic in his 'wild-eyed scheming.'

Scott McNair - A rude young man who can manipulate shadow.

Henry Sutherland - Nephew of Mistress Meredith Brubaker, he possesses the family gift of sonomancy. He can whistle up a variety of effects but is best at projecting a painful noise or his aunt's signature vertigo.

Some Aspirants of House Owl

Elleanor Fortescue - Mentioned during the first choosing.

Hannah Brownyng - New head of House Owl since the first choosing.

<u>Master Wizards of Note</u> - In no particular order

Luther Prowd - Has presided over the conclave for many years as its headmaster. A bit of a stuffed shirt, he is a master at working with the various factions and bringing about consensus. He has fashioned a title for himself - 'Preeminence'. He is a geomancer and invented the spell 'diamond shield' (scutum iaspis). Luther had a fling with Abigale back in the day when he was but a young journeyman. His memories of her are not fond.

Puquabeth Chosha Julia (pronounced jo-LEE-ah) - The sole Elven master to reside in Conclave. Her name means: 'daughter of the twilight sun'. Among humans, she goes simply by Mistress Julia. She is a wind mage and several centuries old. Her husband resides in Lorédon with her children.

Zaid Guthrie - A wily old coot with an affinity for communion with animals. He is Edgar Englewood's Journeyman Master. His wife is ungifted, but one of their three children shows some promise and is an aspirant in House Owl.

Gunther Brubaker - Nephew to Royland's Grandfather, Hans. Master Gunther is the preeminent pyromancer of conclave. He works in the foundry at Conclave firing the smithies extra hot to produce various high quality items. Along with his wife, Meredith, Gunther is an outspoken autonomist.

Meredith Brubaker née Sutherland - Wife of Gunther, she goes by 'Mistress Meredith'. She is a sound mage and can cause a variety of effects with her singing. One of the most potent of these is extreme vertigo in the listener. She is matron of the conclave's créche, overseeing its finances and rules.

Atticus Skinner - Atticus lives in a large manor overlooking the lake. He has but one journeyman and is known to be rather standoffish. He espouses autonomist leanings and quietly urges dissension among the masters who favor this philosophy.

Christopher Spencer - His magic center is a festering compost heap. His special gift is decay, and he has an affinity for warmth and bad smells. He can cause things to rot rapidly, but can also preserve them from such by rotting other things. He is in charge of the conclave's food stores and visits various farmsteads to speed decomposition in their silos. His wife is the deceased Mistress Halifax. None of the children by their union received magical gifts. One of his children is Miss Spencer who is governess at the créche. He is Bella Gibson's app-master.

Felix Wells - His deceased father was Grandma Abbey's former app-master whom she despised. As a loyalist, he holds Peter Doyle's proxy. His wife left off her training to join his household and have children. She remains a journeyman mage.

Clement Brownyng - Franklin's app-master. Victor Brubaker's current journeyman master. Father to Hannah, head of House Owl. Clement's was caretaker for the Hall of Memory. Upon Luther's death, he serves as headmaster pro tem until a new headmaster can be elected. Clement is an autonomist

Flynn Campbell - Briefly mentioned at the second choosing.

Brayden Sheppard - Head of the conclave's seneschals. As a therianthrope, it is said he can take the form of 'a mighty gorilla.'

Alonso Balderas - The loyalists' contender for the job of headmaster. Originally from Freemark, his gift is for shaping stone. He sculpted the ever-flowing fountain at the end of Aspie Row. Alonso is Ariadne's father.

Martin Bates - Originally from Westarbor, Martin has only recently arisen to his mastery. Master Martin is charged with providing a hostelry for the griffins and their riders. A wishy-washy sort, Martin is being bullied and recruited to serve the autonomist cause.

Frida Willoughby - Master in charge of the special gardens sometimes known as the Perilous Glade. Frida is Royland's great aunt on his mother's side. She also has the family affinity for insects and is a devout loyalist.

Jonathan Reinhardt - As a dendromancer, Jonathan is the conclave's premier worker of wood. He tends the orchards and oversees work at the carpentry shop. Jonathan is a hardened loyalist.

Peter Redmond Doyle - Master Pete is stationed at the war front and provides daily reports on conditions via his brother, Redmond. Peter is known to have strong loyalist leanings.

Redmond Peter Doyle - Twin brother to master Pete, Redmond has been dubbed 'Re-Pete' for his strange ability to channel his brother's speech and gestures. Unlike his brother, Redmond is an autonomist.

Sybell Dunham - An elderly master blessed with oracular visions. She lives in the Hall of Meditation and assists new journeymen in developing their 'inner homunculus.'

Dorithie Stanwix - A water mage in charge of the fire brigade. Described by Lucas as 'a large woman.'

Denis Feininger - A recently deceased master. His wife died several year's ago of 'consumption.' His daughter, Susie, is now orphaned and resides at the créche.

Gretta Brubaker née Willoughby - Gretta arrives later in the story. She was found in a sorry state among a group of hostages liberated from the dark druids' slave pens. She was recognized as a mage of the conclave who disappeared long ago along with her husband, Hans, when they were on a mission in the south. The mages are astonished by her safe return to them after being missing for so many years. Gretta is mother to Robert (Royland's father). She is withdrawn and will not speak.

Outliers - Other Masters are mentioned as not being present at the conclave. Among these are:

3 Elven masters in Lorédon:

> ***Master Shon*** - *Bey Cholith Depa Shon*
> > (Howls Fiercely During Hunt)

> ***Mistress Sithia*** - Baqua Lipo Sithia
> > (Freshness of the Morning Rain)

> ***Mistress Talia*** - Qenga Taliha Shunje Qua
> > (Clarity of Thought and Spirit)

5 Masters serving along the war front
> ***Mark Sutherland*** (Henry's dad)
> ***Harland Reznic*** (Eli's dad)
> ***Dominik Cooke***
> ***Angus Gibbs***
> and Peter Doyle as mentioned earlier

1 in Westarbor:

> ***Elizar Chadwick*** (app-master to Lucas and Royland)

1 in the Indigo Isles:

> ***Marcel Jordan*** (app-master to Sholeena and Galwell)

<u>**Some Journeymen**</u> - Journeymen are the most numerous of the mages at conclave, there being around three for every master. We only met a few as we were focused more on the aspirants and their struggles.

Victor Brubaker - The Brubaker heir, son to Gunther and Meredith. He is a pyromancer and is presently a journeyman for Master Clement Brownyng.

Edgar Englewood - The librarian at the conclave. He has a familiar raven named Lenore and is assigned to Master Christopher Spencer.

Jessica Woodwindle - Having an malleable magic center which she slowly can adjust to suit her mood, Jessica has an actual non-magical gift for painting. Landscapes are her favorite. Presently she is the portraitist for the master wizards. She owns a technique of smearing a droplet of paint around on her canvas such that it blends in smoothly with the surrounding oils. This results in a canvas free of any brush strokes that has an extremely life-like, photographic quality. She is a new discovery, having no family at Conclave. She grew up in Fairglen as the daughter of a famous actor.

Arnold Clark - Journeyman Clark is a therianthrope serving in the seneschals. He is the lone survivor of an attack on Master Prowd's funeral barge. He swam back to Conclave to bear witness to the event. His totem animal is a leopard.

<u>**The Abecedarians**</u> - The children and several apprentices Lucas is teaching to read.

Daisy Sutherland - Age 11. Daughter of Mark and sister to Henry from House Falcon. Her father is deployed at the war front. Her mother manages Sutherland Estates in his absence but was formerly a tavern maid with no magical gifts. She sends daisy to the créche for Lucas' lessons, but daisy doesn't live there.

Susanna Feininger (Susie) - Age 8. Daughter of Denis Feininger (recently 'deceased'). Her mother having pre-deceased him, Susie is now orphaned. She lives at the créche at present while the disposition of her estate and to which mage she will become ward are determined.

Skyler Hendrix - Age 14. Apprenticed to Jonathan Reinhardt. Skyler is from Fairax Duchy (north of the Indigo Isles). His father was the first mate of a sailing vessel in the king's navy. Skyler served for a time as a cabin boy before his gift of aeromancy was discovered. He is apprenticed to Master Reinhardt.

Bella Gibson - Age 13. Bella was found to possess the gift of healing, but this can sometimes go terribly wrong. She travels to outlying farmsteads with her app-Master, Christopher Spencer, practicing on animals suffering from various maladies. Bella was a simple farm girl from a small village in Deerfield Duchy, and cannot read. She seems overwhelmed by Conclave and is struggling to fit in. Bella may be the key to battling the plague that is coming. She calls her magic center her 'inner glow.'

Cassandra Reinhardt - Age 9. Daughter of Jonathan and Rebecca

Ariadna Balderas - Age 8. Daughter of Alonso and Carmen

Sholeena Blorlafargalish - See 'House Blue Jay.'

Terwilliger Brown - See 'Fairy Folk.'

Townspeople - There are many non-magical folk of Conclave Village. In this novel, we met a few:

Roger Anderson - Lefty's journeyman smith at the foundry.

Thorbaldric Anvilthane aka "Lefty McHammerhand" - A Dwarven master smith at the foundry.

Unnamed Apothecary - Lucas last left him being led away from his shop to bear witness against the rowdy who had assaulted him.

Madam Maisie Bridges - Lloyd's mom. Wife of Bertram Bridges. She runs Hightopper's, a haberdashery in the trade district..

Unnamed Herald - Known for his lofty speech, he is described as a venerable and distinguished gentleman with an upturned white mustache. He makes proclamations throughout the conclave and announces those who enter the Hall of Masters.

Stewart Knowlton - A farmer living at the outskirts of Conclave. Bella attempted to heal his cow that had been stricken with murrain.

Cassius Mcclure - The king's emissary to the conclave. Cassius attends the council of masters, keeping the king informed. He can convey the king's commands.

Russell Moore - A dock worker who lived in lowside. He went missing after a stranger attacked the apothecary.

Elisa Spencer - Ungifted daughter of Master Christopher Spencer. Miss Spencer is governess of the créche.

Simon Strangelove - A barber in Conclave Village.

Douglas Weil - Chief physic of Conclave

Fairy Folk - Contains some spoilers! (Read the book first)

Terwilliger - A local brownie and professional bootblack. He is of the Seelie court.

Hazel - A hamadryad living in the Perilous Glade of the conclave. She was transplanted there as a sapling.

Fengári - Described as a 'bespectacled owl creature perched on a hickory branch', Fengári chairs the Seelie Court on behalf of queen Tinatia.

Bogalump, the grudge - Described as a 'frog creature smoking a long pipe, he is actually more of a toad and not amphibious at all.

Kieranos - Orenob's 'most faithful' wight. An imp-like creature of the unseelie court who can become a mass of swirling vapors and possess humans.

Orenob - This be not his true name, but tis near enough to conjure by. Actually, the name of this 'unseelie king' is an anagram for 'Oberon,' of "A Mid-summer Night's Dream" fame. Lucas refers to him as a warty-faced demon.

Queen Tinatia - Although not appearing in the story, Terwilliger swears by her 'green booties and her tall, silk hat.' In a manner similar to Orenob, the queen's name is an anagram for 'Titania,' the fairy queen of Shakespeare's fey fantasy.

Fairy Heralds - A grig playing a vielle, a satyr with pan-pipes, and a singing pixie summon Lucas to the seelie court.

Appendix II
(Spells)

Fun Fact: The 'old tongue' I use for the spell verbalizations is simply Latin. You can usually plug a spell name into a Google translation to find its literal meaning. Below is a fairly comprehensive listing of Spells used in my novels to date:

Old Tongue	Means
aqua exstinguit	Water Quenches
aquam claram	Clear Water
ambulare interitus	Withering Stride
calidus ignis ardentis	Blazing Hot Fire
capturam petram	Catch Rock
cogitationes liberare	liberate thoughts
digitus flamma	Flame Finger
exorcizo spiritus	Exorcize Spirit
frigus metallum in perpetuum	permanently cool metal
geas silentii	Geas of Silence
gloriabitur securis	Force Axe
iactare spheara	Spinning Toss
impedimente	Shield/Protect
inexsuperabilis permanens lignea	Permanent Wooden Impregnability
internum calorem	Inner Warmth
levare et colligentes	Lift and Pull
levare et conicere	Lift and Throw

Old Tongue	Means
lumina in	Lights On
lumina quell	Kill the Lights
manent vigilate	Remain Alert
miscere cogitata	Combine Thoughts
motis cessabit	Calm of the Grave
personalis zephyris spirantibus	Personal Zephyr
podagra flammae	Gout of Fire
praefundo harenae	Dampen Sand
praemium	Explode
pulver in ventis	Dust in the Wind
quaerite mihi amans	Seek My Lover
radet ovium	Sheer Sheep
scripturam vim extermina	Erase Writing
spacium girabit	Rotate
sphera de incineratio	Sphere of Incineration
sternetur tinea munda	Maggot Cleanse
suspendium tenaci	Choking Grip
tenera pluviam	Tender Rain
terram aratro	Earth Furrow
ut reflectum speculum	Glass that reflects
visio tenebris	Darksight
viburnum pugna	Snowball Fight